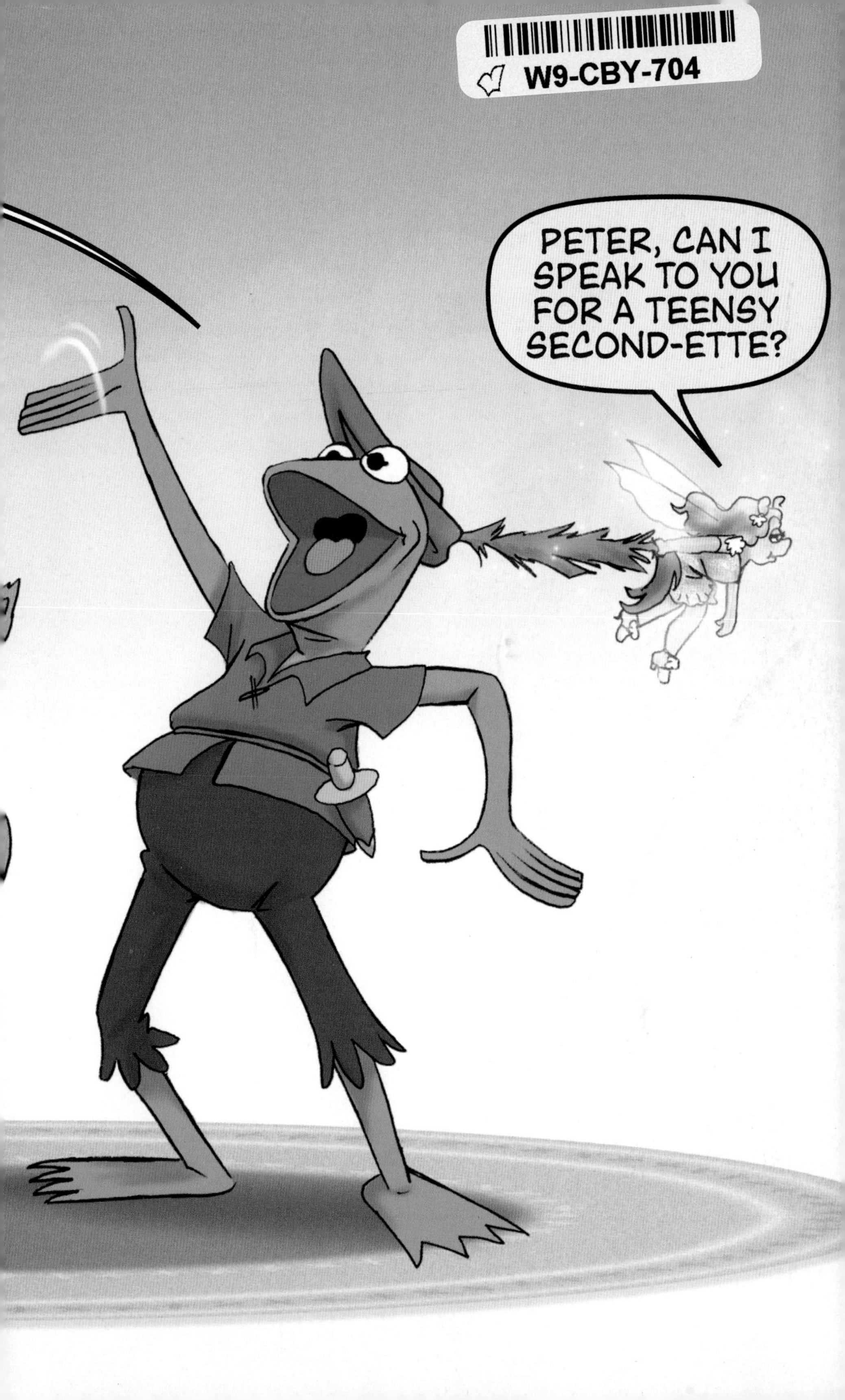
PETER, CAN I SPEAK TO YOU FOR A TEENSY SECOND-ETTE?

Muppet Peter Pan

BOOM KIDS!

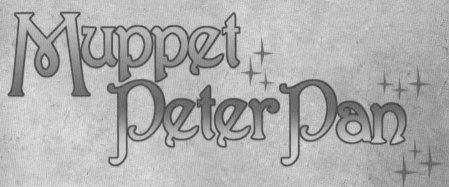

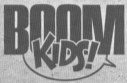

ROSS RICHIE
chief executive officer

MARK WAID
editor-in-chief

ADAM FORTIER
vice president, publishing

CHIP MOSHER
marketing director

MATT GAGNON
managing editor

JENNY CHRISTOPHER
sales director

FIRST EDITION: JANUARY 2010

10 9 8 7 6 5 4 3 2 1

PRINTED BY WORLD COLOR PRESS, INC.,
ST-ROMUALD, QC., CANADA.

Office of publication: 6310 San Vicente Blvd Ste 404, Los Angeles, CA 90048-5457.

A catalog record for this book is available from the Library of Congress and on our website at www.boom-kids.com on the Librarian Resource Page.

Writer:
Grace Randolph

Art and Colors:
Amy Mebberson

Letterer:
Troy Peteri

Editor:
Aaron Sparrow

Assistant Editor:
Christopher Burns

Designer:
Erika Terriquez

Cover:
David Petersen

Hardcover Case Wrap:
Amy Mebberson
& David Rabbitte

"Muppet Wide World
Of Sports" segment by
Amy Mebberson

Special Thanks:
Jesse Post and Lauren Kressel of
Disney Publishing and our friends at
The Muppets Studio

chapter one

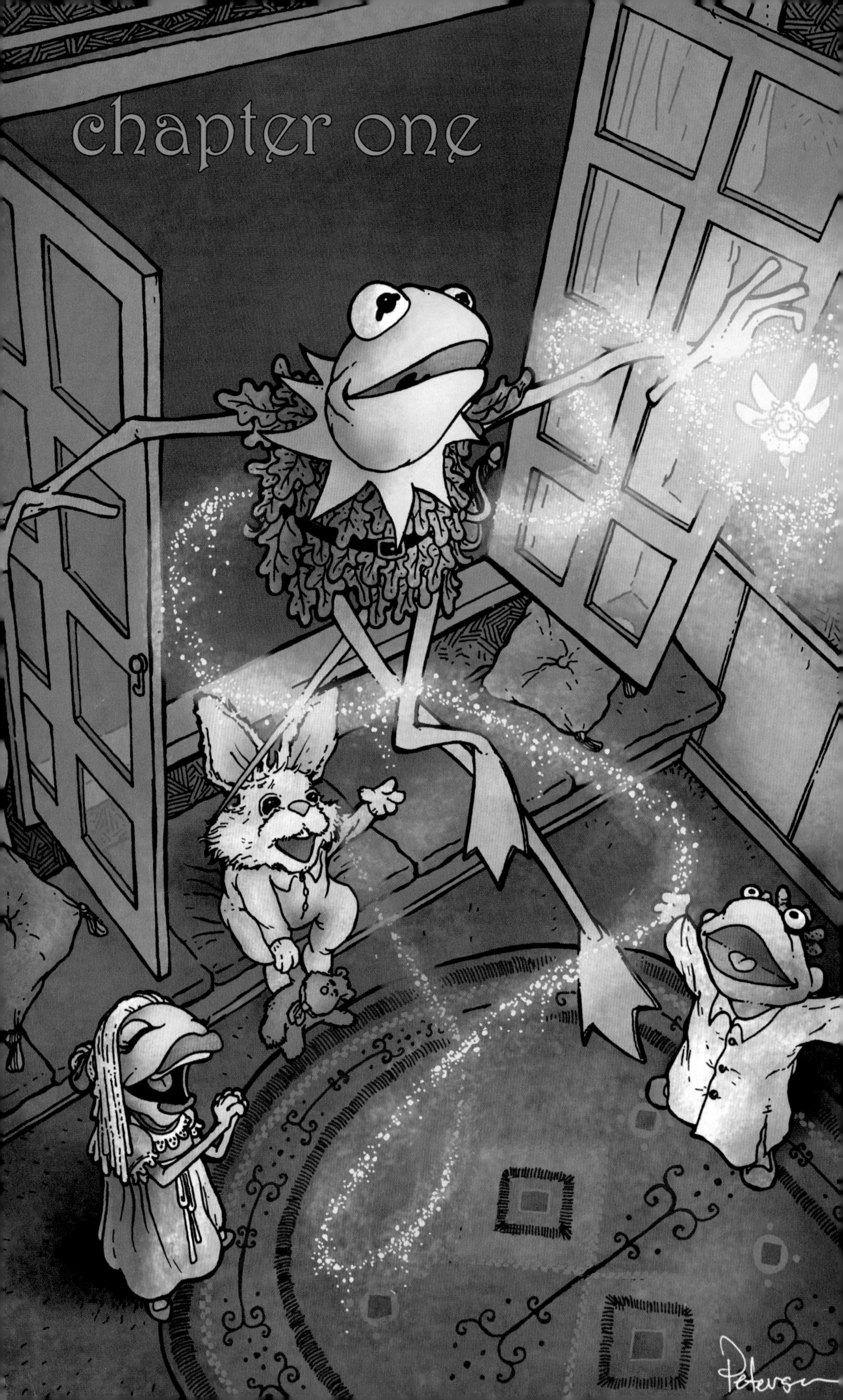

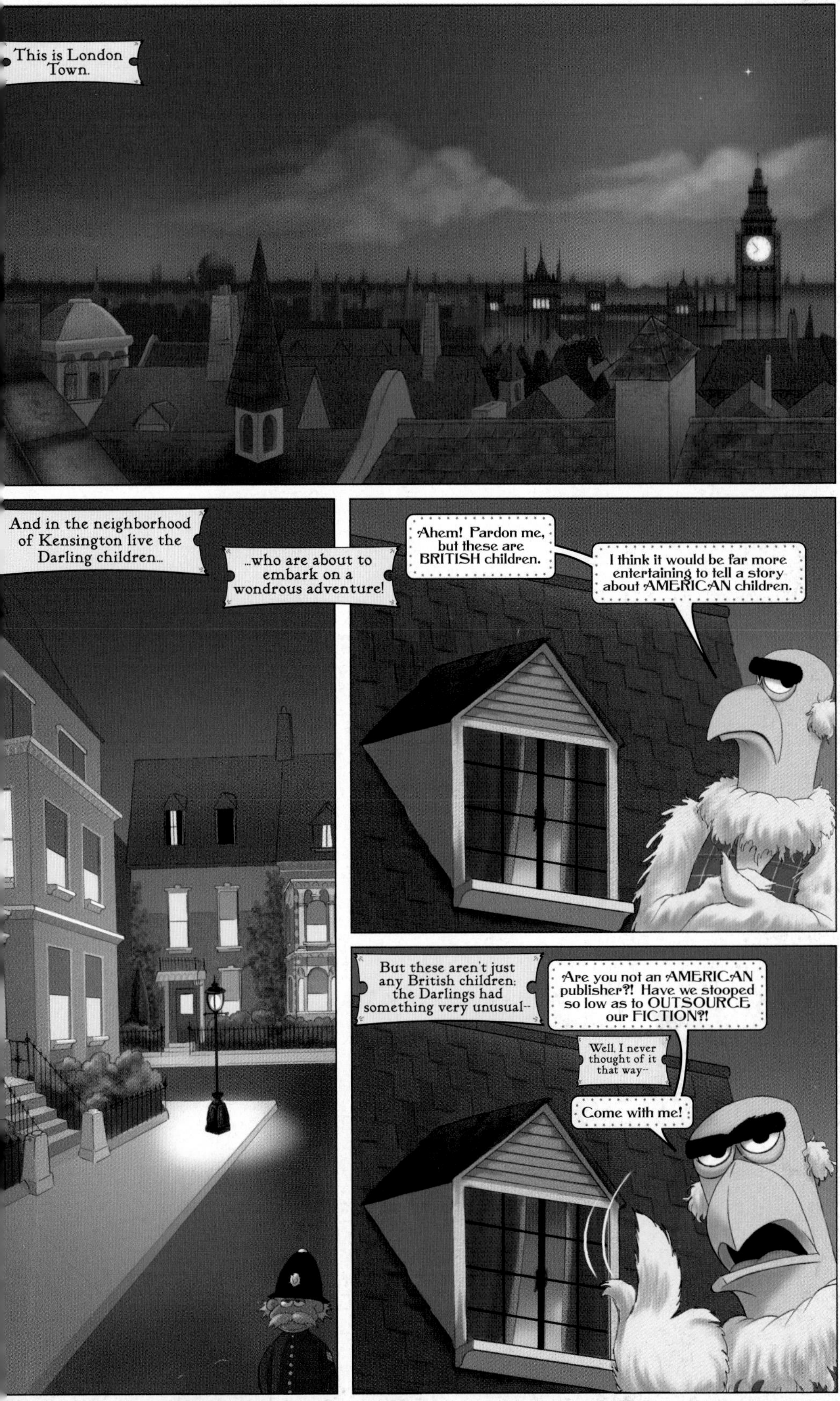
This is London Town.
And in the neighborhood of Kensington live the Darling children...
...who are about to embark on a wondrous adventure!
Ahem! Pardon me, but these are BRITISH children.
I think it would be far more entertaining to tell a story about AMERICAN children.
But these aren't just any British children: the Darlings had something very unusual--
Are you not an AMERICAN publisher?! Have we stooped so low as to OUTSOURCE our FICTION?!
Well, I never thought of it that way--
Come with me!

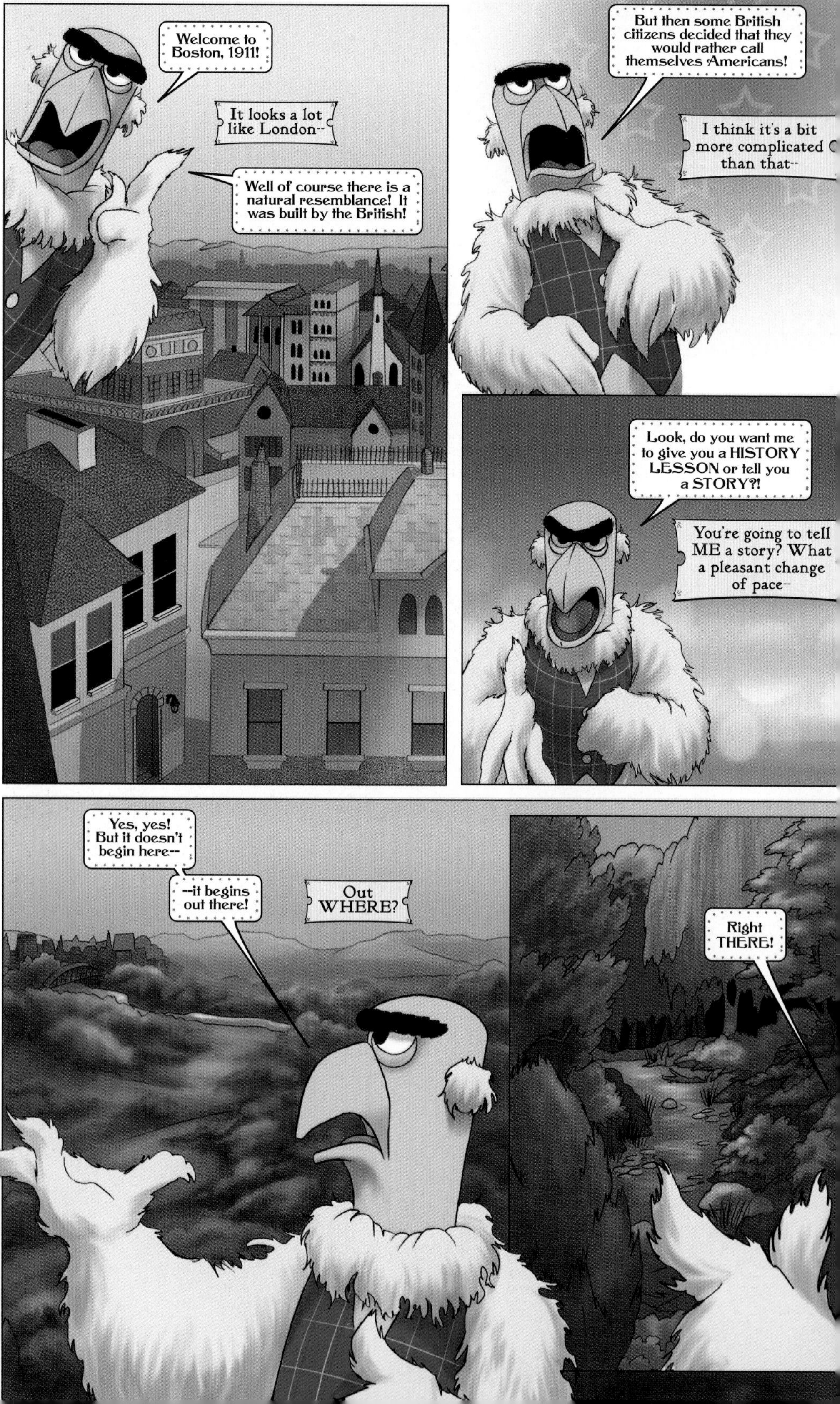
Welcome to Boston, 1911!
It looks a lot like London--
Well of course there is a natural resemblance! It was built by the British!
But then some British citizens decided that they would rather call themselves Americans!
I think it's a bit more complicated than that--
Look, do you want me to give you a HISTORY LESSON or tell you a STORY?!
You're going to tell ME a story? What a pleasant change of pace--
Yes, yes! But it doesn't begin here--
--it begins out there!
Out WHERE?
Right THERE!

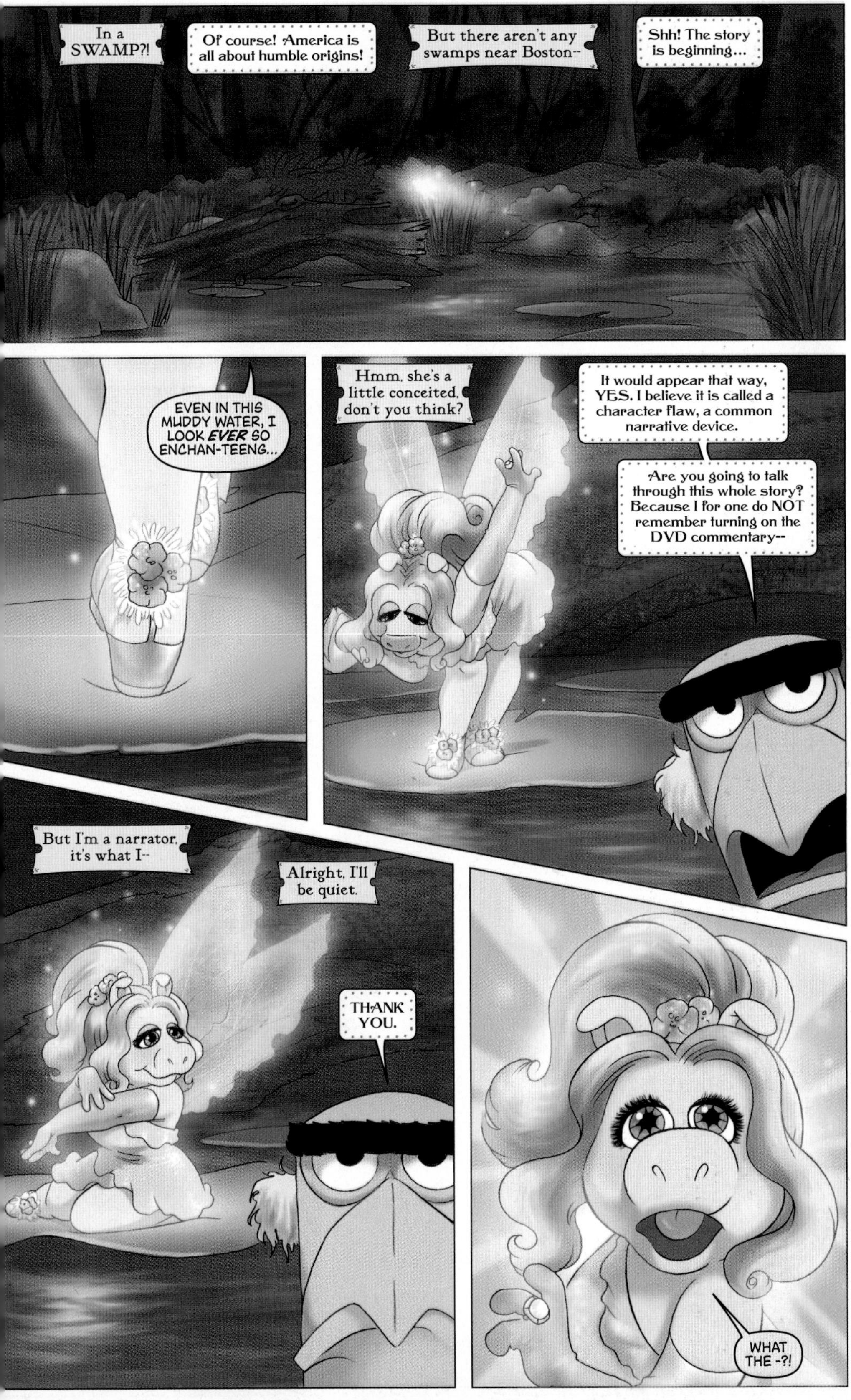
In a SWAMP?!
Of course! America is all about humble origins!
But there aren't any swamps near Boston--
Shh! The story is beginning...
EVEN IN THIS MUDDY WATER, I LOOK EVER SO ENCHAN-TEENG...
Hmm, she's a little conceited, don't you think?
It would appear that way, YES. I believe it is called a character flaw, a common narrative device.
Are you going to talk through this whole story? Because I for one do NOT remember turning on the DVD commentary--
But I'm a narrator, it's what I--
Alright, I'll be quiet.
THANK YOU.
WHAT THE -?!

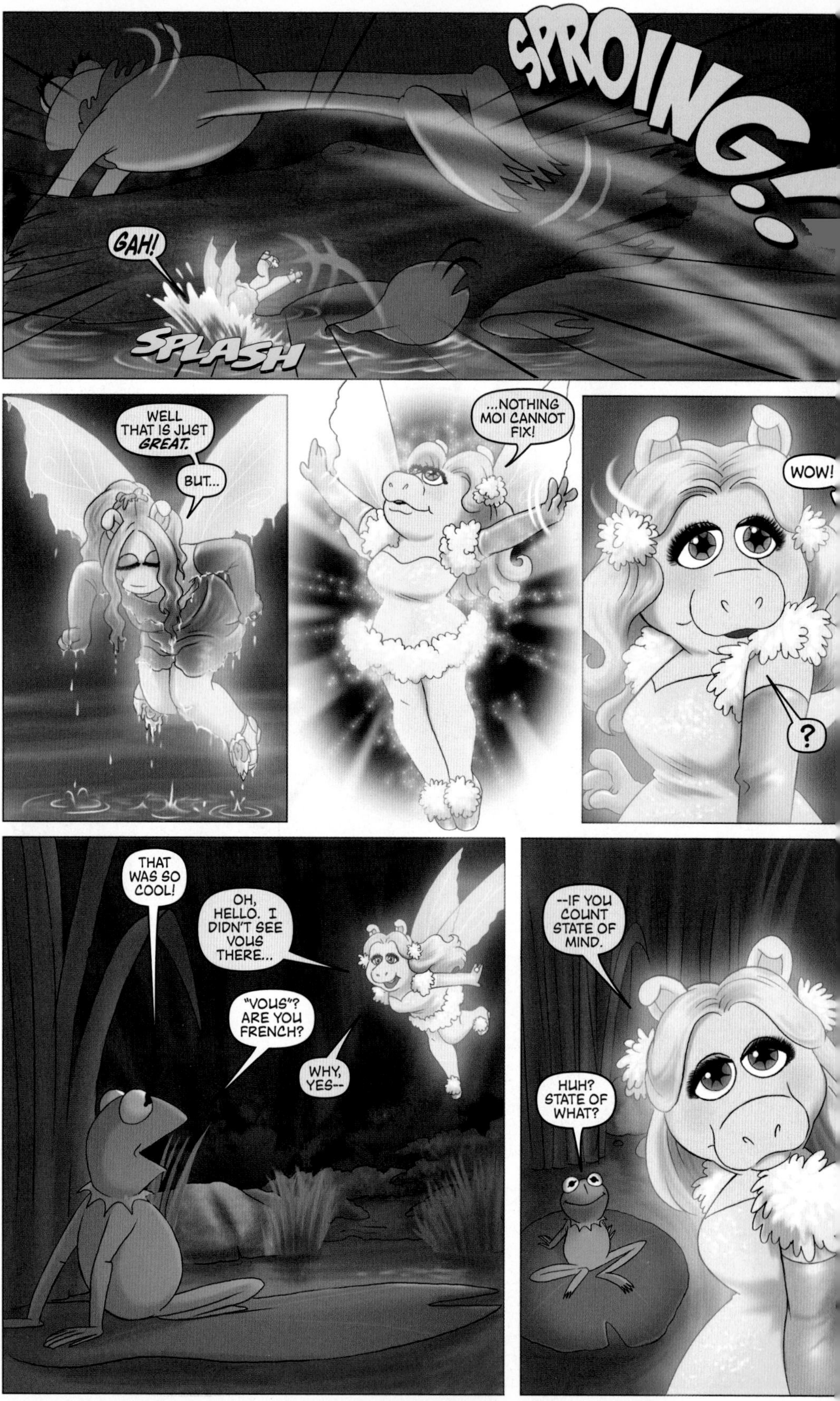
SPROING!!
GAH!
SPLASH
WELL THAT IS JUST *GREAT.*
BUT...
...NOTHING MOI CANNOT FIX!
WOW!
?
THAT WAS SO COOL!
OH, HELLO. I DIDN'T SEE VOUS THERE...
"VOUS"? ARE YOU FRENCH?
WHY, YES--
--IF YOU COUNT STATE OF MIND.
HUH? STATE OF WHAT?

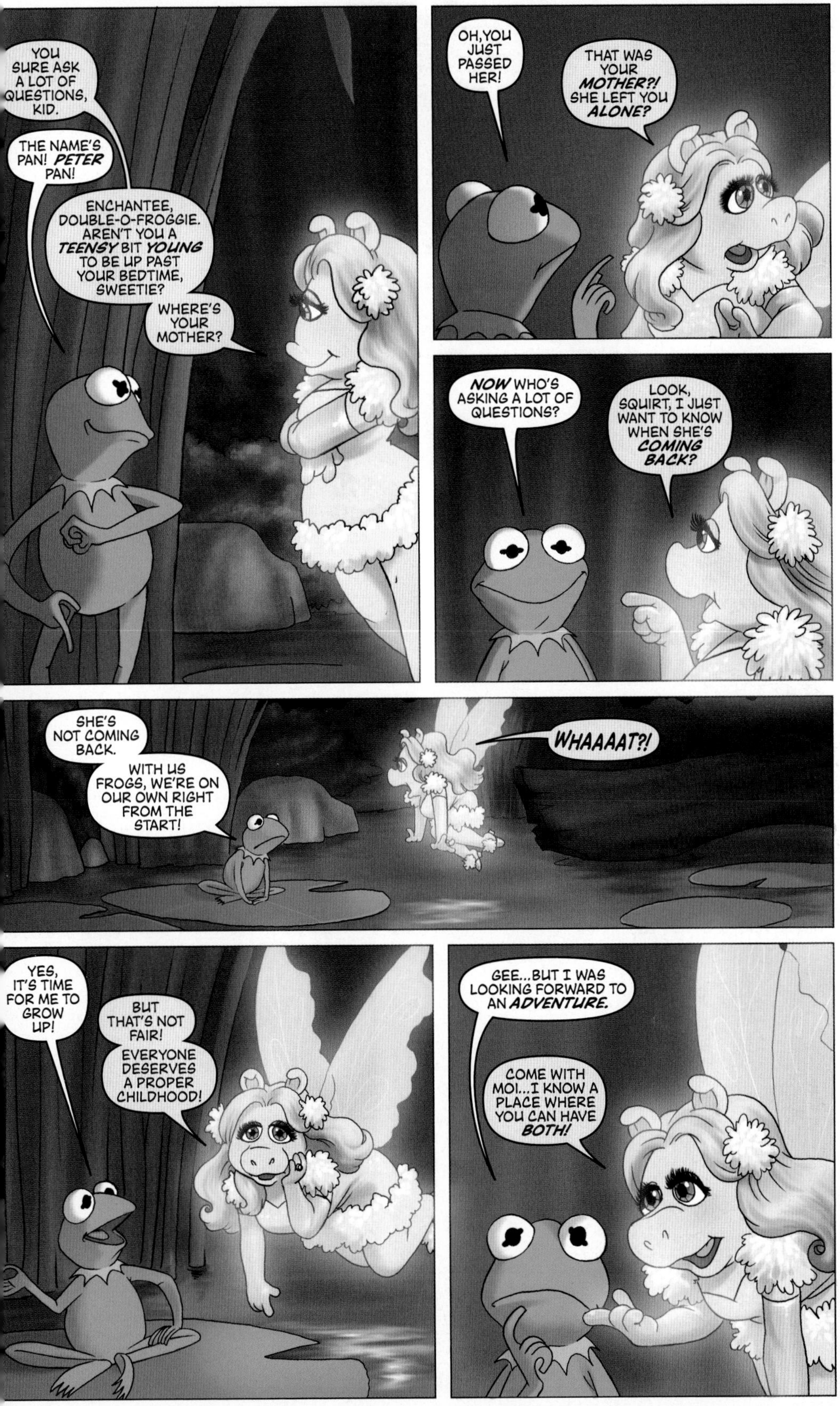
YOU SURE ASK A LOT OF QUESTIONS, KID.
THE NAME'S PAN! PETER PAN!
ENCHANTEE, DOUBLE-O-FROGGIE. AREN'T YOU A TEENSY BIT YOUNG TO BE UP PAST YOUR BEDTIME, SWEETIE?
WHERE'S YOUR MOTHER?
OH, YOU JUST PASSED HER!
THAT WAS YOUR MOTHER?! SHE LEFT YOU ALONE?
NOW WHO'S ASKING A LOT OF QUESTIONS?
LOOK, SQUIRT, I JUST WANT TO KNOW WHEN SHE'S COMING BACK?
SHE'S NOT COMING BACK.
WITH US FROGS, WE'RE ON OUR OWN RIGHT FROM THE START!
WHAAAAT?!
YES, IT'S TIME FOR ME TO GROW UP!
BUT THAT'S NOT FAIR!
EVERYONE DESERVES A PROPER CHILDHOOD!
GEE...BUT I WAS LOOKING FORWARD TO AN ADVENTURE.
COME WITH MOI...I KNOW A PLACE WHERE YOU CAN HAVE BOTH!

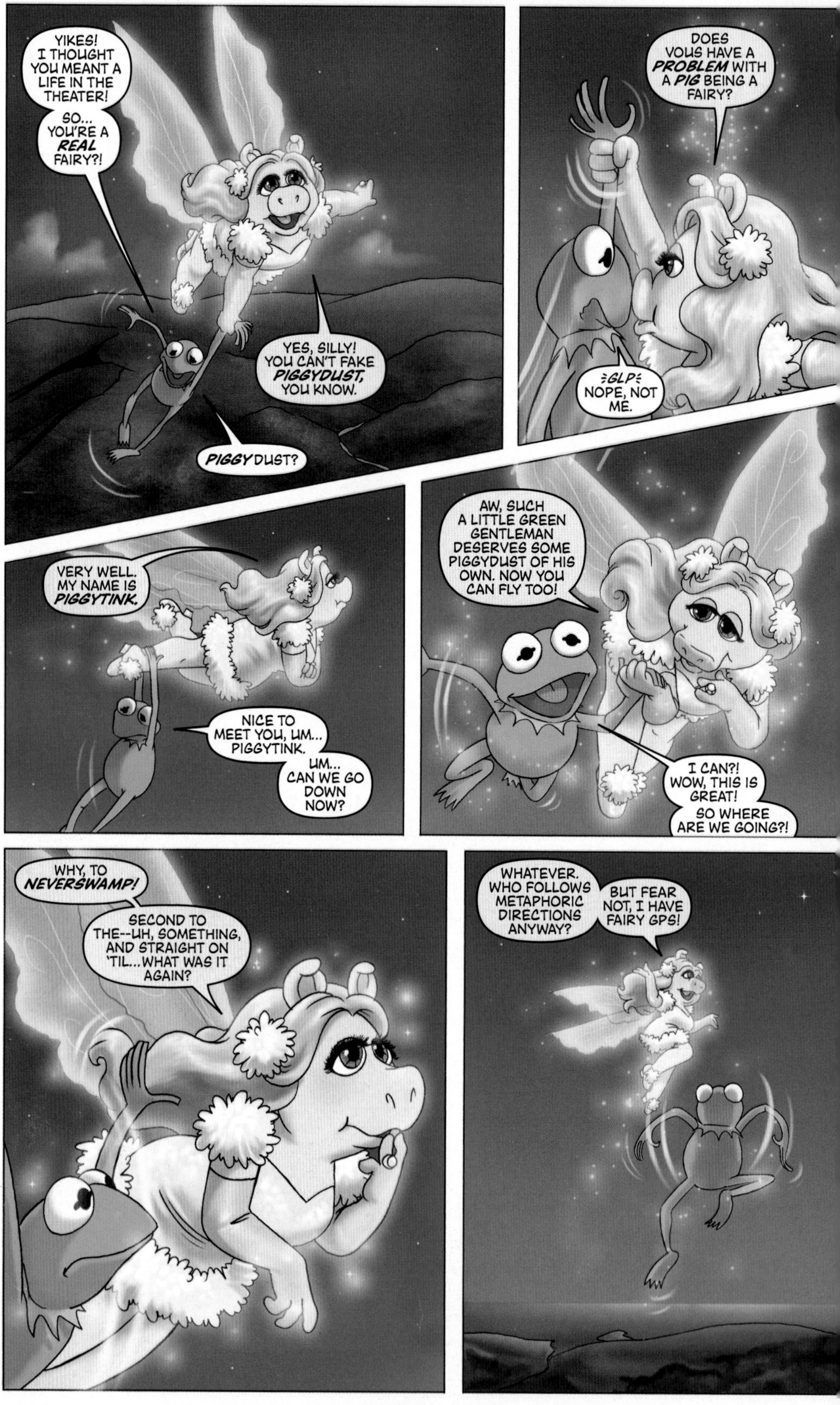

YIKES! I THOUGHT YOU MEANT A LIFE IN THE THEATER!
SO... YOU'RE A REAL FAIRY?!
YES, SILLY! YOU CAN'T FAKE PIGGYDUST, YOU KNOW.
PIGGY DUST?
DOES VOUS HAVE A PROBLEM WITH A PIG BEING A FAIRY?
GLP
NOPE, NOT ME.
VERY WELL. MY NAME IS PIGGYTINK.
NICE TO MEET YOU, UM... PIGGYTINK.
UM... CAN WE GO DOWN NOW?
AW, SUCH A LITTLE GREEN GENTLEMAN DESERVES SOME PIGGYDUST OF HIS OWN. NOW YOU CAN FLY TOO!
I CAN?! WOW, THIS IS GREAT!
SO WHERE ARE WE GOING?!
WHY, TO NEVERSWAMP!
SECOND TO THE--UH, SOMETHING, AND STRAIGHT ON 'TIL...WHAT WAS IT AGAIN?
WHATEVER. WHO FOLLOWS METAPHORIC DIRECTIONS ANYWAY?
BUT FEAR NOT, I HAVE FAIRY GPS!

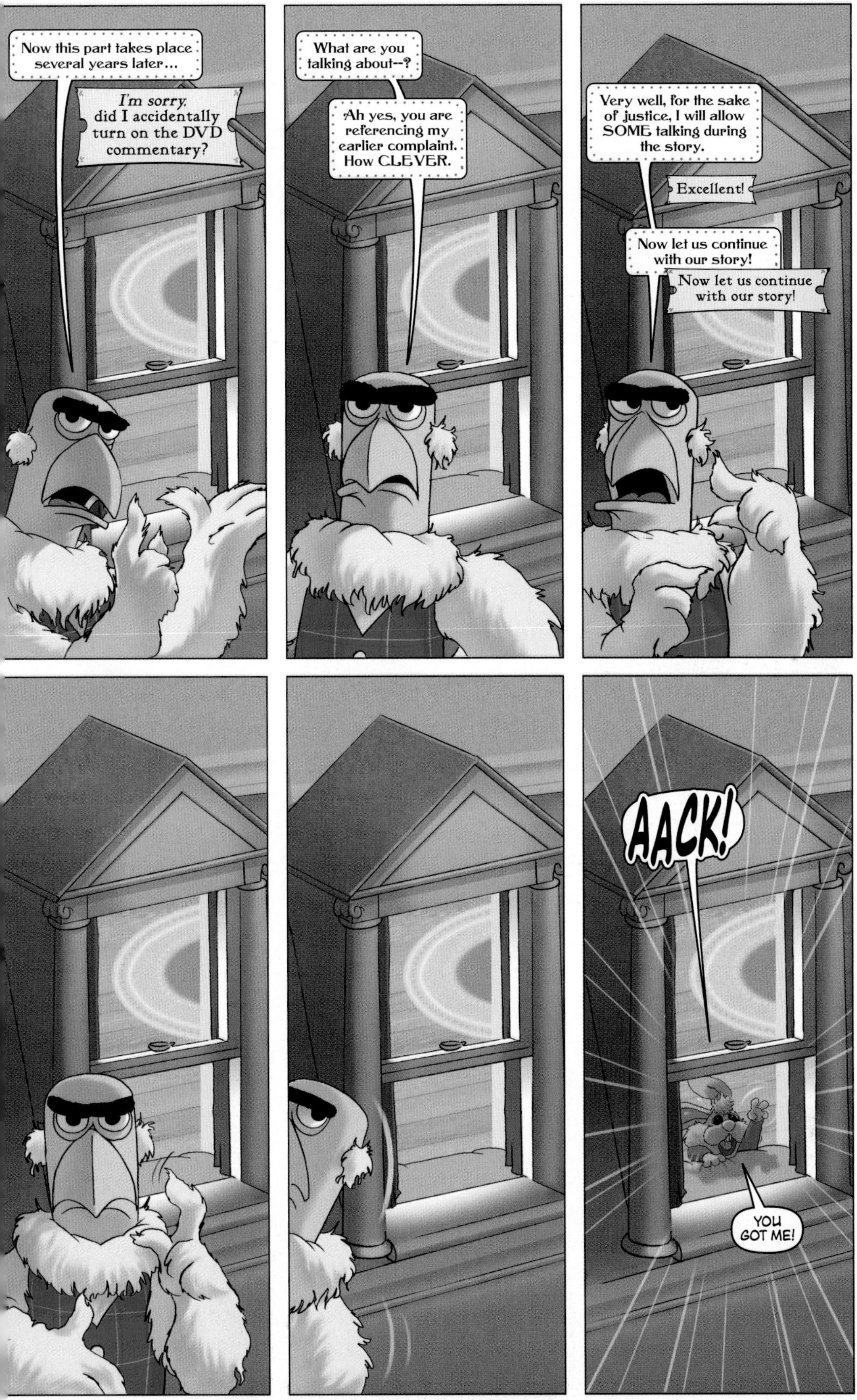
Now this part takes place several years later...
I'm sorry, did I accidentally turn on the DVD commentary?
What are you talking about--?
Ah yes, you are referencing my earlier complaint. How CLEVER.
Very well, for the sake of justice, I will allow SOME talking during the story.
Excellent!
Now let us continue with our story!
Now let us continue with our story!
AACK!
YOU GOT ME!

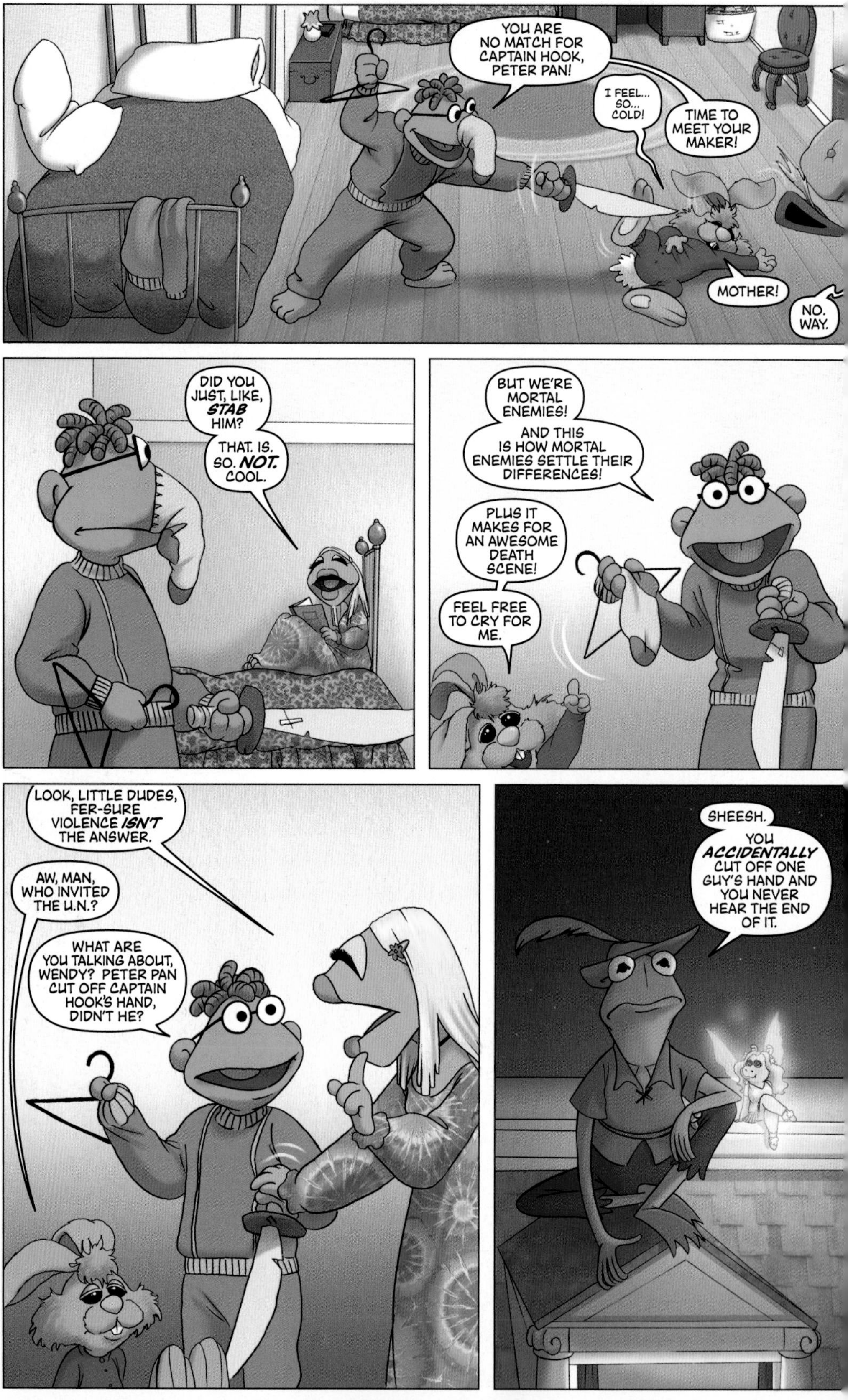

YOU ARE NO MATCH FOR CAPTAIN HOOK, PETER PAN!
I FEEL... SO... COLD!
TIME TO MEET YOUR MAKER!
MOTHER!
NO. WAY.
DID YOU JUST, LIKE, STAB HIM?
THAT. IS. SO. NOT. COOL.
BUT WE'RE MORTAL ENEMIES!
AND THIS IS HOW MORTAL ENEMIES SETTLE THEIR DIFFERENCES!
PLUS IT MAKES FOR AN AWESOME DEATH SCENE!
FEEL FREE TO CRY FOR ME.
LOOK, LITTLE DUDES, FER-SURE VIOLENCE ISN'T THE ANSWER.
AW, MAN, WHO INVITED THE U.N.?
WHAT ARE YOU TALKING ABOUT, WENDY? PETER PAN CUT OFF CAPTAIN HOOK'S HAND, DIDN'T HE?
SHEESH.
YOU ACCIDENTALLY CUT OFF ONE GUY'S HAND AND YOU NEVER HEAR THE END OF IT.

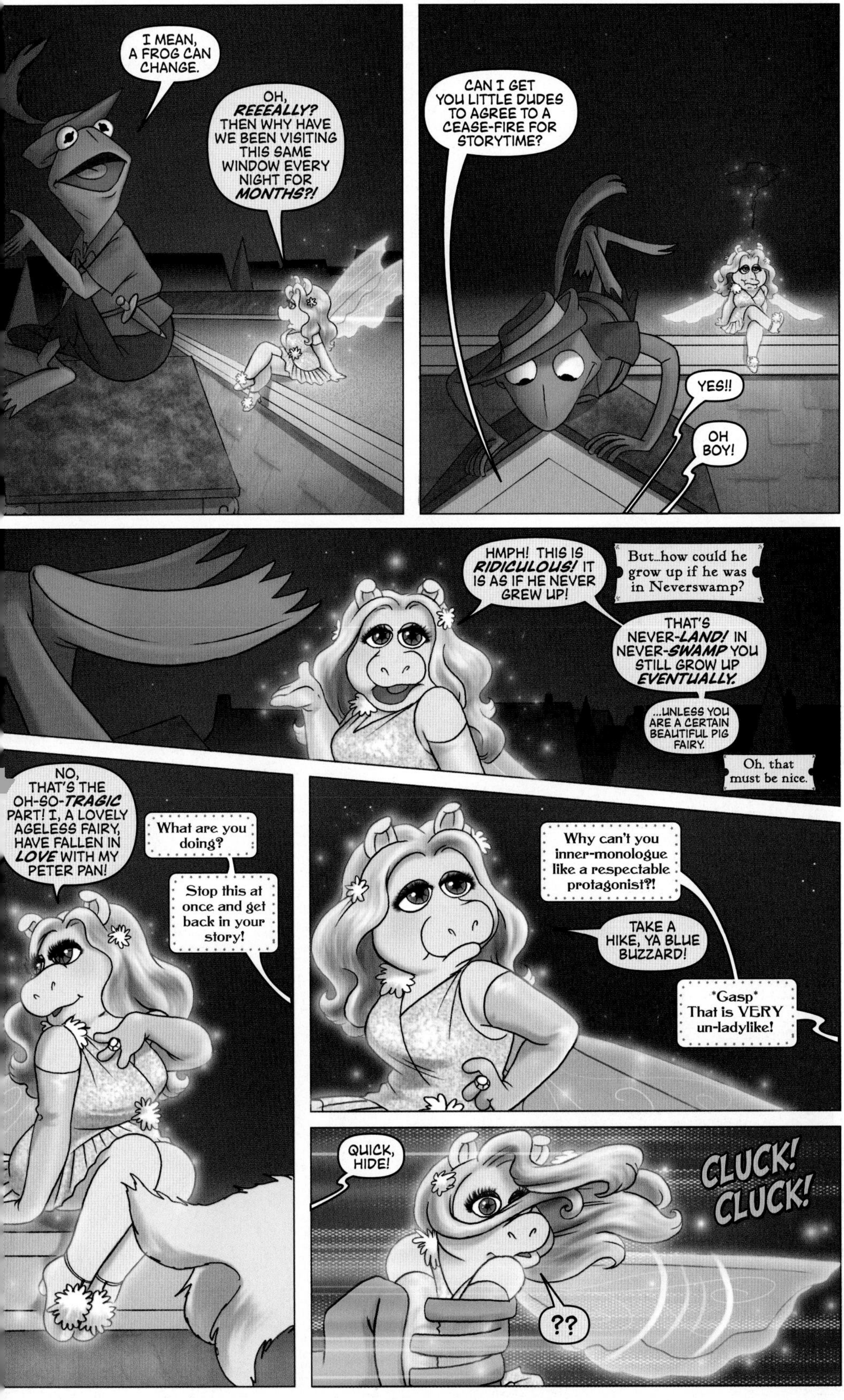

I MEAN, A FROG CAN CHANGE.
OH, REEEALLY? THEN WHY HAVE WE BEEN VISITING THIS SAME WINDOW EVERY NIGHT FOR MONTHS?!
CAN I GET YOU LITTLE DUDES TO AGREE TO A CEASE-FIRE FOR STORYTIME?
YES!!
OH BOY!
HMPH! THIS IS RIDICULOUS! IT IS AS IF HE NEVER GREW UP!
But...how could he grow up if he was in Neverswamp?
THAT'S NEVER-LAND! IN NEVER-SWAMP YOU STILL GROW UP EVENTUALLY.
...UNLESS YOU ARE A CERTAIN BEAUTIFUL PIG FAIRY.
Oh, that must be nice.
NO, THAT'S THE OH-SO-TRAGIC PART! I, A LOVELY AGELESS FAIRY, HAVE FALLEN IN LOVE WITH MY PETER PAN!
What are you doing?
Stop this at once and get back in your story!
Why can't you inner-monologue like a respectable protagonist?!
TAKE A HIKE, YA BLUE BUZZARD!
Gasp That is VERY un-ladylike!
QUICK, HIDE!
CLUCK! CLUCK!
??

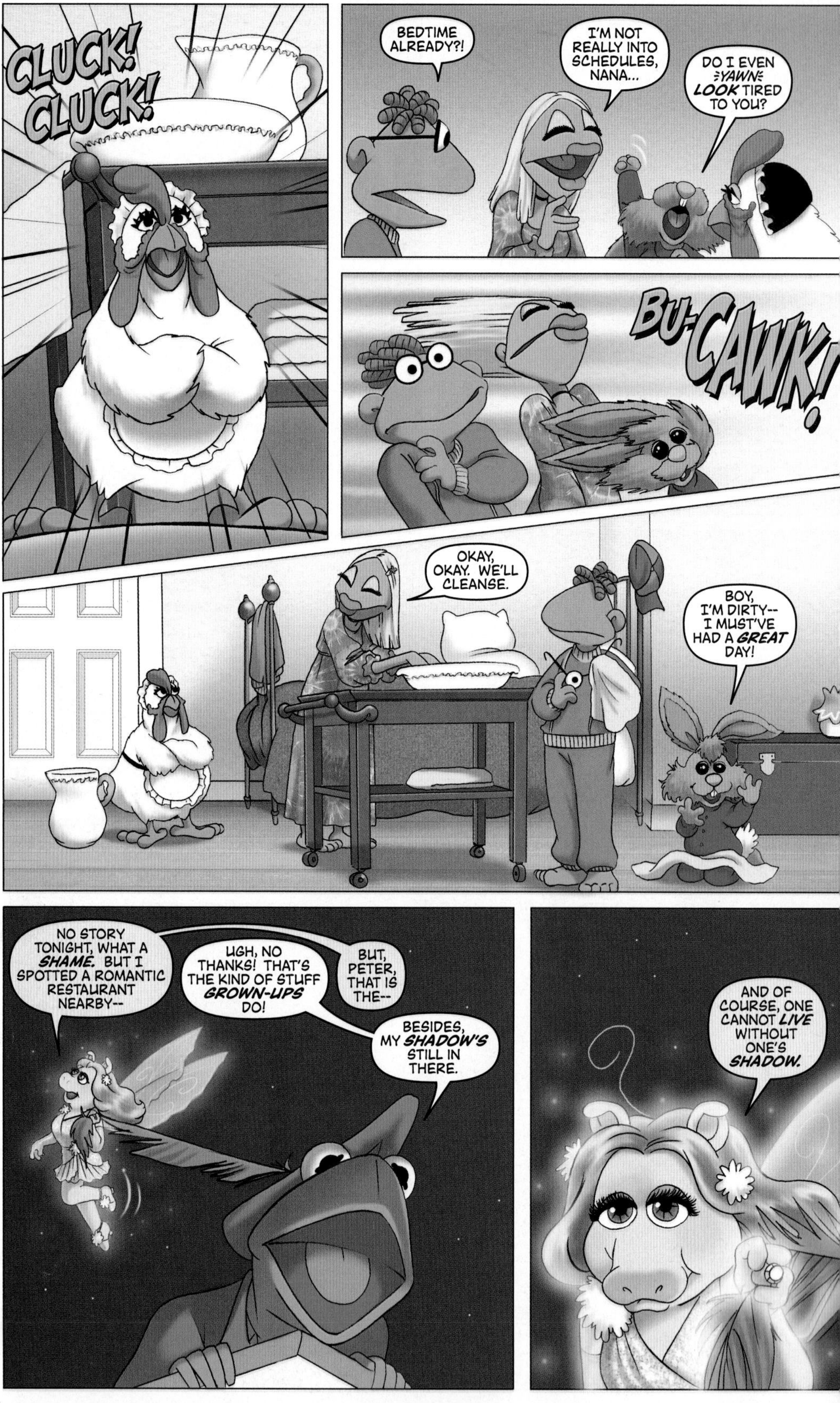
CLUCK! CLUCK!
BEDTIME ALREADY?!
I'M NOT REALLY INTO SCHEDULES, NANA...
DO I EVEN ≈YAWN≈ LOOK TIRED TO YOU?
BU-CAWK!
OKAY, OKAY. WE'LL CLEANSE.
BOY, I'M DIRTY-- I MUST'VE HAD A GREAT DAY!
NO STORY TONIGHT, WHAT A SHAME. BUT I SPOTTED A ROMANTIC RESTAURANT NEARBY--
UGH, NO THANKS! THAT'S THE KIND OF STUFF GROWN-UPS DO!
BUT, PETER, THAT IS THE--
BESIDES, MY SHADOW'S STILL IN THERE.
AND OF COURSE, ONE CANNOT LIVE WITHOUT ONE'S SHADOW.

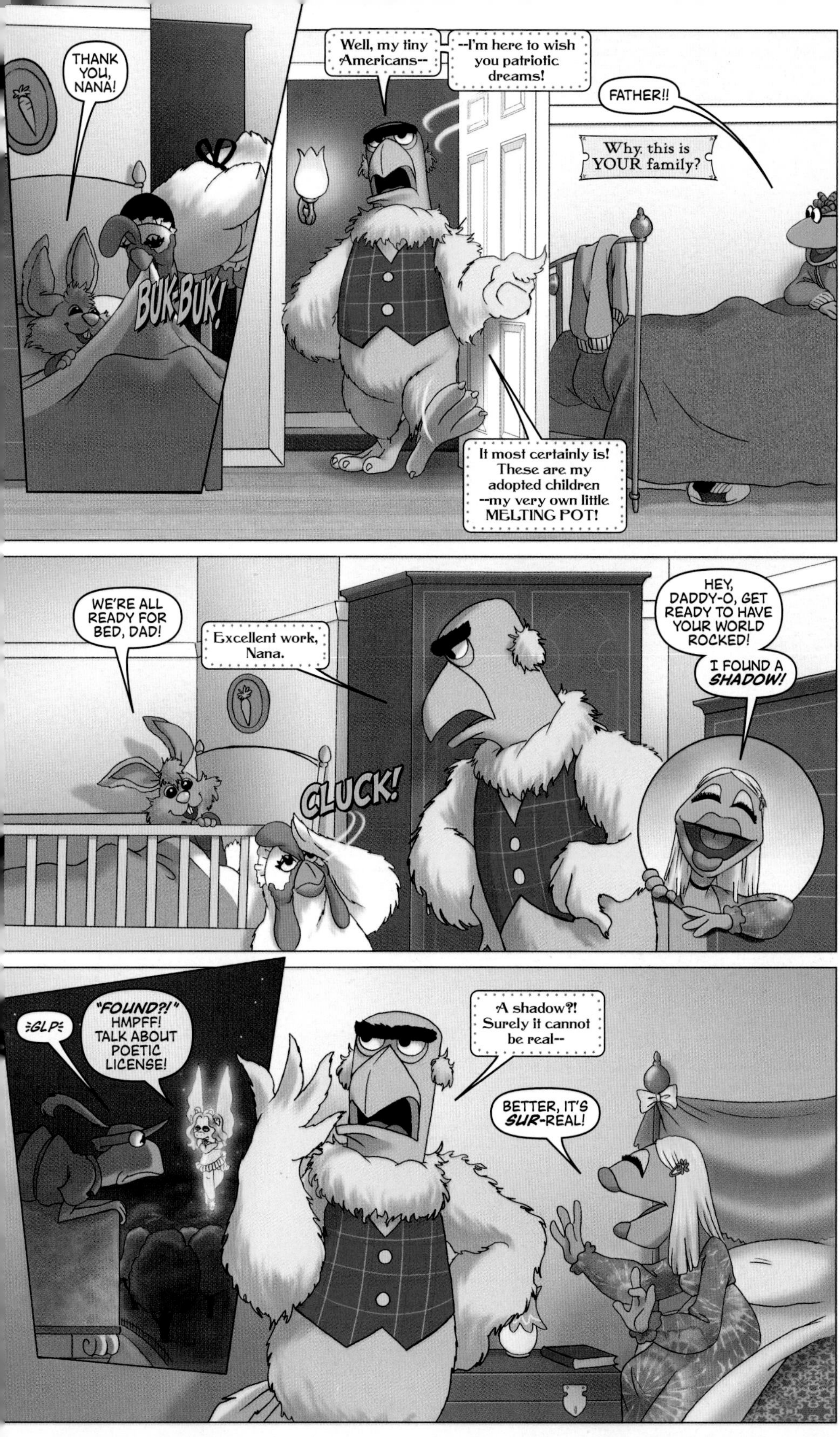

THANK YOU, NANA!
BUK-BUK!
Well, my tiny Americans--
--I'm here to wish you patriotic dreams!
FATHER!!
Why, this is YOUR family?
It most certainly is! These are my adopted children --my very own little MELTING POT!
WE'RE ALL READY FOR BED, DAD!
Excellent work, Nana.
CLUCK!
HEY, DADDY-O, GET READY TO HAVE YOUR WORLD ROCKED!
I FOUND A SHADOW!
=GLP=
"FOUND?!" HMPFF! TALK ABOUT POETIC LICENSE!
A shadow?! Surely it cannot be real--
BETTER, IT'S SUR-REAL!

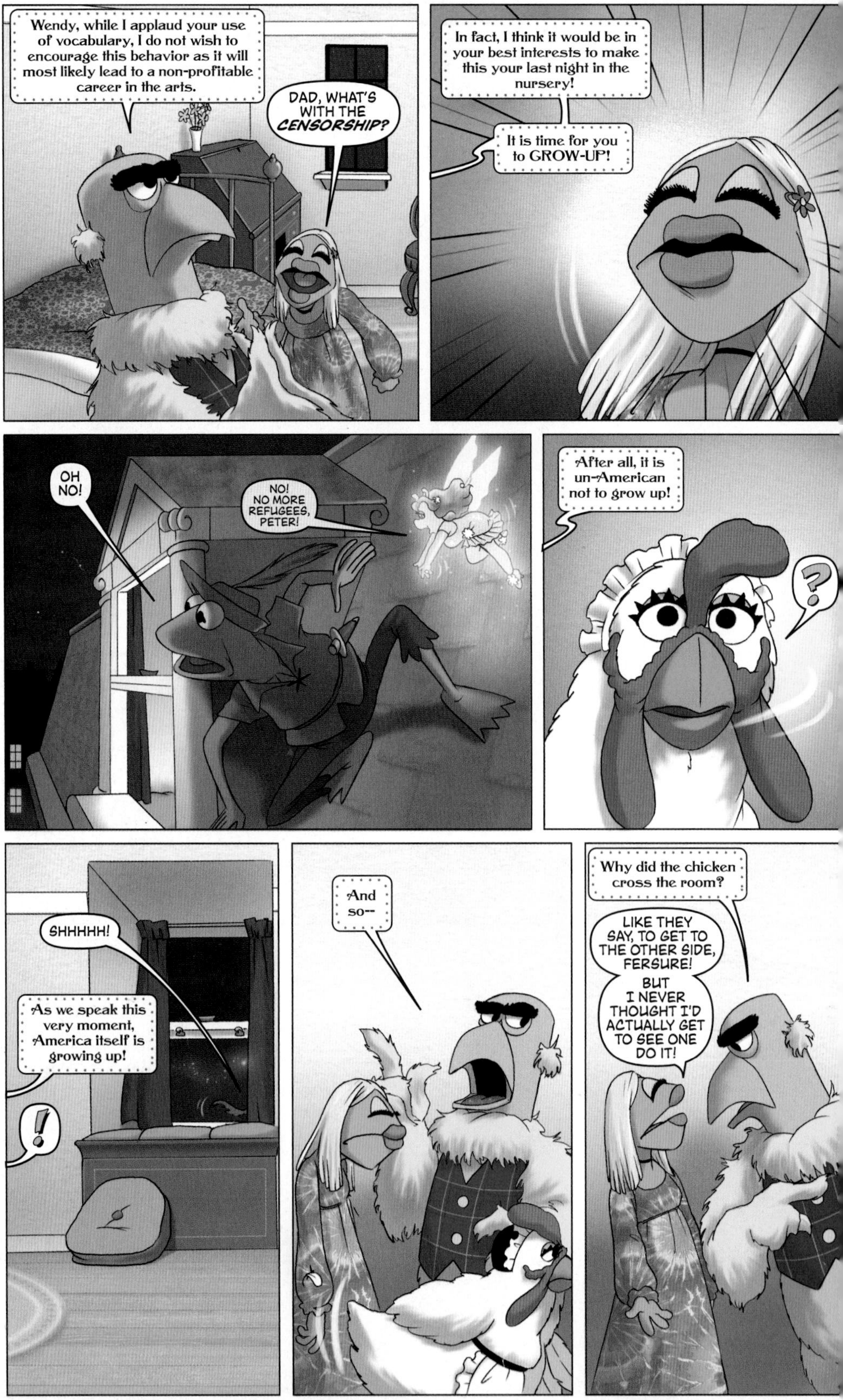
Wendy, while I applaud your use of vocabulary, I do not wish to encourage this behavior as it will most likely lead to a non-profitable career in the arts.
DAD, WHAT'S WITH THE CENSORSHIP?
In fact, I think it would be in your best interests to make this your last night in the nursery!
It is time for you to GROW-UP!
OH NO!
NO! NO MORE REFUGEES, PETER!
After all, it is un-American not to grow up!
?
SHHHHH!
As we speak this very moment, America itself is growing up!
!
And so--
Why did the chicken cross the room?
LIKE THEY SAY, TO GET TO THE OTHER SIDE, FERSURE!
BUT I NEVER THOUGHT I'D ACTUALLY GET TO SEE ONE DO IT!

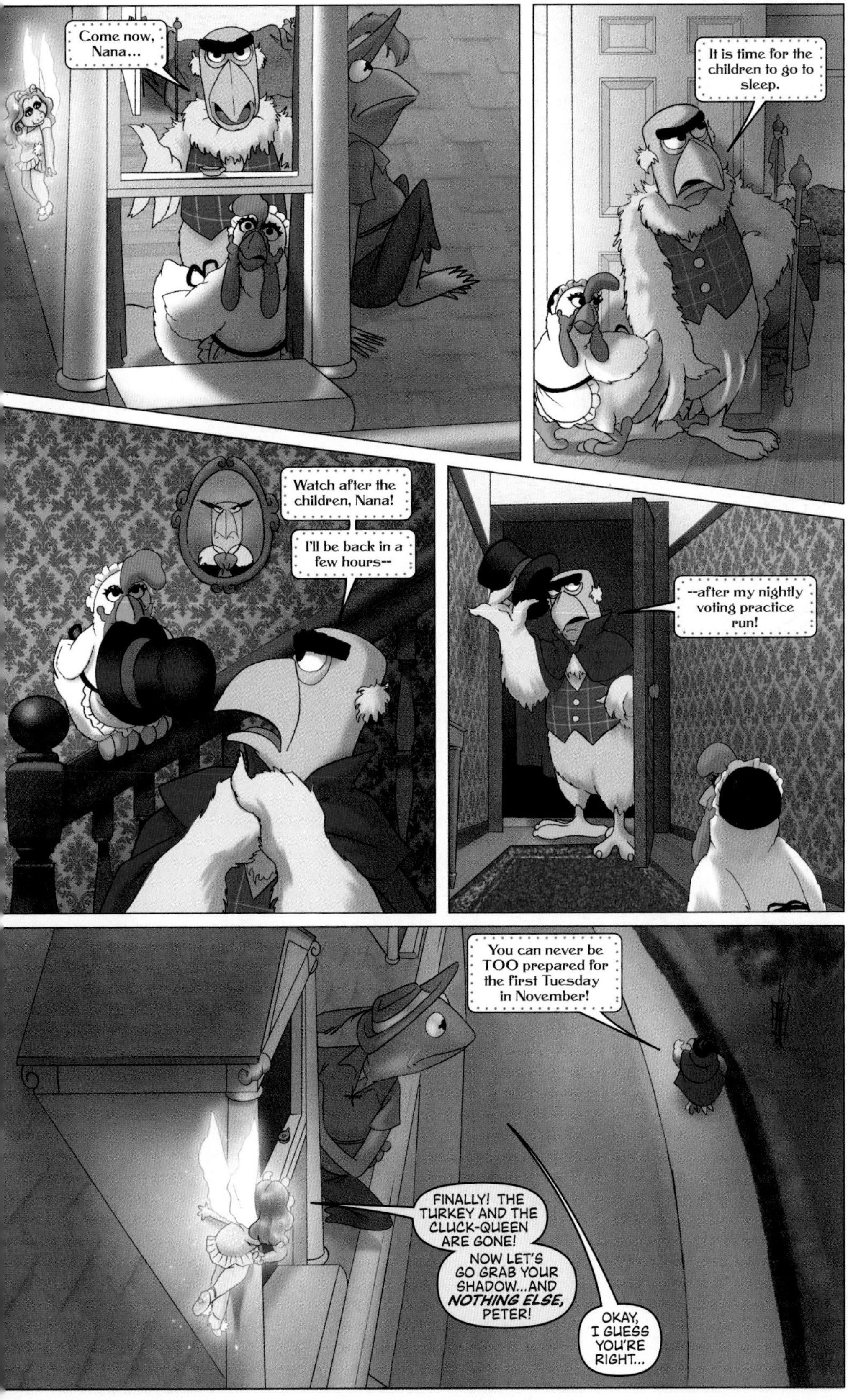
Come now, Nana...
It is time for the children to go to sleep.
Watch after the children, Nana!
I'll be back in a few hours--
--after my nightly voting practice run!
You can never be TOO prepared for the first Tuesday in November!
FINALLY! THE TURKEY AND THE CLUCK-QUEEN ARE GONE!
NOW LET'S GO GRAB YOUR SHADOW...AND *NOTHING ELSE,* PETER!
OKAY, I GUESS YOU'RE RIGHT...

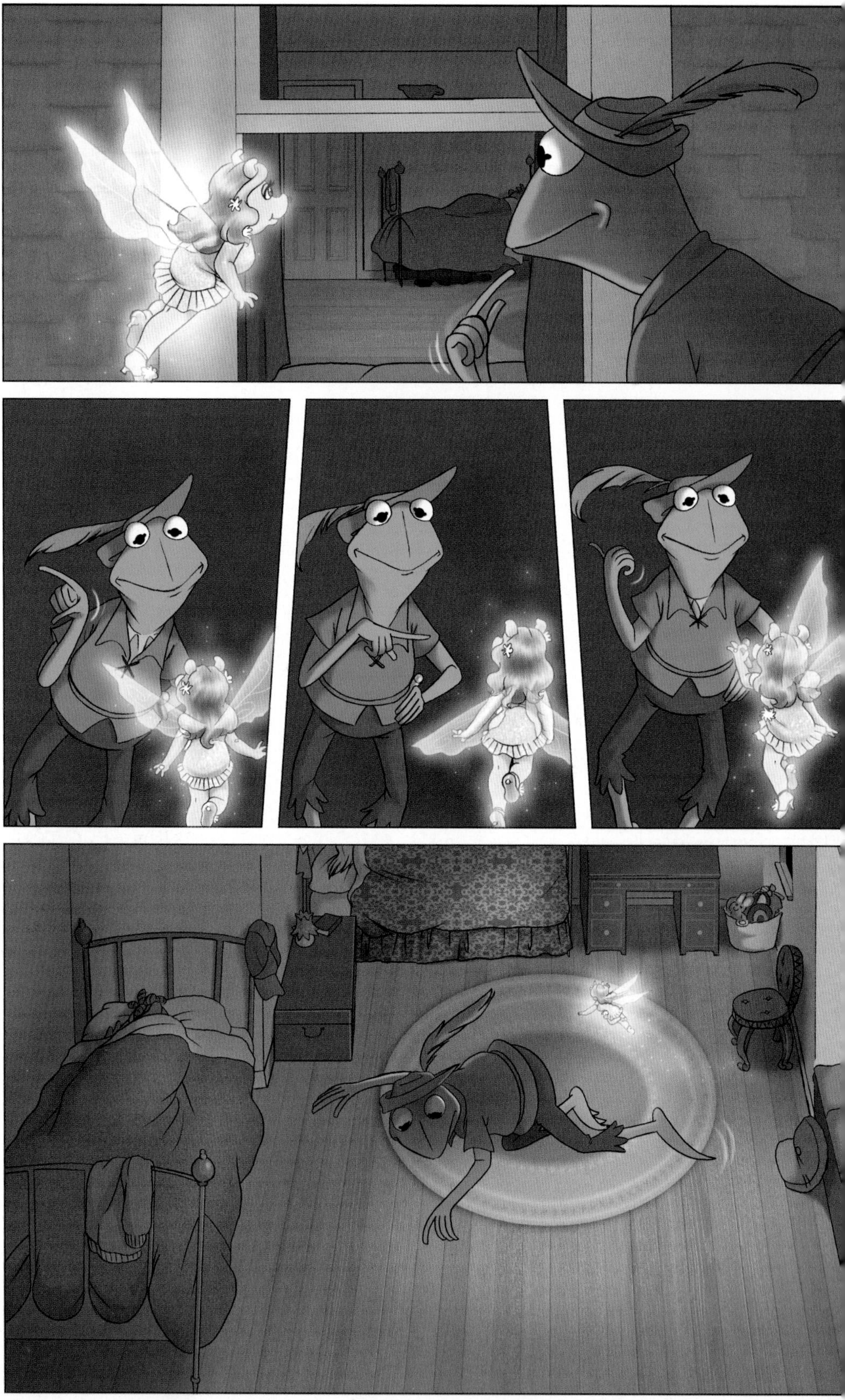

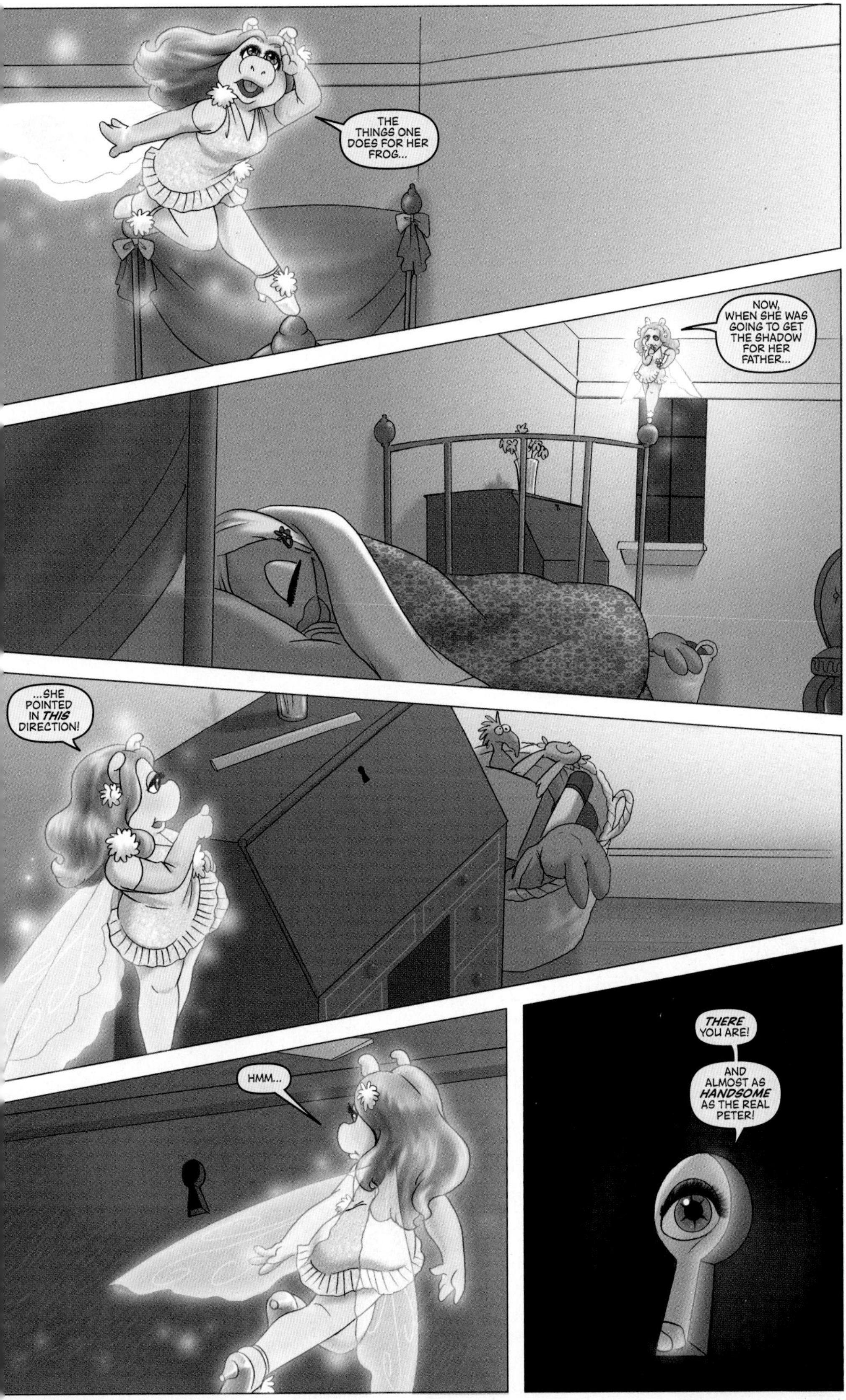
THE THINGS ONE DOES FOR HER FROG...
NOW, WHEN SHE WAS GOING TO GET THE SHADOW FOR HER FATHER...
...SHE POINTED IN *THIS* DIRECTION!
HMM...
THERE YOU ARE!
AND ALMOST AS *HANDSOME* AS THE REAL PETER!

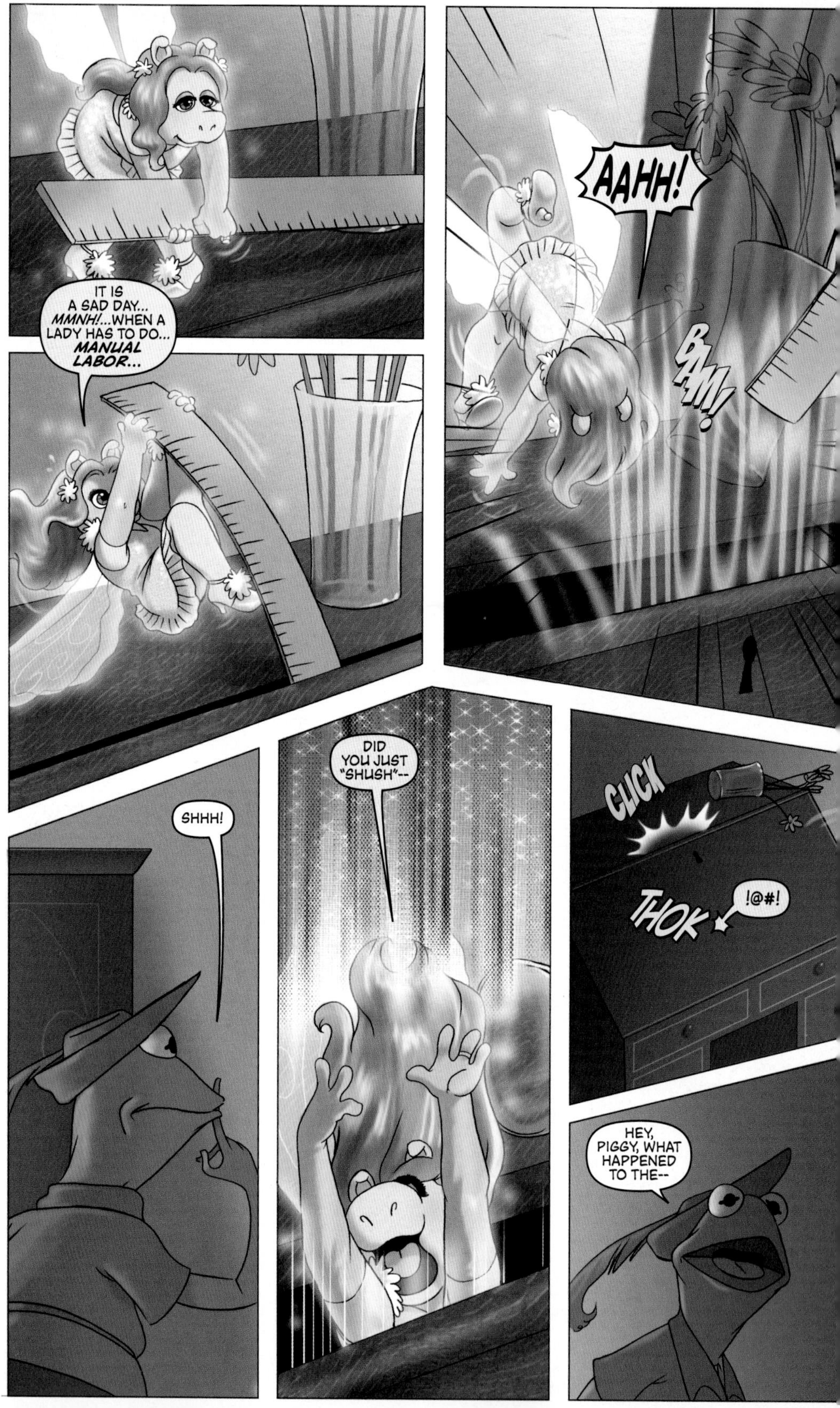
IT IS A SAD DAY... MMNH!...WHEN A LADY HAS TO DO... MANUAL LABOR...
AAHH!
BAM!
WHOOM!
SHHH!
DID YOU JUST "SHUSH"--
CLICK
THOK
!@#!
HEY, PIGGY, WHAT HAPPENED TO THE--

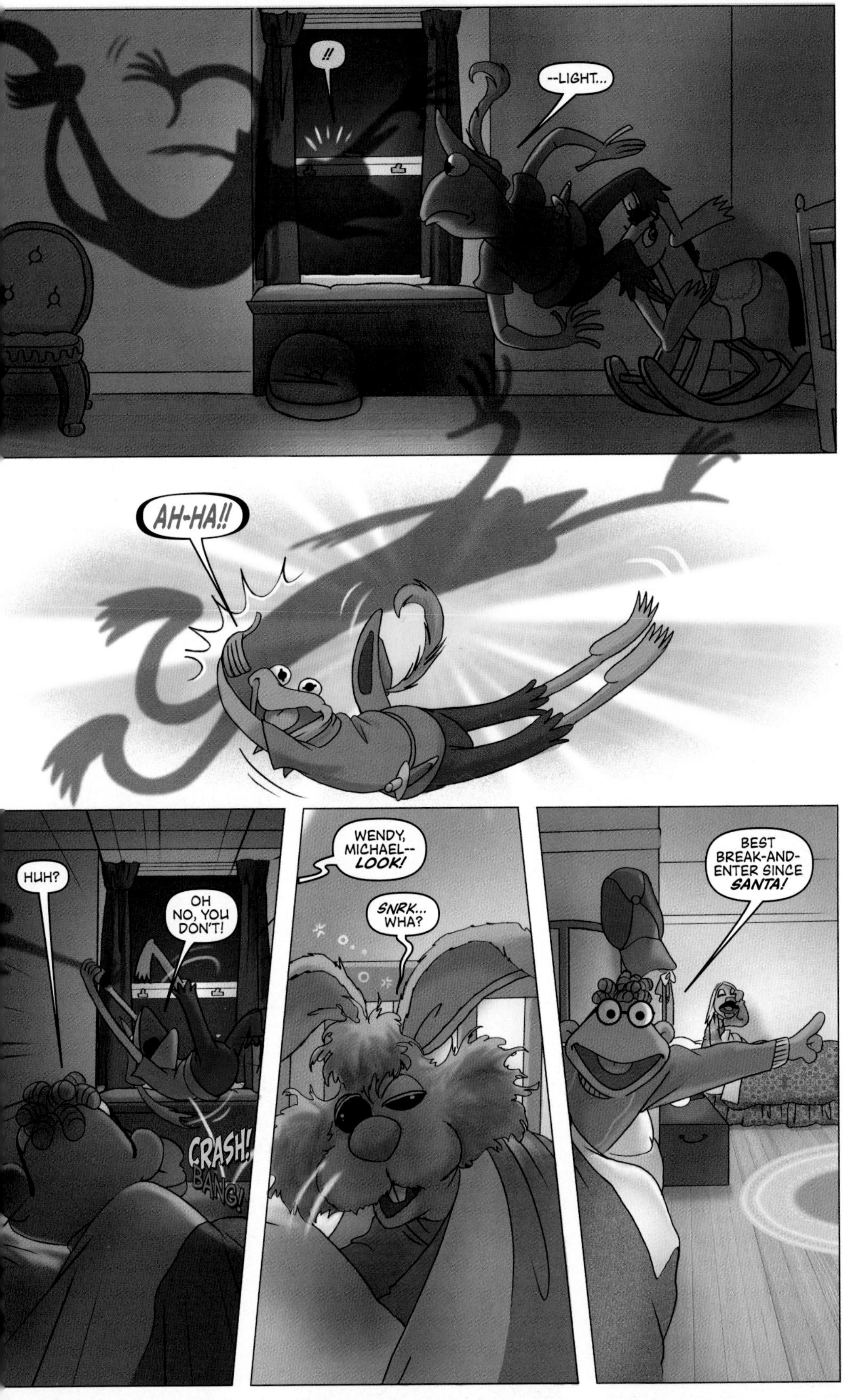
!!
--LIGHT...
AH-HA!!
HUH?
OH NO, YOU DON'T!
CRASH!
BANG!
WENDY, MICHAEL-- LOOK!
SNRK... WHA?
BEST BREAK-AND-ENTER SINCE SANTA!

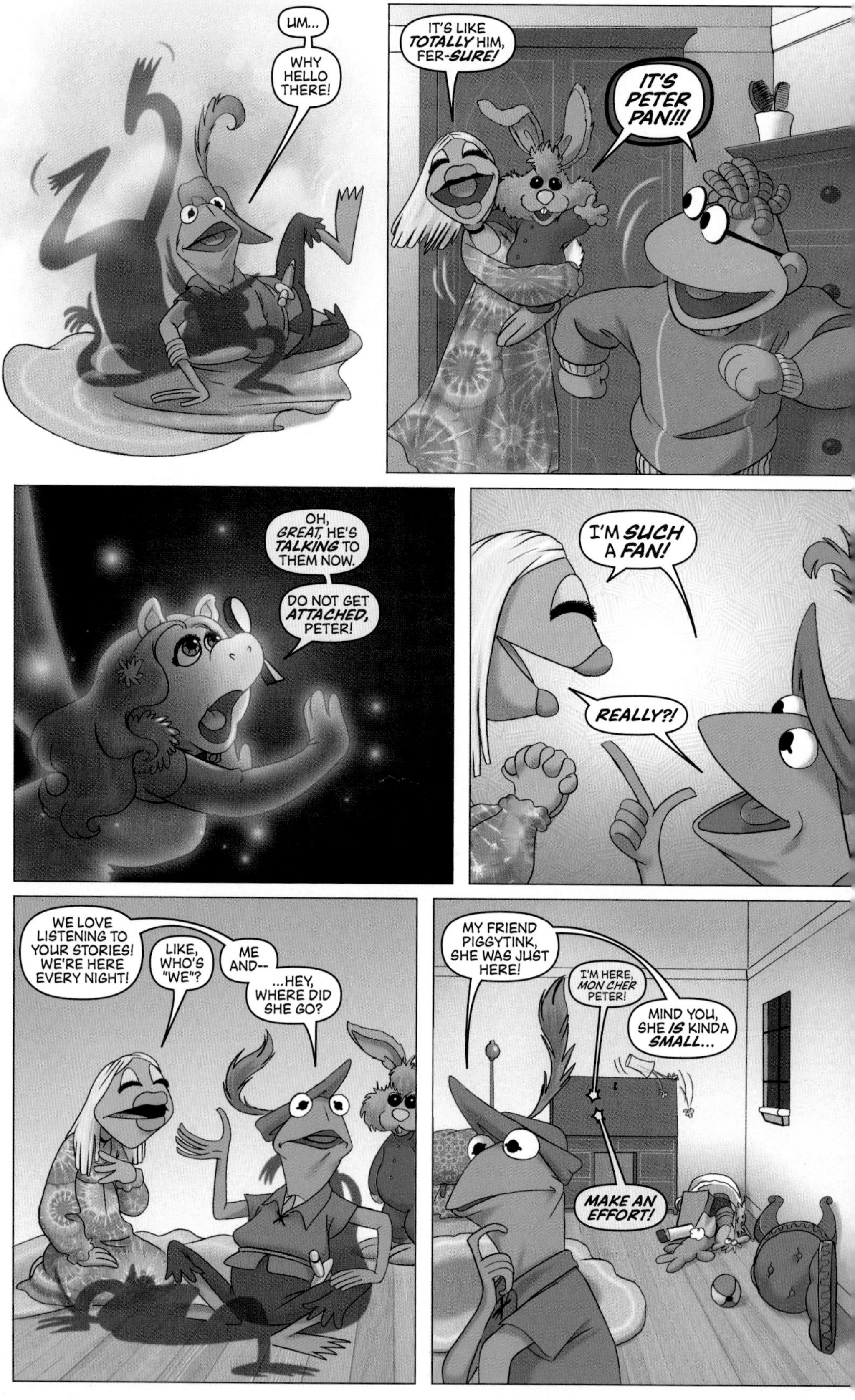
UM...
WHY HELLO THERE!
IT'S LIKE TOTALLY HIM, FER-SURE!
IT'S PETER PAN!!!
OH, GREAT, HE'S TALKING TO THEM NOW.
DO NOT GET ATTACHED, PETER!
I'M SUCH A FAN!
REALLY?!
WE LOVE LISTENING TO YOUR STORIES! WE'RE HERE EVERY NIGHT!
LIKE, WHO'S "WE"?
ME AND--
...HEY, WHERE DID SHE GO?
MY FRIEND PIGGYTINK, SHE WAS JUST HERE!
I'M HERE, MON CHER PETER!
MIND YOU, SHE IS KINDA SMALL...
MAKE AN EFFORT!

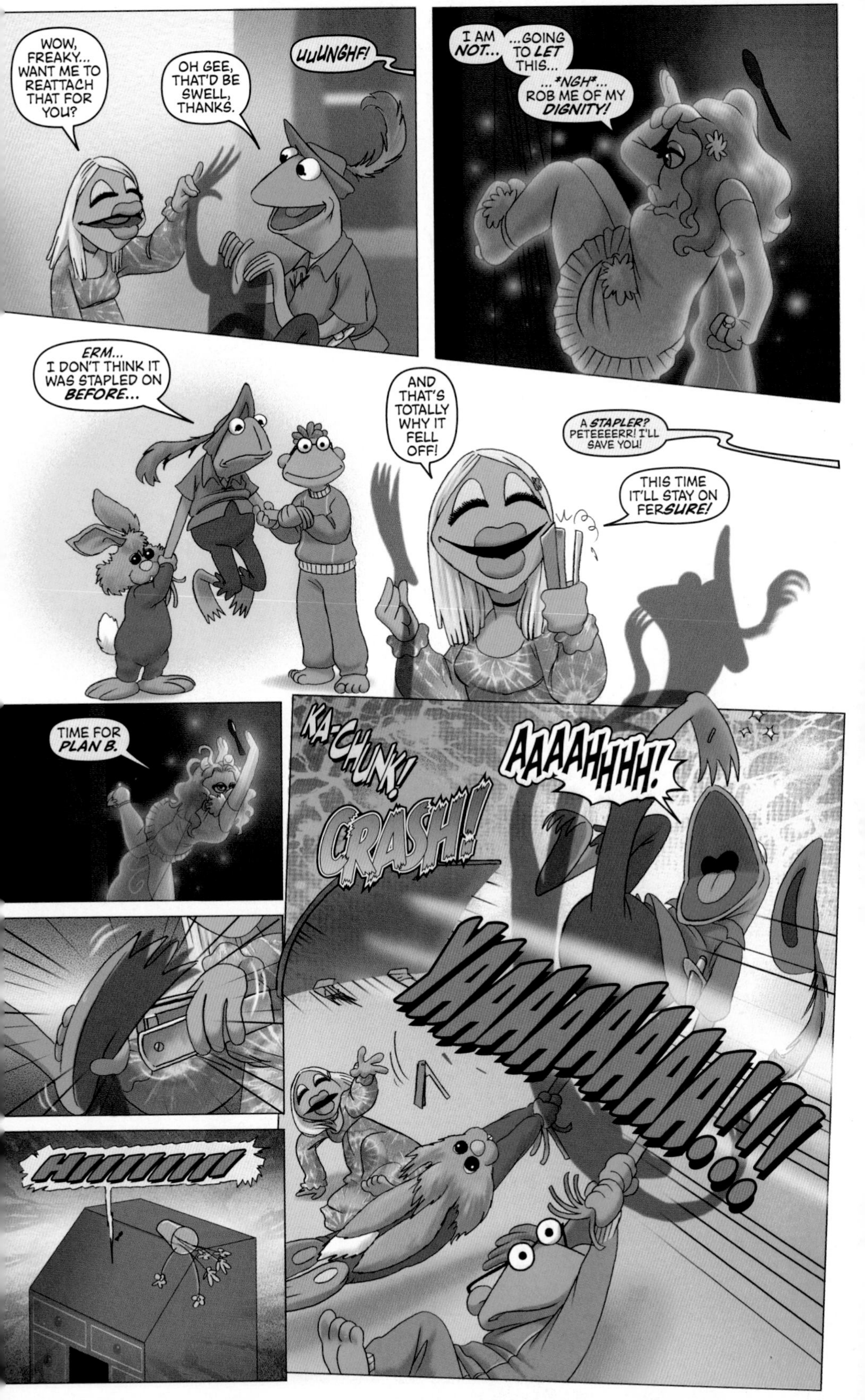
WOW, FREAKY... WANT ME TO REATTACH THAT FOR YOU?
OH GEE, THAT'D BE SWELL, THANKS.
UUUNGHF!
I AM NOT...
...GOING TO LET THIS...
...*NGH*... ROB ME OF MY DIGNITY!
ERM... I DON'T THINK IT WAS STAPLED ON BEFORE...
AND THAT'S TOTALLY WHY IT FELL OFF!
A STAPLER? PETEEEERR! I'LL SAVE YOU!
THIS TIME IT'LL STAY ON FERSURE!
TIME FOR PLAN B.
KA-CHUNK!
CRASH!
AAAAHHHH!
HIIIIIII!
YAAAAAAAA!!!...

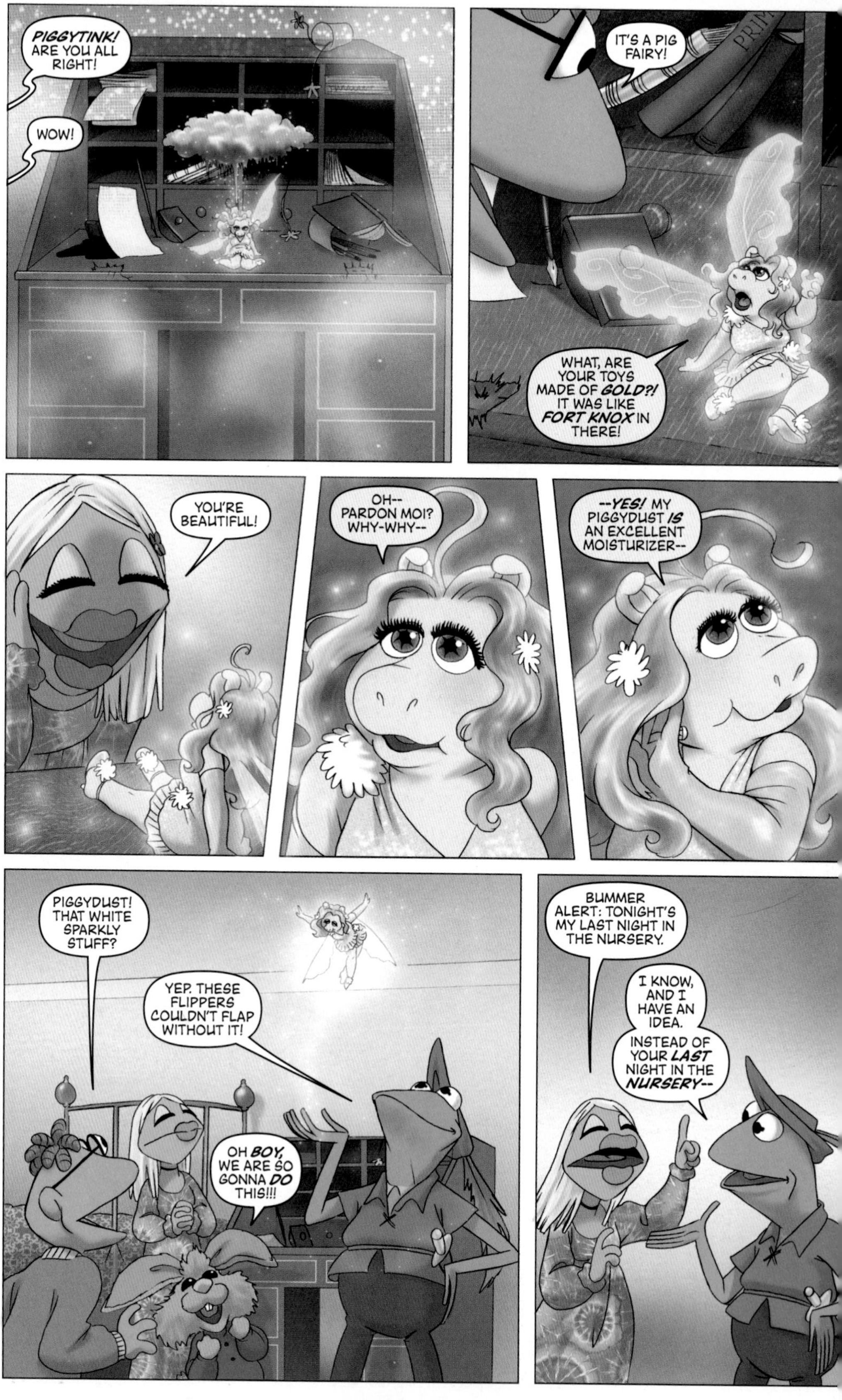
PIGGYTINK! ARE YOU ALL RIGHT!
WOW!
IT'S A PIG FAIRY!
WHAT, ARE YOUR TOYS MADE OF ***GOLD?!*** IT WAS LIKE ***FORT KNOX*** IN THERE!
YOU'RE BEAUTIFUL!
OH-- PARDON MOI? WHY-WHY--
--***YES!*** MY PIGGYDUST ***IS*** AN EXCELLENT MOISTURIZER--
PIGGYDUST! THAT WHITE SPARKLY STUFF?
YEP. THESE FLIPPERS COULDN'T FLAP WITHOUT IT!
OH ***BOY,*** WE ARE SO GONNA ***DO*** THIS!!!
BUMMER ALERT: TONIGHT'S MY LAST NIGHT IN THE NURSERY.
I KNOW, AND I HAVE AN IDEA.
INSTEAD OF YOUR ***LAST*** NIGHT IN THE ***NURSERY***--

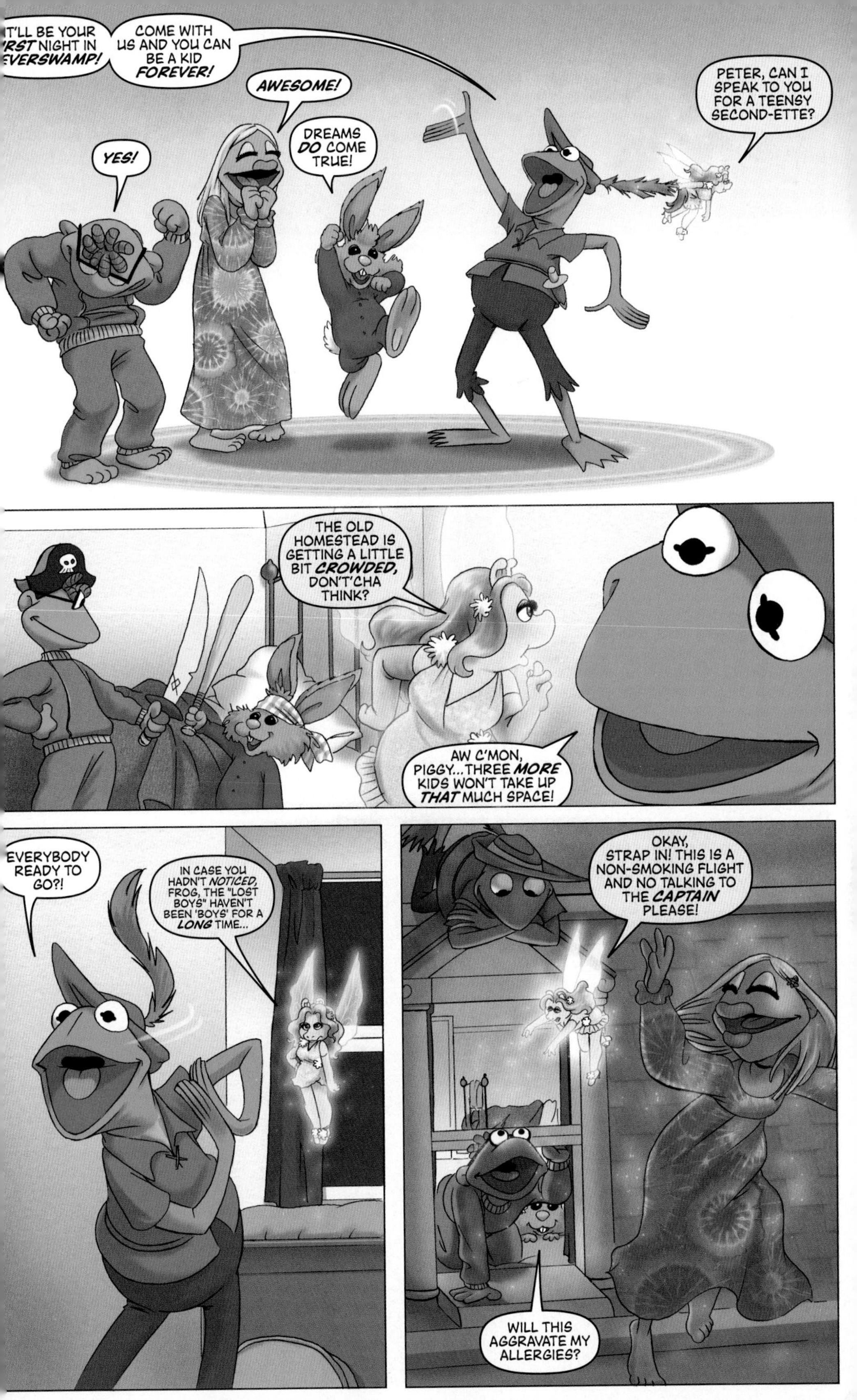
T'LL BE YOUR RST NIGHT IN EVERSWAMP!
COME WITH US AND YOU CAN BE A KID FOREVER!
AWESOME!
YES!
DREAMS DO COME TRUE!
PETER, CAN I SPEAK TO YOU FOR A TEENSY SECOND-ETTE?
THE OLD HOMESTEAD IS GETTING A LITTLE BIT CROWDED, DON'T'CHA THINK?
AW C'MON, PIGGY...THREE MORE KIDS WON'T TAKE UP THAT MUCH SPACE!
EVERYBODY READY TO GO?!
IN CASE YOU HADN'T NOTICED, FROG, THE "LOST BOYS" HAVEN'T BEEN 'BOYS' FOR A LONG TIME...
OKAY, STRAP IN! THIS IS A NON-SMOKING FLIGHT AND NO TALKING TO THE CAPTAIN PLEASE!
WILL THIS AGGRAVATE MY ALLERGIES?

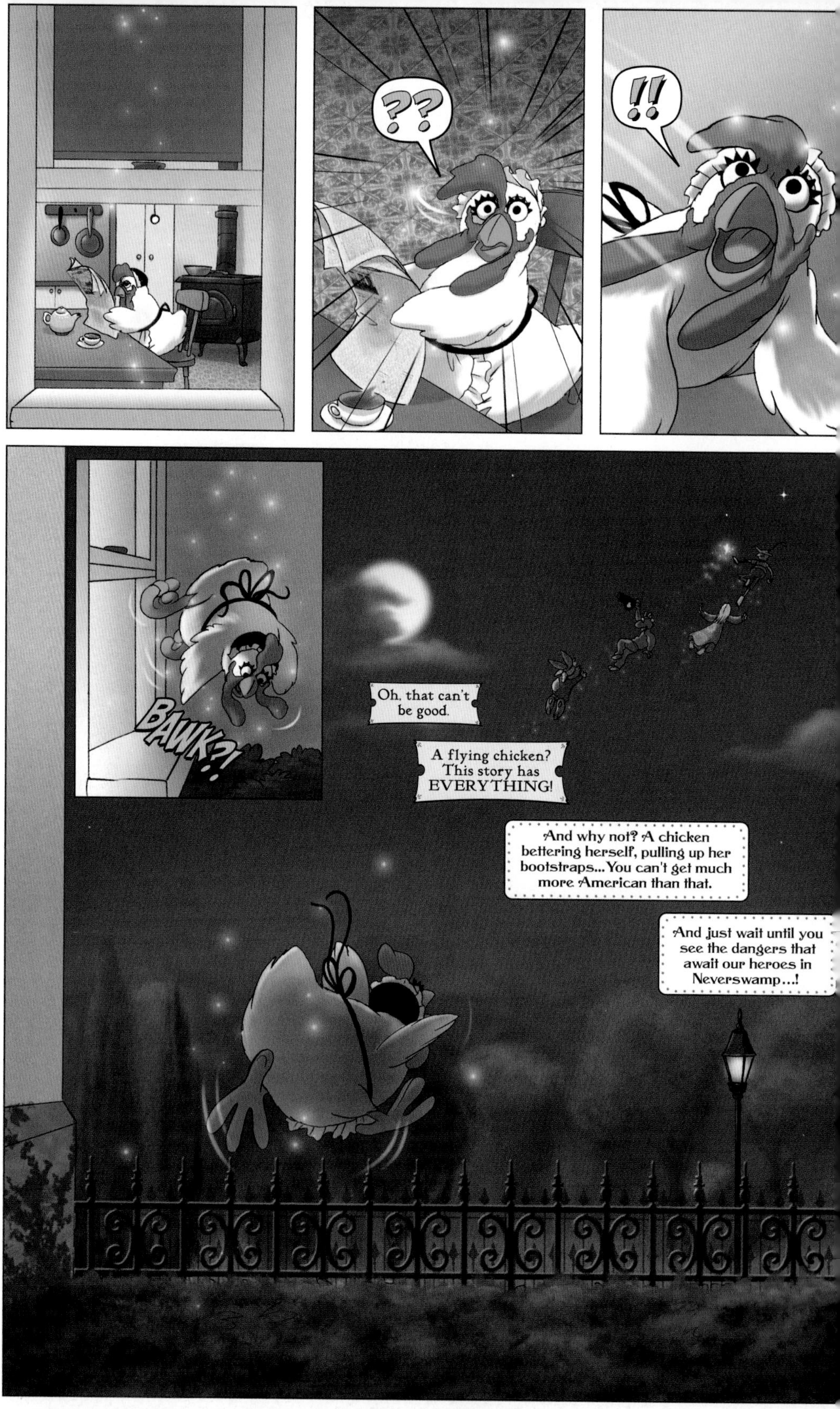
??
!!
BAWK?!
Oh, that can't be good.
A flying chicken? This story has EVERYTHING!
And why not? A chicken bettering herself, pulling up her bootstraps... You can't get much more American than that.
And just wait until you see the dangers that await our heroes in Neverswamp...!

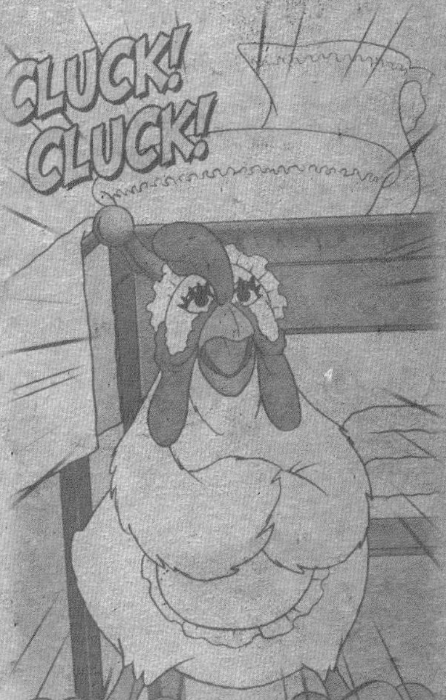
CLUCK!
CLUCK!

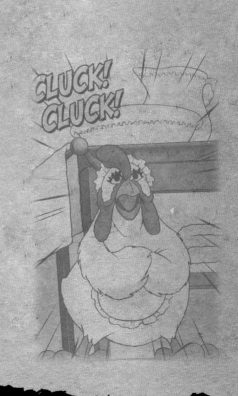

chapter two

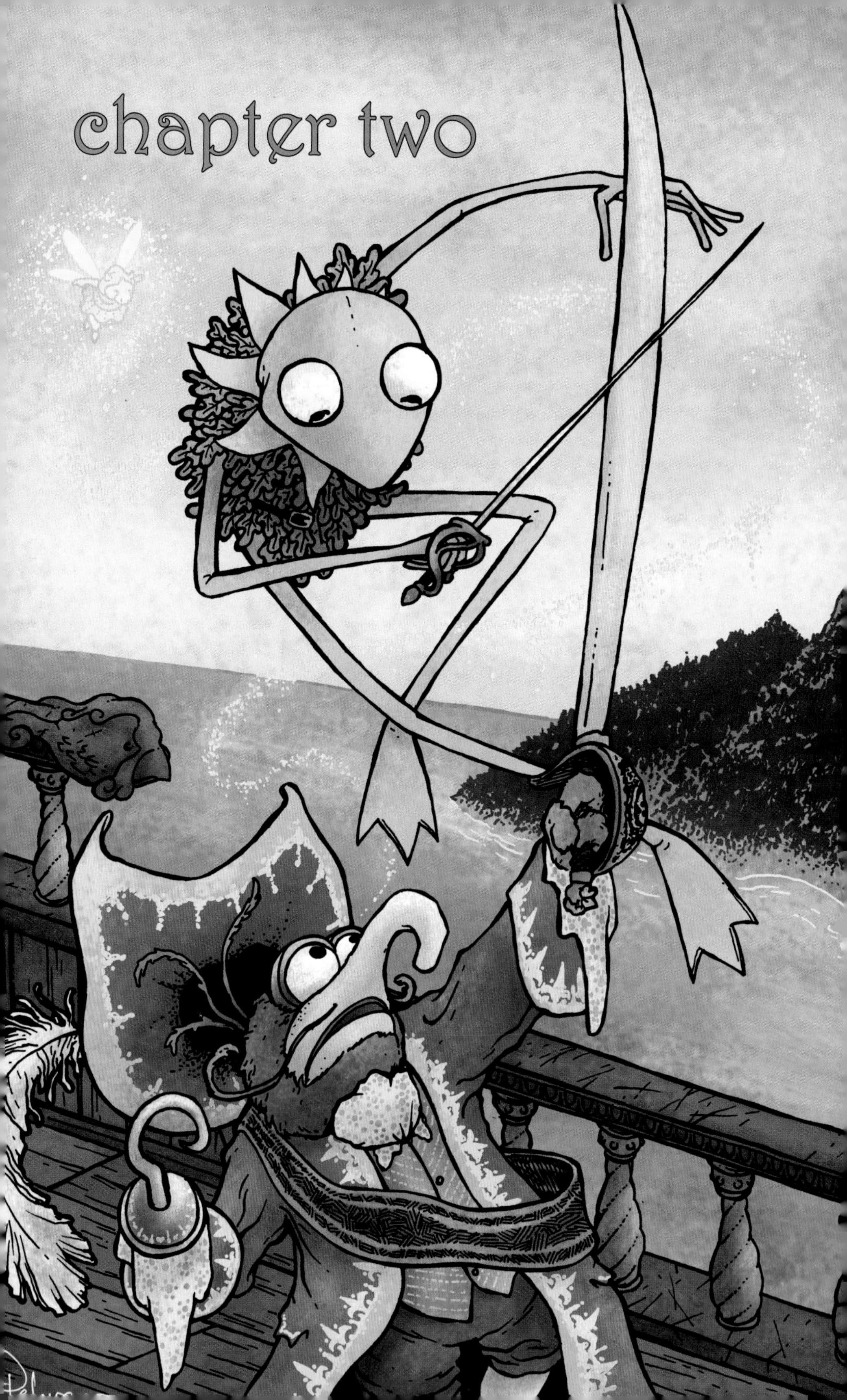

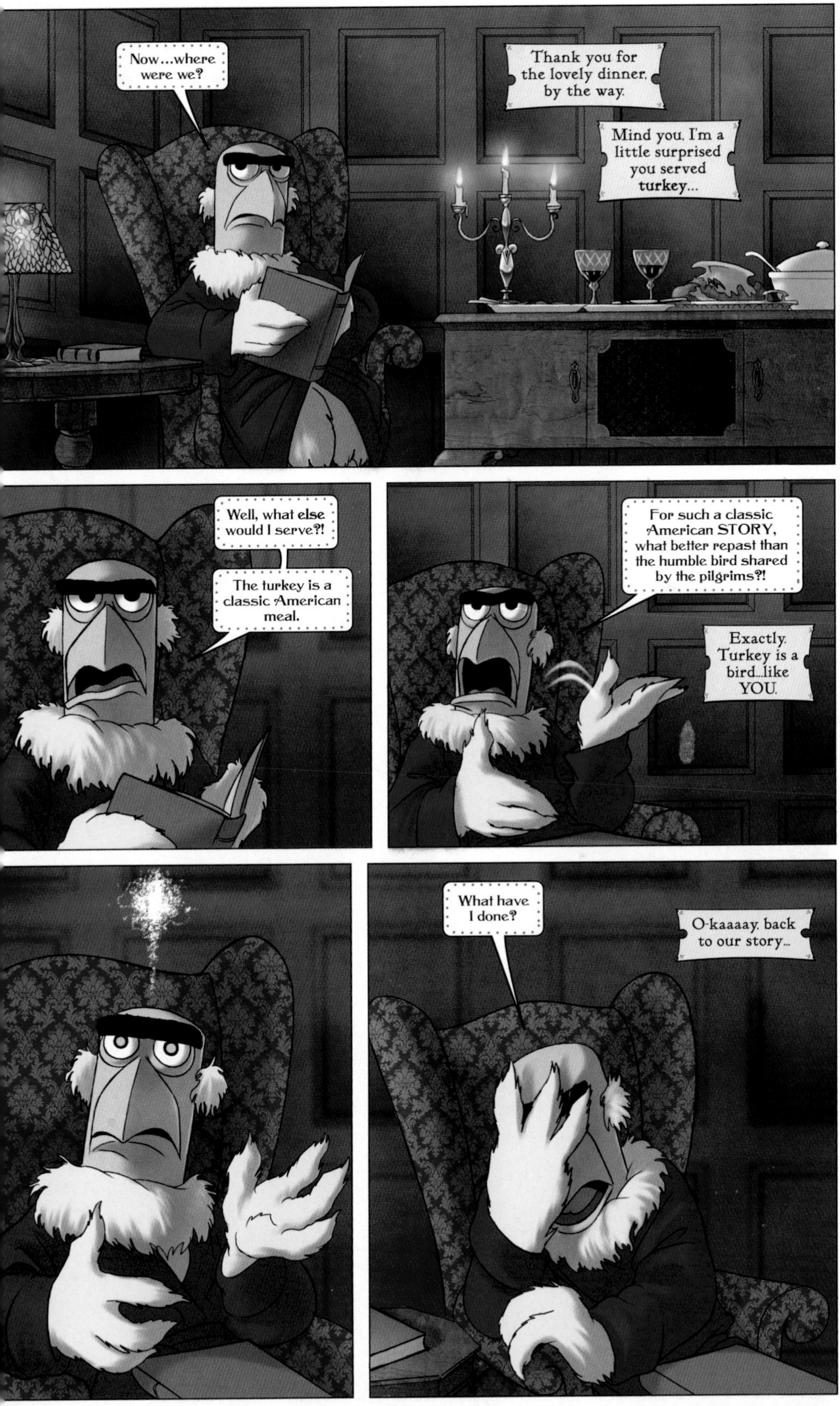
Now...where were we?
Thank you for the lovely dinner, by the way.
Mind you, I'm a little surprised you served turkey...
Well, what else would I serve?!
The turkey is a classic American meal.
For such a classic American STORY, what better repast than the humble bird shared by the pilgrims?!
Exactly. Turkey is a bird...like YOU.
What have I done?
O-kaaaay, back to our story...

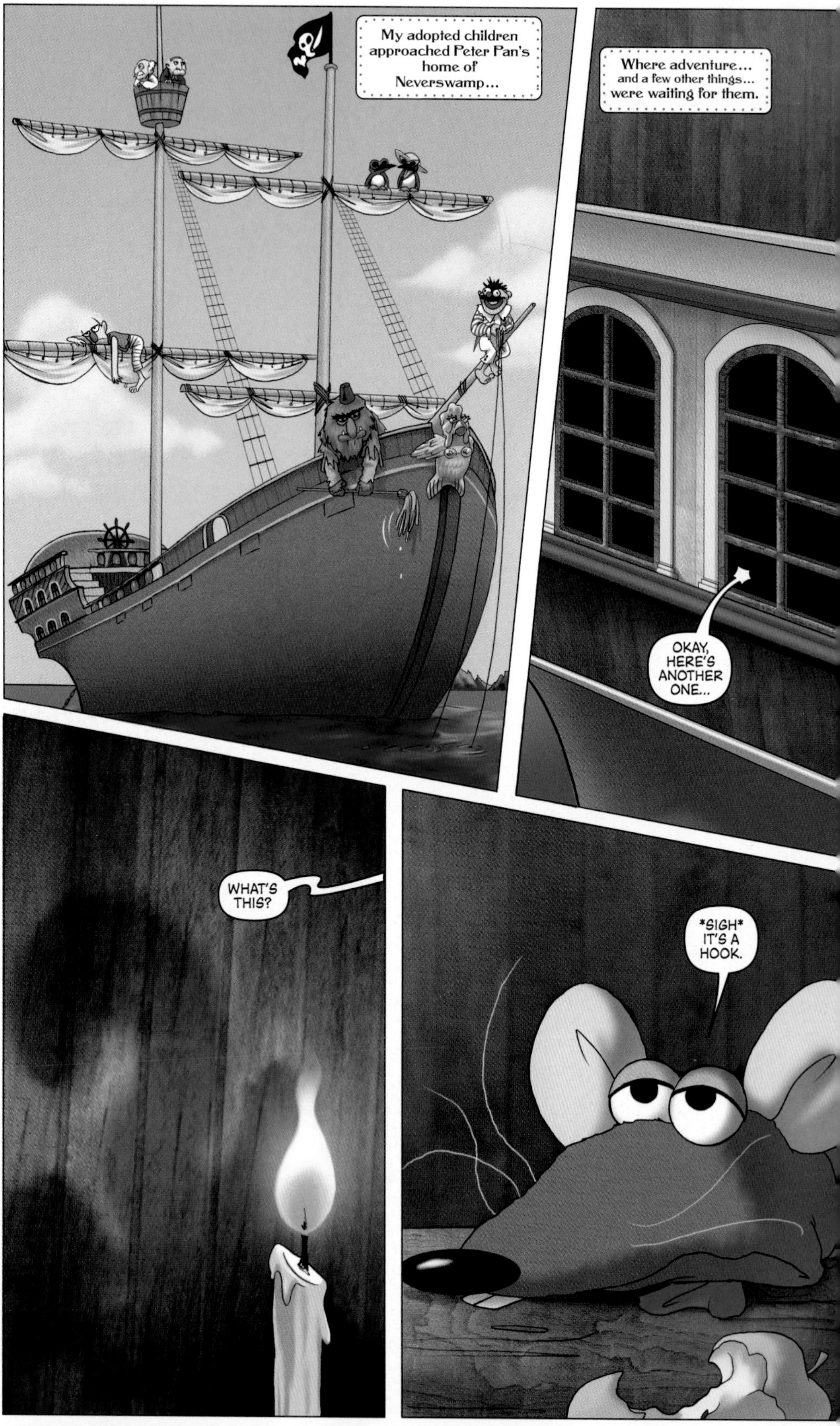
My adopted children approached Peter Pan's home of Neverswamp...
Where adventure... and a few other things... were waiting for them.
OKAY, HERE'S ANOTHER ONE...
WHAT'S THIS?
SIGH IT'S A HOOK.

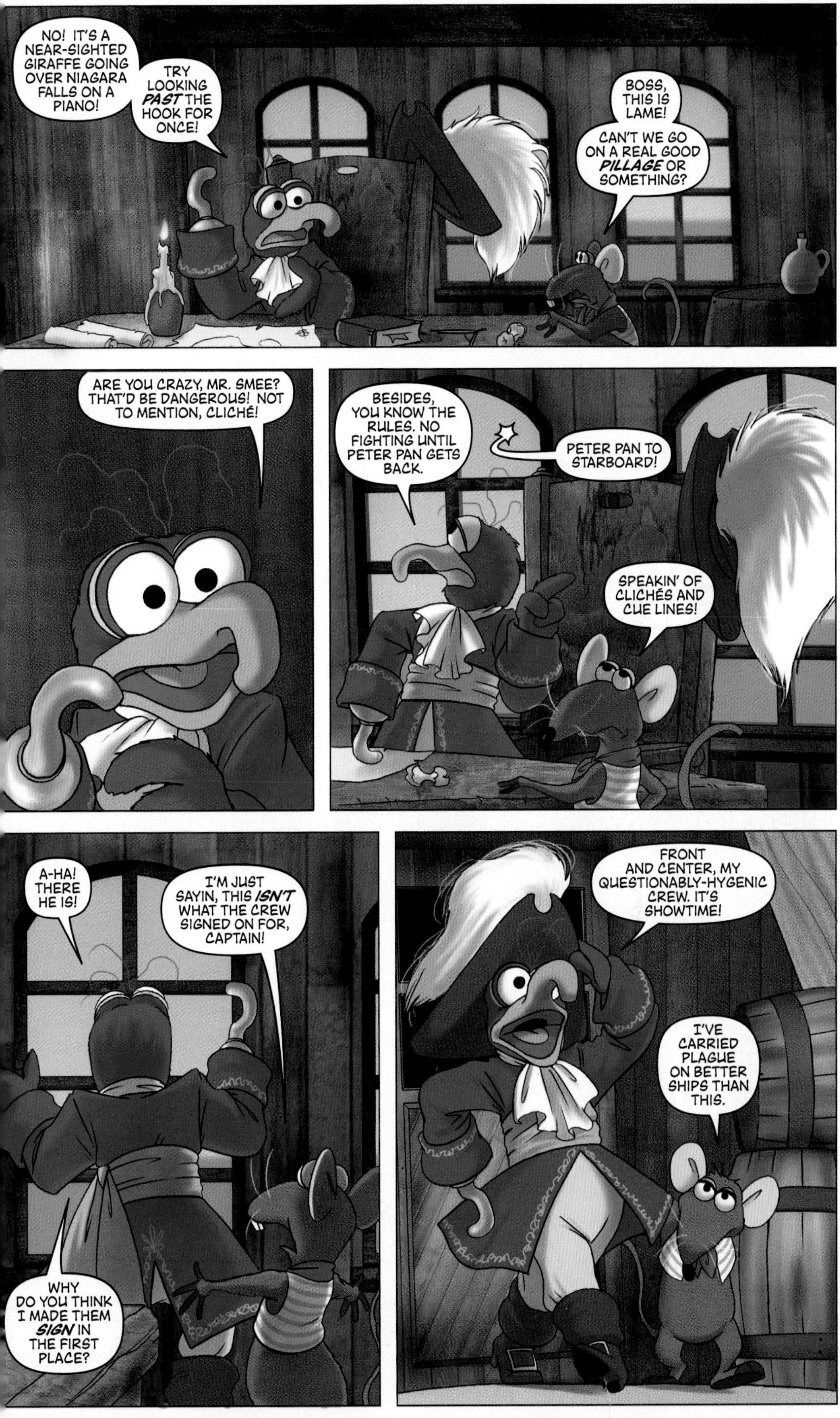
NO! IT'S A NEAR-SIGHTED GIRAFFE GOING OVER NIAGARA FALLS ON A PIANO!
TRY LOOKING *PAST* THE HOOK FOR ONCE!
BOSS, THIS IS LAME!
CAN'T WE GO ON A REAL GOOD *PILLAGE* OR SOMETHING?
ARE YOU CRAZY, MR. SMEE? THAT'D BE DANGEROUS! NOT TO MENTION, CLICHÉ!
BESIDES, YOU KNOW THE RULES. NO FIGHTING UNTIL PETER PAN GETS BACK.
PETER PAN TO STARBOARD!
SPEAKIN' OF CLICHÉS AND CUE LINES!
A-HA! THERE HE IS!
I'M JUST SAYIN, THIS *ISN'T* WHAT THE CREW SIGNED ON FOR, CAPTAIN!
WHY DO YOU THINK I MADE THEM *SIGN* IN THE FIRST PLACE?
FRONT AND CENTER, MY QUESTIONABLY-HYGENIC CREW. IT'S SHOWTIME!
I'VE CARRIED PLAGUE ON BETTER SHIPS THAN THIS.

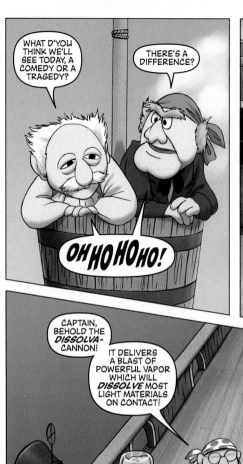

WHAT D'YOU THINK WE'LL SEE TODAY, A COMEDY OR A TRAGEDY?

THERE'S A DIFFERENCE?

OH HO HO HO!

IS IT READY, GUNNER BUNSEN?

AW, WHAT DID THEY DO TO THE CANNON?

CAPTAIN, BEHOLD THE DISSOLVA-CANNON!

IT DELIVERS A BLAST OF POWERFUL VAPOR WHICH WILL DISSOLVE MOST LIGHT MATERIALS ON CONTACT!

SO HOW DID HE TEST THIS ONE?

SIGH

EXCELLENT! LET PETER PAN TRY HIDING FROM ME NOW!

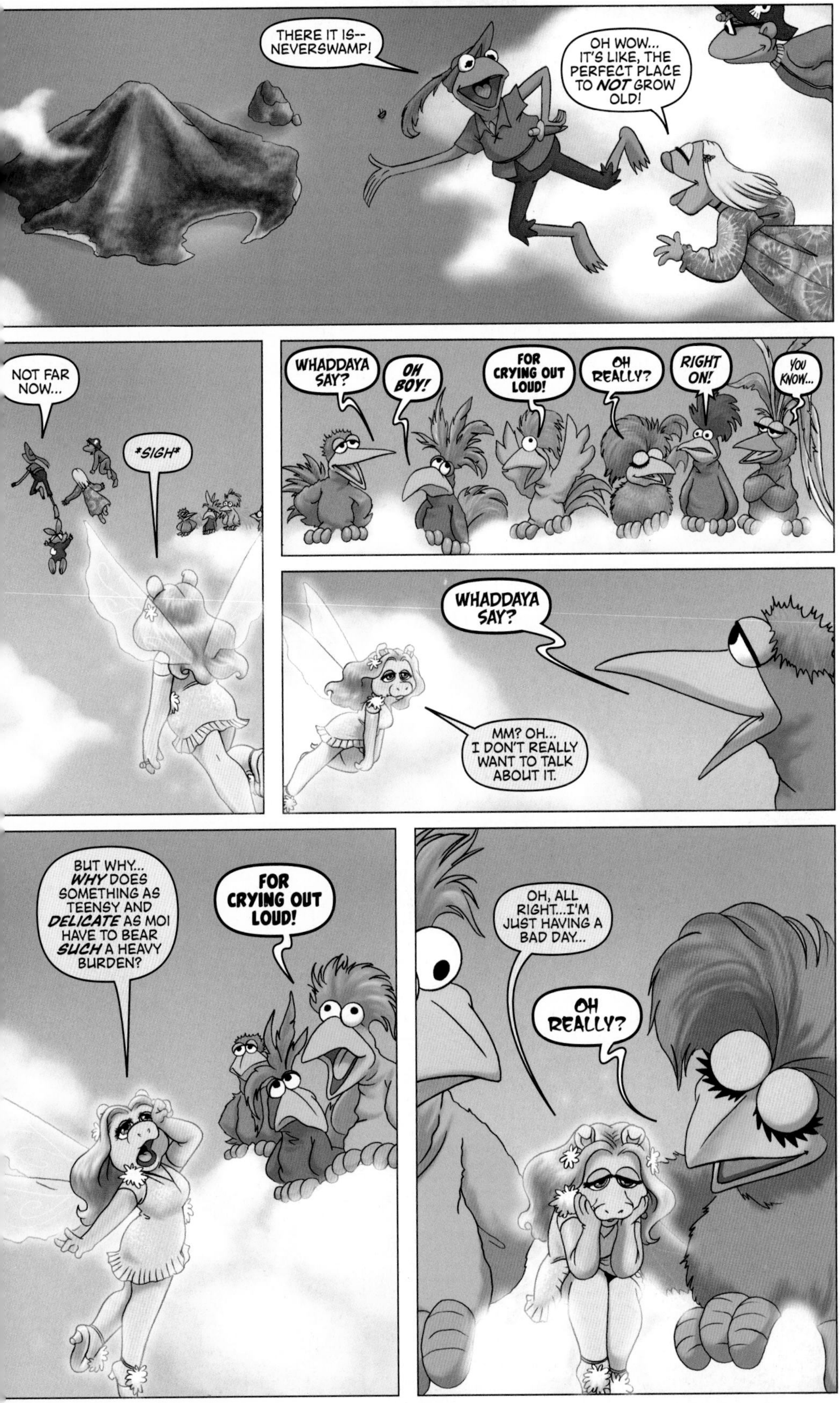
THERE IT IS-- NEVERSWAMP!
OH WOW... IT'S LIKE, THE PERFECT PLACE TO NOT GROW OLD!
NOT FAR NOW...
SIGH
WHADDAYA SAY?
OH BOY!
FOR CRYING OUT LOUD!
OH REALLY?
RIGHT ON!
YOU KNOW...
WHADDAYA SAY?
MM? OH... I DON'T REALLY WANT TO TALK ABOUT IT.
BUT WHY... WHY DOES SOMETHING AS TEENSY AND DELICATE AS MOI HAVE TO BEAR SUCH A HEAVY BURDEN?
FOR CRYING OUT LOUD!
OH, ALL RIGHT...I'M JUST HAVING A BAD DAY...
OH REALLY?

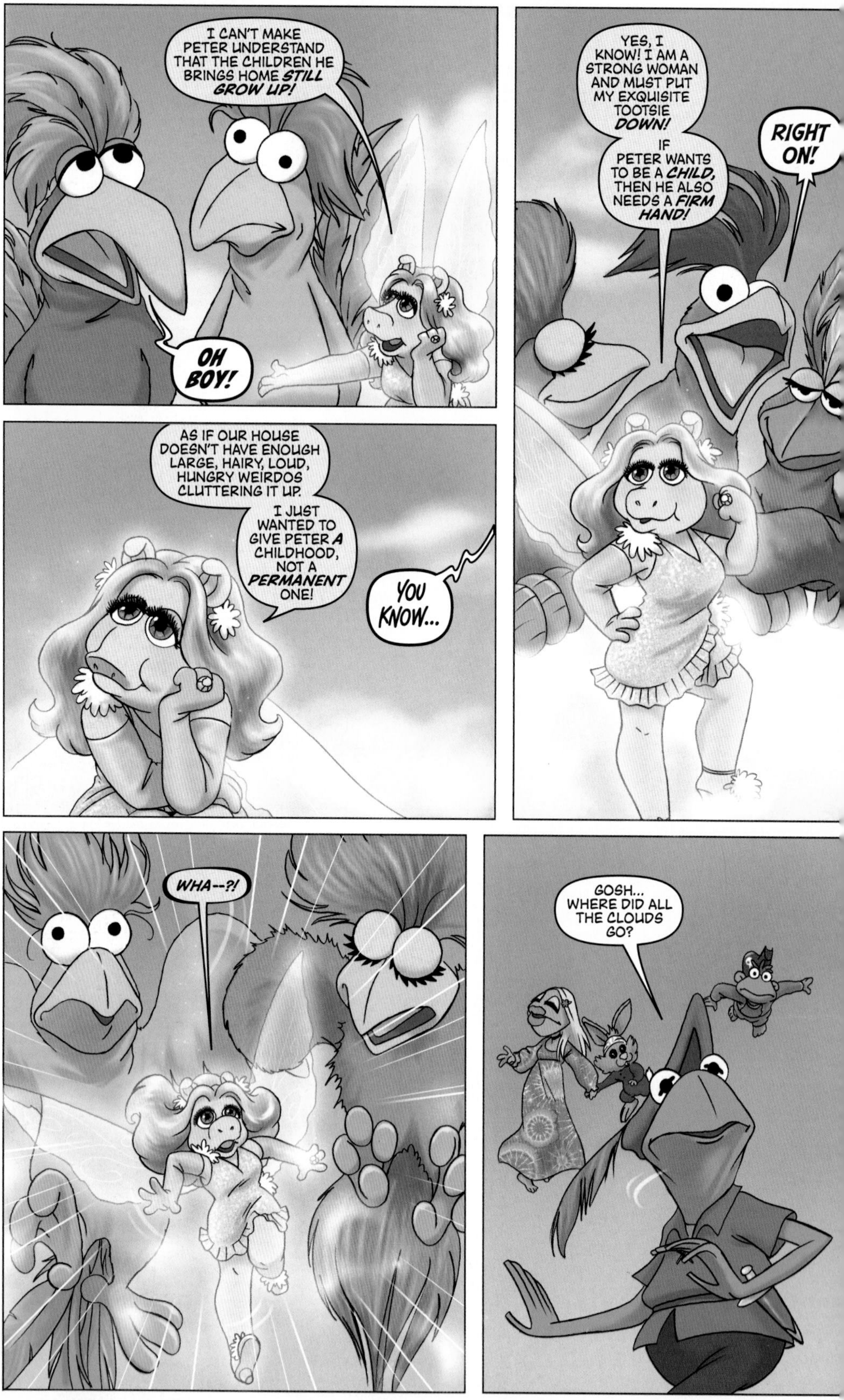

I CAN'T MAKE PETER UNDERSTAND THAT THE CHILDREN HE BRINGS HOME *STILL GROW UP!*
OH BOY!
YES, I KNOW! I AM A STRONG WOMAN AND MUST PUT MY EXQUISITE TOOTSIE *DOWN!*
IF PETER WANTS TO BE A *CHILD,* THEN HE ALSO NEEDS A *FIRM HAND!*
RIGHT ON!
AS IF OUR HOUSE DOESN'T HAVE ENOUGH LARGE, HAIRY, LOUD, HUNGRY WEIRDOS CLUTTERING IT UP.
I JUST WANTED TO GIVE PETER *A* CHILDHOOD, NOT A *PERMANENT* ONE!
YOU KNOW...
WHA--?!
GOSH... WHERE DID ALL THE CLOUDS GO?

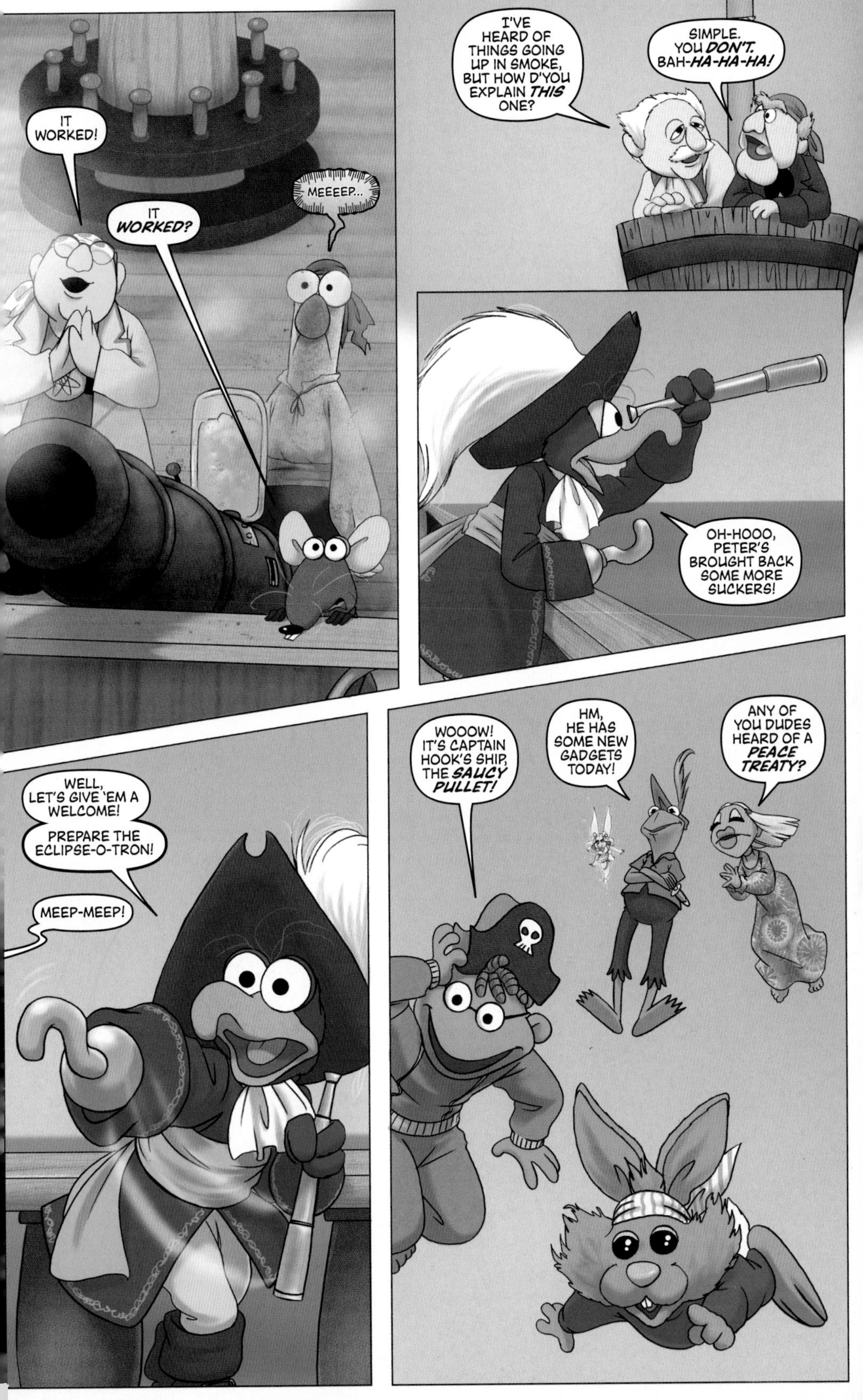
IT WORKED!
IT WORKED?
MEEEEP...
I'VE HEARD OF THINGS GOING UP IN SMOKE, BUT HOW D'YOU EXPLAIN THIS ONE?
SIMPLE. YOU DON'T. BAH-HA-HA-HA!
OH-HOOO, PETER'S BROUGHT BACK SOME MORE SUCKERS!
WELL, LET'S GIVE 'EM A WELCOME!
PREPARE THE ECLIPSE-O-TRON!
MEEP-MEEP!
WOOOW! IT'S CAPTAIN HOOK'S SHIP, THE SAUCY PULLET!
HM, HE HAS SOME NEW GADGETS TODAY!
ANY OF YOU DUDES HEARD OF A PEACE TREATY?

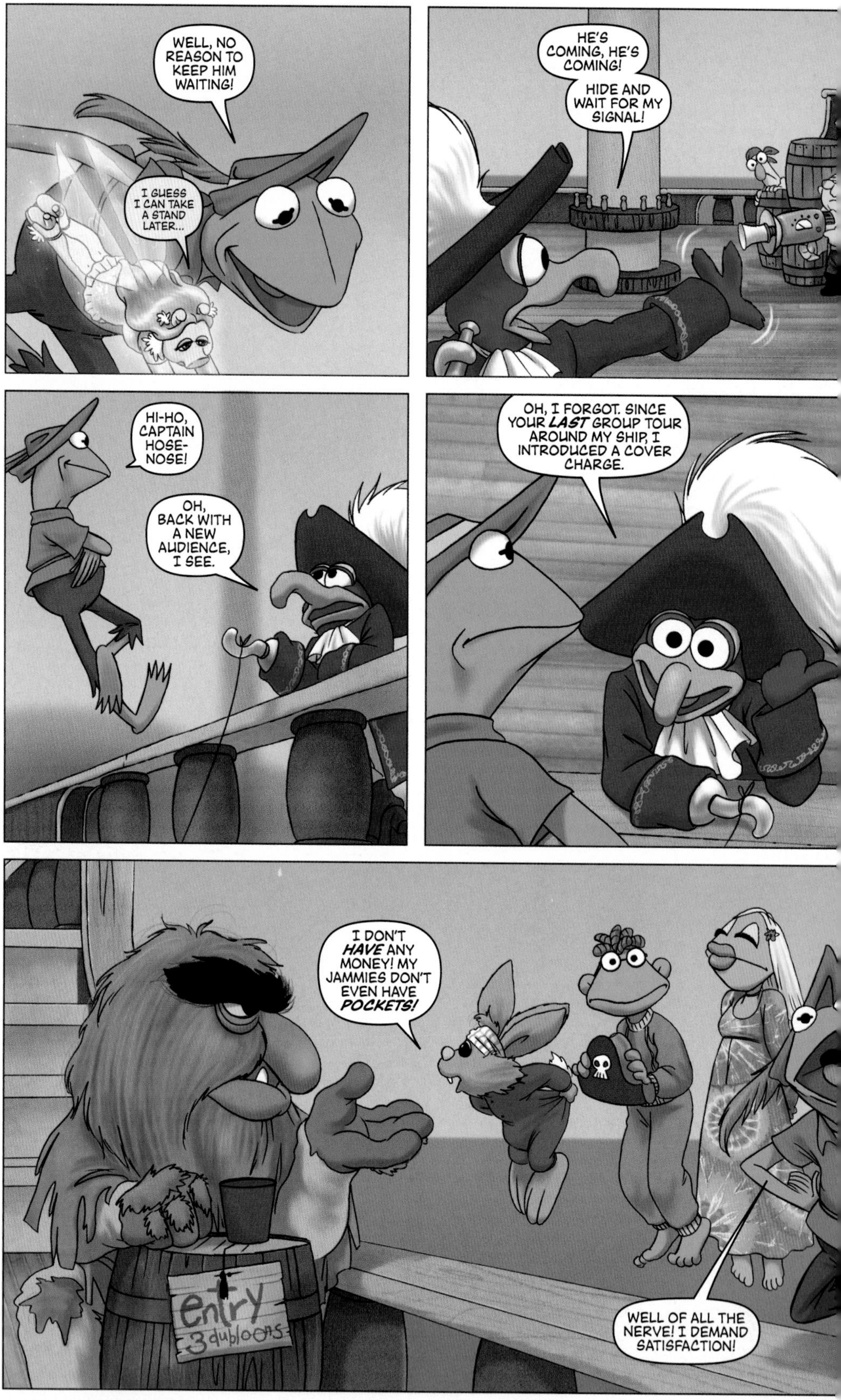
WELL, NO REASON TO KEEP HIM WAITING!
I GUESS I CAN TAKE A STAND LATER...
HE'S COMING, HE'S COMING!
HIDE AND WAIT FOR MY SIGNAL!
HI-HO, CAPTAIN HOSE-NOSE!
OH, BACK WITH A NEW AUDIENCE, I SEE.
OH, I FORGOT. SINCE YOUR *LAST* GROUP TOUR AROUND MY SHIP, I INTRODUCED A COVER CHARGE.
I DON'T *HAVE* ANY MONEY! MY JAMMIES DON'T EVEN HAVE *POCKETS!*
entry 3 dubloons
WELL OF ALL THE NERVE! I DEMAND SATISFACTION!

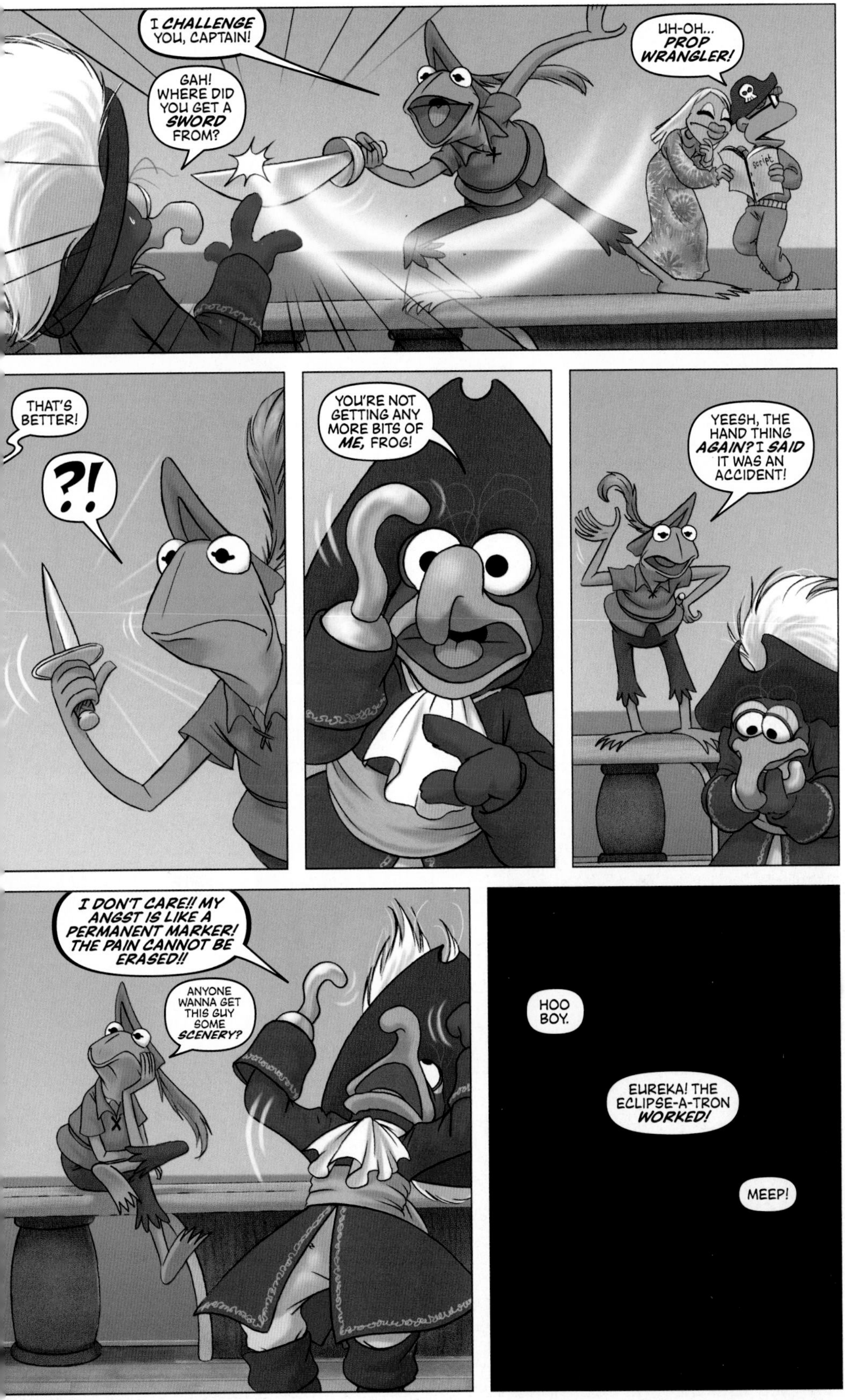
I CHALLENGE YOU, CAPTAIN!
GAH! WHERE DID YOU GET A SWORD FROM?
UH-OH... PROP WRANGLER!
SCRIPT
THAT'S BETTER!
?!
YOU'RE NOT GETTING ANY MORE BITS OF ME, FROG!
YEESH, THE HAND THING AGAIN? I SAID IT WAS AN ACCIDENT!
I DON'T CARE!! MY ANGST IS LIKE A PERMANENT MARKER! THE PAIN CANNOT BE ERASED!!
ANYONE WANNA GET THIS GUY SOME SCENERY?
HOO BOY.
EUREKA! THE ECLIPSE-A-TRON WORKED!
MEEP!

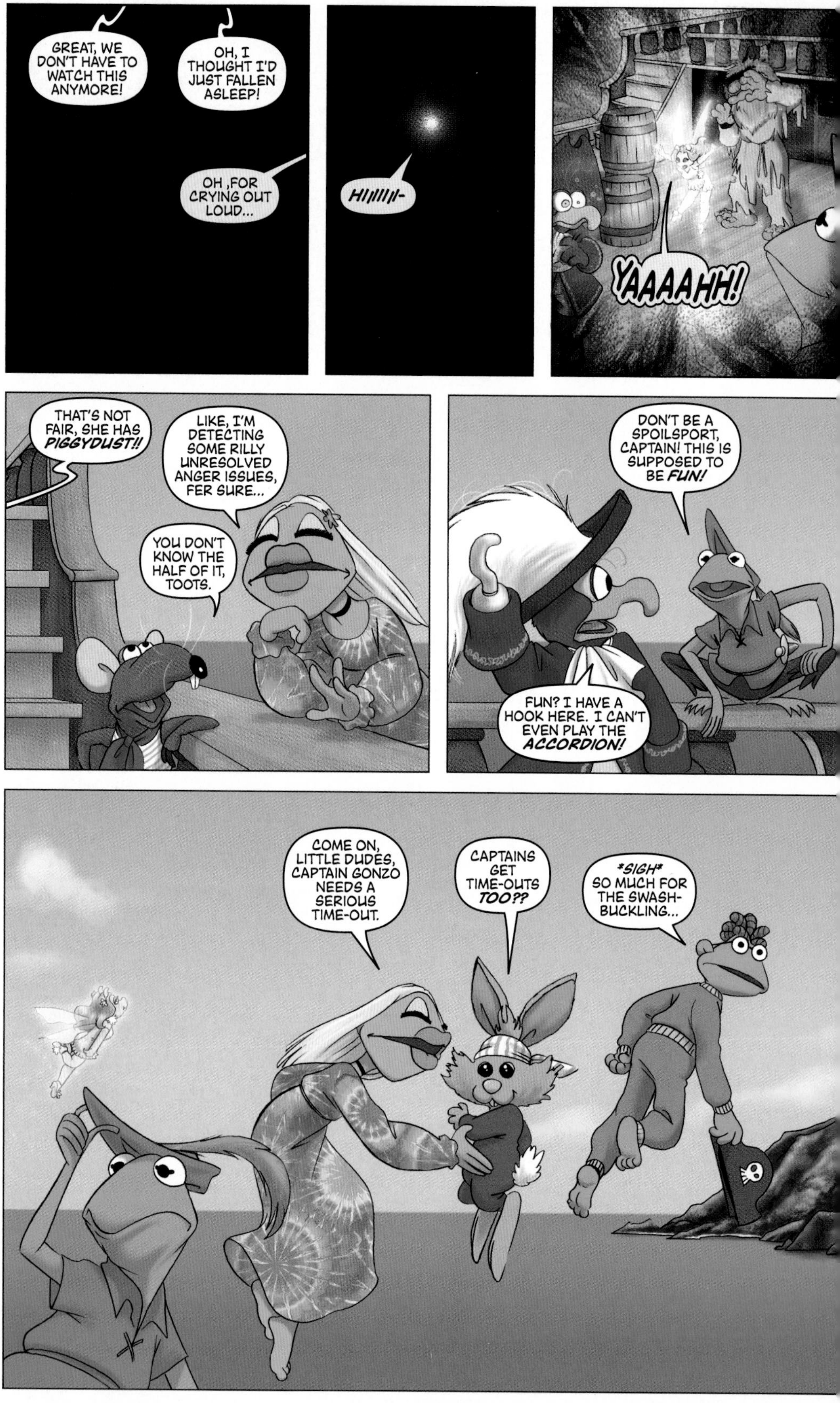
GREAT, WE DON'T HAVE TO WATCH THIS ANYMORE!
OH, I THOUGHT I'D JUST FALLEN ASLEEP!
OH ,FOR CRYING OUT LOUD...
HI!!!!!!-
YAAAAHH!
THAT'S NOT FAIR, SHE HAS PIGGYDUST!!
LIKE, I'M DETECTING SOME RILLY UNRESOLVED ANGER ISSUES, FER SURE...
YOU DON'T KNOW THE HALF OF IT, TOOTS.
DON'T BE A SPOILSPORT, CAPTAIN! THIS IS SUPPOSED TO BE FUN!
FUN? I HAVE A HOOK HERE. I CAN'T EVEN PLAY THE ACCORDION!
COME ON, LITTLE DUDES, CAPTAIN GONZO NEEDS A SERIOUS TIME-OUT.
CAPTAINS GET TIME-OUTS TOO??
SIGH SO MUCH FOR THE SWASH-BUCKLING...

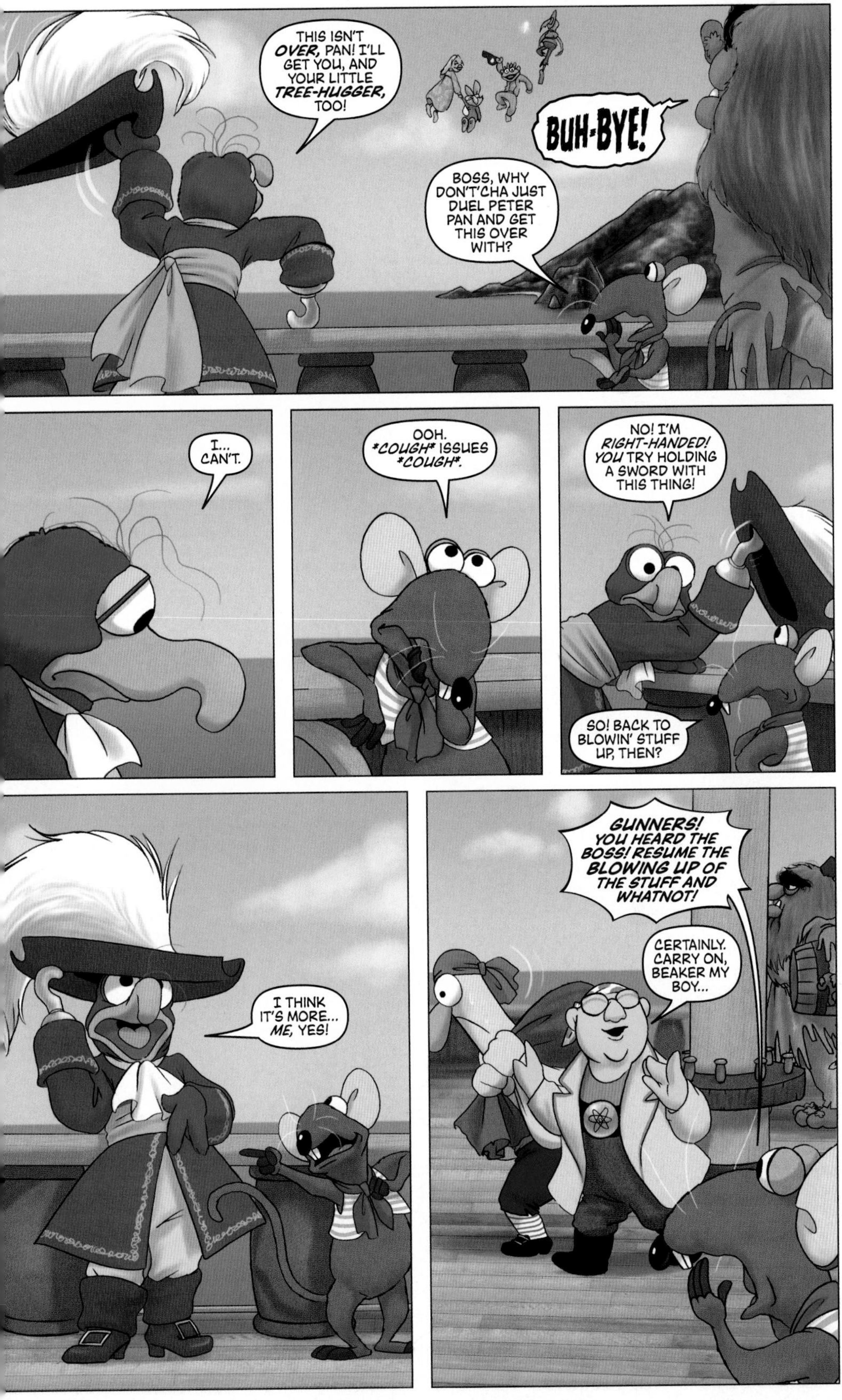
THIS ISN'T *OVER*, PAN! I'LL GET YOU, AND YOUR LITTLE *TREE-HUGGER*, TOO!
BUH-BYE!
BOSS, WHY DON'T'CHA JUST DUEL PETER PAN AND GET THIS OVER WITH?
I... CAN'T.
OOH. *COUGH* ISSUES *COUGH*.
NO! I'M *RIGHT-HANDED! YOU* TRY HOLDING A SWORD WITH THIS THING!
SO! BACK TO BLOWIN' STUFF UP, THEN?
I THINK IT'S MORE... *ME*, YES!
GUNNERS! YOU HEARD THE BOSS! RESUME THE **BLOWING UP** *OF THE STUFF AND WHATNOT!*
CERTAINLY. CARRY ON, BEAKER MY BOY...

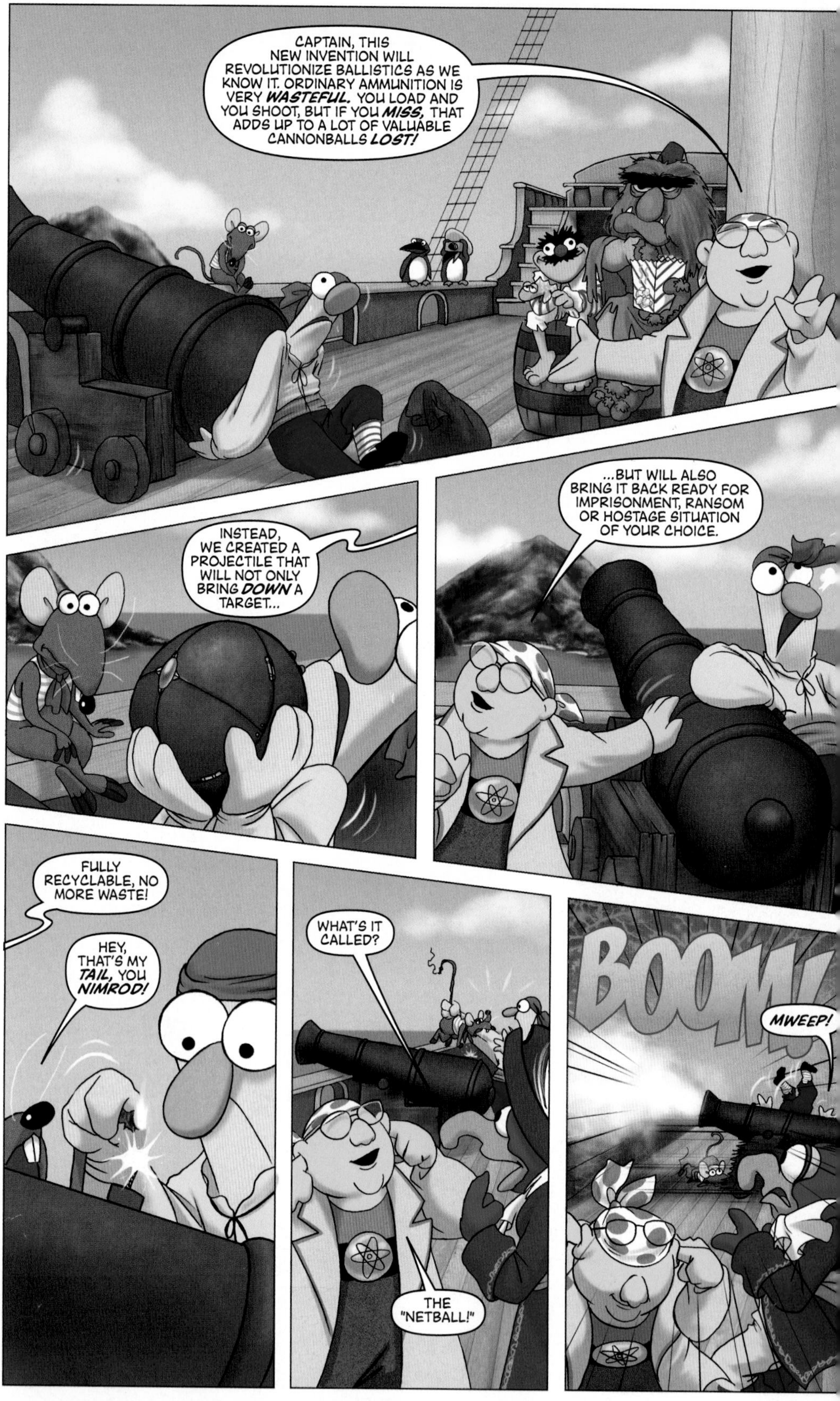
CAPTAIN, THIS NEW INVENTION WILL REVOLUTIONIZE BALLISTICS AS WE KNOW IT. ORDINARY AMMUNITION IS VERY *WASTEFUL.* YOU LOAD AND YOU SHOOT, BUT IF YOU *MISS,* THAT ADDS UP TO A LOT OF VALUABLE CANNONBALLS *LOST!*
INSTEAD, WE CREATED A PROJECTILE THAT WILL NOT ONLY BRING *DOWN* A TARGET...
...BUT WILL ALSO BRING IT BACK READY FOR IMPRISONMENT, RANSOM OR HOSTAGE SITUATION OF YOUR CHOICE.
FULLY RECYCLABLE, NO MORE WASTE!
HEY, THAT'S MY *TAIL,* YOU *NIMROD!*
WHAT'S IT CALLED?
THE "NETBALL!"
BOOM!
MWEEP!

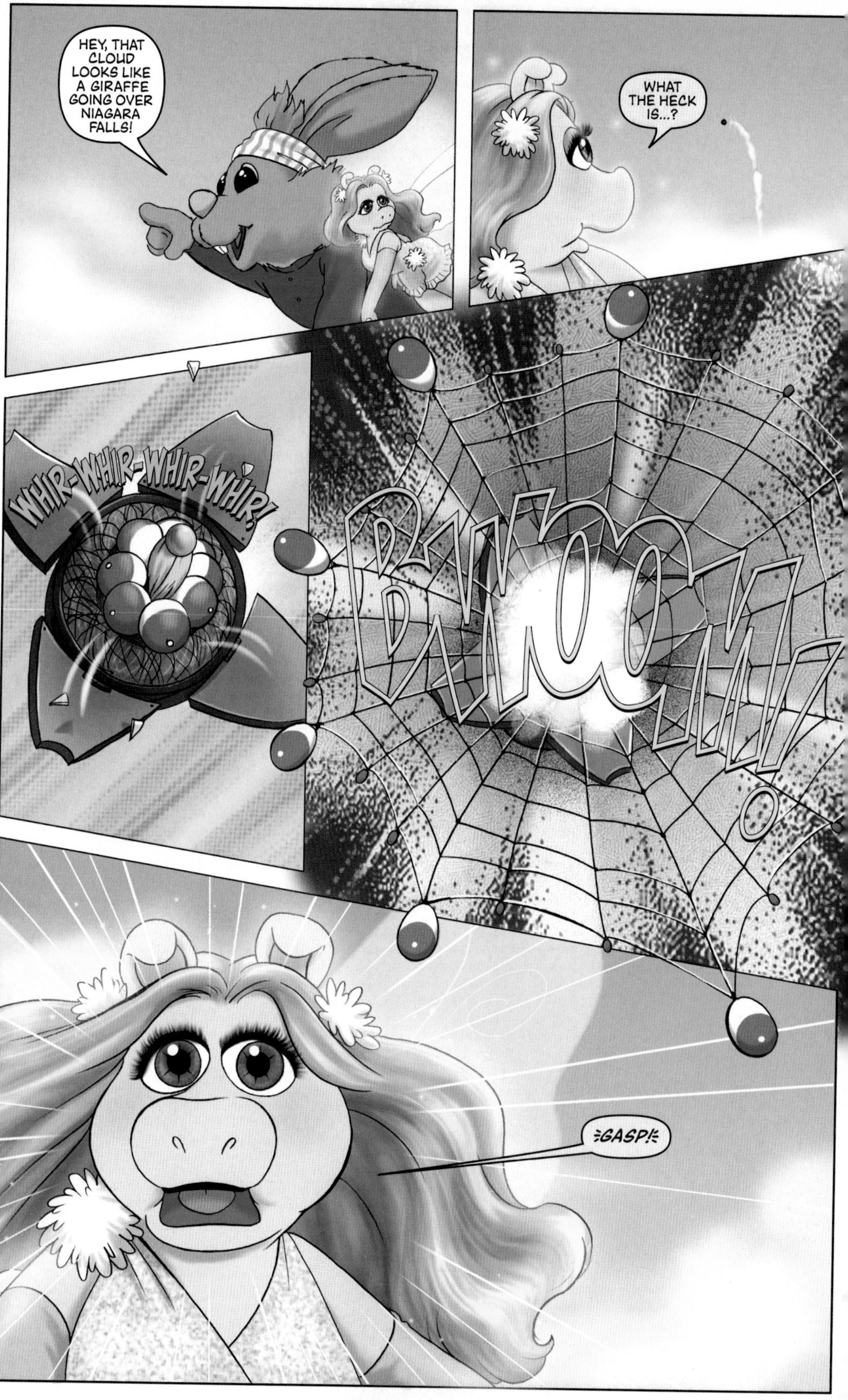
HEY, THAT CLOUD LOOKS LIKE A GIRAFFE GOING OVER NIAGARA FALLS!
WHAT THE HECK IS...?
WHIR-WHIR-WHIR-WHIR!
BAWOOOM!
GASP!

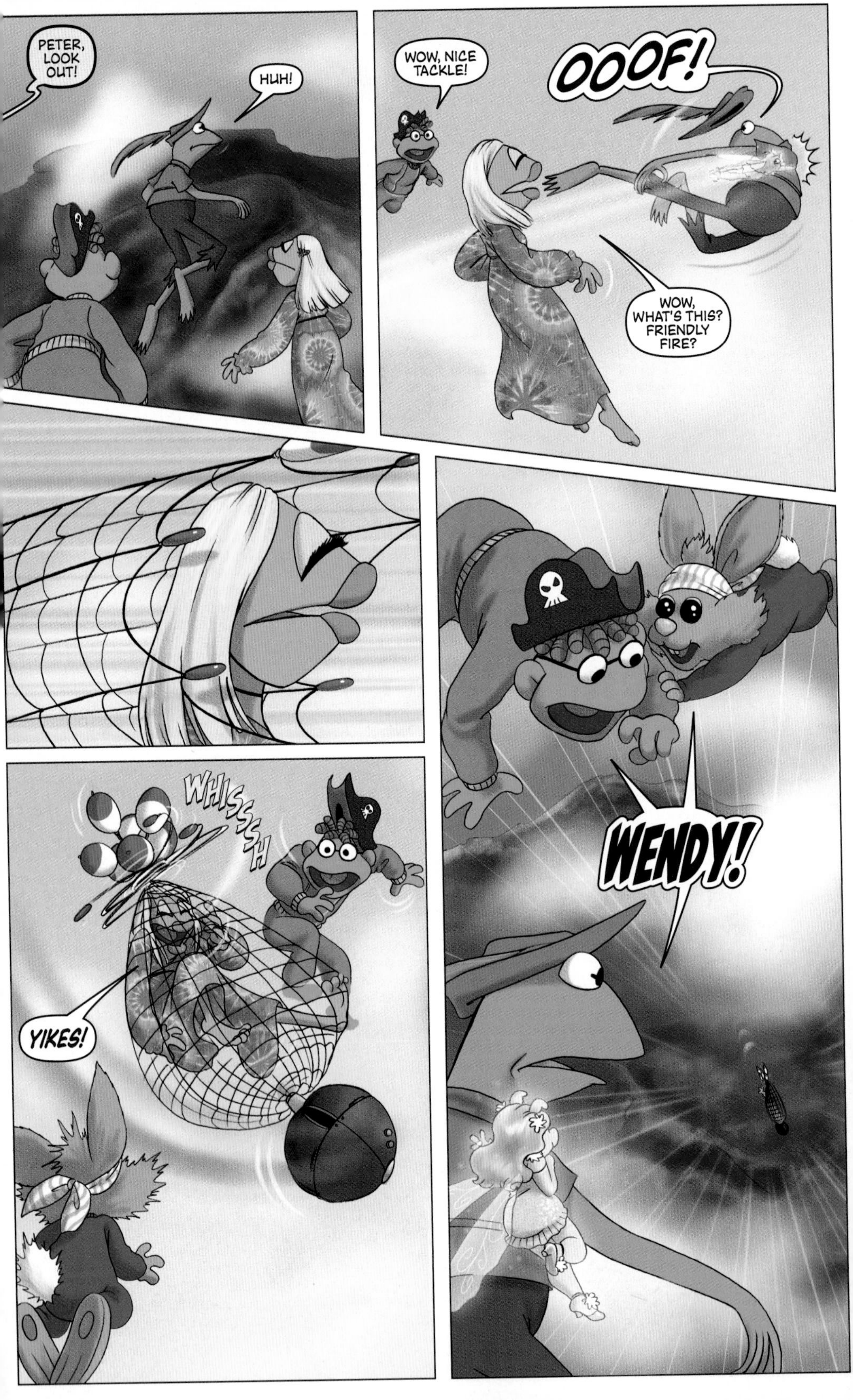
PETER, LOOK OUT!
HUH!
WOW, NICE TACKLE!
OOOF!
WOW, WHAT'S THIS? FRIENDLY FIRE?
WHISSSH
WENDY!
YIKES!

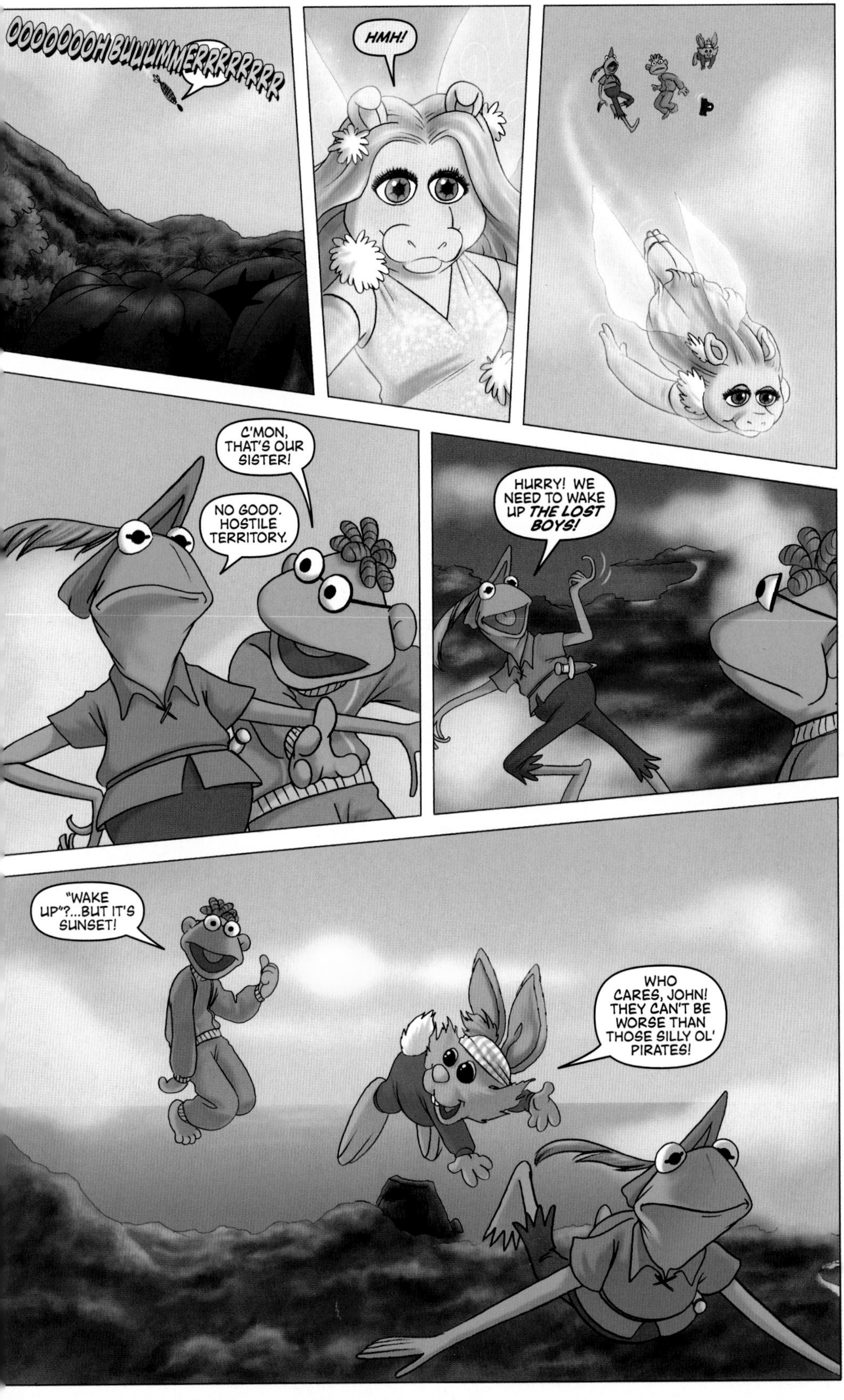
OOOOOOOOH BUUUMMERRRRRRR
HMH!
C'MON, THAT'S OUR SISTER!
NO GOOD. HOSTILE TERRITORY.
HURRY! WE NEED TO WAKE UP THE LOST BOYS!
"WAKE UP"?...BUT IT'S SUNSET!
WHO CARES, JOHN! THEY CAN'T BE WORSE THAN THOSE SILLY OL' PIRATES!

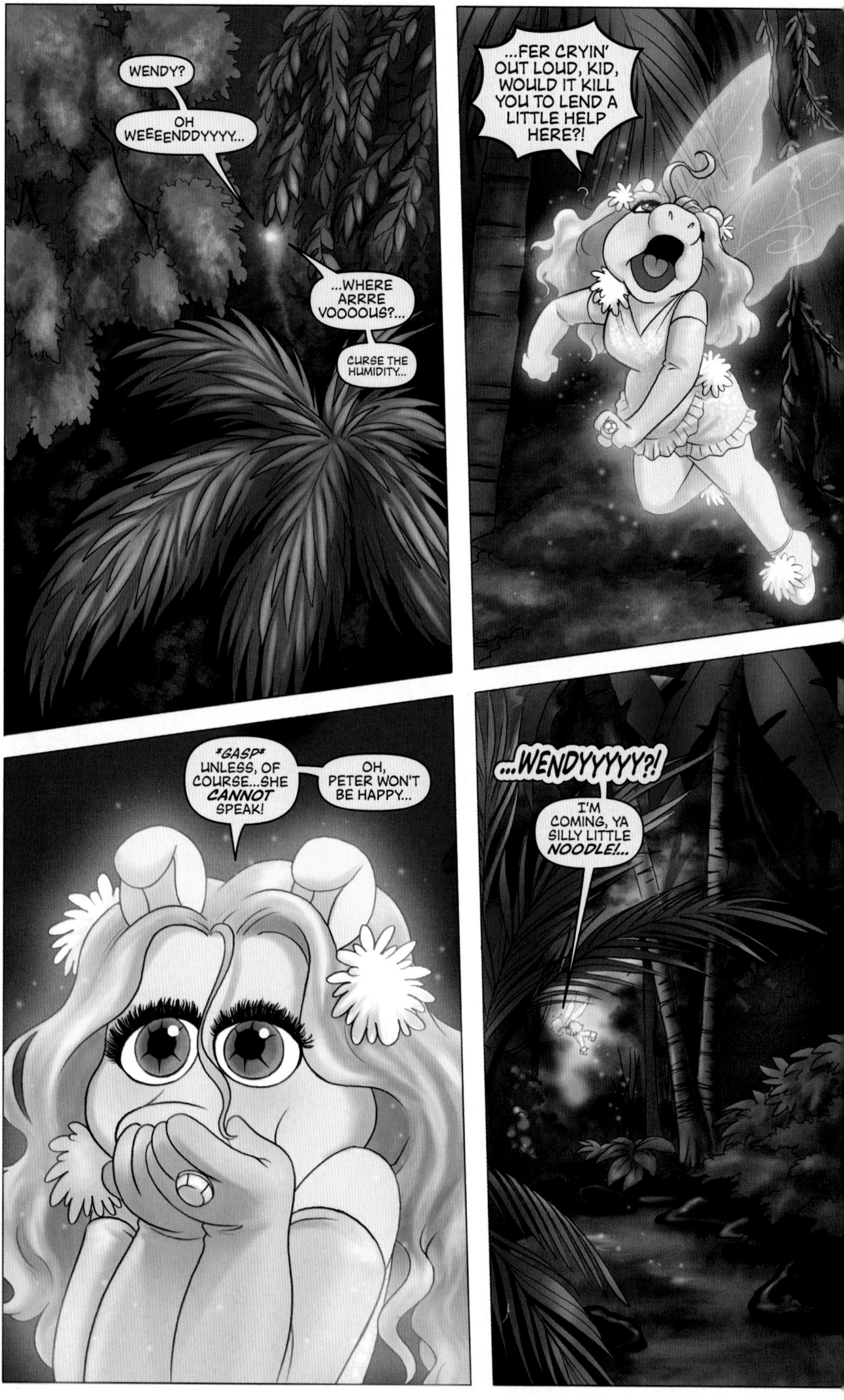
WENDY?
OH WEEEENDDYYYY...
...WHERE ARRRE VOOOOUS?...
CURSE THE HUMIDITY...
...FER CRYIN' OUT LOUD, KID, WOULD IT KILL YOU TO LEND A LITTLE HELP HERE?!
GASP UNLESS, OF COURSE...SHE *CANNOT* SPEAK!
OH, PETER WON'T BE HAPPY...
...WENDYYYYY?!
I'M COMING, YA SILLY LITTLE *NOODLE!*...

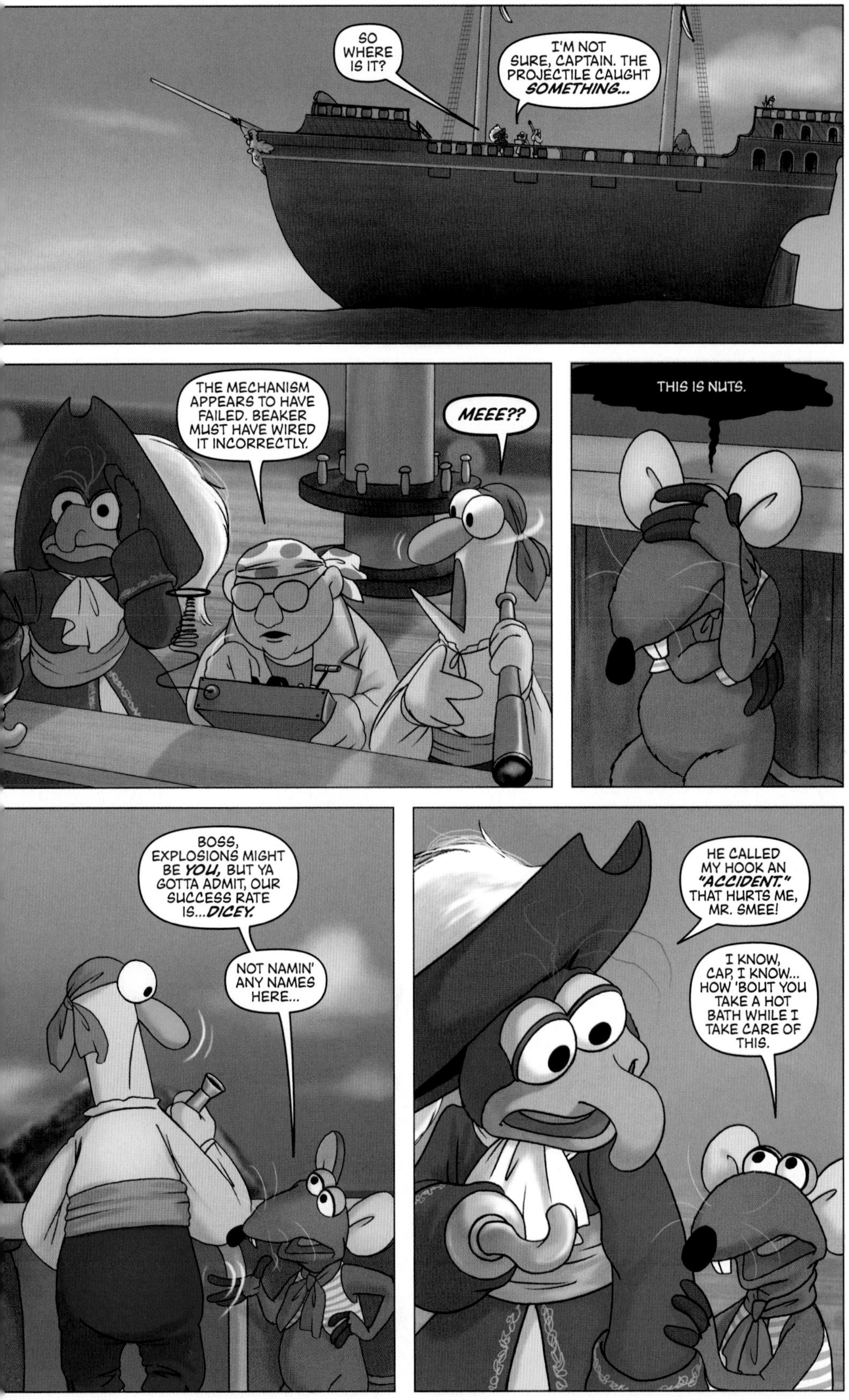
SO WHERE IS IT?
I'M NOT SURE, CAPTAIN. THE PROJECTILE CAUGHT *SOMETHING...*
THE MECHANISM APPEARS TO HAVE FAILED. BEAKER MUST HAVE WIRED IT INCORRECTLY.
MEEE??
THIS IS NUTS.
BOSS, EXPLOSIONS MIGHT BE *YOU,* BUT YA GOTTA ADMIT, OUR SUCCESS RATE IS...*DICEY.*
NOT NAMIN' ANY NAMES HERE...
HE CALLED MY HOOK AN *"ACCIDENT."* THAT HURTS ME, MR. SMEE!
I KNOW, CAP, I KNOW... HOW 'BOUT YOU TAKE A HOT BATH WHILE I TAKE CARE OF THIS.

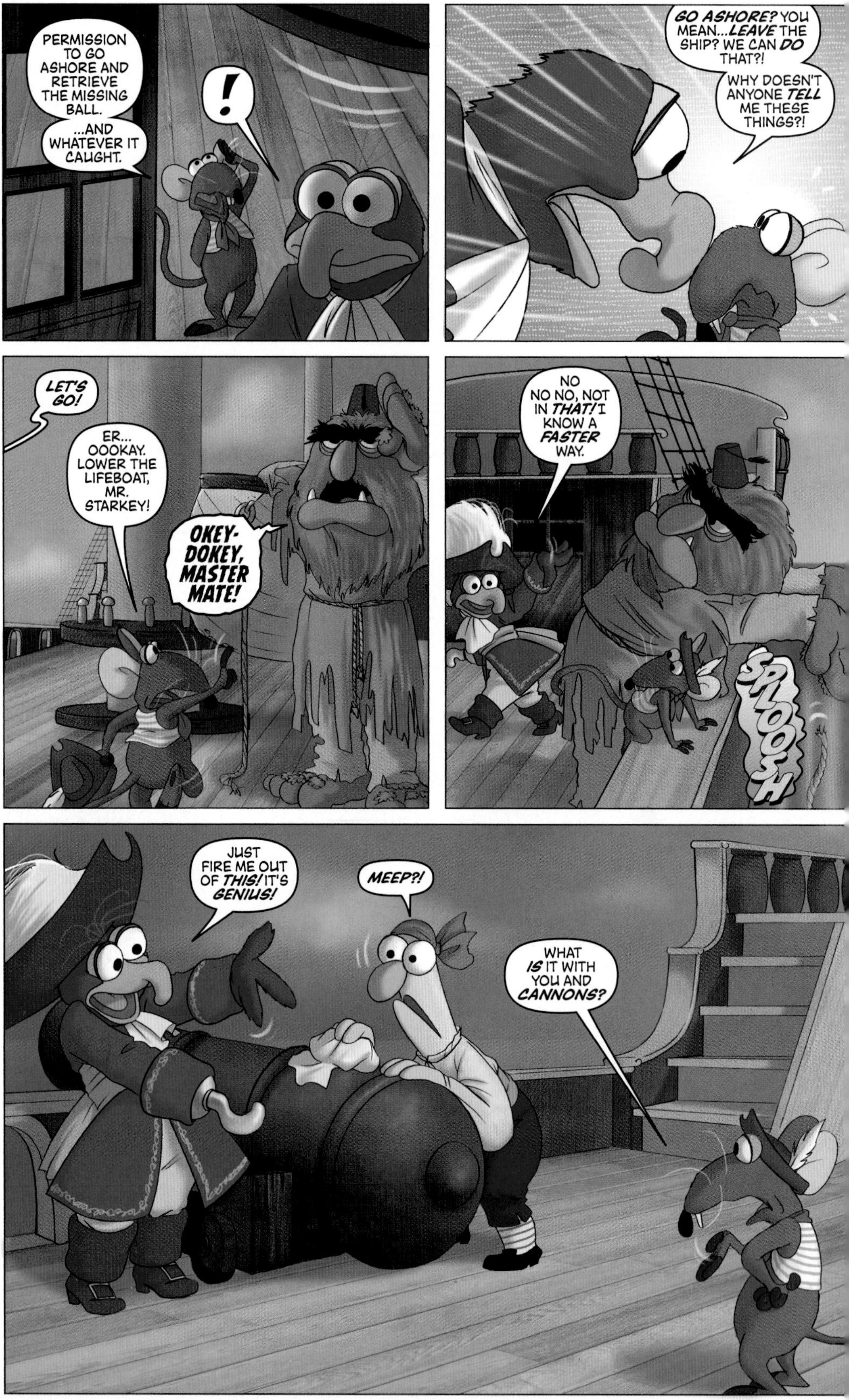
PERMISSION TO GO ASHORE AND RETRIEVE THE MISSING BALL.
...AND WHATEVER IT CAUGHT.
!
GO ASHORE? YOU MEAN...LEAVE THE SHIP? WE CAN DO THAT?!
WHY DOESN'T ANYONE TELL ME THESE THINGS?!
LET'S GO!
ER... OOOKAY. LOWER THE LIFEBOAT, MR. STARKEY!
OKEY-DOKEY, MASTER MATE!
NO NO NO, NOT IN THAT! I KNOW A FASTER WAY.
SPLOOSH
JUST FIRE ME OUT OF THIS! IT'S GENIUS!
MEEP?!
WHAT IS IT WITH YOU AND CANNONS?

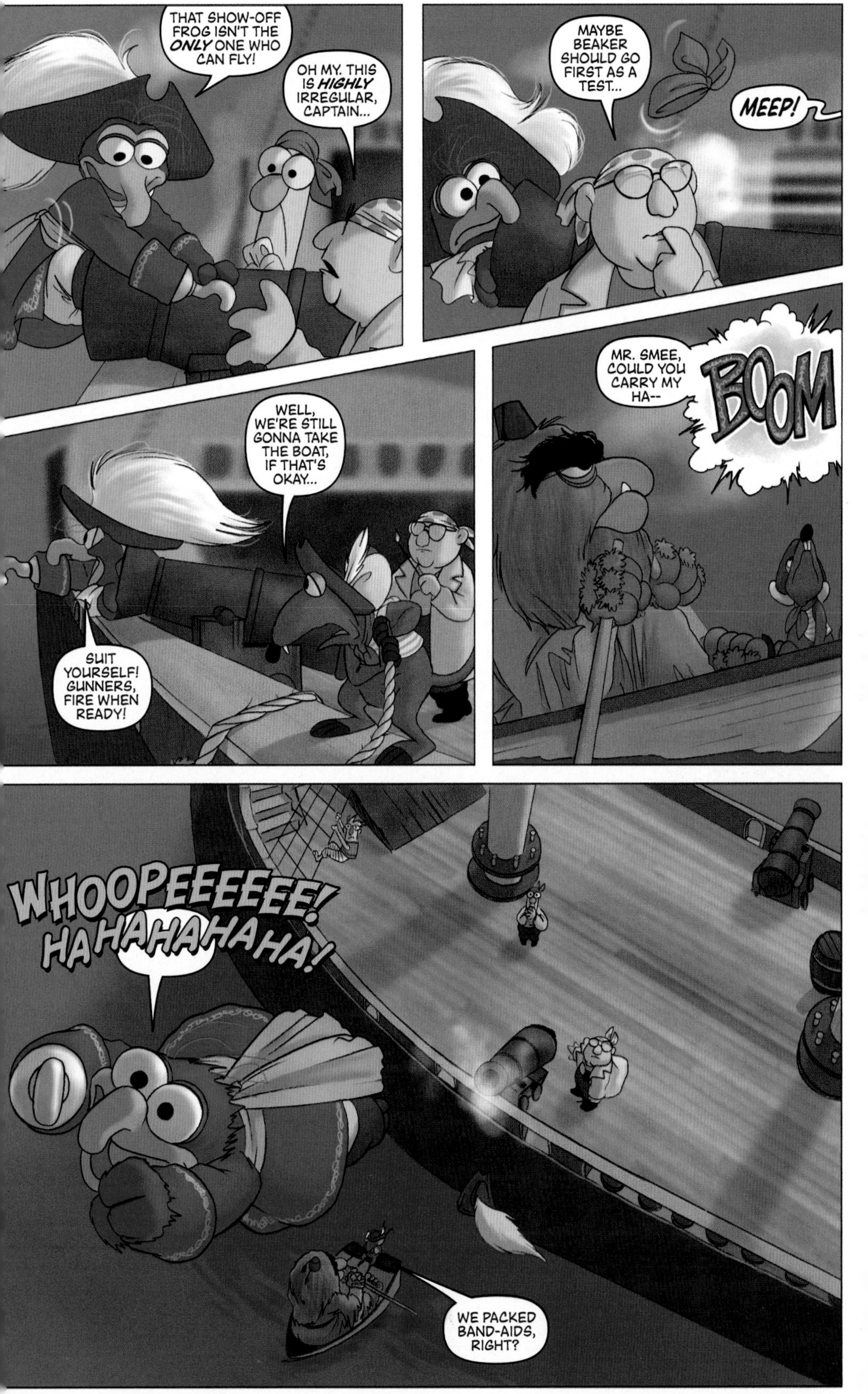
THAT SHOW-OFF FROG ISN'T THE ONLY ONE WHO CAN FLY!
OH MY. THIS IS HIGHLY IRREGULAR, CAPTAIN...
MAYBE BEAKER SHOULD GO FIRST AS A TEST...
MEEP!
WELL, WE'RE STILL GONNA TAKE THE BOAT, IF THAT'S OKAY...
SUIT YOURSELF! GUNNERS, FIRE WHEN READY!
MR. SMEE, COULD YOU CARRY MY HA--
BOOM
WHOOPEEEEEEE! HAHAHAHAHAHA!
WE PACKED BAND-AIDS, RIGHT?

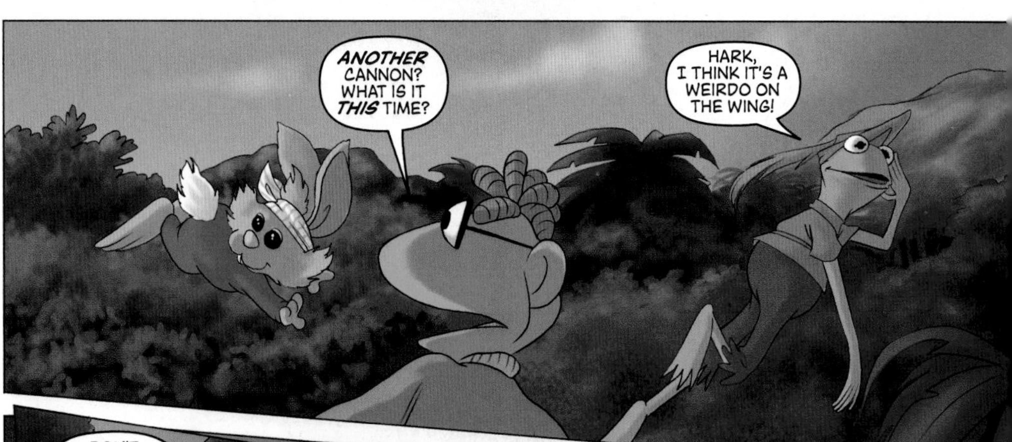
ANOTHER CANNON? WHAT IS IT THIS TIME?
HARK, I THINK IT'S A WEIRDO ON THE WING!

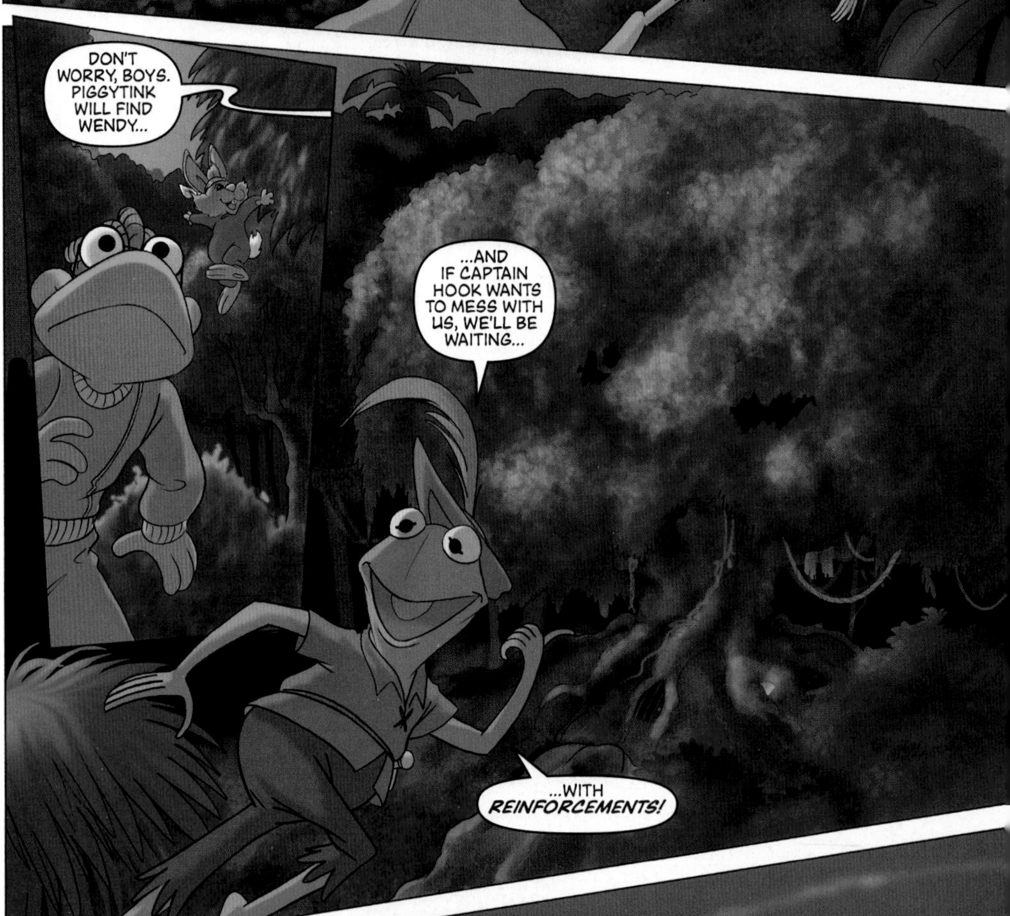
DON'T WORRY, BOYS. PIGGYTINK WILL FIND WENDY...
...AND IF CAPTAIN HOOK WANTS TO MESS WITH US, WE'LL BE WAITING...
...WITH REINFORCEMENTS!

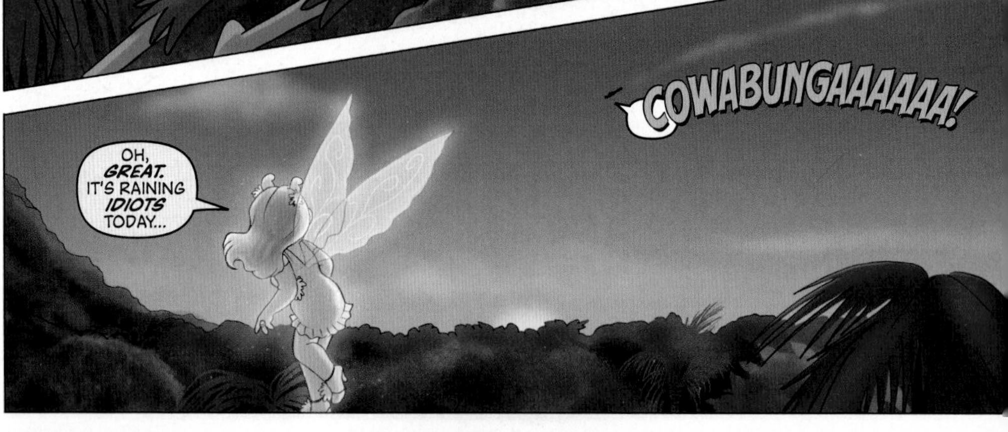
COWABUNGAAAAAA!
OH, GREAT. IT'S RAINING IDIOTS TODAY...

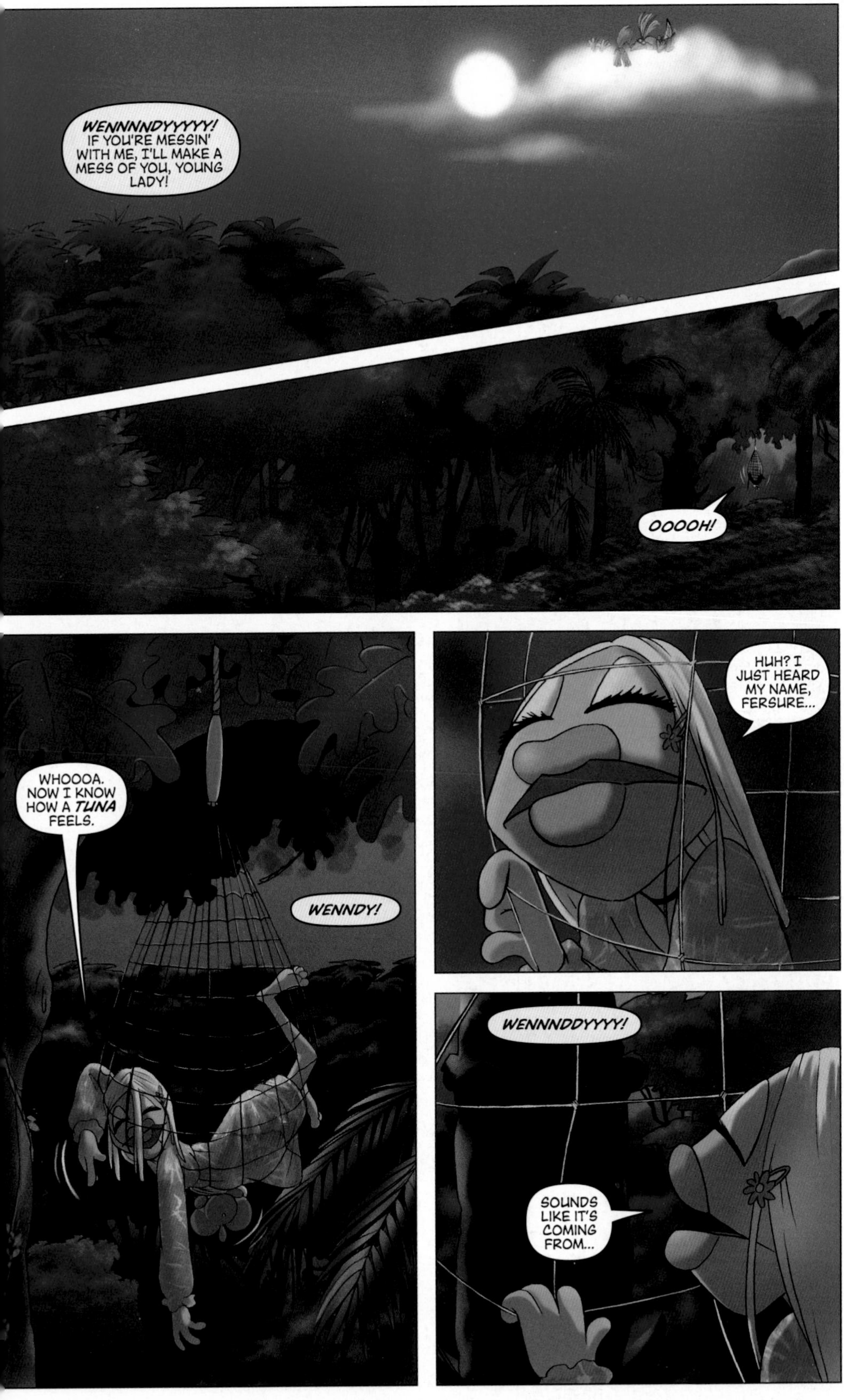
WENNNNDYYYYY! IF YOU'RE MESSIN' WITH ME, I'LL MAKE A MESS OF YOU, YOUNG LADY!
OOOOH!
WHOOOA. NOW I KNOW HOW A TUNA FEELS.
WENNDY!
HUH? I JUST HEARD MY NAME, FERSURE...
WENNNDDYYYY!
SOUNDS LIKE IT'S COMING FROM...

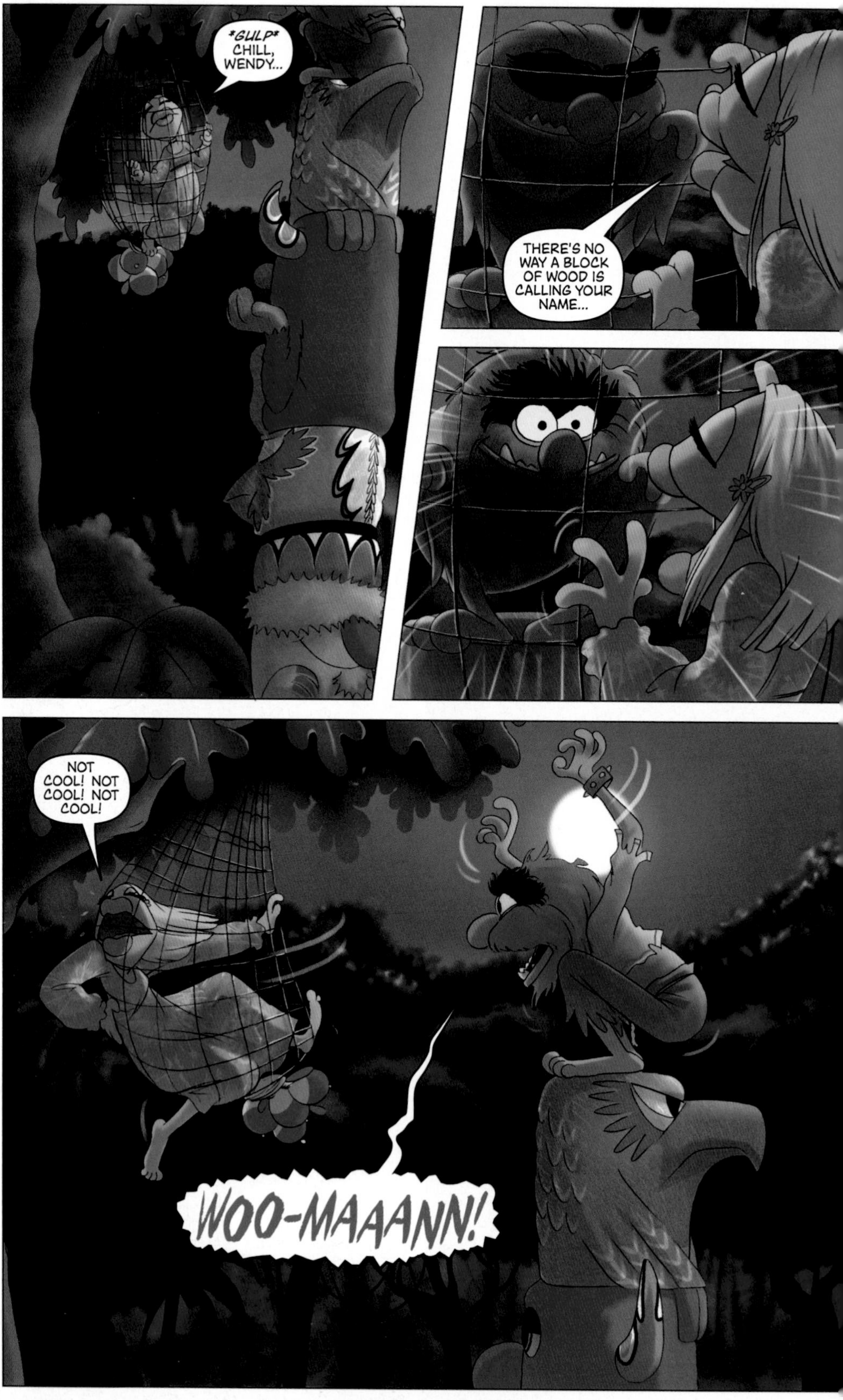
GULP CHILL, WENDY...
THERE'S NO WAY A BLOCK OF WOOD IS CALLING YOUR NAME...
NOT COOL! NOT COOL! NOT COOL!
WOO-MAAANN!

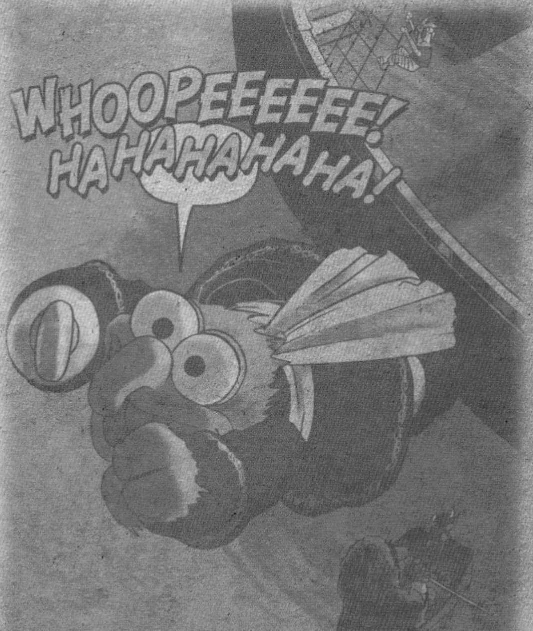
WHOOPEEEEEEE!
HA HAHAHAHAHA!

chapter three

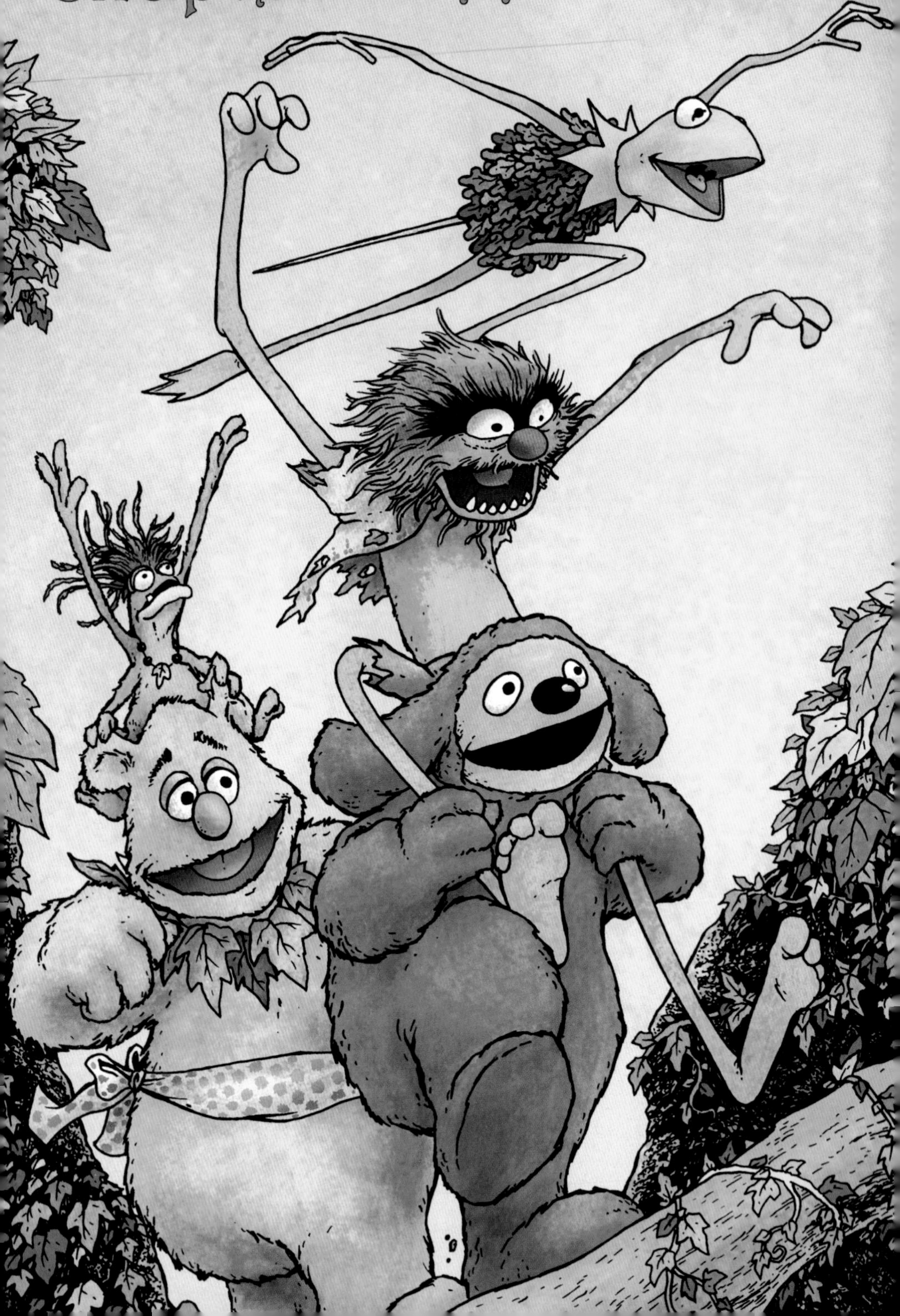

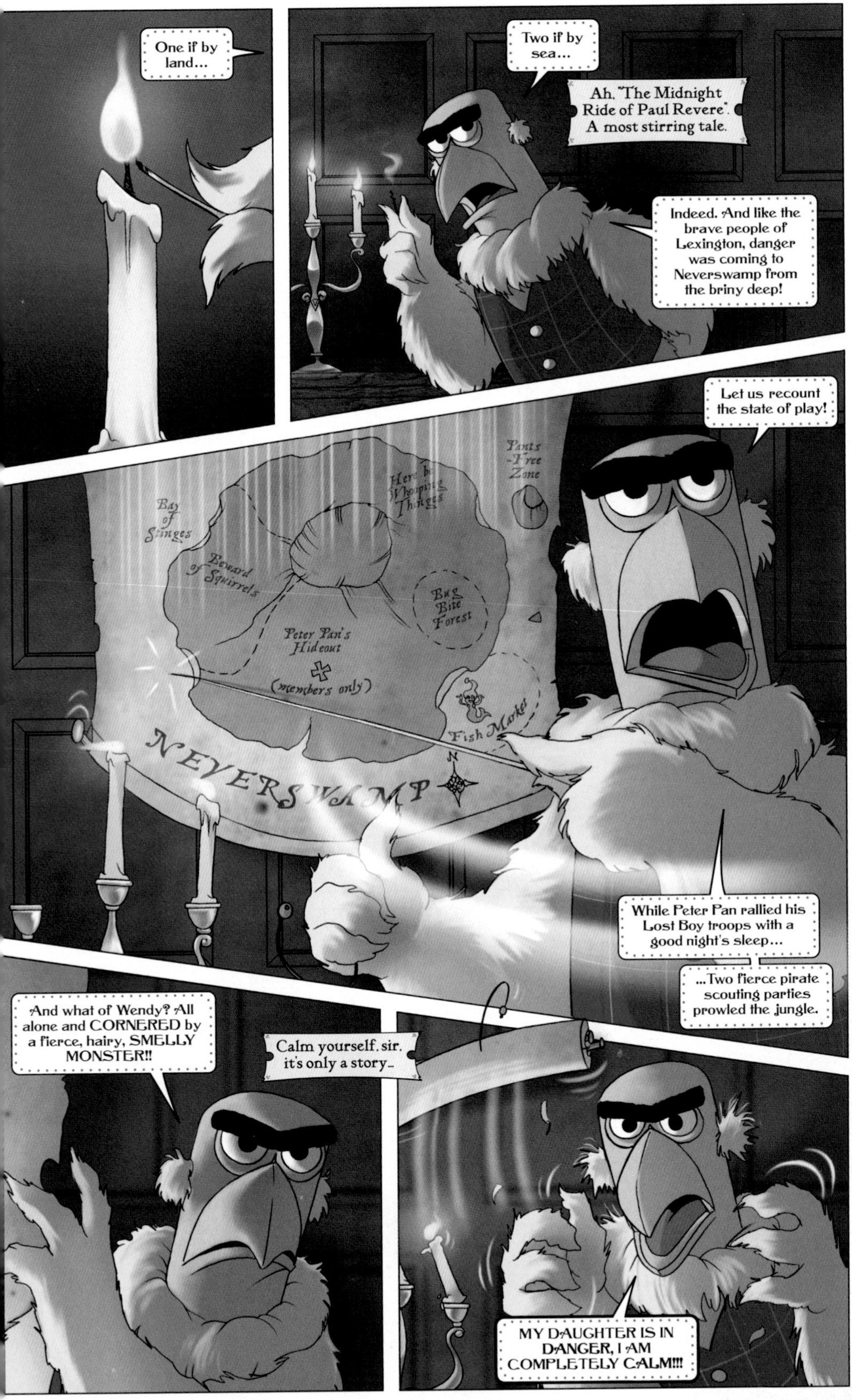
One if by land...
Two if by sea...
Ah, "The Midnight Ride of Paul Revere". A most stirring tale.
Indeed. And like the brave people of Lexington, danger was coming to Neverswamp from the briny deep!
Let us recount the state of play!
Pants -Free Zone
Here be Whooping Thinges
Bay of Stinges
Beward of Squirrels
Bug Bite Forest
Peter Pan's Hideout
(members only)
Fish Market
NEVERSWAMP
N
While Peter Pan rallied his Lost Boy troops with a good night's sleep...
...Two fierce pirate scouting parties prowled the jungle.
And what of Wendy? All alone and CORNERED by a fierce, hairy, SMELLY MONSTER!!
Calm yourself, sir, it's only a story...
MY DAUGHTER IS IN DANGER, I AM COMPLETELY CALM!!!

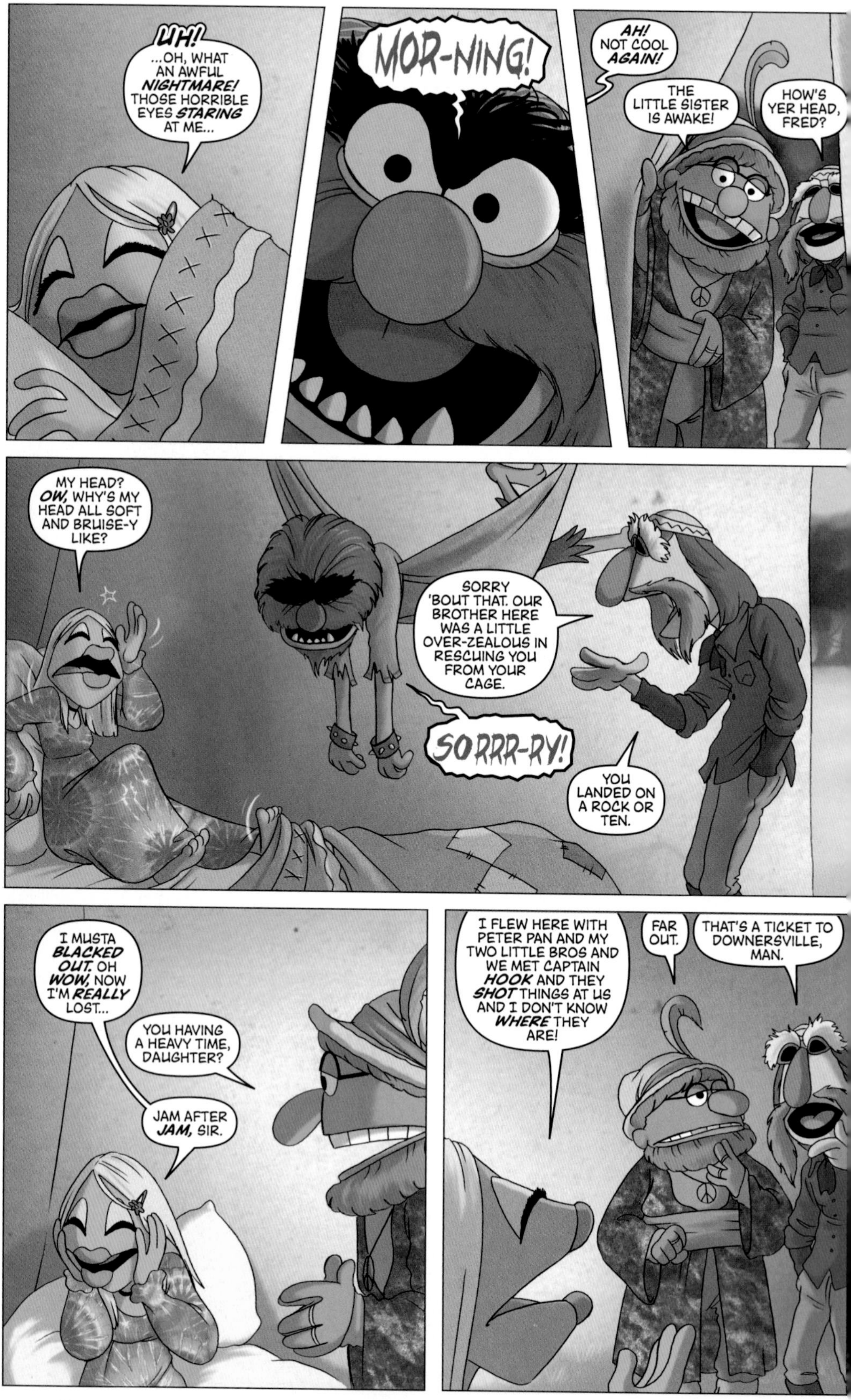
UH! ...OH, WHAT AN AWFUL NIGHTMARE! THOSE HORRIBLE EYES STARING AT ME...
MOR-NING!
AH! NOT COOL AGAIN!
THE LITTLE SISTER IS AWAKE!
HOW'S YER HEAD, FRED?
MY HEAD? OW, WHY'S MY HEAD ALL SOFT AND BRUISE-Y LIKE?
SORRY 'BOUT THAT. OUR BROTHER HERE WAS A LITTLE OVER-ZEALOUS IN RESCUING YOU FROM YOUR CAGE.
SORRR-RY!
YOU LANDED ON A ROCK OR TEN.
I MUSTA BLACKED OUT. OH WOW, NOW I'M REALLY LOST...
YOU HAVING A HEAVY TIME, DAUGHTER?
JAM AFTER JAM, SIR.
I FLEW HERE WITH PETER PAN AND MY TWO LITTLE BROS AND WE MET CAPTAIN HOOK AND THEY SHOT THINGS AT US AND I DON'T KNOW WHERE THEY ARE!
FAR OUT.
THAT'S A TICKET TO DOWNERSVILLE, MAN.

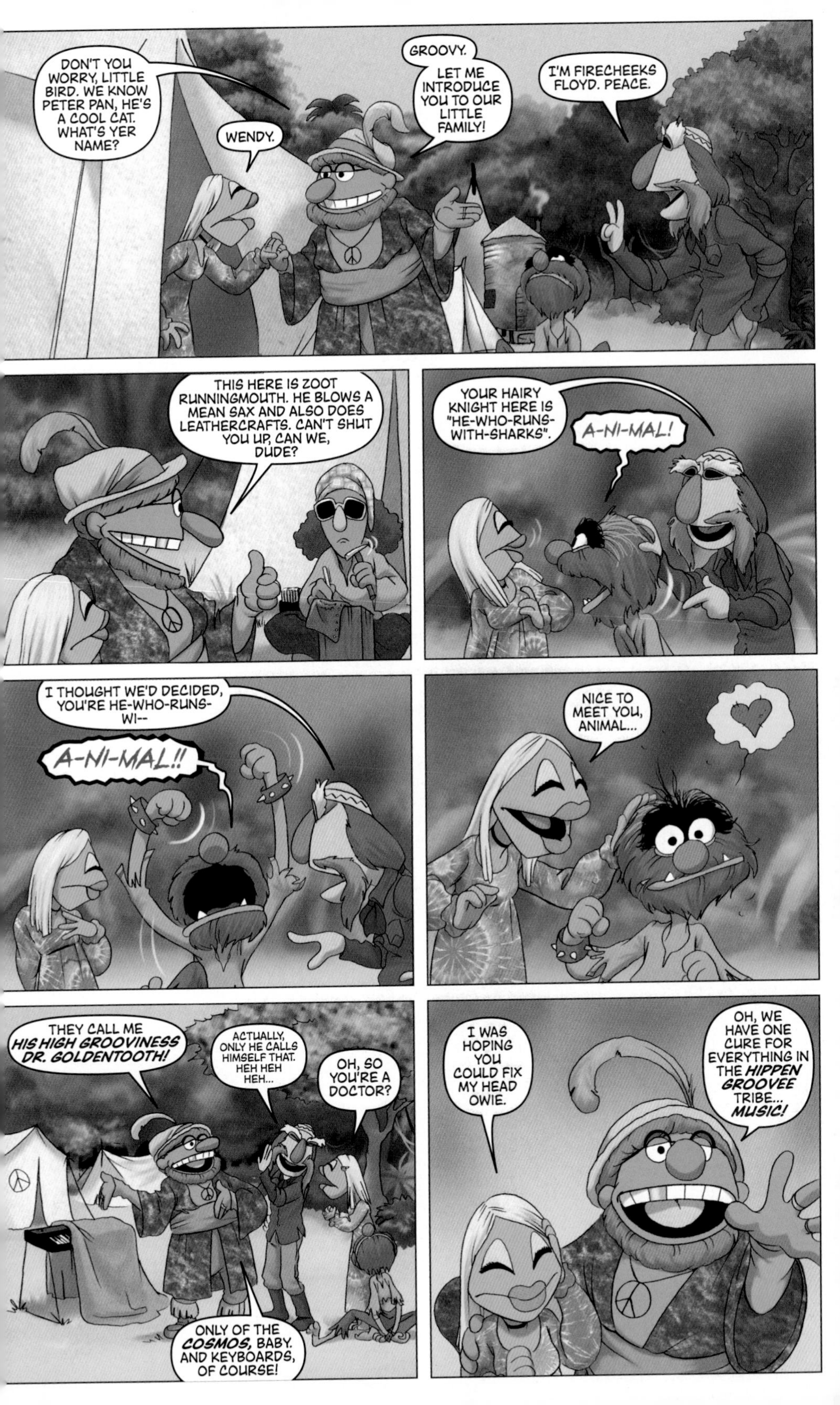

DON'T YOU WORRY, LITTLE BIRD. WE KNOW PETER PAN, HE'S A COOL CAT. WHAT'S YER NAME?
WENDY.
GROOVY.
LET ME INTRODUCE YOU TO OUR LITTLE FAMILY!
I'M FIRECHEEKS FLOYD. PEACE.
THIS HERE IS ZOOT RUNNINGMOUTH. HE BLOWS A MEAN SAX AND ALSO DOES LEATHERCRAFTS. CAN'T SHUT YOU UP, CAN WE, DUDE?
YOUR HAIRY KNIGHT HERE IS "HE-WHO-RUNS-WITH-SHARKS".
A-NI-MAL!
I THOUGHT WE'D DECIDED, YOU'RE HE-WHO-RUNS-WI--
A-NI-MAL!!
NICE TO MEET YOU, ANIMAL...
THEY CALL ME *HIS HIGH GROOVINESS DR. GOLDENTOOTH!*
ACTUALLY, ONLY HE CALLS HIMSELF THAT. HEH HEH HEH...
OH, SO YOU'RE A DOCTOR?
ONLY OF THE *COSMOS,* BABY. AND KEYBOARDS, OF COURSE!
I WAS HOPING YOU COULD FIX MY HEAD OWIE.
OH, WE HAVE ONE CURE FOR EVERYTHING IN THE *HIPPEN GROOVEE* TRIBE... *MUSIC!*

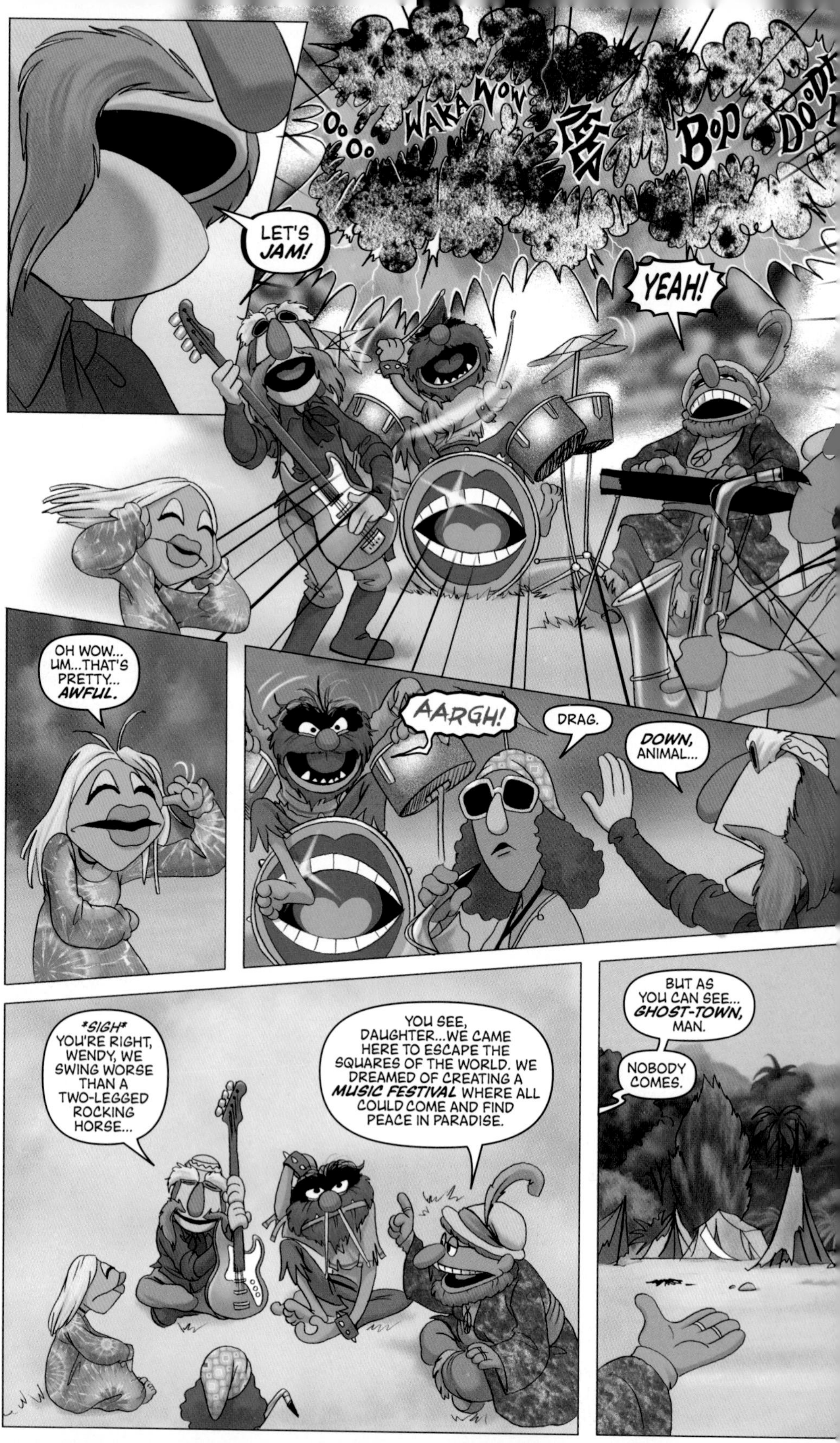
OoOo WAKA WOW ZEE BOP DOOD
LET'S JAM!
YEAH!
OH WOW... UM...THAT'S PRETTY... AWFUL.
AARGH!
DRAG.
DOWN, ANIMAL...
SIGH YOU'RE RIGHT, WENDY, WE SWING WORSE THAN A TWO-LEGGED ROCKING HORSE...
YOU SEE, DAUGHTER...WE CAME HERE TO ESCAPE THE SQUARES OF THE WORLD. WE DREAMED OF CREATING A MUSIC FESTIVAL WHERE ALL COULD COME AND FIND PEACE IN PARADISE.
BUT AS YOU CAN SEE... GHOST-TOWN, MAN.
NOBODY COMES.

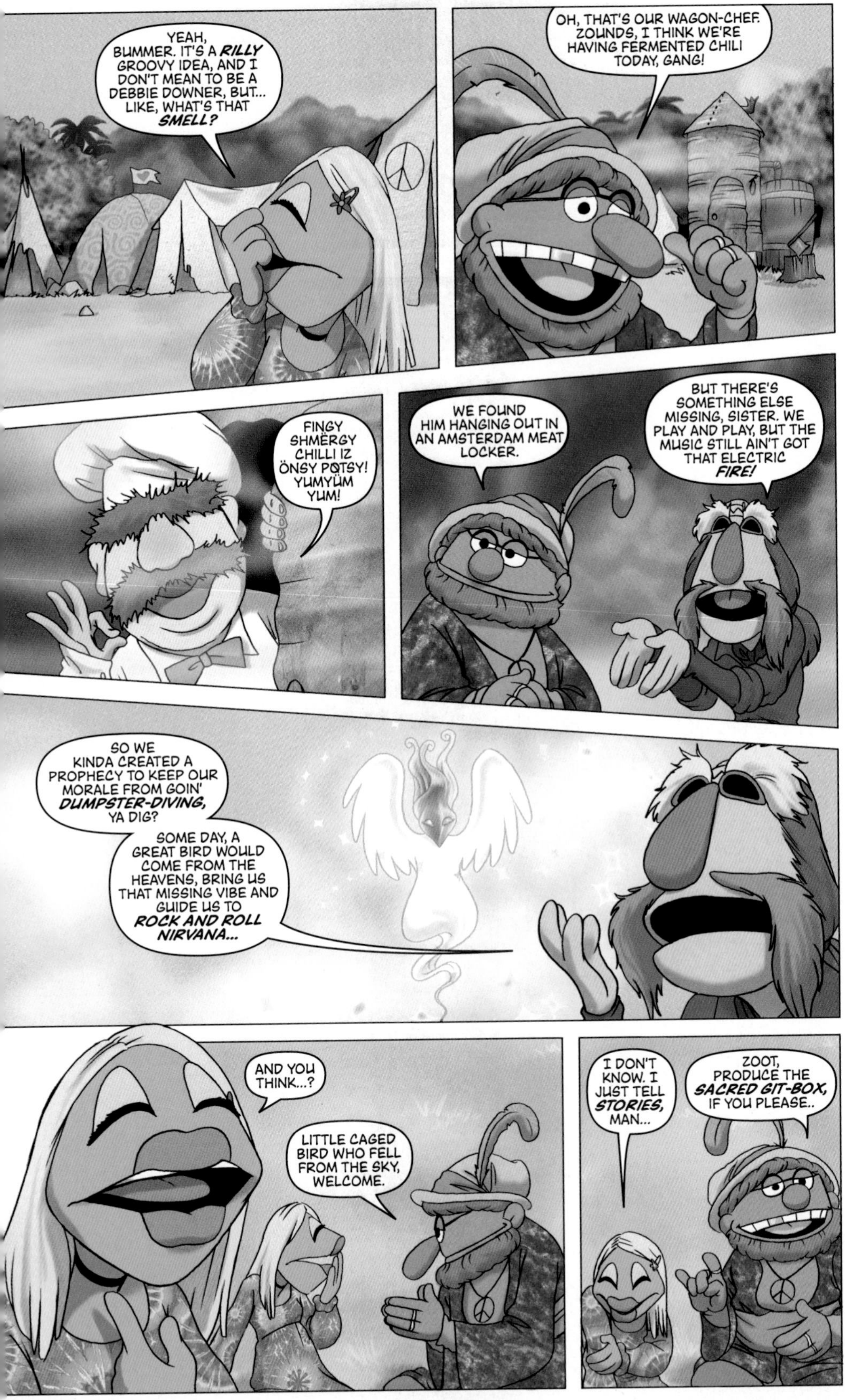
YEAH, BUMMER. IT'S A RILLY GROOVY IDEA, AND I DON'T MEAN TO BE A DEBBIE DOWNER, BUT... LIKE, WHAT'S THAT SMELL?
OH, THAT'S OUR WAGON-CHEF. ZOUNDS, I THINK WE'RE HAVING FERMENTED CHILI TODAY, GANG!
FINGY SHMËRGY CHILLI IZ ÖNSY PØTSY! YUMYÜM YUM!
WE FOUND HIM HANGING OUT IN AN AMSTERDAM MEAT LOCKER.
BUT THERE'S SOMETHING ELSE MISSING, SISTER. WE PLAY AND PLAY, BUT THE MUSIC STILL AIN'T GOT THAT ELECTRIC FIRE!
SO WE KINDA CREATED A PROPHECY TO KEEP OUR MORALE FROM GOIN' DUMPSTER-DIVING, YA DIG?
SOME DAY, A GREAT BIRD WOULD COME FROM THE HEAVENS, BRING US THAT MISSING VIBE AND GUIDE US TO ROCK AND ROLL NIRVANA...
AND YOU THINK...?
LITTLE CAGED BIRD WHO FELL FROM THE SKY, WELCOME.
I DON'T KNOW. I JUST TELL STORIES, MAN...
ZOOT, PRODUCE THE SACRED GIT-BOX, IF YOU PLEASE..

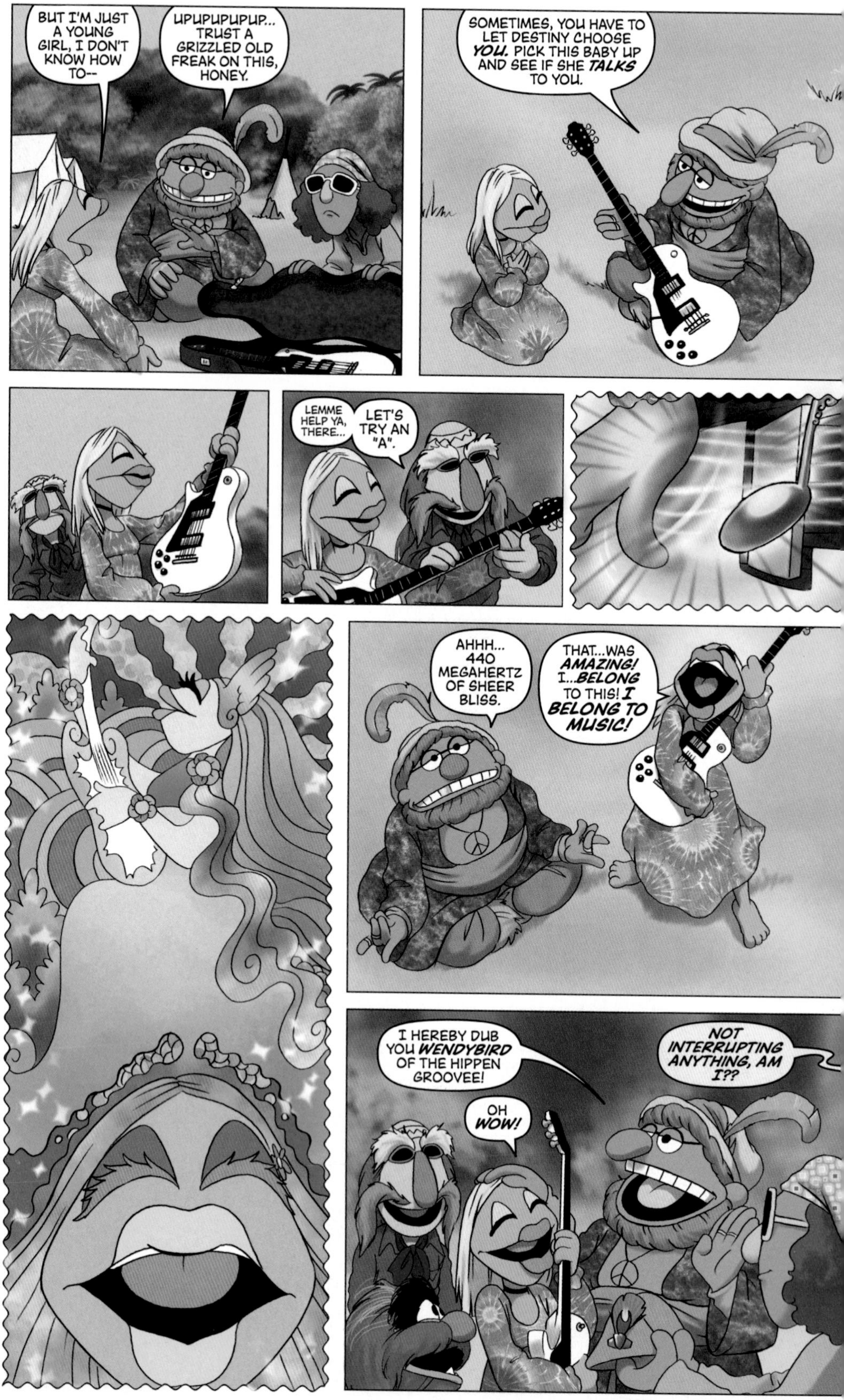
BUT I'M JUST A YOUNG GIRL, I DON'T KNOW HOW TO--
UPUPUPUPUP... TRUST A GRIZZLED OLD FREAK ON THIS, HONEY.
SOMETIMES, YOU HAVE TO LET DESTINY CHOOSE YOU. PICK THIS BABY UP AND SEE IF SHE TALKS TO YOU.
LEMME HELP YA, THERE...
LET'S TRY AN "A".
AHHH... 440 MEGAHERTZ OF SHEER BLISS.
THAT...WAS AMAZING! I...BELONG TO THIS! I BELONG TO MUSIC!
I HEREBY DUB YOU WENDYBIRD OF THE HIPPEN GROOVEE!
NOT INTERRUPTING ANYTHING, AM I??
OH WOW!

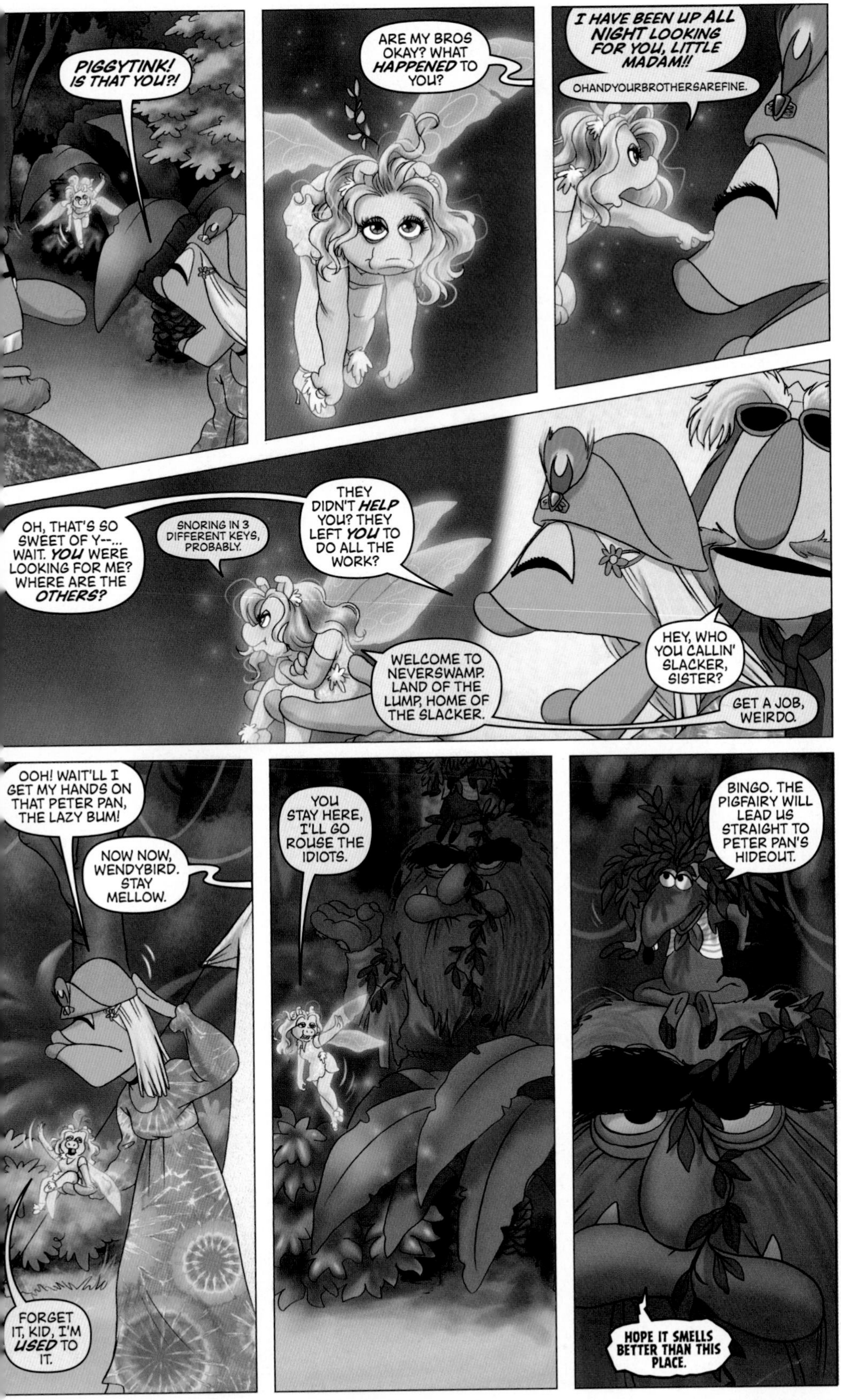
PIGGYTINK! IS THAT YOU?!
ARE MY BROS OKAY? WHAT HAPPENED TO YOU?
I HAVE BEEN UP ALL NIGHT LOOKING FOR YOU, LITTLE MADAM!!
OHANDYOURBROTHERSAREFINE.
OH, THAT'S SO SWEET OF Y--... WAIT. YOU WERE LOOKING FOR ME? WHERE ARE THE OTHERS?
SNORING IN 3 DIFFERENT KEYS, PROBABLY.
THEY DIDN'T HELP YOU? THEY LEFT YOU TO DO ALL THE WORK?
WELCOME TO NEVERSWAMP. LAND OF THE LUMP, HOME OF THE SLACKER.
HEY, WHO YOU CALLIN' SLACKER, SISTER?
GET A JOB, WEIRDO.
OOH! WAIT'LL I GET MY HANDS ON THAT PETER PAN, THE LAZY BUM!
NOW NOW, WENDYBIRD. STAY MELLOW.
FORGET IT, KID, I'M USED TO IT.
YOU STAY HERE, I'LL GO ROUSE THE IDIOTS.
BINGO. THE PIGFAIRY WILL LEAD US STRAIGHT TO PETER PAN'S HIDEOUT.
HOPE IT SMELLS BETTER THAN THIS PLACE.

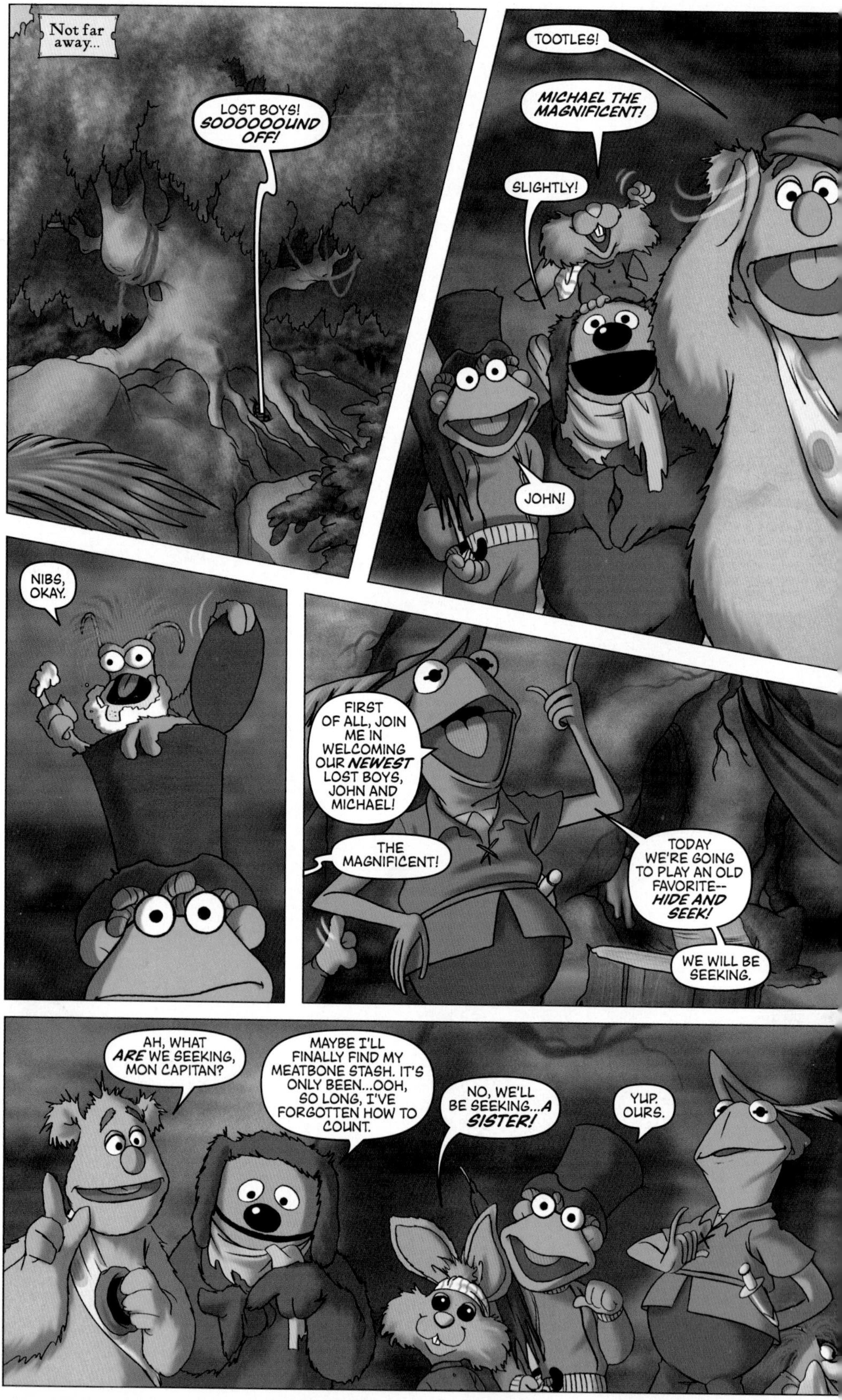
Not far away...
LOST BOYS! SOOOOOOUND OFF!
TOOTLES!
MICHAEL THE MAGNIFICENT!
SLIGHTLY!
JOHN!
NIBS, OKAY.
FIRST OF ALL, JOIN ME IN WELCOMING OUR NEWEST LOST BOYS, JOHN AND MICHAEL!
THE MAGNIFICENT!
TODAY WE'RE GOING TO PLAY AN OLD FAVORITE-- HIDE AND SEEK!
WE WILL BE SEEKING.
AH, WHAT ARE WE SEEKING, MON CAPITAN?
MAYBE I'LL FINALLY FIND MY MEATBONE STASH. IT'S ONLY BEEN...OOH, SO LONG, I'VE FORGOTTEN HOW TO COUNT.
NO, WE'LL BE SEEKING...A SISTER!
YUP. OURS.

OOH, A *CHIQUITA*, EH? EEEENTERESTING...

SHE DOES NOT LOOK LIKE EITHER OF *YOU*, DOES SHE?

NAW, SHE'S TALL, WITH LONG BLONDE HA--

OKAY, WE SEEK NOW!!

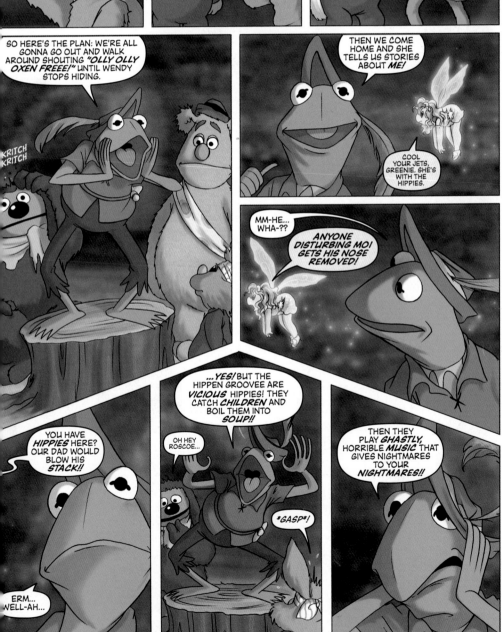

SO HERE'S THE PLAN: WE'RE ALL GONNA GO OUT AND WALK AROUND SHOUTING *"OLLY OLLY OXEN FREEE!"* UNTIL WENDY STOPS HIDING.

KRITCH KRITCH

THEN WE COME HOME AND SHE TELLS US STORIES ABOUT *ME!*

COOL YOUR JETS, GREENIE. SHE'S WITH THE HIPPIES.

MM-HE... WHA-??

ANYONE DISTURBING MOI GETS HIS NOSE REMOVED!

YOU HAVE *HIPPIES* HERE? OUR DAD WOULD BLOW HIS *STACK!!*

ERM... WELL-AH...

...*YES!* BUT THE HIPPEN GROOVEE ARE *VICIOUS* HIPPIES! THEY CATCH *CHILDREN* AND BOIL THEM INTO *SOUP!!*

OH HEY ROSCOE...

GASP!

THEN THEY PLAY *GHASTLY*, HORRIBLE *MUSIC* THAT GIVES NIGHTMARES TO YOUR *NIGHTMARES!!*

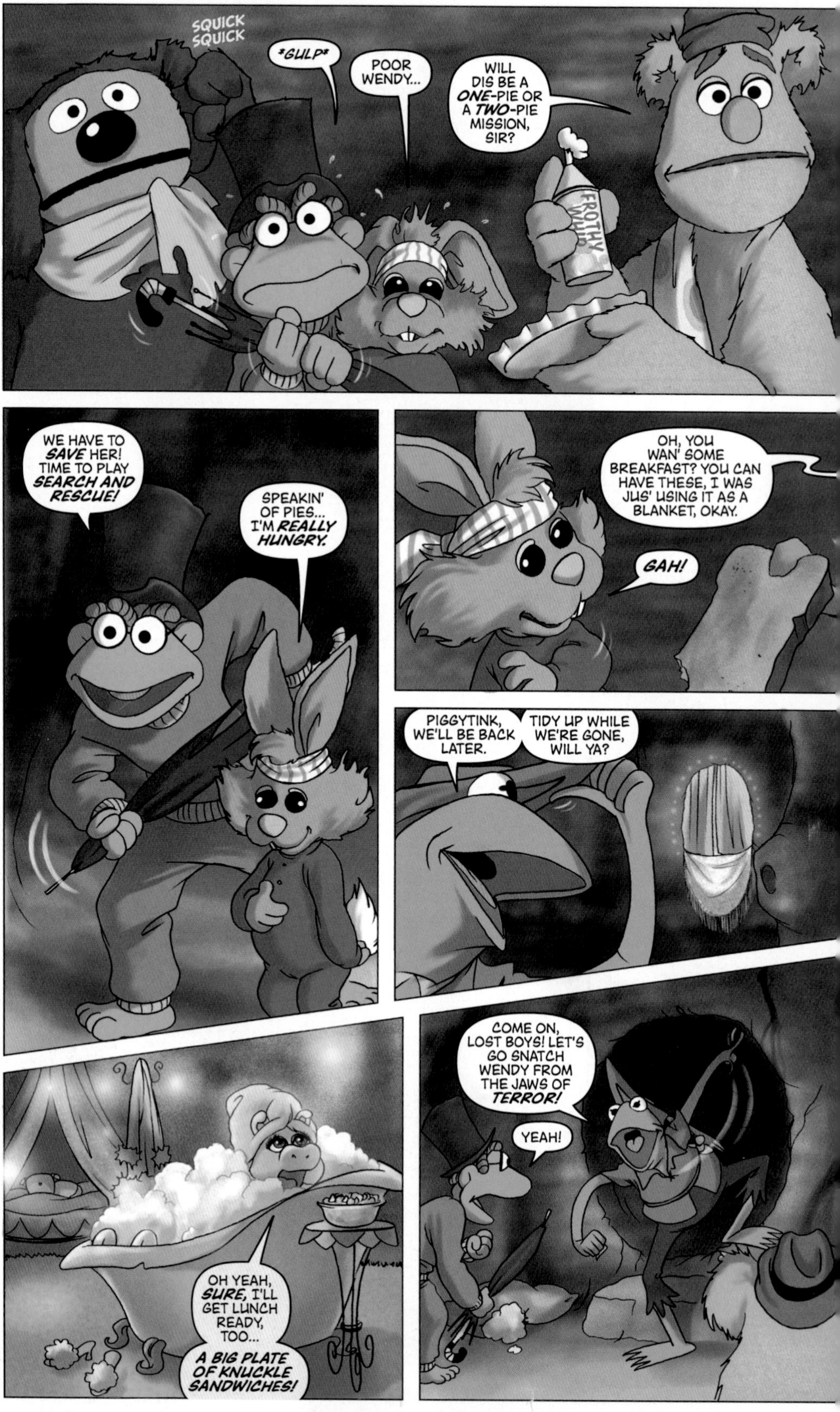
SQUICK SQUICK
GULP
POOR WENDY...
WILL DIS BE A ONE-PIE OR A TWO-PIE MISSION, SIR?
FROTHY WHIP
WE HAVE TO SAVE HER! TIME TO PLAY SEARCH AND RESCUE!
SPEAKIN' OF PIES... I'M REALLY HUNGRY.
OH, YOU WAN' SOME BREAKFAST? YOU CAN HAVE THESE, I WAS JUS' USING IT AS A BLANKET, OKAY.
GAH!
PIGGYTINK, WE'LL BE BACK LATER.
TIDY UP WHILE WE'RE GONE, WILL YA?
OH YEAH, SURE, I'LL GET LUNCH READY, TOO...
A BIG PLATE OF KNUCKLE SANDWICHES!
COME ON, LOST BOYS! LET'S GO SNATCH WENDY FROM THE JAWS OF TERROR!
YEAH!

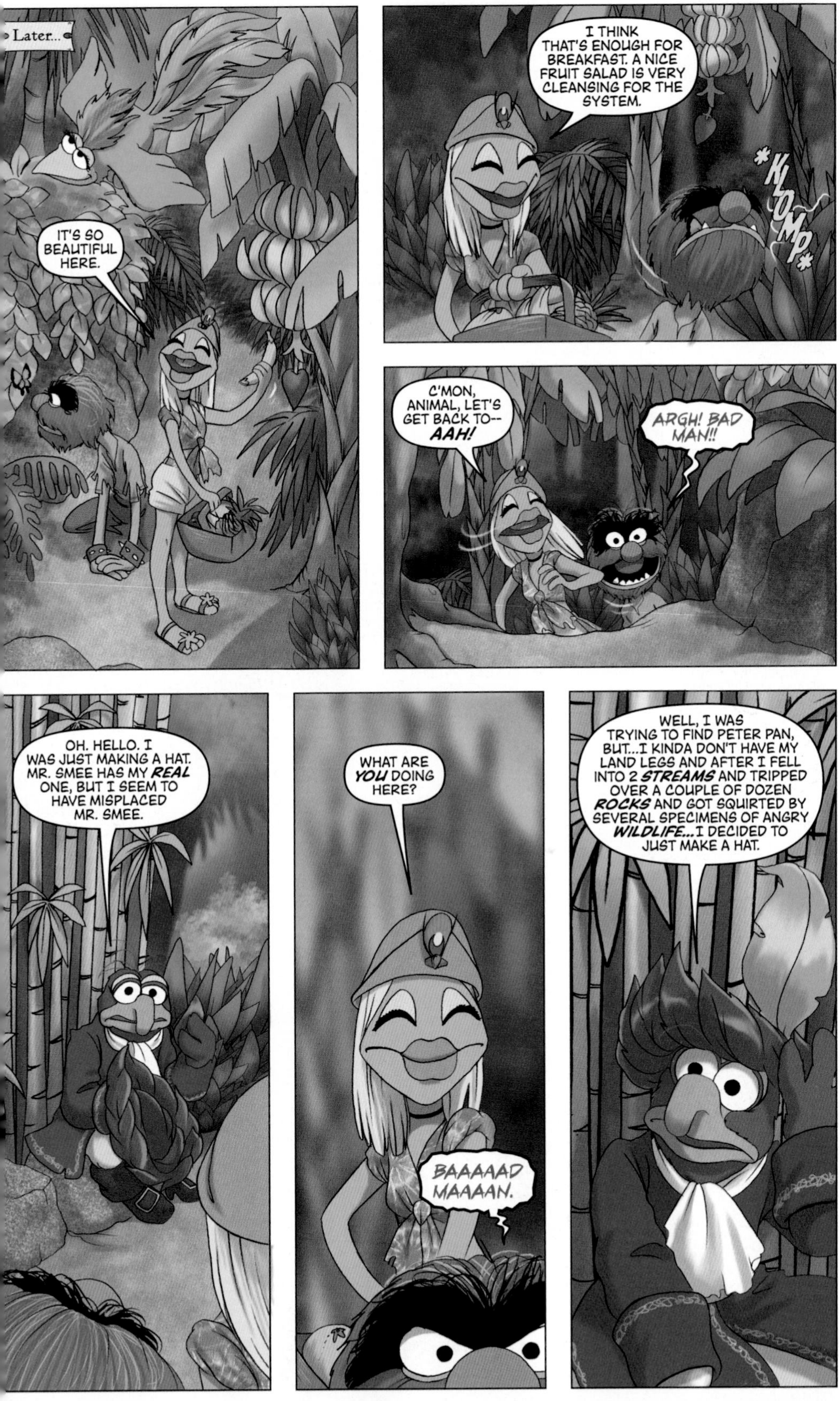
Later...
IT'S SO BEAUTIFUL HERE.
I THINK THAT'S ENOUGH FOR BREAKFAST. A NICE FRUIT SALAD IS VERY CLEANSING FOR THE SYSTEM.
KLOMP
C'MON, ANIMAL, LET'S GET BACK TO-- AAH!
ARGH! BAD MAN!!
OH. HELLO. I WAS JUST MAKING A HAT. MR. SMEE HAS MY REAL ONE, BUT I SEEM TO HAVE MISPLACED MR. SMEE.
WHAT ARE YOU DOING HERE?
BAAAAAD MAAAAN.
WELL, I WAS TRYING TO FIND PETER PAN, BUT...I KINDA DON'T HAVE MY LAND LEGS AND AFTER I FELL INTO 2 STREAMS AND TRIPPED OVER A COUPLE OF DOZEN ROCKS AND GOT SQUIRTED BY SEVERAL SPECIMENS OF ANGRY WILDLIFE...I DECIDED TO JUST MAKE A HAT.

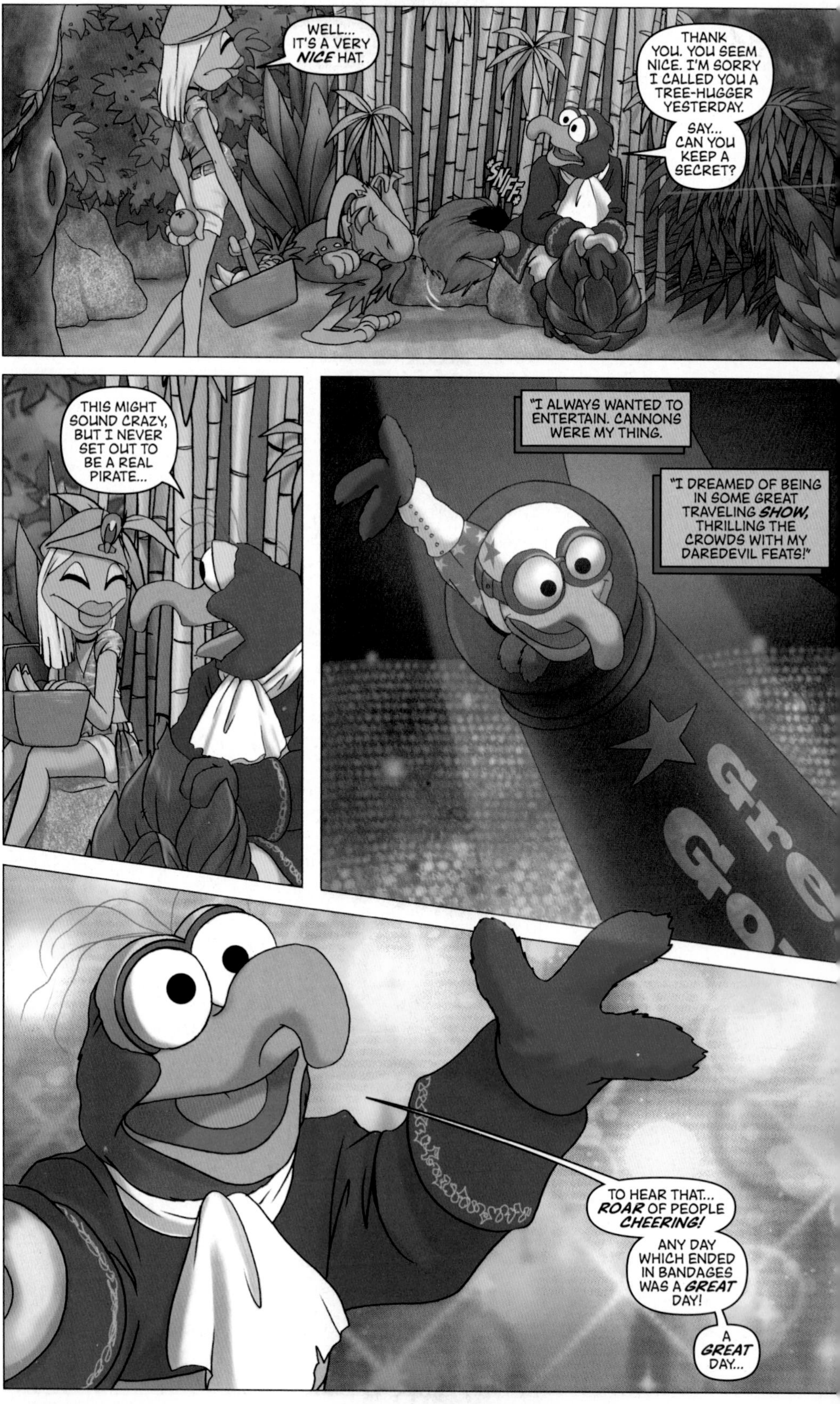
WELL... IT'S A VERY NICE HAT.
THANK YOU. YOU SEEM NICE. I'M SORRY I CALLED YOU A TREE-HUGGER YESTERDAY.
SAY... CAN YOU KEEP A SECRET?
SNIFF
THIS MIGHT SOUND CRAZY, BUT I NEVER SET OUT TO BE A REAL PIRATE...
"I ALWAYS WANTED TO ENTERTAIN. CANNONS WERE MY THING.
"I DREAMED OF BEING IN SOME GREAT TRAVELING SHOW, THRILLING THE CROWDS WITH MY DAREDEVIL FEATS!"
TO HEAR THAT... ROAR OF PEOPLE CHEERING!
ANY DAY WHICH ENDED IN BANDAGES WAS A GREAT DAY!
A GREAT DAY...

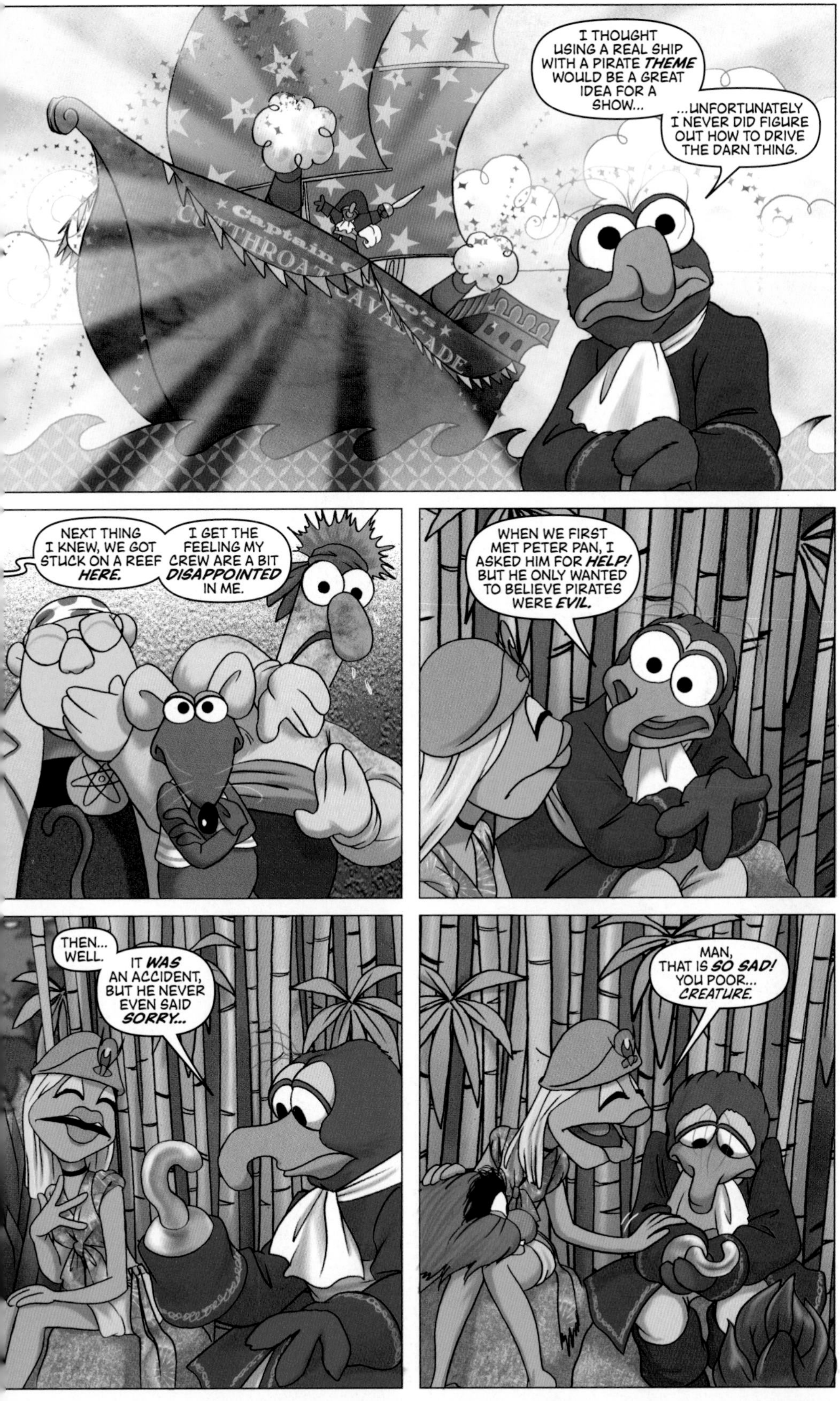

I THOUGHT USING A REAL SHIP WITH A PIRATE THEME WOULD BE A GREAT IDEA FOR A SHOW...
...UNFORTUNATELY I NEVER DID FIGURE OUT HOW TO DRIVE THE DARN THING.
Captain Gonzo's CUTTHROAT CAVALCADE
NEXT THING I KNEW, WE GOT STUCK ON A REEF HERE.
I GET THE FEELING MY CREW ARE A BIT DISAPPOINTED IN ME.
WHEN WE FIRST MET PETER PAN, I ASKED HIM FOR HELP! BUT HE ONLY WANTED TO BELIEVE PIRATES WERE EVIL.
THEN... WELL.
IT WAS AN ACCIDENT, BUT HE NEVER EVEN SAID SORRY...
MAN, THAT IS SO SAD! YOU POOR... CREATURE.

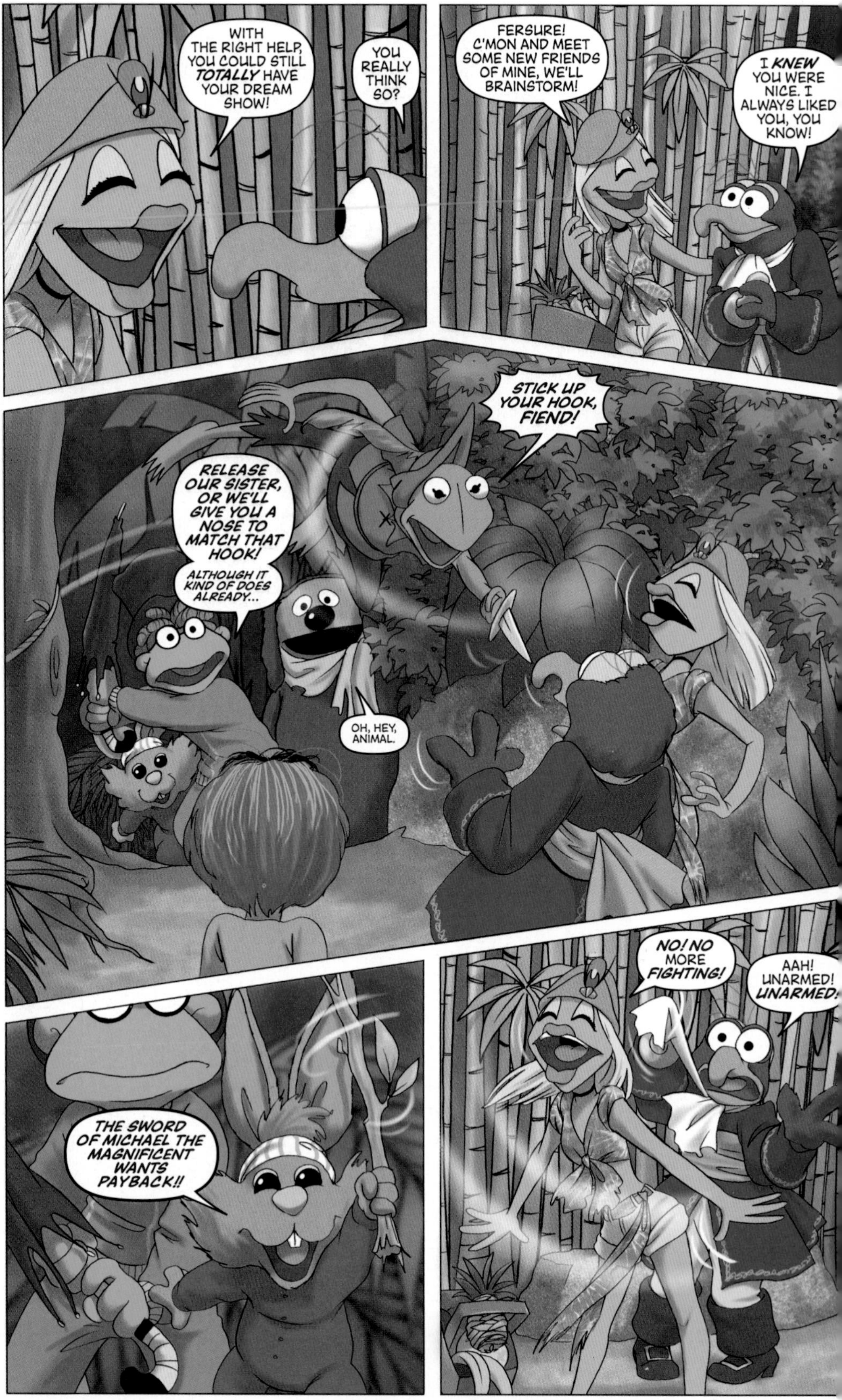
WITH THE RIGHT HELP, YOU COULD STILL *TOTALLY* HAVE YOUR DREAM SHOW!
YOU REALLY THINK SO?
FERSURE! C'MON AND MEET SOME NEW FRIENDS OF MINE, WE'LL BRAINSTORM!
I *KNEW* YOU WERE NICE. I ALWAYS LIKED YOU, YOU KNOW!
STICK UP YOUR HOOK, FIEND!
RELEASE OUR SISTER, OR WE'LL GIVE YOU A NOSE TO MATCH THAT HOOK!
ALTHOUGH IT KIND OF DOES ALREADY...
OH, HEY, ANIMAL.
THE SWORD OF MICHAEL THE MAGNIFICENT WANTS PAYBACK!!
NO! NO MORE FIGHTING!
AAH! UNARMED! *UNARMED!*

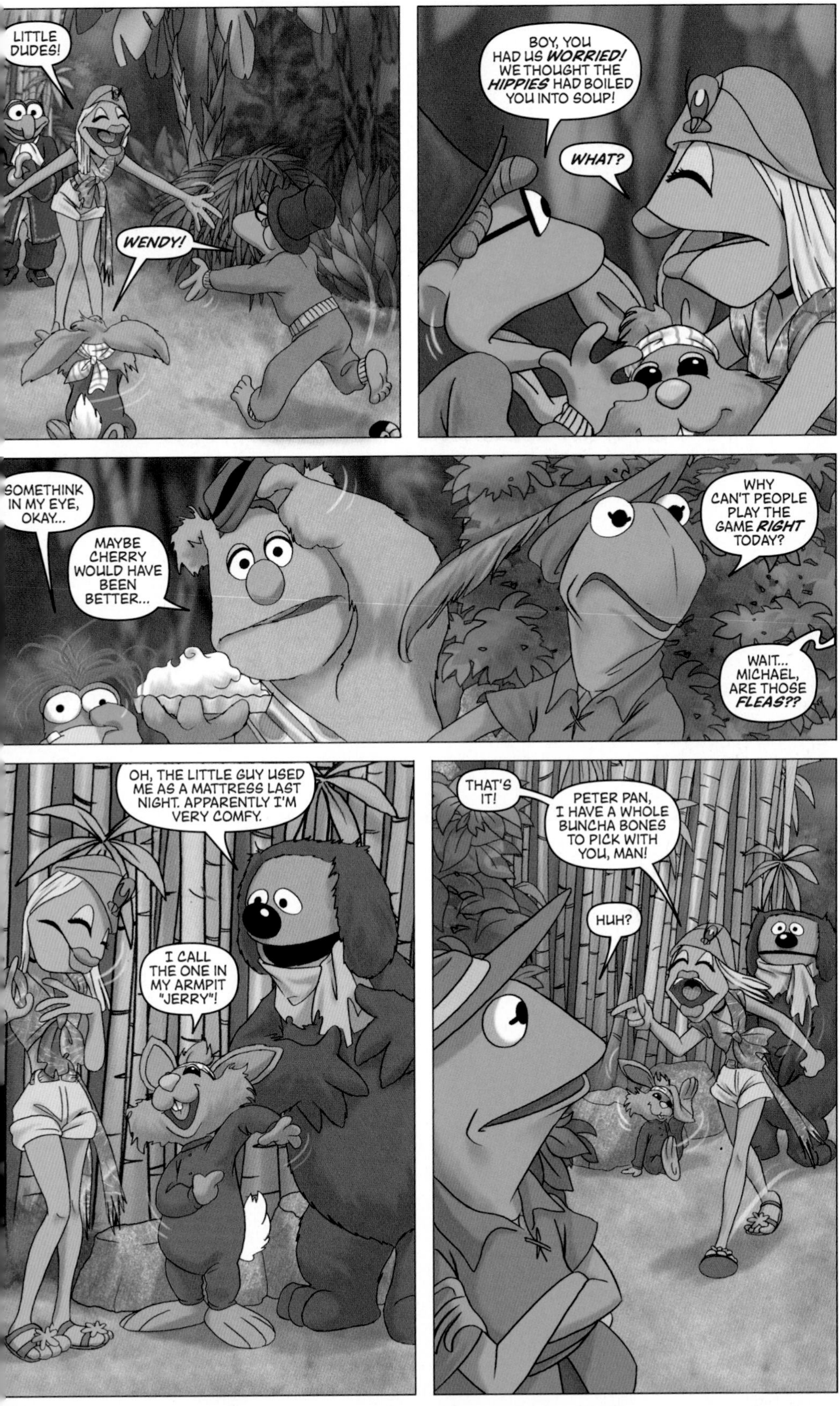
LITTLE DUDES!
WENDY!
BOY, YOU HAD US WORRIED! WE THOUGHT THE HIPPIES HAD BOILED YOU INTO SOUP!
WHAT?
SOMETHINK IN MY EYE, OKAY...
MAYBE CHERRY WOULD HAVE BEEN BETTER...
WHY CAN'T PEOPLE PLAY THE GAME RIGHT TODAY?
WAIT... MICHAEL, ARE THOSE FLEAS??
OH, THE LITTLE GUY USED ME AS A MATTRESS LAST NIGHT. APPARENTLY I'M VERY COMFY.
I CALL THE ONE IN MY ARMPIT "JERRY"!
THAT'S IT!
PETER PAN, I HAVE A WHOLE BUNCHA BONES TO PICK WITH YOU, MAN!
HUH?

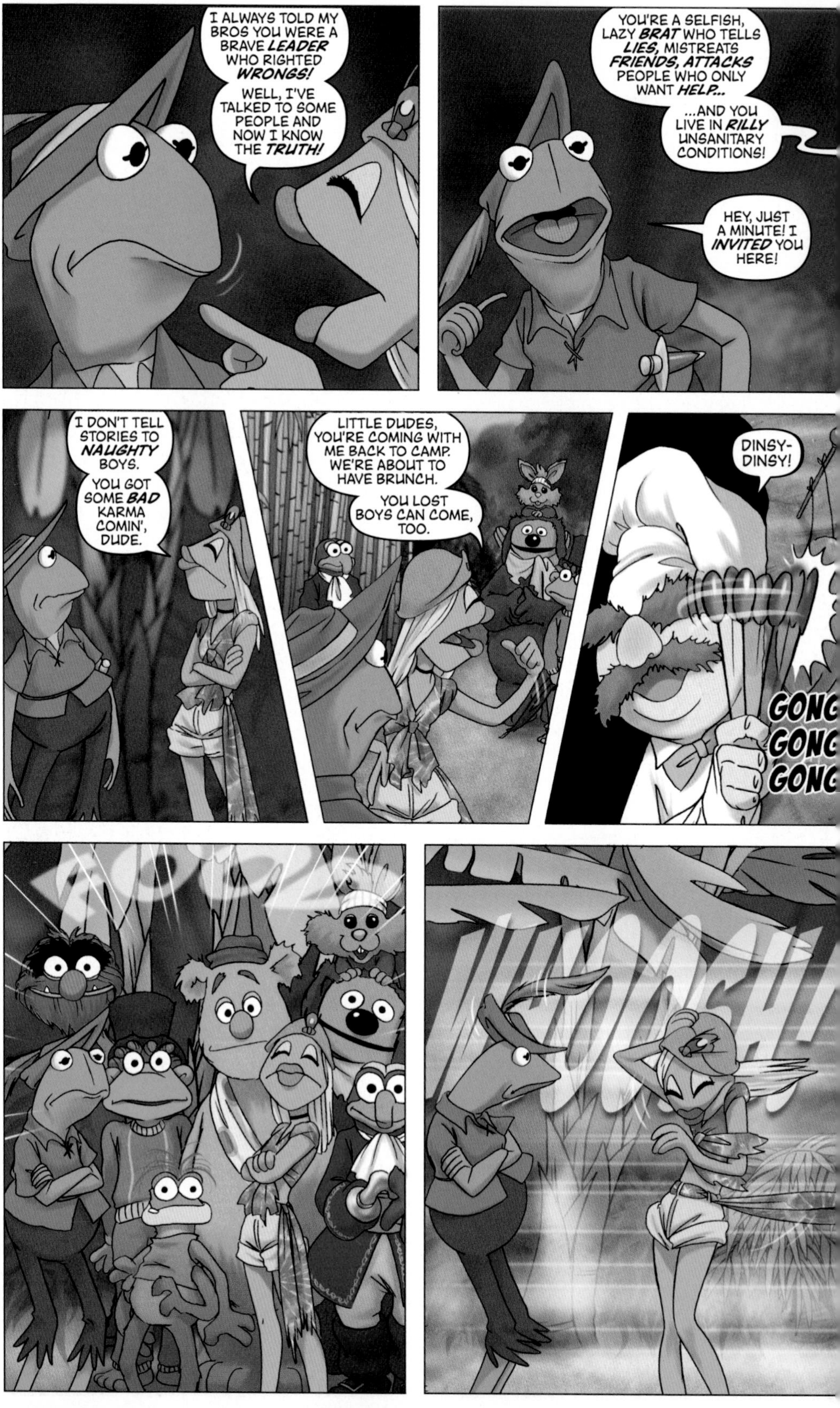
I ALWAYS TOLD MY BROS YOU WERE A BRAVE LEADER WHO RIGHTED WRONGS!
WELL, I'VE TALKED TO SOME PEOPLE AND NOW I KNOW THE TRUTH!
YOU'RE A SELFISH, LAZY BRAT WHO TELLS LIES, MISTREATS FRIENDS, ATTACKS PEOPLE WHO ONLY WANT HELP...
...AND YOU LIVE IN RILLY UNSANITARY CONDITIONS!
HEY, JUST A MINUTE! I INVITED YOU HERE!
I DON'T TELL STORIES TO NAUGHTY BOYS.
YOU GOT SOME BAD KARMA COMIN', DUDE.
LITTLE DUDES, YOU'RE COMING WITH ME BACK TO CAMP. WE'RE ABOUT TO HAVE BRUNCH.
YOU LOST BOYS CAN COME, TOO.
DINSY-DINSY!
GONG GONG GONG

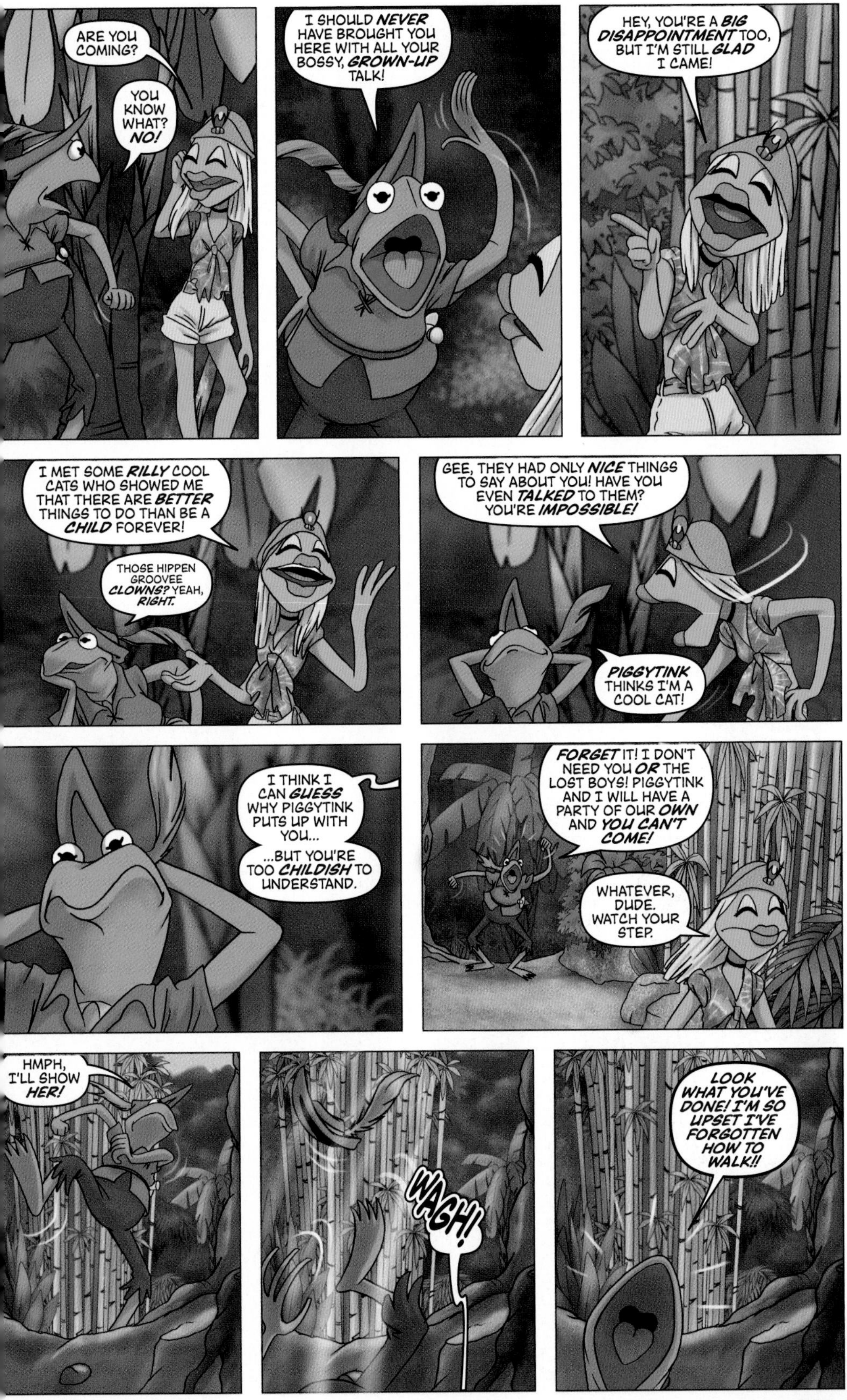
ARE YOU COMING?
YOU KNOW WHAT? NO!
I SHOULD NEVER HAVE BROUGHT YOU HERE WITH ALL YOUR BOSSY, GROWN-UP TALK!
HEY, YOU'RE A BIG DISAPPOINTMENT TOO, BUT I'M STILL GLAD I CAME!
I MET SOME RILLY COOL CATS WHO SHOWED ME THAT THERE ARE BETTER THINGS TO DO THAN BE A CHILD FOREVER!
THOSE HIPPEN GROOVEE CLOWNS? YEAH, RIGHT.
GEE, THEY HAD ONLY NICE THINGS TO SAY ABOUT YOU! HAVE YOU EVEN TALKED TO THEM? YOU'RE IMPOSSIBLE!
PIGGYTINK THINKS I'M A COOL CAT!
I THINK I CAN GUESS WHY PIGGYTINK PUTS UP WITH YOU...
...BUT YOU'RE TOO CHILDISH TO UNDERSTAND.
FORGET IT! I DON'T NEED YOU OR THE LOST BOYS! PIGGYTINK AND I WILL HAVE A PARTY OF OUR OWN AND YOU CAN'T COME!
WHATEVER, DUDE. WATCH YOUR STEP.
HMPH, I'LL SHOW HER!
WAGH!
LOOK WHAT YOU'VE DONE! I'M SO UPSET I'VE FORGOTTEN HOW TO WALK!!

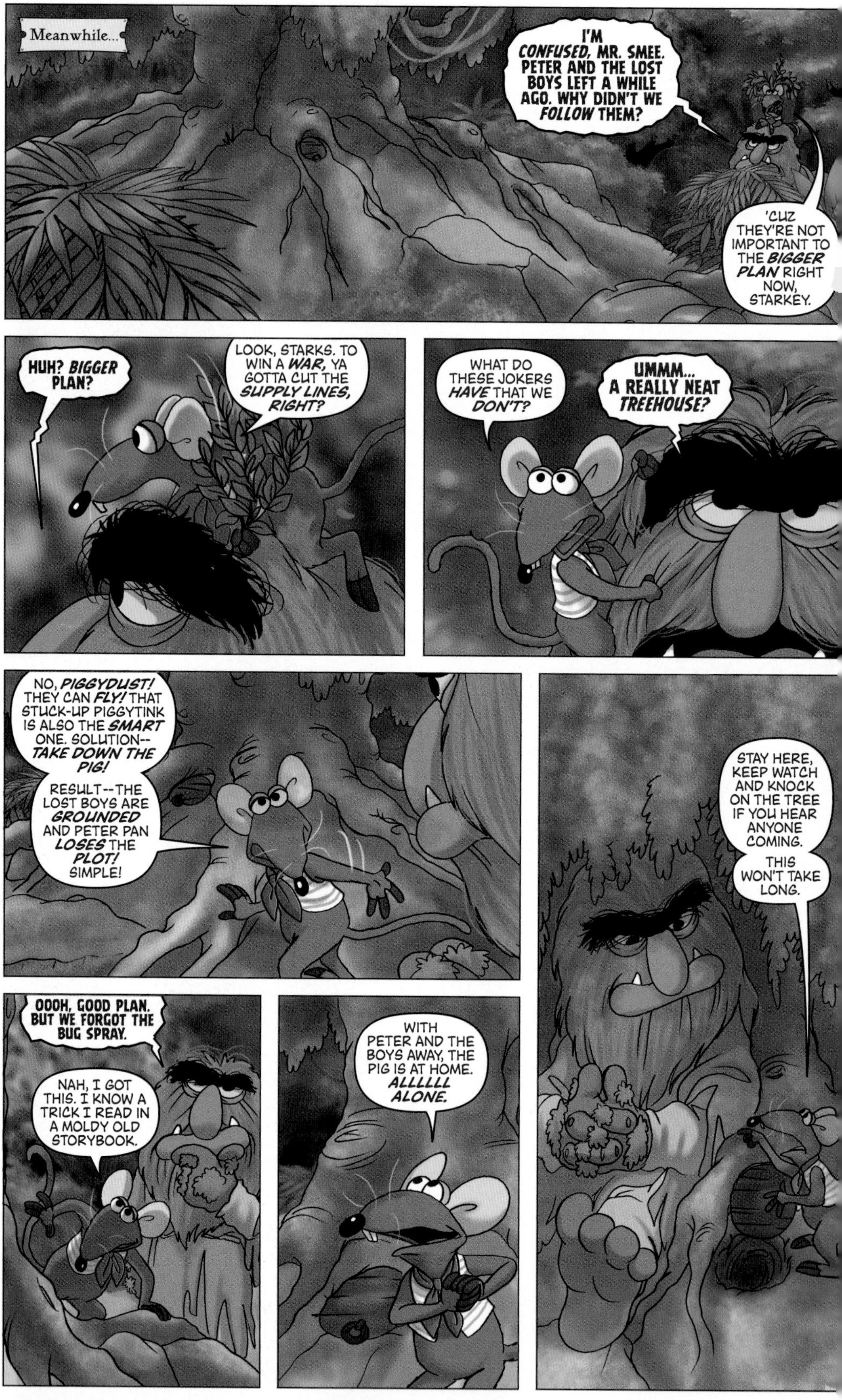
Meanwhile...
I'M *CONFUSED,* MR. SMEE. PETER AND THE LOST BOYS LEFT A WHILE AGO. WHY DIDN'T WE *FOLLOW* THEM?
'CUZ THEY'RE NOT IMPORTANT TO THE *BIGGER PLAN* RIGHT NOW, STARKEY.
HUH? *BIGGER* PLAN?
LOOK, STARKS. TO WIN A *WAR,* YA GOTTA CUT THE *SUPPLY LINES, RIGHT?*
WHAT DO THESE JOKERS *HAVE* THAT WE *DON'T?*
UMMM... A REALLY NEAT *TREEHOUSE?*
NO, *PIGGYDUST!* THEY CAN *FLY!* THAT STUCK-UP PIGGYTINK IS ALSO THE *SMART* ONE. SOLUTION-- *TAKE DOWN THE PIG!*
RESULT--THE LOST BOYS ARE *GROUNDED* AND PETER PAN *LOSES* THE *PLOT!* SIMPLE!
STAY HERE, KEEP WATCH AND KNOCK ON THE TREE IF YOU HEAR ANYONE COMING.
THIS WON'T TAKE LONG.
OOOH, GOOD PLAN. BUT WE FORGOT THE BUG SPRAY.
NAH, I GOT THIS. I KNOW A TRICK I READ IN A MOLDY OLD STORYBOOK.
WITH PETER AND THE BOYS AWAY, THE PIG IS AT HOME. *ALLLLLL ALONE.*

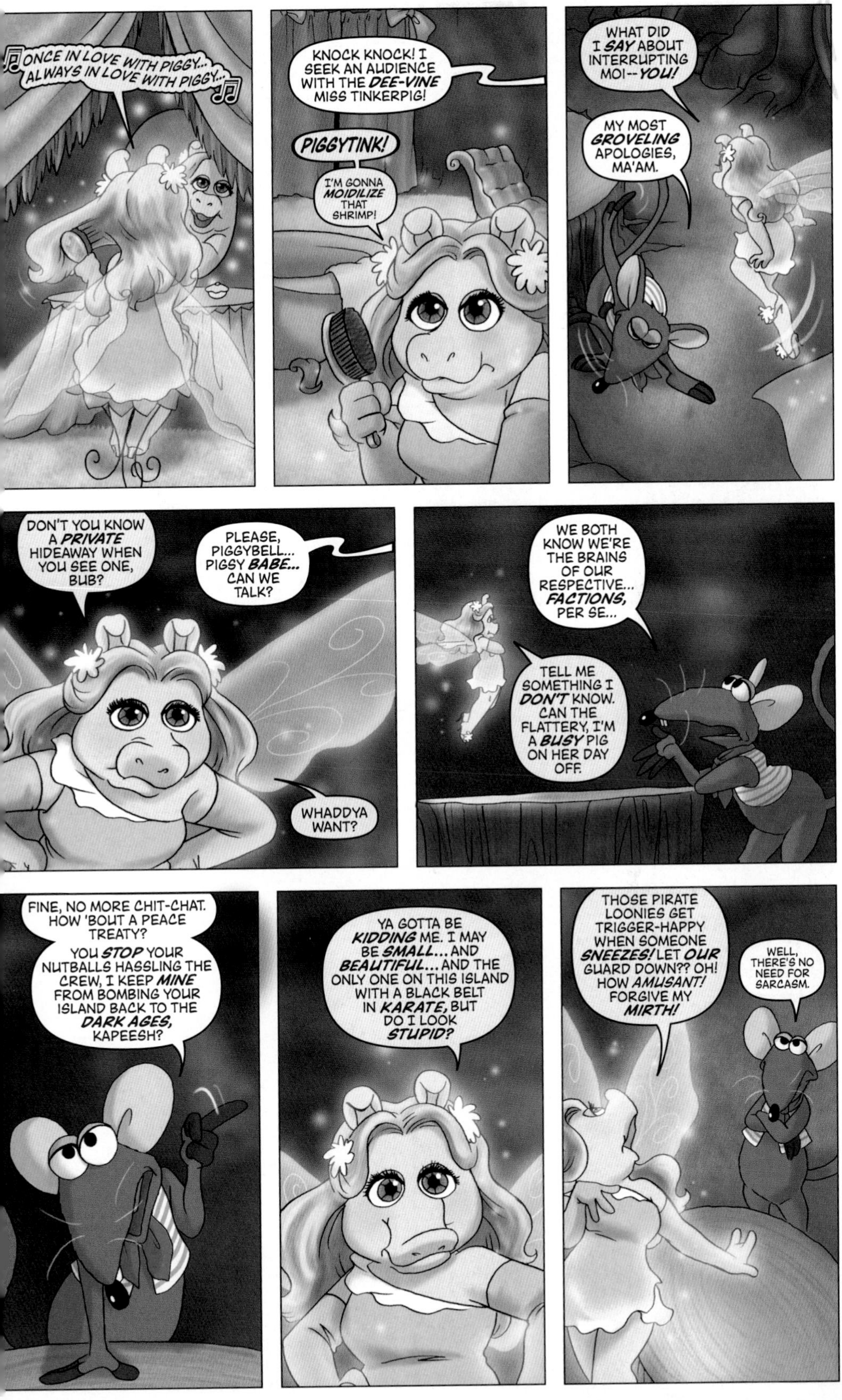
♫ONCE IN LOVE WITH PIGGY... ALWAYS IN LOVE WITH PIGGY...♫
KNOCK KNOCK! I SEEK AN AUDIENCE WITH THE DEE-VINE MISS TINKERPIG!
PIGGYTINK!
I'M GONNA MOIDILIZE THAT SHRIMP!
WHAT DID I SAY ABOUT INTERRUPTING MOI--YOU!
MY MOST GROVELING APOLOGIES, MA'AM.
DON'T YOU KNOW A PRIVATE HIDEAWAY WHEN YOU SEE ONE, BUB?
PLEASE, PIGGYBELL... PIGSY BABE... CAN WE TALK?
WHADDYA WANT?
WE BOTH KNOW WE'RE THE BRAINS OF OUR RESPECTIVE... FACTIONS, PER SE...
TELL ME SOMETHING I DON'T KNOW. CAN THE FLATTERY, I'M A BUSY PIG ON HER DAY OFF.
FINE, NO MORE CHIT-CHAT. HOW 'BOUT A PEACE TREATY?
YOU STOP YOUR NUTBALLS HASSLING THE CREW, I KEEP MINE FROM BOMBING YOUR ISLAND BACK TO THE DARK AGES, KAPEESH?
YA GOTTA BE KIDDING ME. I MAY BE SMALL... AND BEAUTIFUL... AND THE ONLY ONE ON THIS ISLAND WITH A BLACK BELT IN KARATE, BUT DO I LOOK STUPID?
THOSE PIRATE LOONIES GET TRIGGER-HAPPY WHEN SOMEONE SNEEZES! LET OUR GUARD DOWN?? OH! HOW AMUSANT! FORGIVE MY MIRTH!
WELL, THERE'S NO NEED FOR SARCASM.

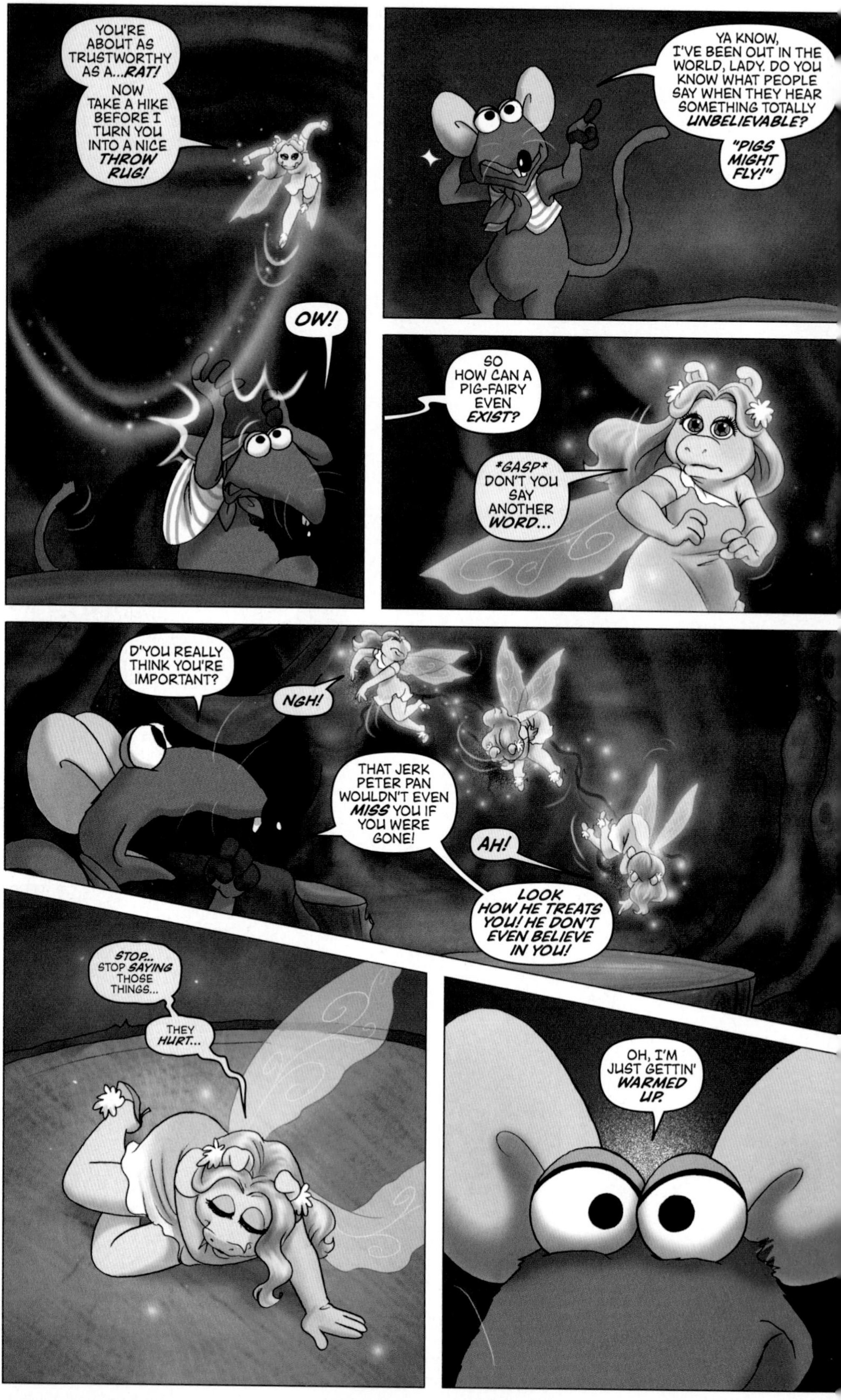

YOU'RE ABOUT AS TRUSTWORTHY AS A...RAT! NOW TAKE A HIKE BEFORE I TURN YOU INTO A NICE THROW RUG!
OW!
YA KNOW, I'VE BEEN OUT IN THE WORLD, LADY. DO YOU KNOW WHAT PEOPLE SAY WHEN THEY HEAR SOMETHING TOTALLY UNBELIEVABLE?
"PIGS MIGHT FLY!"
SO HOW CAN A PIG-FAIRY EVEN EXIST?
GASP DON'T YOU SAY ANOTHER WORD...
D'YOU REALLY THINK YOU'RE IMPORTANT?
NGH!
THAT JERK PETER PAN WOULDN'T EVEN MISS YOU IF YOU WERE GONE!
AH!
LOOK HOW HE TREATS YOU! HE DON'T EVEN BELIEVE IN YOU!
STOP... STOP SAYING THOSE THINGS...
THEY HURT...
OH, I'M JUST GETTIN' WARMED UP.

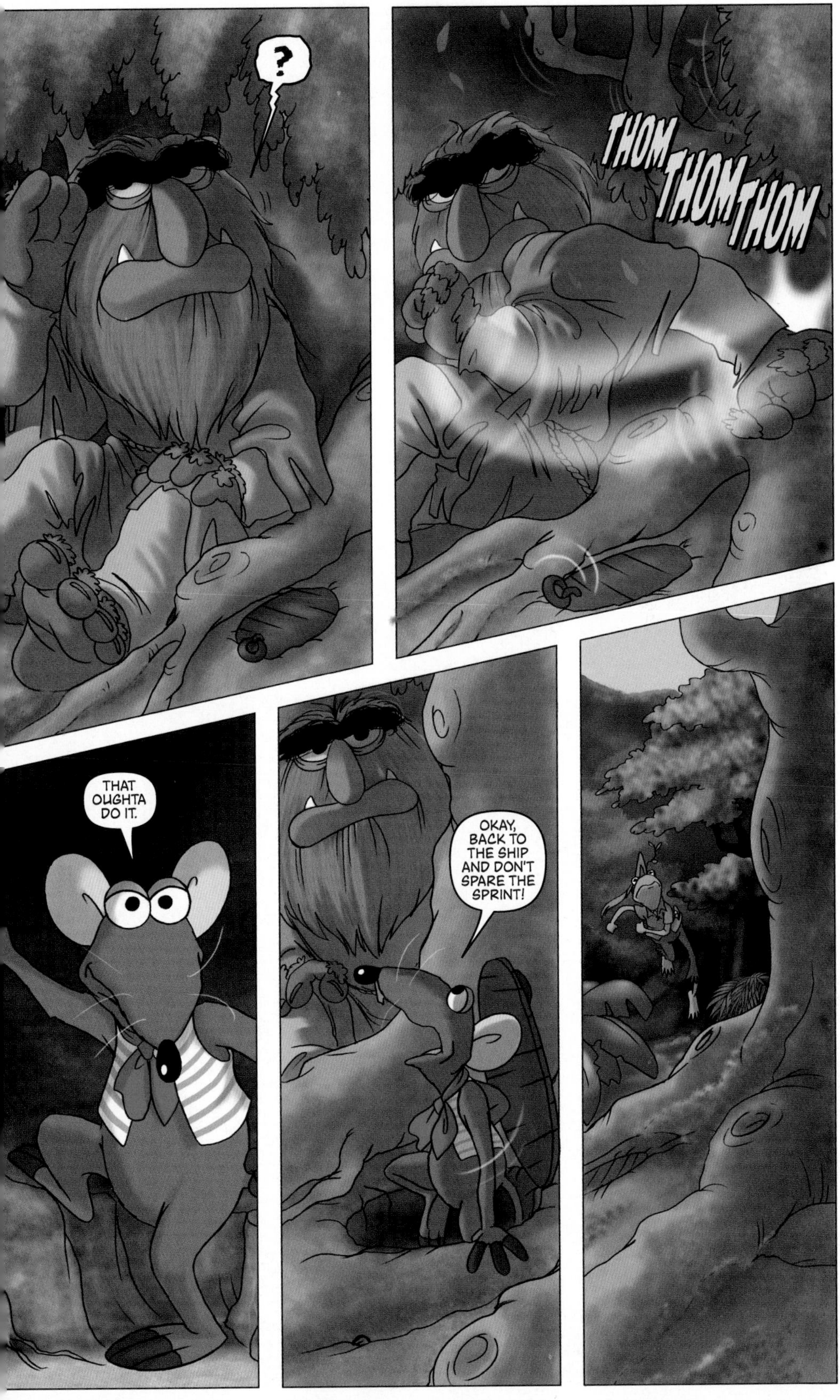
?
THOM THOM THOM
THAT OUGHTA DO IT.
OKAY, BACK TO THE SHIP AND DON'T SPARE THE SPRINT!

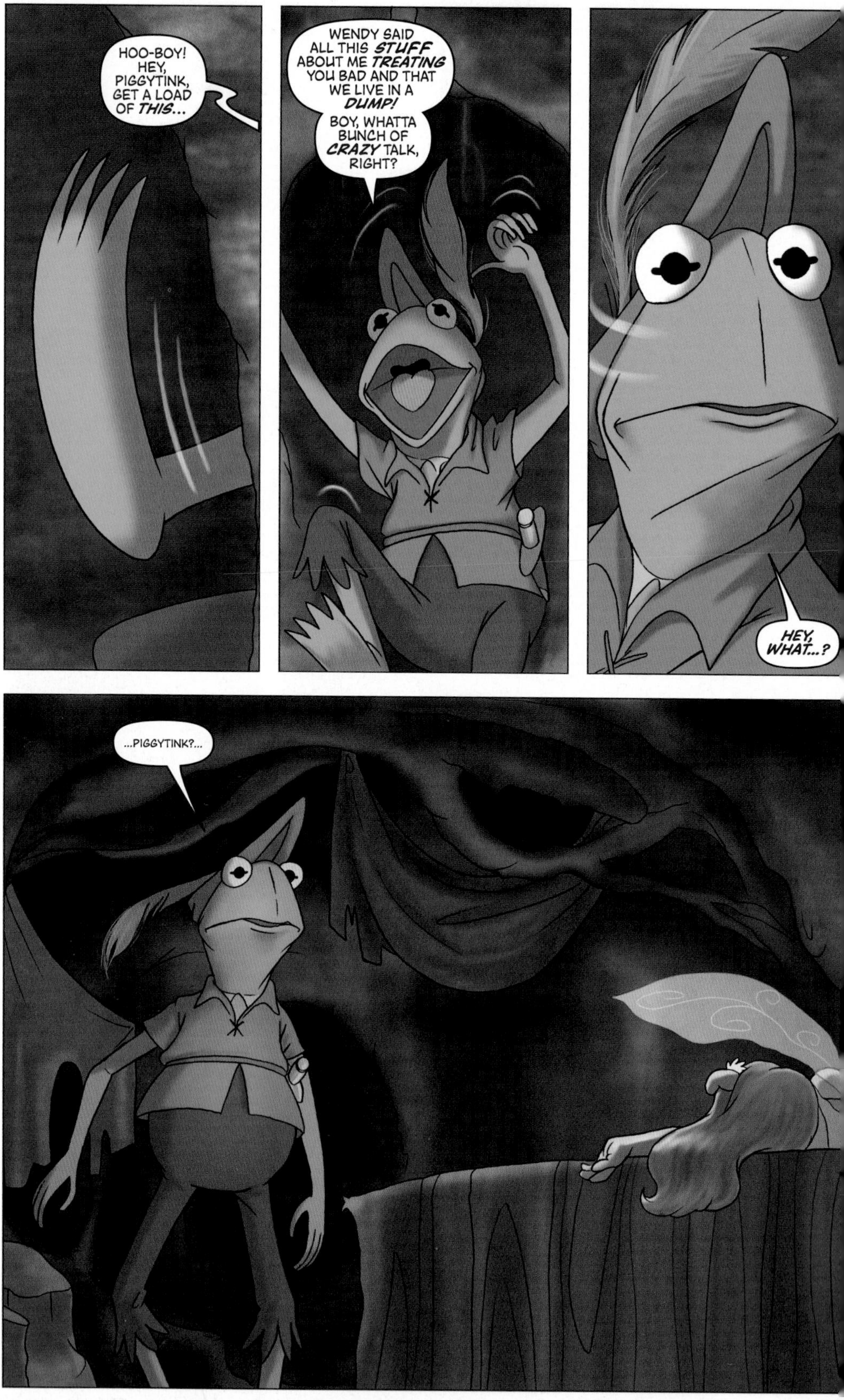
HOO-BOY! HEY, PIGGYTINK, GET A LOAD OF THIS...
WENDY SAID ALL THIS STUFF ABOUT ME TREATING YOU BAD AND THAT WE LIVE IN A DUMP!
BOY, WHATTA BUNCH OF CRAZY TALK, RIGHT?
HEY, WHAT...?
...PIGGYTINK?...

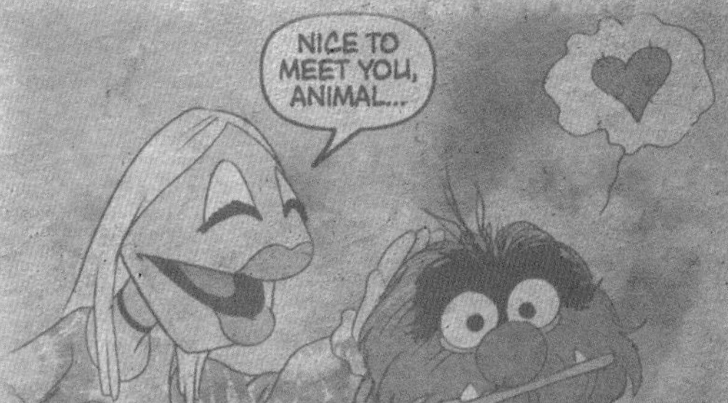
NICE TO MEET YOU, ANIMAL...

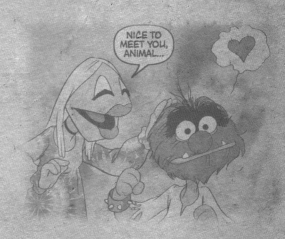

chapter four

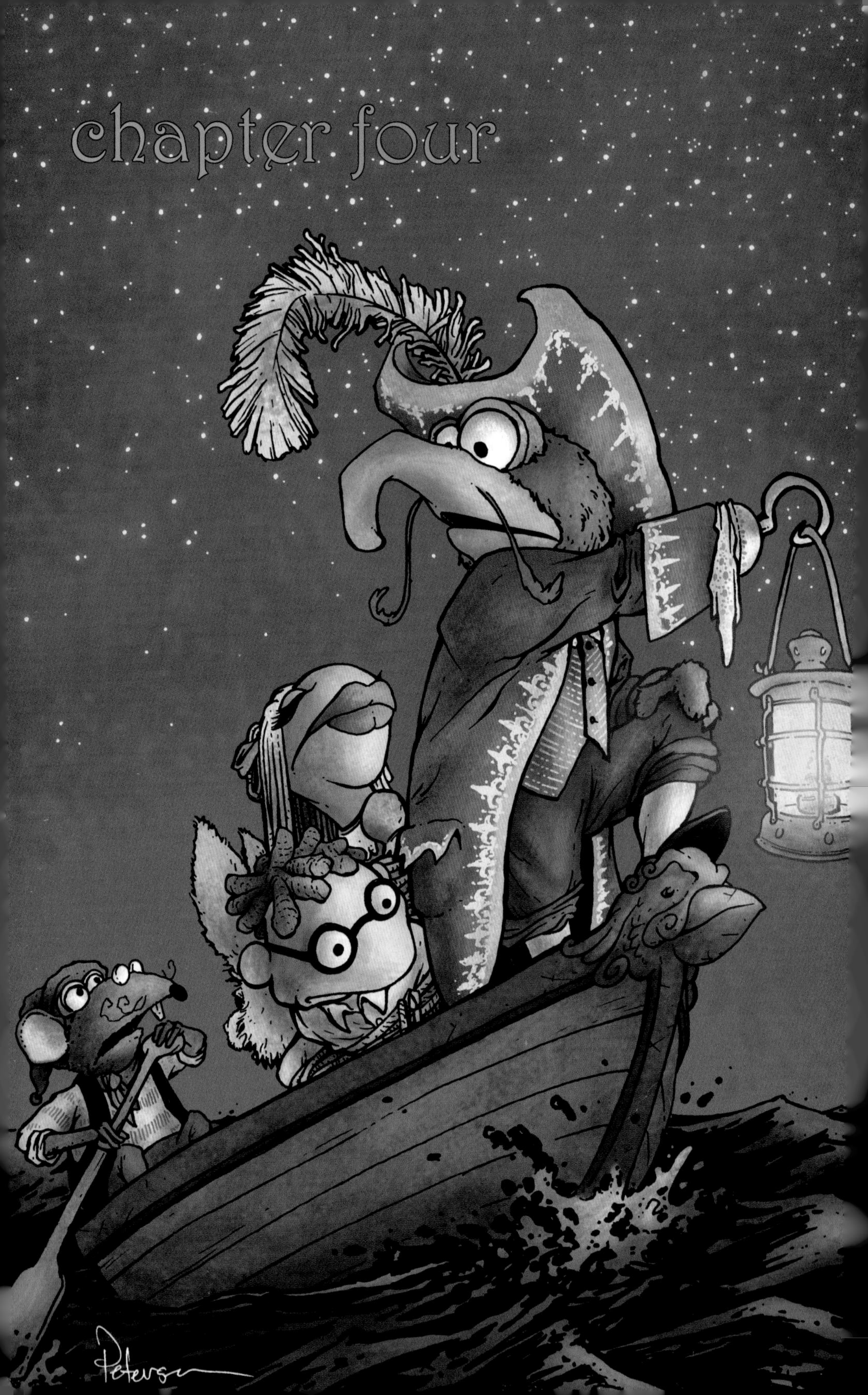

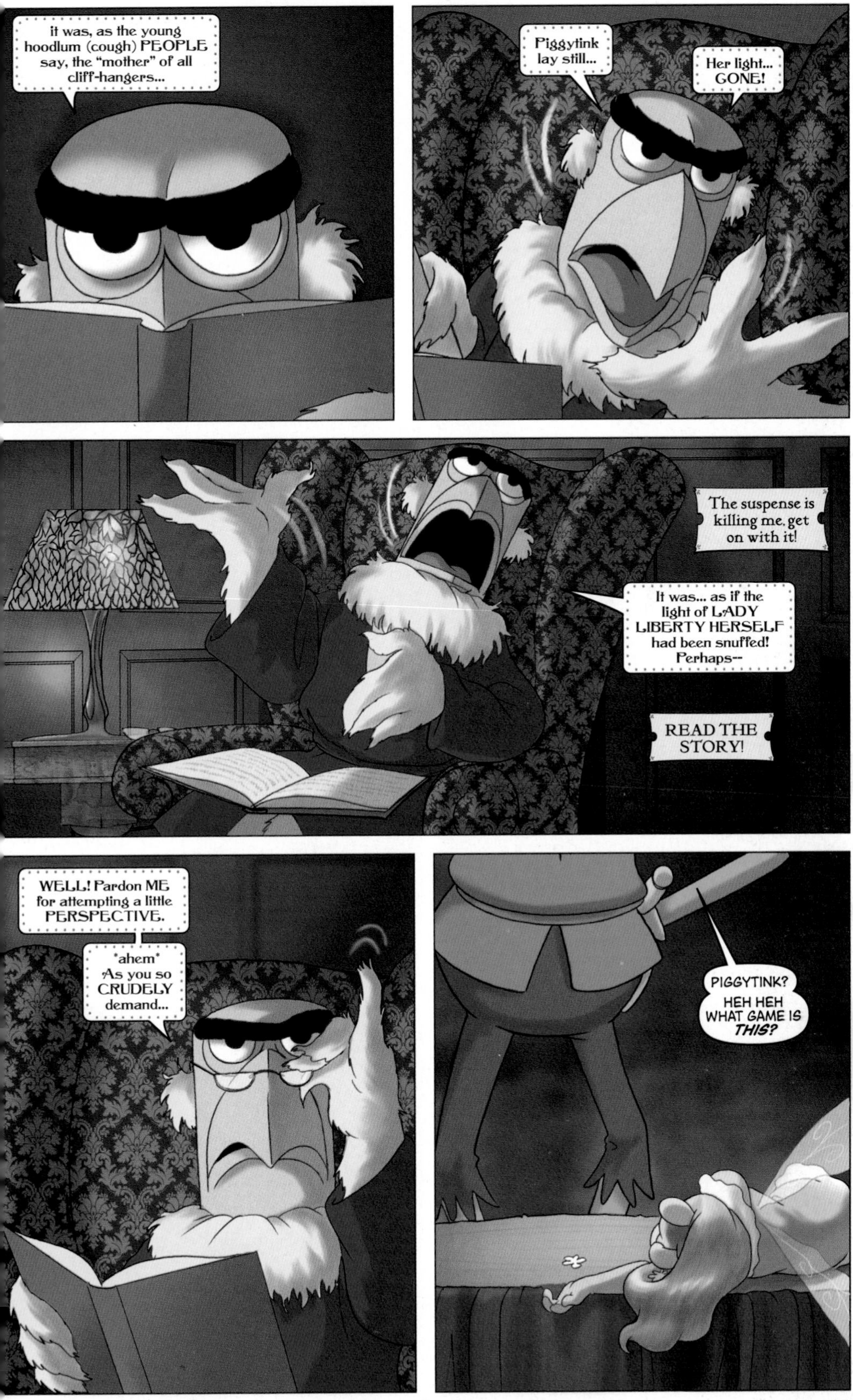
it was, as the young hoodlum (cough) PEOPLE say, the "mother" of all cliff-hangers...
Piggytink lay still...
Her light... GONE!
The suspense is killing me, get on with it!
It was... as if the light of LADY LIBERTY HERSELF had been snuffed! Perhaps--
READ THE STORY!
WELL! Pardon ME for attempting a little PERSPECTIVE.
ahem As you so CRUDELY demand...
PIGGYTINK? HEH HEH WHAT GAME IS *THIS?*

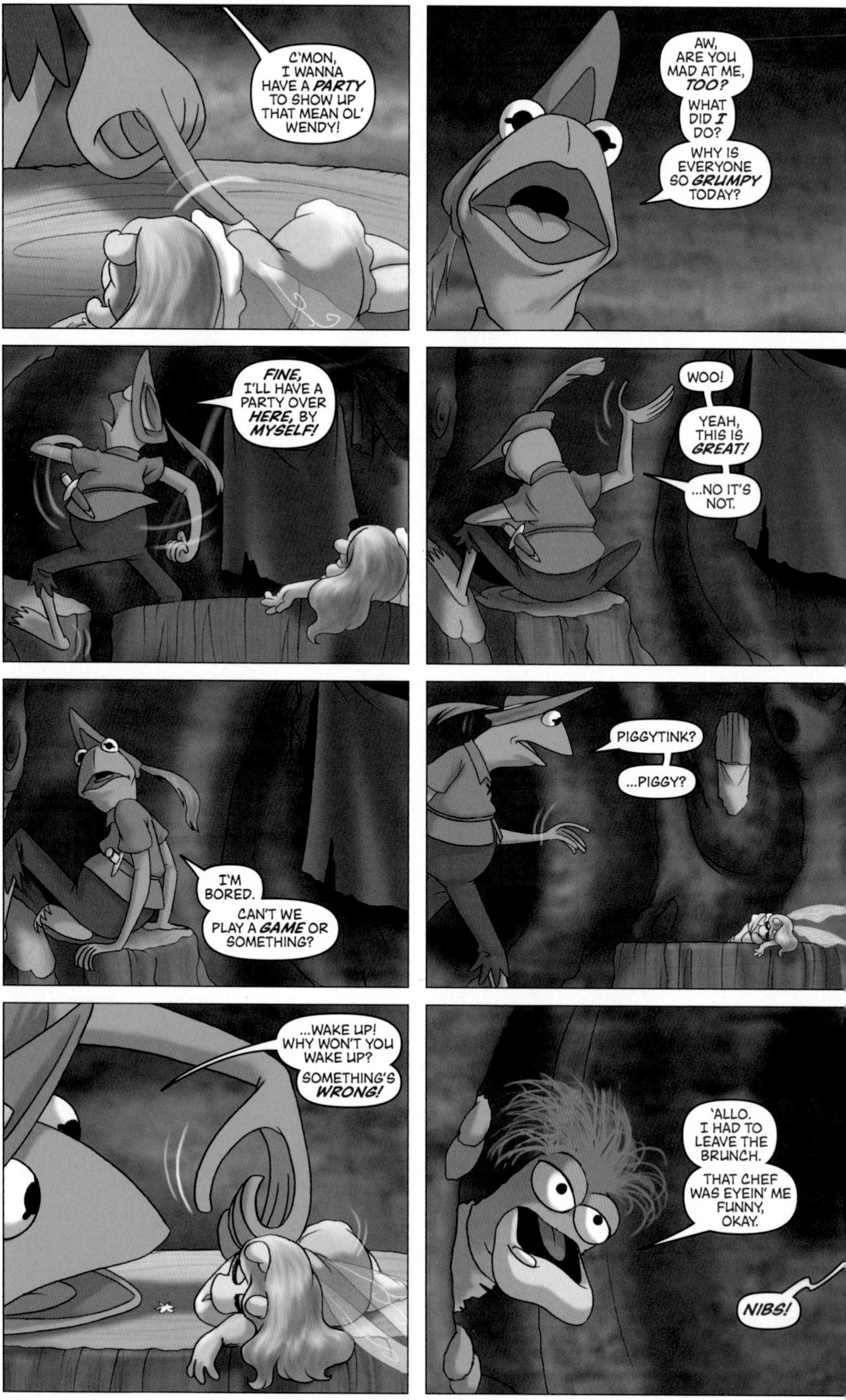

C'MON, I WANNA HAVE A PARTY TO SHOW UP THAT MEAN OL' WENDY!
AW, ARE YOU MAD AT ME, TOO?
WHAT DID I DO?
WHY IS EVERYONE SO GRUMPY TODAY?
FINE, I'LL HAVE A PARTY OVER HERE, BY MYSELF!
WOO!
YEAH, THIS IS GREAT!
...NO IT'S NOT.
I'M BORED.
CAN'T WE PLAY A GAME OR SOMETHING?
PIGGYTINK?
...PIGGY?
...WAKE UP! WHY WON'T YOU WAKE UP?
SOMETHING'S WRONG!
'ALLO. I HAD TO LEAVE THE BRUNCH.
THAT CHEF WAS EYEIN' ME FUNNY, OKAY.
NIBS!

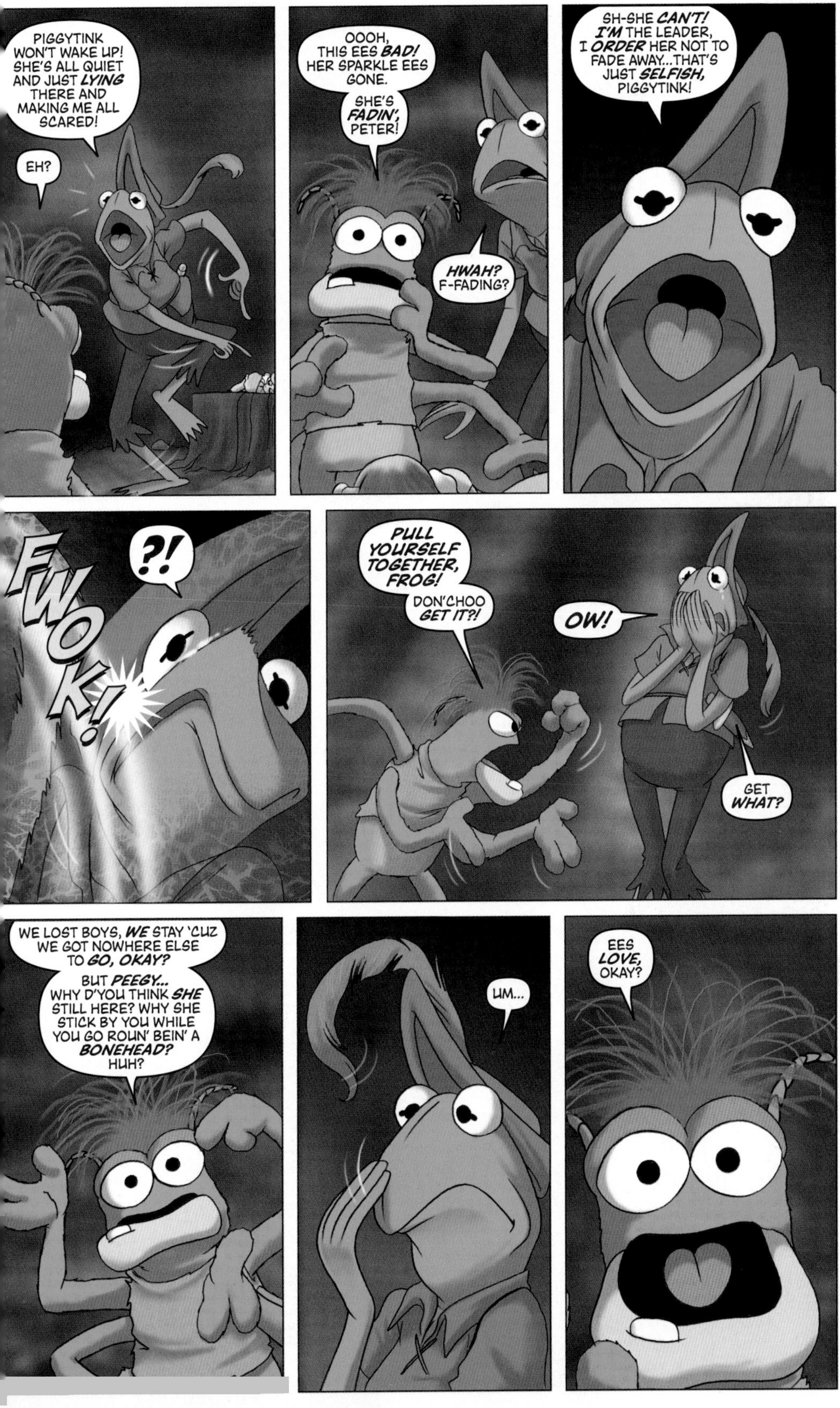
PIGGYTINK WON'T WAKE UP! SHE'S ALL QUIET AND JUST LYING THERE AND MAKING ME ALL SCARED!
EH?
OOOH, THIS EES BAD! HER SPARKLE EES GONE.
SHE'S FADIN', PETER!
HWAH? F-FADING?
SH-SHE CAN'T! I'M THE LEADER, I ORDER HER NOT TO FADE AWAY...THAT'S JUST SELFISH, PIGGYTINK!
?!
FWOK!
PULL YOURSELF TOGETHER, FROG!
DON'CHOO GET IT?!
OW!
GET WHAT?
WE LOST BOYS, WE STAY 'CUZ WE GOT NOWHERE ELSE TO GO, OKAY?
BUT PEEGY... WHY D'YOU THINK SHE STILL HERE? WHY SHE STICK BY YOU WHILE YOU GO ROUN' BEIN' A BONEHEAD? HUH?
UM...
EES LOVE, OKAY?

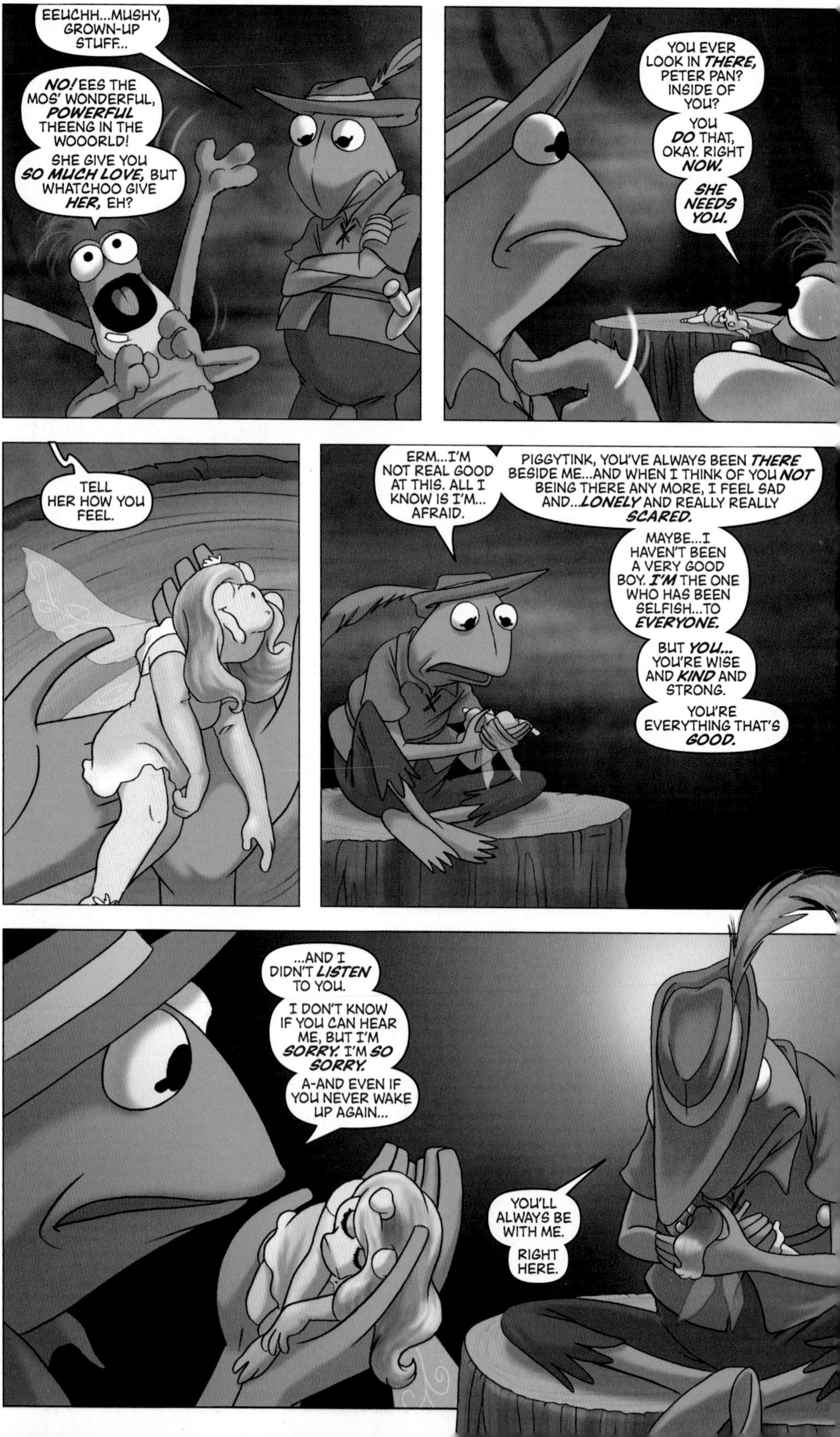

EEUCHH...MUSHY, GROWN-UP STUFF...
NO! EES THE MOS' WONDERFUL, POWERFUL THEENG IN THE WOOORLD!
SHE GIVE YOU SO MUCH LOVE, BUT WHATCHOO GIVE HER, EH?
YOU EVER LOOK IN THERE, PETER PAN? INSIDE OF YOU?
YOU DO THAT, OKAY. RIGHT NOW.
SHE NEEDS YOU.
TELL HER HOW YOU FEEL.
ERM...I'M NOT REAL GOOD AT THIS. ALL I KNOW IS I'M... AFRAID.
PIGGYTINK, YOU'VE ALWAYS BEEN THERE BESIDE ME...AND WHEN I THINK OF YOU NOT BEING THERE ANY MORE, I FEEL SAD AND...LONELY AND REALLY REALLY SCARED.
MAYBE...I HAVEN'T BEEN A VERY GOOD BOY. I'M THE ONE WHO HAS BEEN SELFISH...TO EVERYONE.
BUT YOU... YOU'RE WISE AND KIND AND STRONG.
YOU'RE EVERYTHING THAT'S GOOD.
...AND I DIDN'T LISTEN TO YOU.
I DON'T KNOW IF YOU CAN HEAR ME, BUT I'M SORRY. I'M SO SORRY.
A-AND EVEN IF YOU NEVER WAKE UP AGAIN...
YOU'LL ALWAYS BE WITH ME.
RIGHT HERE.

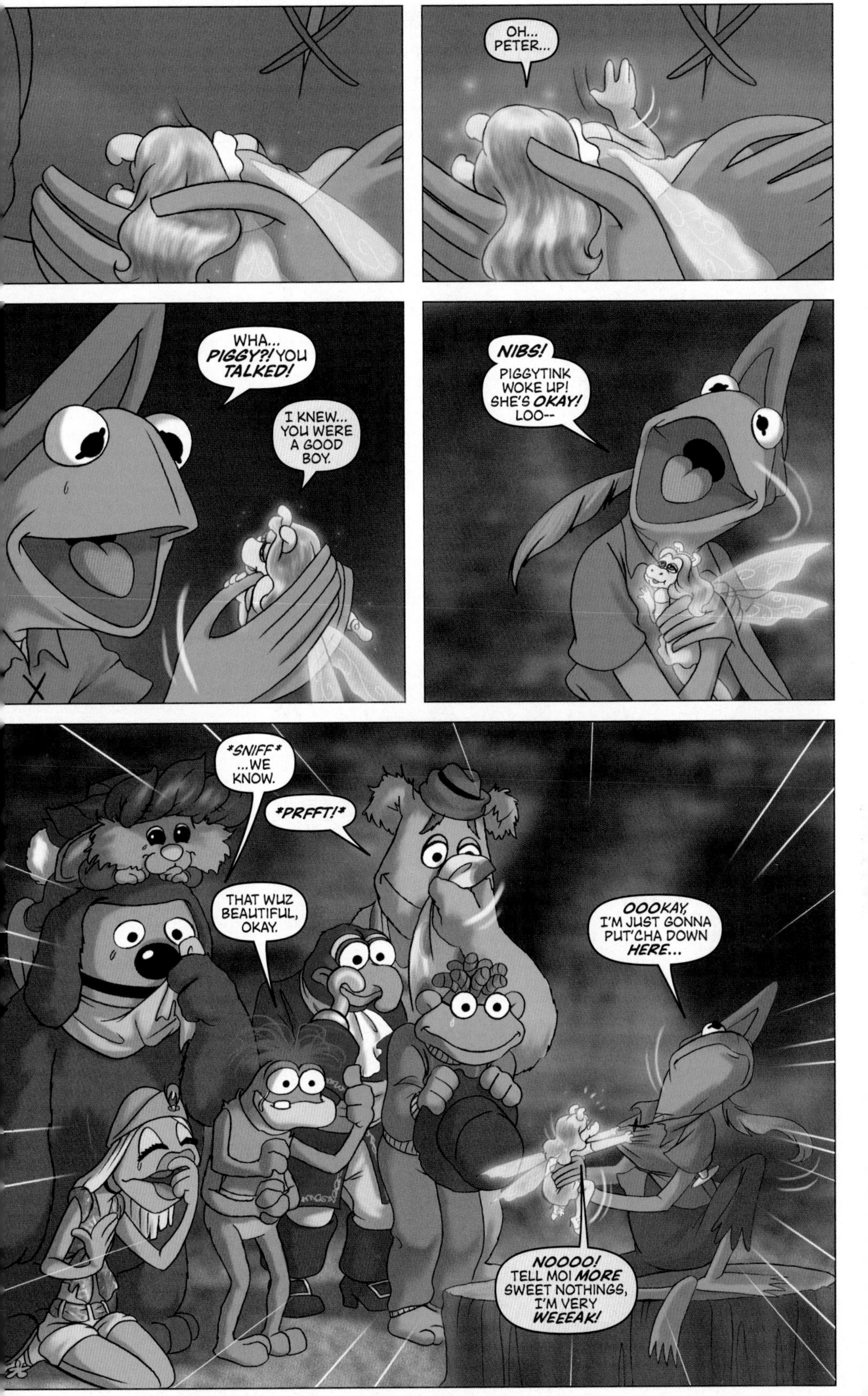
OH... PETER...
WHA... PIGGY?! YOU TALKED!
I KNEW... YOU WERE A GOOD BOY.
NIBS! PIGGYTINK WOKE UP! SHE'S OKAY! LOO--
SNIFF ...WE KNOW.
PRFFT!
THAT WUZ BEAUTIFUL, OKAY.
OOOKAY, I'M JUST GONNA PUT'CHA DOWN HERE...
NOOOO! TELL MOI MORE SWEET NOTHINGS, I'M VERY WEEEAK!

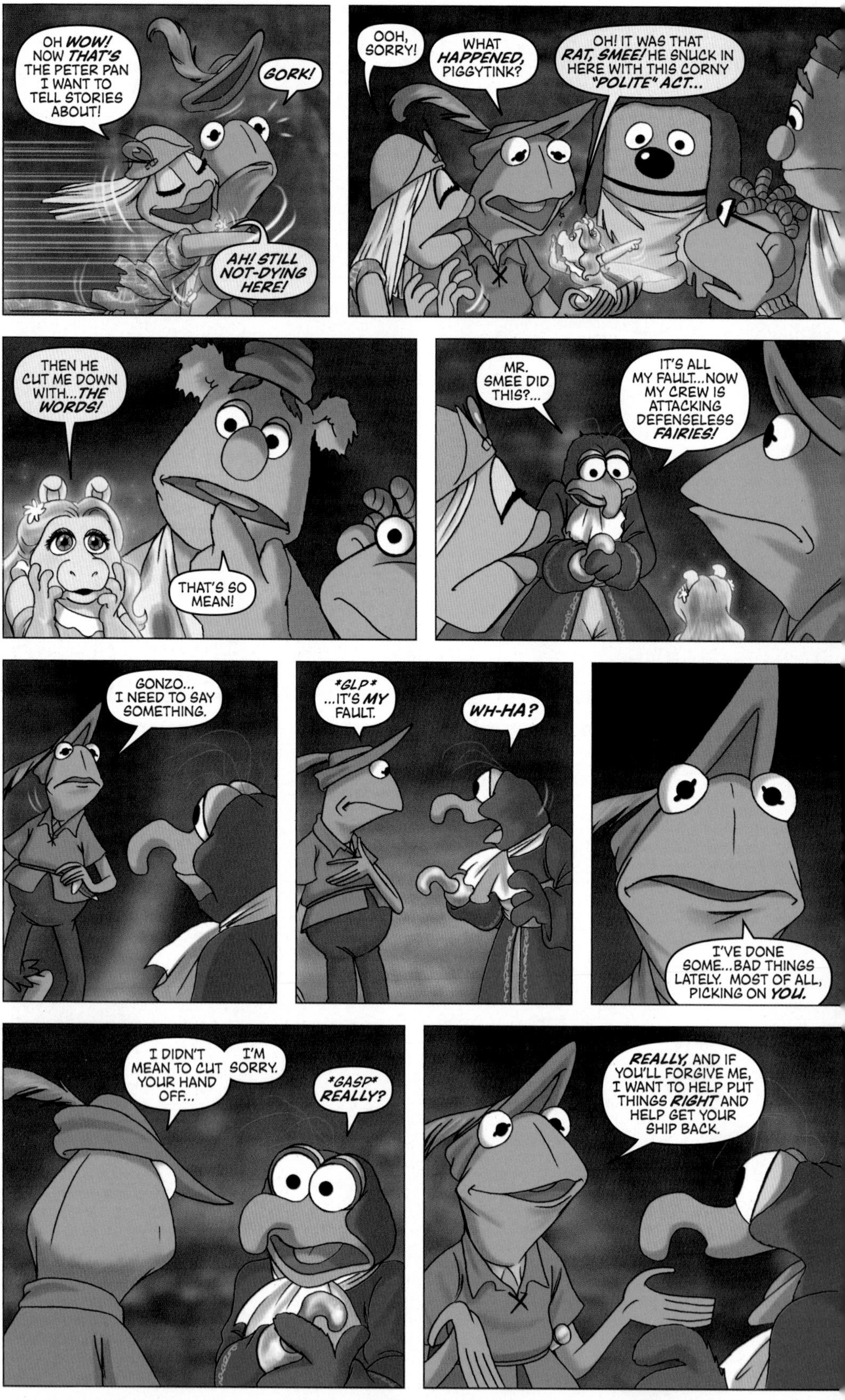

OH WOW! NOW THAT'S THE PETER PAN I WANT TO TELL STORIES ABOUT!
GORK!
AH! STILL NOT-DYING HERE!
OOH, SORRY!
WHAT HAPPENED, PIGGYTINK?
OH! IT WAS THAT RAT, SMEE! HE SNUCK IN HERE WITH THIS CORNY "POLITE" ACT...
THEN HE CUT ME DOWN WITH...THE WORDS!
THAT'S SO MEAN!
MR. SMEE DID THIS?...
IT'S ALL MY FAULT...NOW MY CREW IS ATTACKING DEFENSELESS FAIRIES!
GONZO... I NEED TO SAY SOMETHING.
GLP ...IT'S MY FAULT.
WH-HA?
I'VE DONE SOME...BAD THINGS LATELY. MOST OF ALL, PICKING ON YOU.
I DIDN'T MEAN TO CUT YOUR HAND OFF...
I'M SORRY.
GASP REALLY?
REALLY, AND IF YOU'LL FORGIVE ME, I WANT TO HELP PUT THINGS RIGHT AND HELP GET YOUR SHIP BACK.

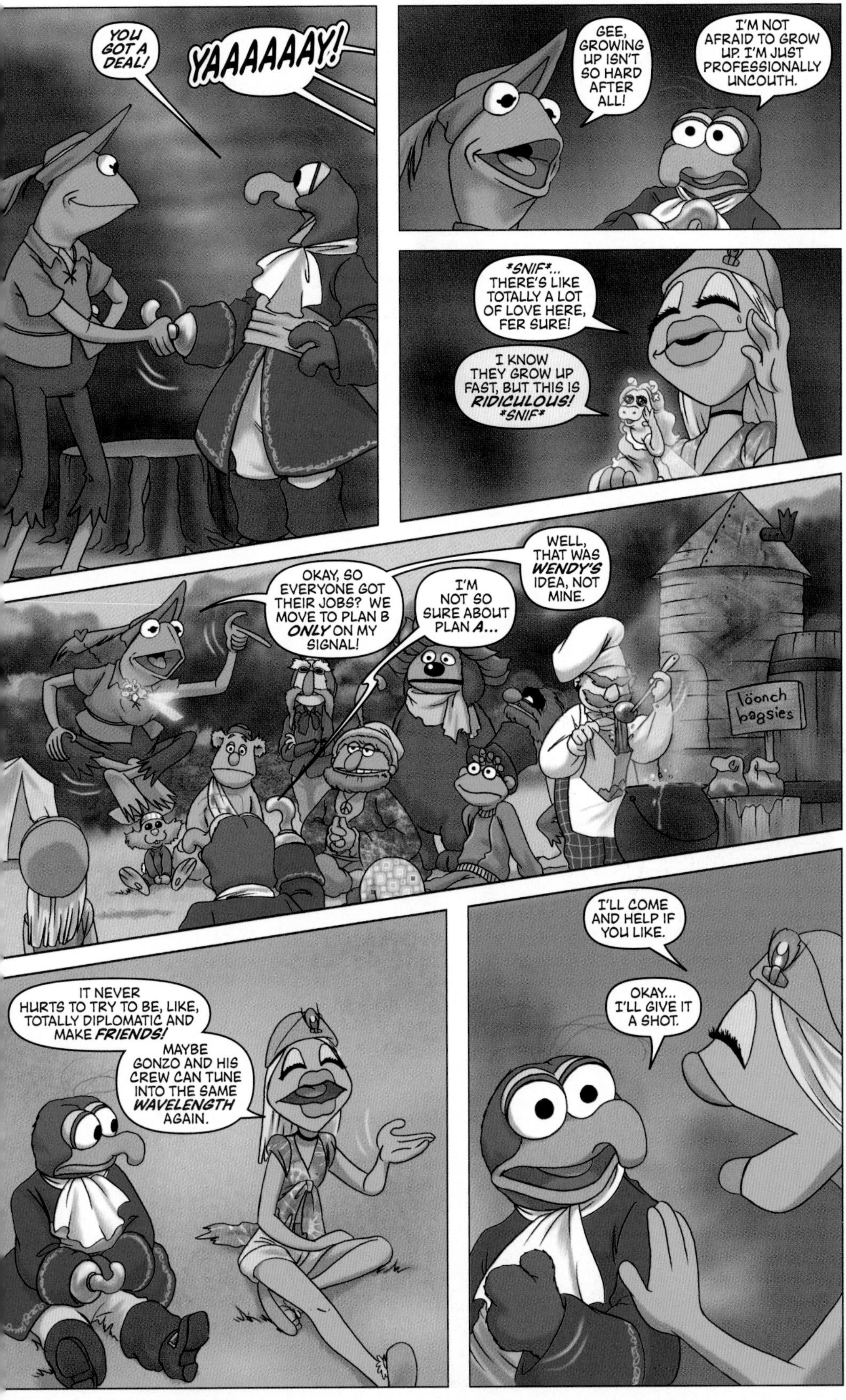

YOU GOT A DEAL!
YAAAAAAY!
GEE, GROWING UP ISN'T SO HARD AFTER ALL!
I'M NOT AFRAID TO GROW UP. I'M JUST PROFESSIONALLY UNCOUTH.
SNIF... THERE'S LIKE TOTALLY A LOT OF LOVE HERE, FER SURE!
I KNOW THEY GROW UP FAST, BUT THIS IS RIDICULOUS! *SNIF*
OKAY, SO EVERYONE GOT THEIR JOBS? WE MOVE TO PLAN B ONLY ON MY SIGNAL!
I'M NOT SO SURE ABOUT PLAN A...
WELL, THAT WAS WENDY'S IDEA, NOT MINE.
löonch bagsies
IT NEVER HURTS TO TRY TO BE, LIKE, TOTALLY DIPLOMATIC AND MAKE FRIENDS!
MAYBE GONZO AND HIS CREW CAN TUNE INTO THE SAME WAVELENGTH AGAIN.
I'LL COME AND HELP IF YOU LIKE.
OKAY... I'LL GIVE IT A SHOT.

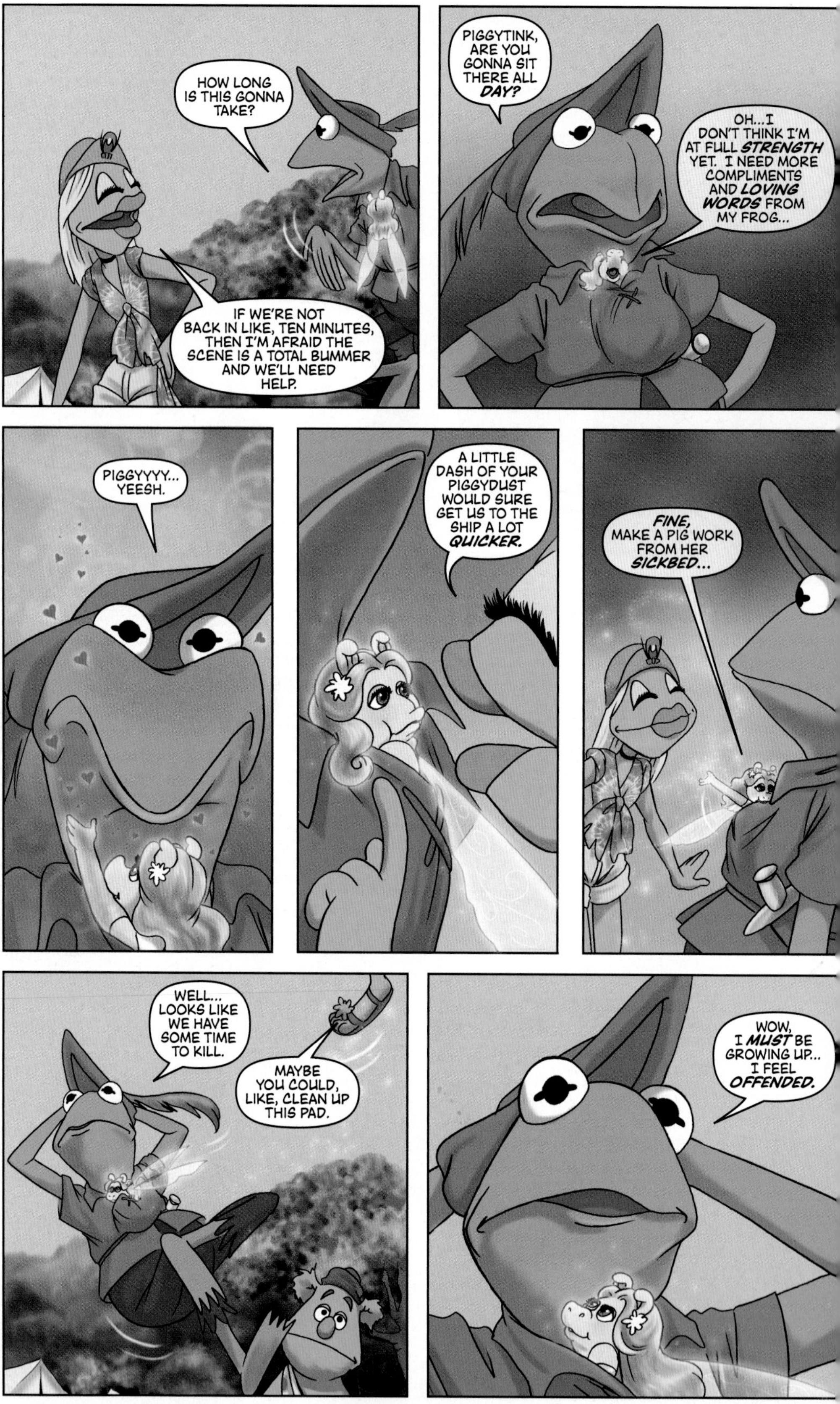
HOW LONG IS THIS GONNA TAKE?
IF WE'RE NOT BACK IN LIKE, TEN MINUTES, THEN I'M AFRAID THE SCENE IS A TOTAL BUMMER AND WE'LL NEED HELP.
PIGGYTINK, ARE YOU GONNA SIT THERE ALL DAY?
OH...I DON'T THINK I'M AT FULL STRENGTH YET. I NEED MORE COMPLIMENTS AND LOVING WORDS FROM MY FROG...
PIGGYYYY... YEESH.
A LITTLE DASH OF YOUR PIGGYDUST WOULD SURE GET US TO THE SHIP A LOT QUICKER.
FINE, MAKE A PIG WORK FROM HER SICKBED...
WELL... LOOKS LIKE WE HAVE SOME TIME TO KILL.
MAYBE YOU COULD, LIKE, CLEAN UP THIS PAD.
WOW, I MUST BE GROWING UP... I FEEL OFFENDED.

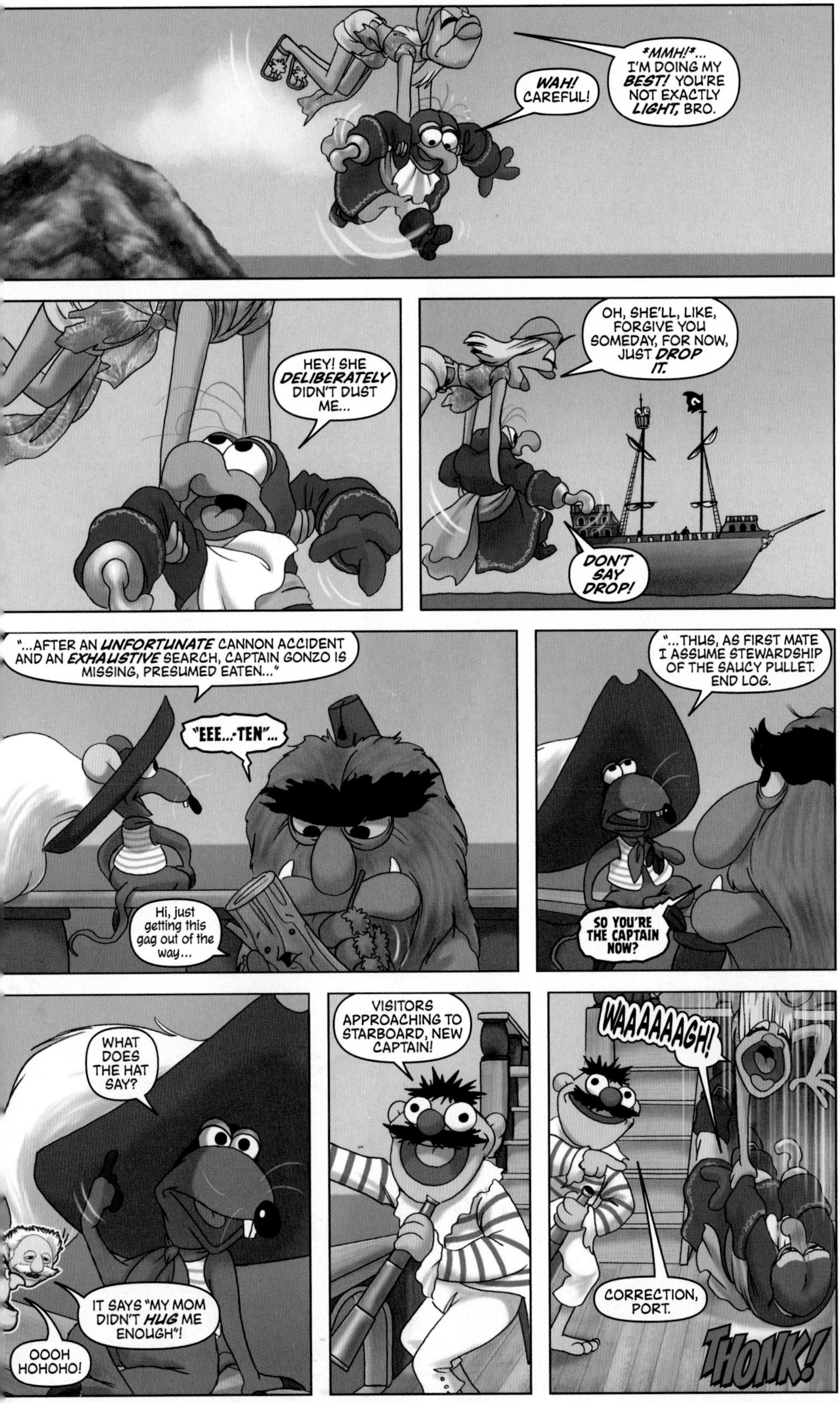
WAH! CAREFUL!
MMH!... I'M DOING MY BEST! YOU'RE NOT EXACTLY LIGHT, BRO.
HEY! SHE DELIBERATELY DIDN'T DUST ME...
OH, SHE'LL, LIKE, FORGIVE YOU SOMEDAY. FOR NOW, JUST DROP IT.
DON'T SAY DROP!
"...AFTER AN UNFORTUNATE CANNON ACCIDENT AND AN EXHAUSTIVE SEARCH, CAPTAIN GONZO IS MISSING, PRESUMED EATEN..."
"EEE...-TEN"...
Hi, just getting this gag out of the way...
"...THUS, AS FIRST MATE I ASSUME STEWARDSHIP OF THE SAUCY PULLET. END LOG.
SO YOU'RE THE CAPTAIN NOW?
WHAT DOES THE HAT SAY?
IT SAYS "MY MOM DIDN'T HUG ME ENOUGH"!
OOOH HOHOHO!
VISITORS APPROACHING TO STARBOARD, NEW CAPTAIN!
WAAAAAAGH!
CORRECTION, PORT.
THONK!

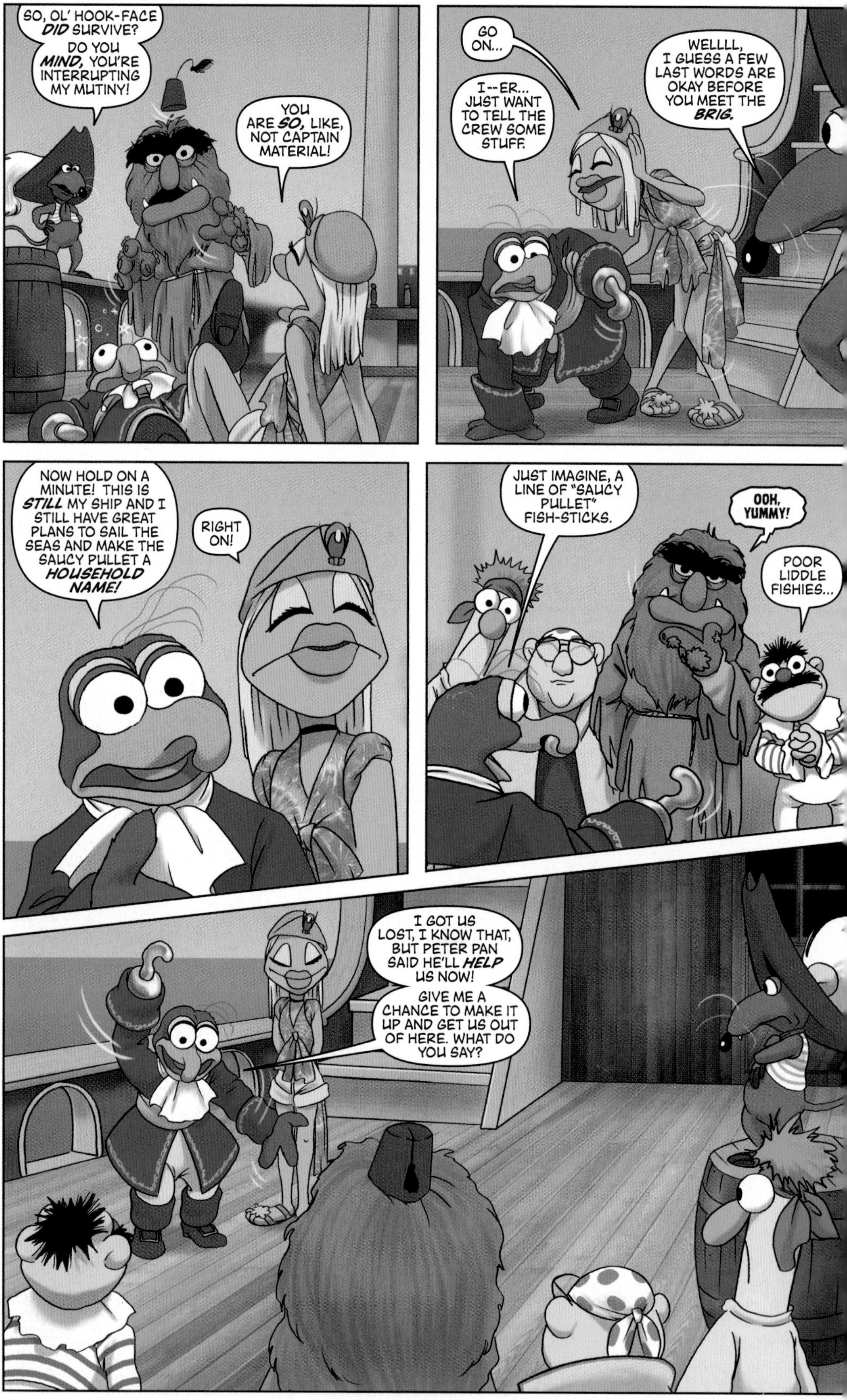
SO, OL' HOOK-FACE *DID* SURVIVE?
DO YOU *MIND,* YOU'RE INTERRUPTING MY MUTINY!
YOU ARE *SO,* LIKE, NOT CAPTAIN MATERIAL!
GO ON...
I--ER... JUST WANT TO TELL THE CREW SOME STUFF.
WELLLL, I GUESS A FEW LAST WORDS ARE OKAY BEFORE YOU MEET THE *BRIG.*
NOW HOLD ON A MINUTE! THIS IS *STILL* MY SHIP AND I STILL HAVE GREAT PLANS TO SAIL THE SEAS AND MAKE THE SAUCY PULLET A *HOUSEHOLD NAME!*
RIGHT ON!
JUST IMAGINE, A LINE OF "SAUCY PULLET" FISH-STICKS.
OOH, YUMMY!
POOR LIDDLE FISHIES...
I GOT US LOST, I KNOW THAT, BUT PETER PAN SAID HE'LL *HELP* US NOW!
GIVE ME A CHANCE TO MAKE IT UP AND GET US OUT OF HERE. WHAT DO YOU SAY?

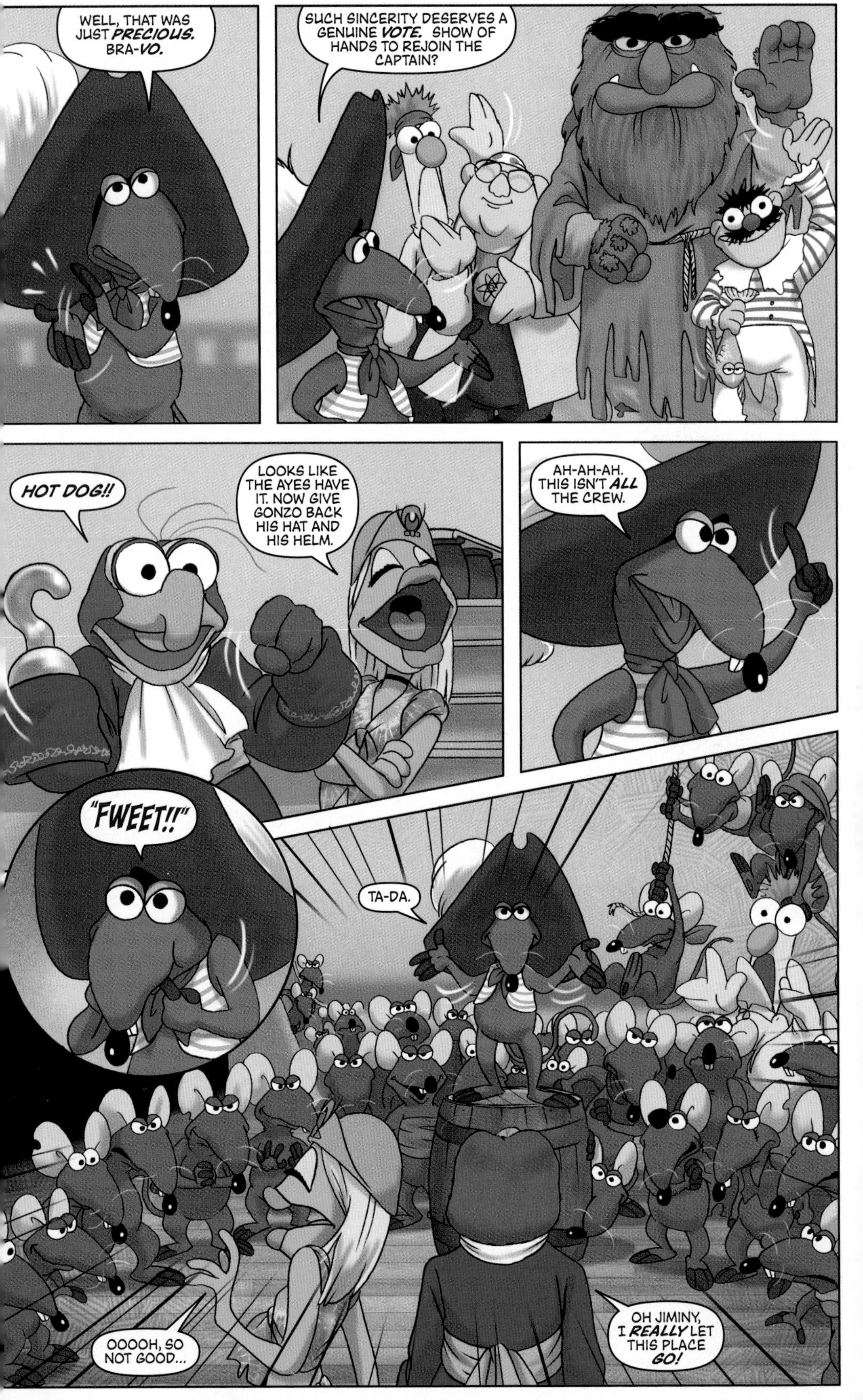
WELL, THAT WAS JUST *PRECIOUS.* BRA-*VO.*
SUCH SINCERITY DESERVES A GENUINE *VOTE.* SHOW OF HANDS TO REJOIN THE CAPTAIN?
HOT DOG!!
LOOKS LIKE THE AYES HAVE IT. NOW GIVE GONZO BACK HIS HAT AND HIS HELM.
AH-AH-AH. THIS ISN'T *ALL* THE CREW.
"FWEET!!"
TA-DA.
OOOOH, SO NOT GOOD...
OH JIMINY, I *REALLY* LET THIS PLACE *GO!*

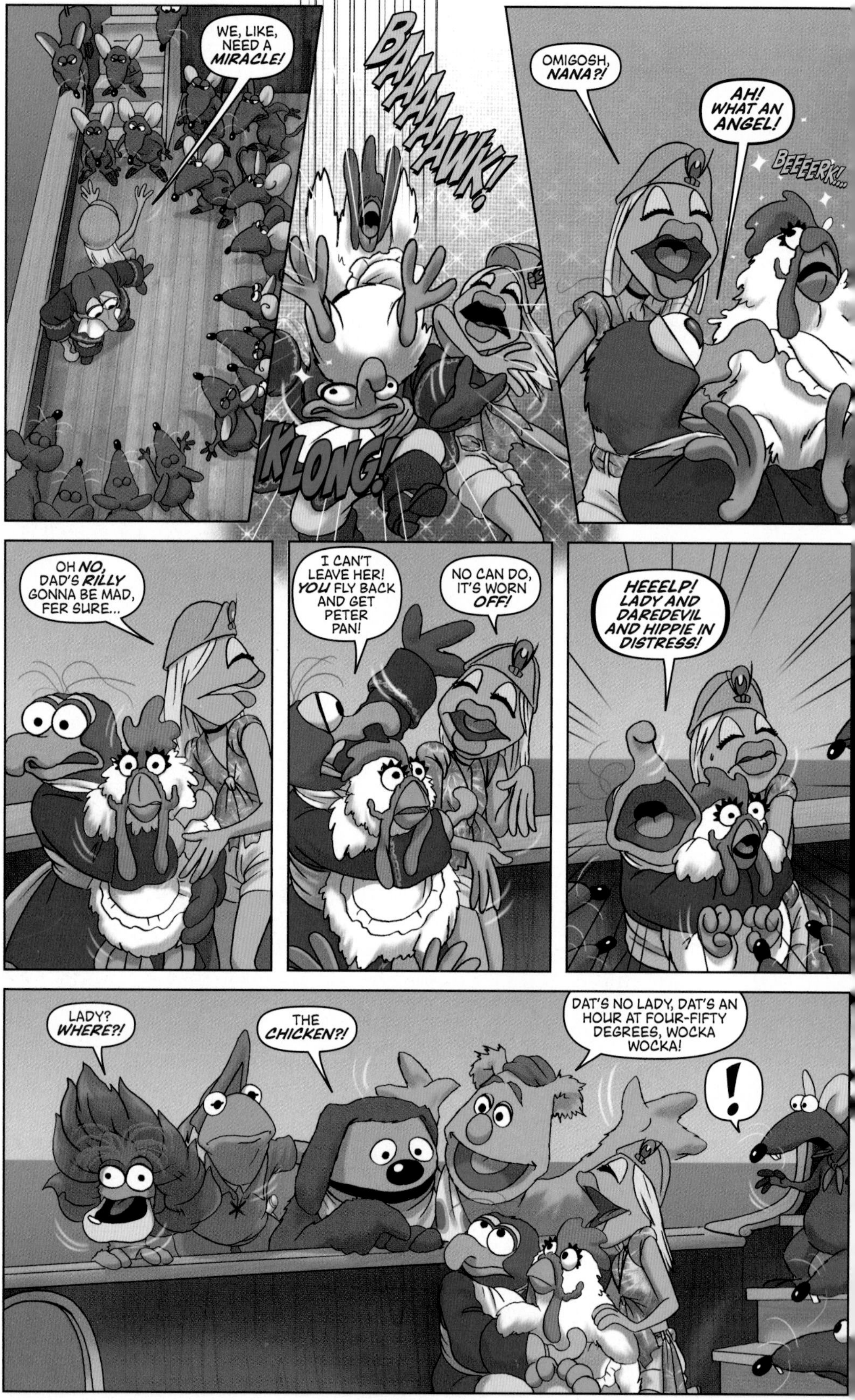

WE, LIKE, NEED A MIRACLE!
BAAAAAWK!!
KLONG!
OMIGOSH, NANA?!
AH! WHAT AN ANGEL!
BEEEERK!...
OH NO, DAD'S RILLY GONNA BE MAD, FER SURE...
I CAN'T LEAVE HER! YOU FLY BACK AND GET PETER PAN!
NO CAN DO, IT'S WORN OFF!
HEEELP! LADY AND DAREDEVIL AND HIPPIE IN DISTRESS!
LADY? WHERE?!
THE CHICKEN?!
DAT'S NO LADY, DAT'S AN HOUR AT FOUR-FIFTY DEGREES, WOCKA WOCKA!
!

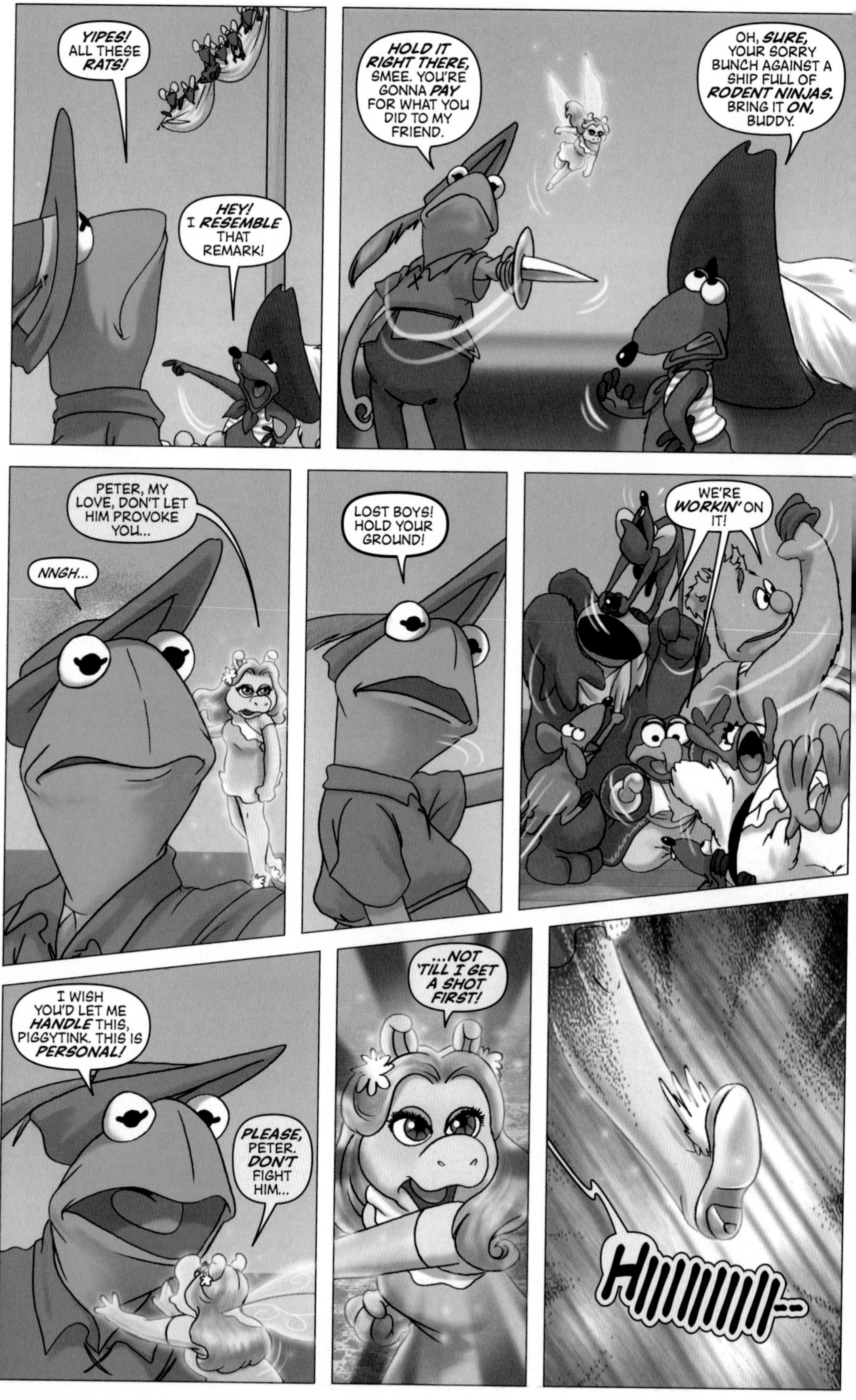
YIPES! ALL THESE RATS!
HEY! I RESEMBLE THAT REMARK!
HOLD IT RIGHT THERE, SMEE. YOU'RE GONNA PAY FOR WHAT YOU DID TO MY FRIEND.
OH, SURE, YOUR SORRY BUNCH AGAINST A SHIP FULL OF RODENT NINJAS. BRING IT ON, BUDDY.
PETER, MY LOVE, DON'T LET HIM PROVOKE YOU...
NNGH...
LOST BOYS! HOLD YOUR GROUND!
WE'RE WORKIN' ON IT!
I WISH YOU'D LET ME HANDLE THIS, PIGGYTINK. THIS IS PERSONAL!
PLEASE, PETER. DON'T FIGHT HIM...
...NOT 'TILL I GET A SHOT FIRST!
HIIIIIIII--

AND WITH THAT *BLINDING* OPENING SHOT, WE WELCOME YOU TO THIS SPECIAL EDITION OF THE *WIIILD* WORLD OF MUPPET SPORTS!

IT'S GRUDGE MATCH CENTRAL HERE IN NEVERSWAMP WITH *SEASON LOSERS* THE LOST BOYS GOING HEAD-TO-HEAD WITH GLOBAL CHAMPIONS THE RATTUS RAIDERS. LET'S LOOK AT SOME HIGHLIGHTS SO FAR.

THE ONE-TWO OPENER OF COACH PETER PAN AND RUNNING BACK PIGGYTINK GOT OFFENSE OFF TO A GOOD START BUT THAT WAS QUICKLY STEAMROLLERED BY 6 OF THE RAIDERS' 40 CORNERBACKS.

hi mom!

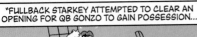

"FULLBACK STARKEY ATTEMPTED TO CLEAR AN OPENING FOR QB GONZO TO GAIN POSSESSION...

"...BUT GONZO FAILED TO SCORE WHEN HE FUMBLED JUST SHORT OF THE END ZONE.

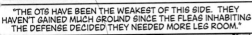

"THE OTS HAVE BEEN THE WEAKEST OF THIS SIDE. THEY HAVEN'T GAINED MUCH GROUND SINCE THE FLEAS INHABITING THE DEFENSE DECIDED THEY NEEDED MORE LEG ROOM."

COACH PAN, ARE WE GOING TO SEE ANY CHANGE IN STRATEGY FOR THE REMAINDER OF THIS FIRST HALF?

WELL...*NGH!* I DON'T THINK YOU SHOULD INTERPRET LACK OF...*UMH*...*FORM* TO MEAN A LACK OF *STRATEGY.*

WE'D BE MORE THAN HAPPY TO USE STRATEGY IF...*WAH!*... WE DIDN'T SUSPECT WE WERE PLAYING AGAINST A SLIGHTLY STACKED DECK HERE, IF YOU KNOW WHAT I'M SAYIN'!

WELL, CAUTIOUS SKEPTICISM FROM THE OFFENSIVE COACH THERE. WILL THE LOST BOYS MANAGE TO BREAK THROUGH OR IS THE BALL LOOKING DOWN THE BARREL OF A BASTING WAND? LET'S CROSS LIVE TO THE SECOND HALF. LOUIS KAZAGGER, MUPPET SPORTS.

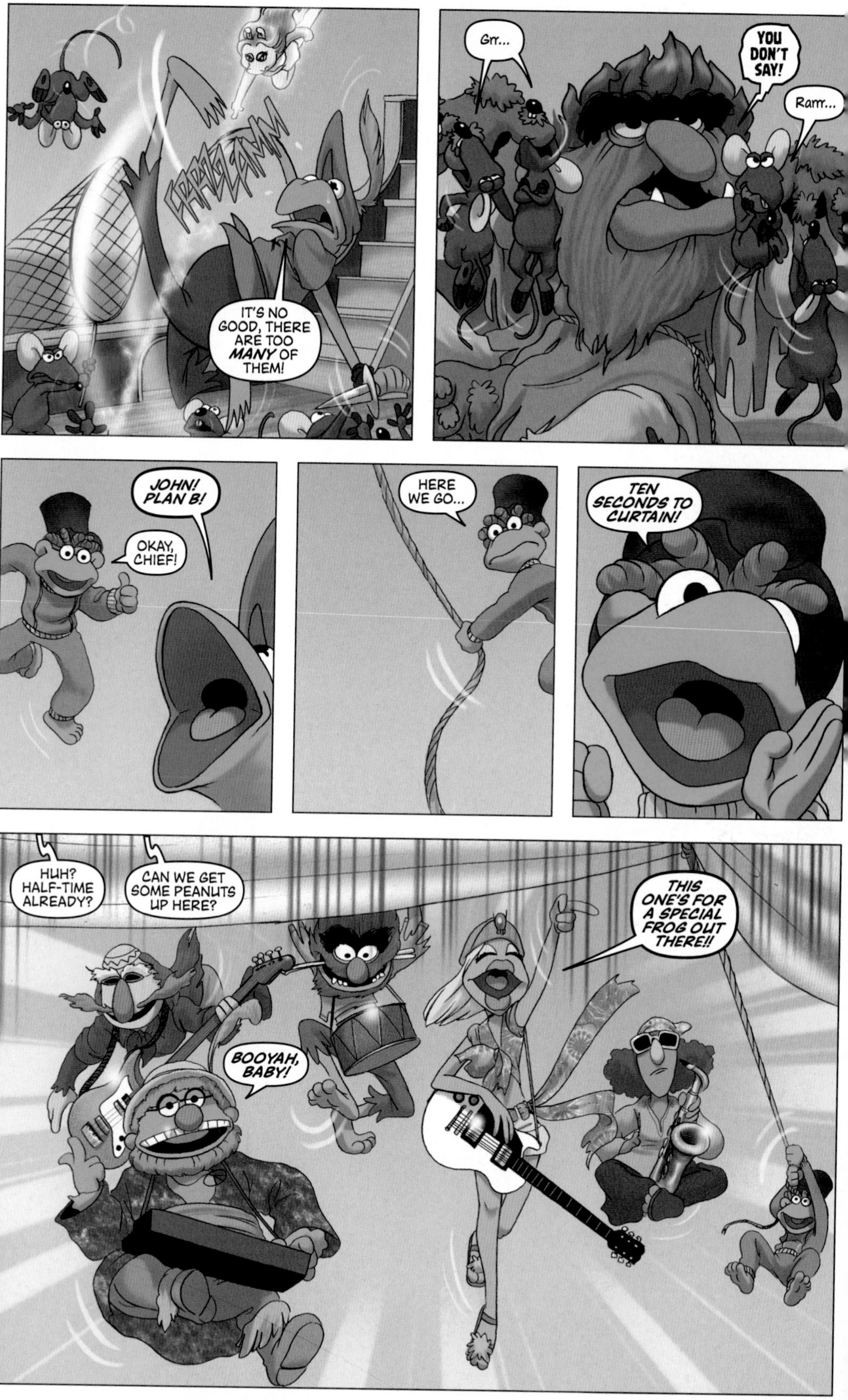
CRAAACKOW
IT'S NO GOOD, THERE ARE TOO MANY OF THEM!
Grr...
YOU DON'T SAY!
Rarrr...
JOHN! PLAN B!
OKAY, CHIEF!
HERE WE GO...
TEN SECONDS TO CURTAIN!
HUH? HALF-TIME ALREADY?
CAN WE GET SOME PEANUTS UP HERE?
THIS ONE'S FOR A SPECIAL FROG OUT THERE!!
BOOYAH, BABY!

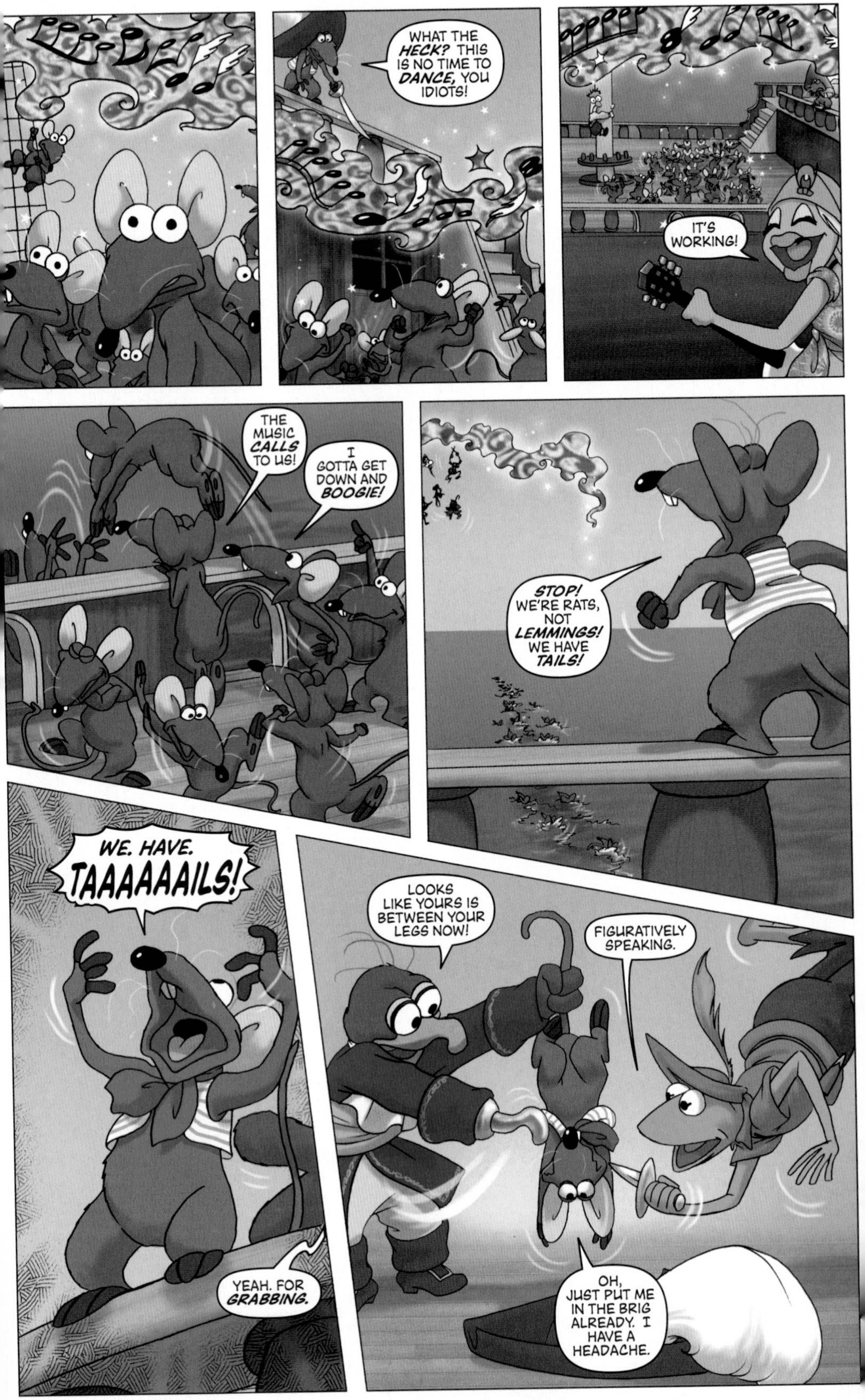
WHAT THE HECK? THIS IS NO TIME TO DANCE, YOU IDIOTS!
IT'S WORKING!
THE MUSIC CALLS TO US!
I GOTTA GET DOWN AND BOOGIE!
STOP! WE'RE RATS, NOT LEMMINGS! WE HAVE TAILS!
WE. HAVE. TAAAAAAILS!
YEAH. FOR GRABBING.
LOOKS LIKE YOURS IS BETWEEN YOUR LEGS NOW!
FIGURATIVELY SPEAKING.
OH, JUST PUT ME IN THE BRIG ALREADY. I HAVE A HEADACHE.

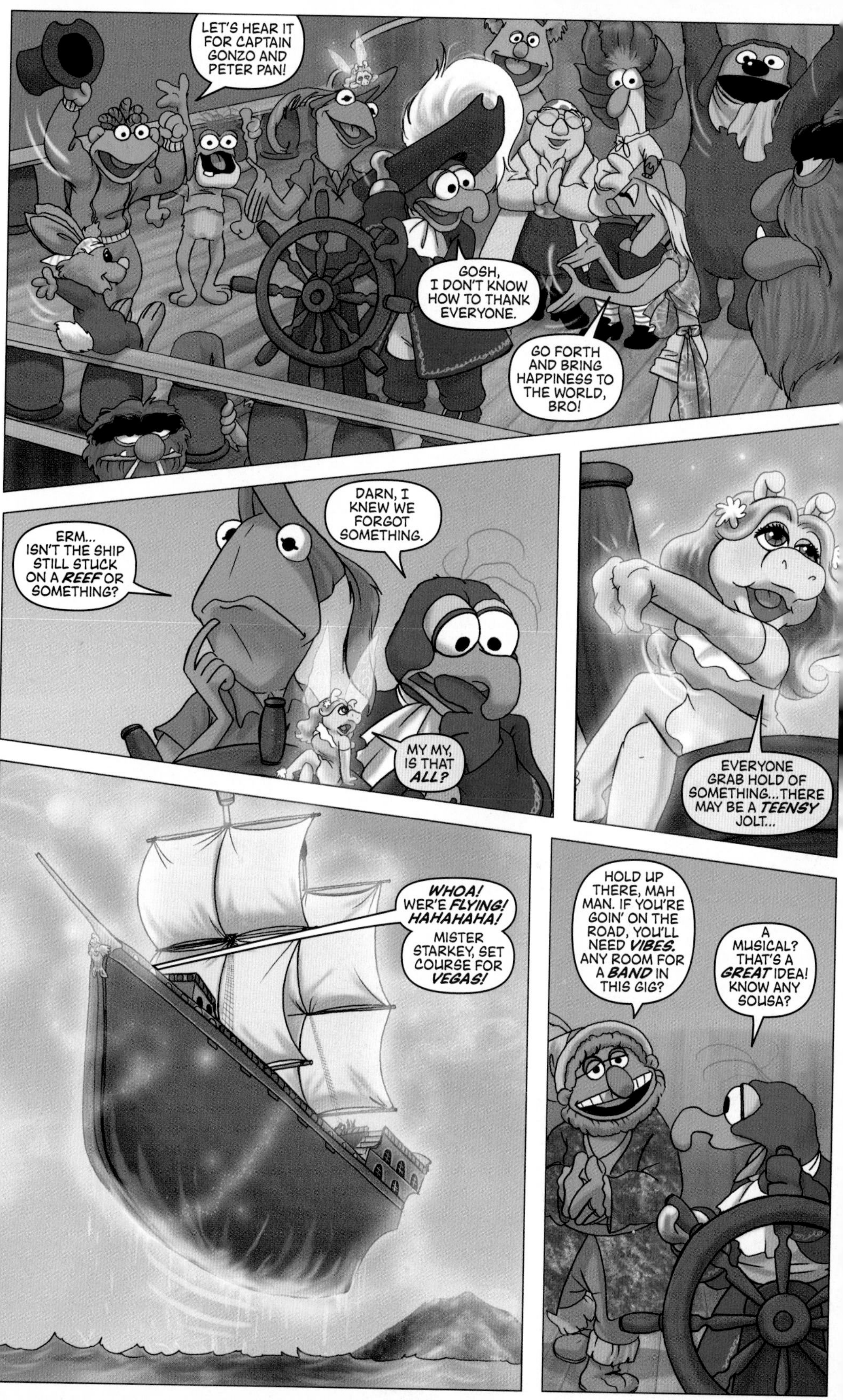
LET'S HEAR IT FOR CAPTAIN GONZO AND PETER PAN!
GOSH, I DON'T KNOW HOW TO THANK EVERYONE.
GO FORTH AND BRING HAPPINESS TO THE WORLD, BRO!
ERM... ISN'T THE SHIP STILL STUCK ON A *REEF* OR SOMETHING?
DARN, I KNEW WE FORGOT SOMETHING.
MY MY, IS THAT *ALL?*
EVERYONE GRAB HOLD OF SOMETHING...THERE MAY BE A *TEENSY* JOLT...
WHOA! WE'RE *FLYING!* *HAHAHAHA!*
MISTER STARKEY, SET COURSE FOR *VEGAS!*
HOLD UP THERE, MAH MAN. IF YOU'RE GOIN' ON THE ROAD, YOU'LL NEED *VIBES.* ANY ROOM FOR A *BAND* IN THIS GIG?
A MUSICAL? THAT'S A *GREAT* IDEA! KNOW ANY SOUSA?

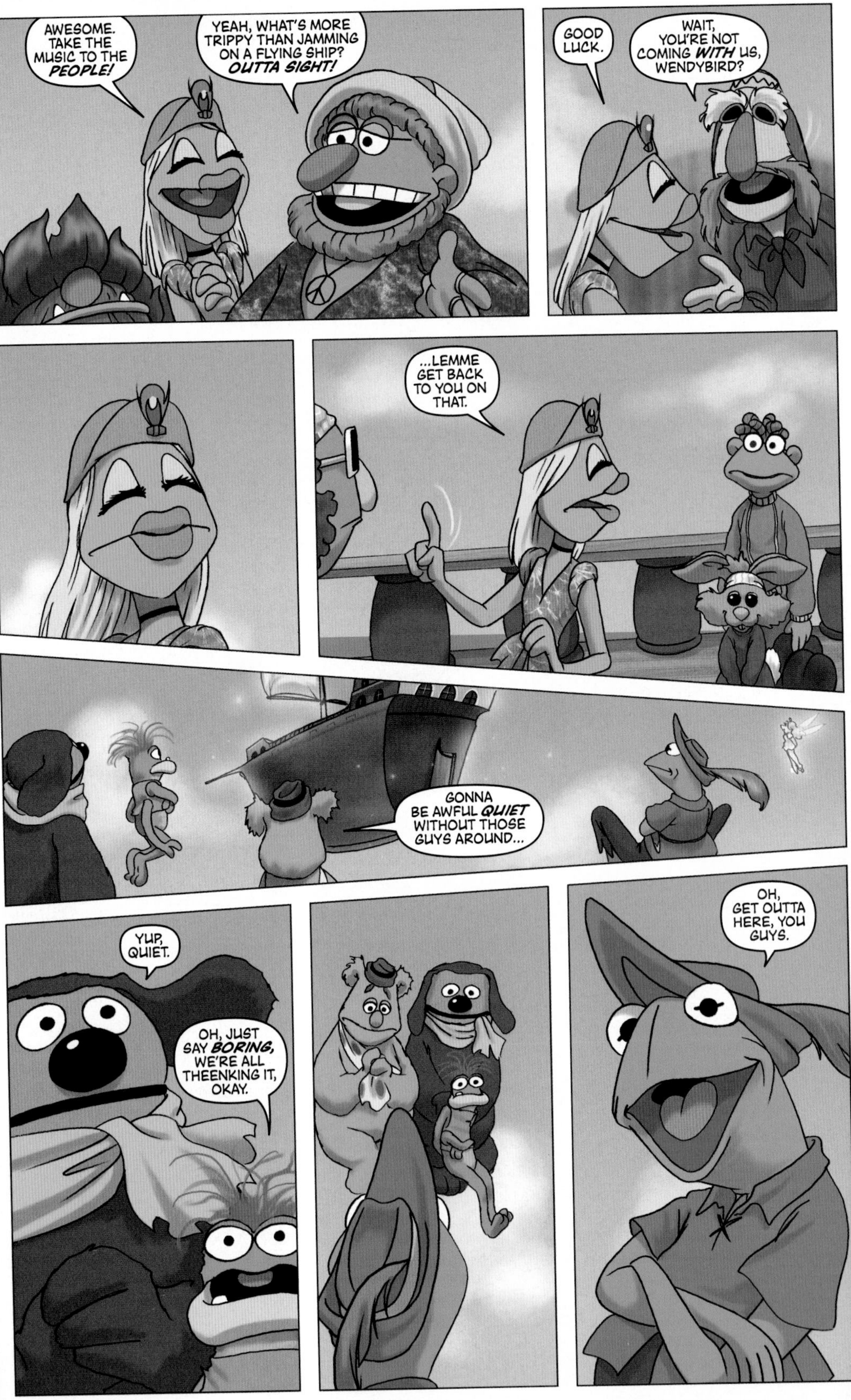
AWESOME. TAKE THE MUSIC TO THE *PEOPLE!*
YEAH, WHAT'S MORE TRIPPY THAN JAMMING ON A FLYING SHIP? *OUTTA SIGHT!*
GOOD LUCK.
WAIT, YOU'RE NOT COMING *WITH* US, WENDYBIRD?
...LEMME GET BACK TO YOU ON THAT.
GONNA BE AWFUL *QUIET* WITHOUT THOSE GUYS AROUND...
YUP, QUIET.
OH, JUST SAY *BORING,* WE'RE ALL THEENKING IT, OKAY.
OH, GET OUTTA HERE, YOU GUYS.

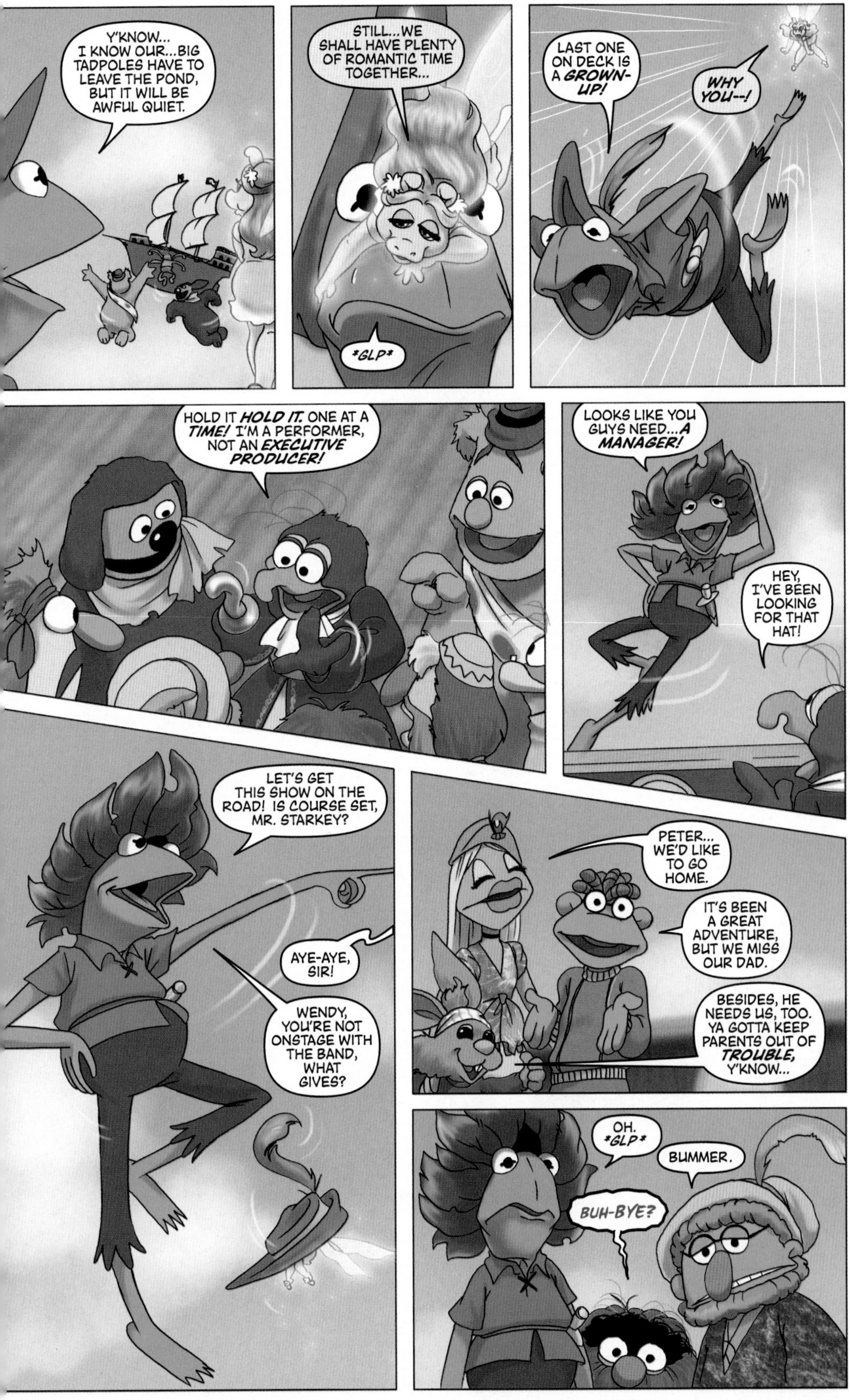

Y'KNOW... I KNOW OUR...BIG TADPOLES HAVE TO LEAVE THE POND, BUT IT WILL BE AWFUL QUIET.
STILL...WE SHALL HAVE PLENTY OF ROMANTIC TIME TOGETHER...
GLP
LAST ONE ON DECK IS A GROWN-UP!
WHY YOU--!
HOLD IT HOLD IT. ONE AT A TIME! I'M A PERFORMER, NOT AN EXECUTIVE PRODUCER!
LOOKS LIKE YOU GUYS NEED...A MANAGER!
HEY, I'VE BEEN LOOKING FOR THAT HAT!
LET'S GET THIS SHOW ON THE ROAD! IS COURSE SET, MR. STARKEY?
AYE-AYE, SIR!
WENDY, YOU'RE NOT ONSTAGE WITH THE BAND, WHAT GIVES?
PETER... WE'D LIKE TO GO HOME.
IT'S BEEN A GREAT ADVENTURE, BUT WE MISS OUR DAD.
BESIDES, HE NEEDS US, TOO. YA GOTTA KEEP PARENTS OUT OF TROUBLE, Y'KNOW...
OH. *GLP*
BUMMER.
BUH-BYE?

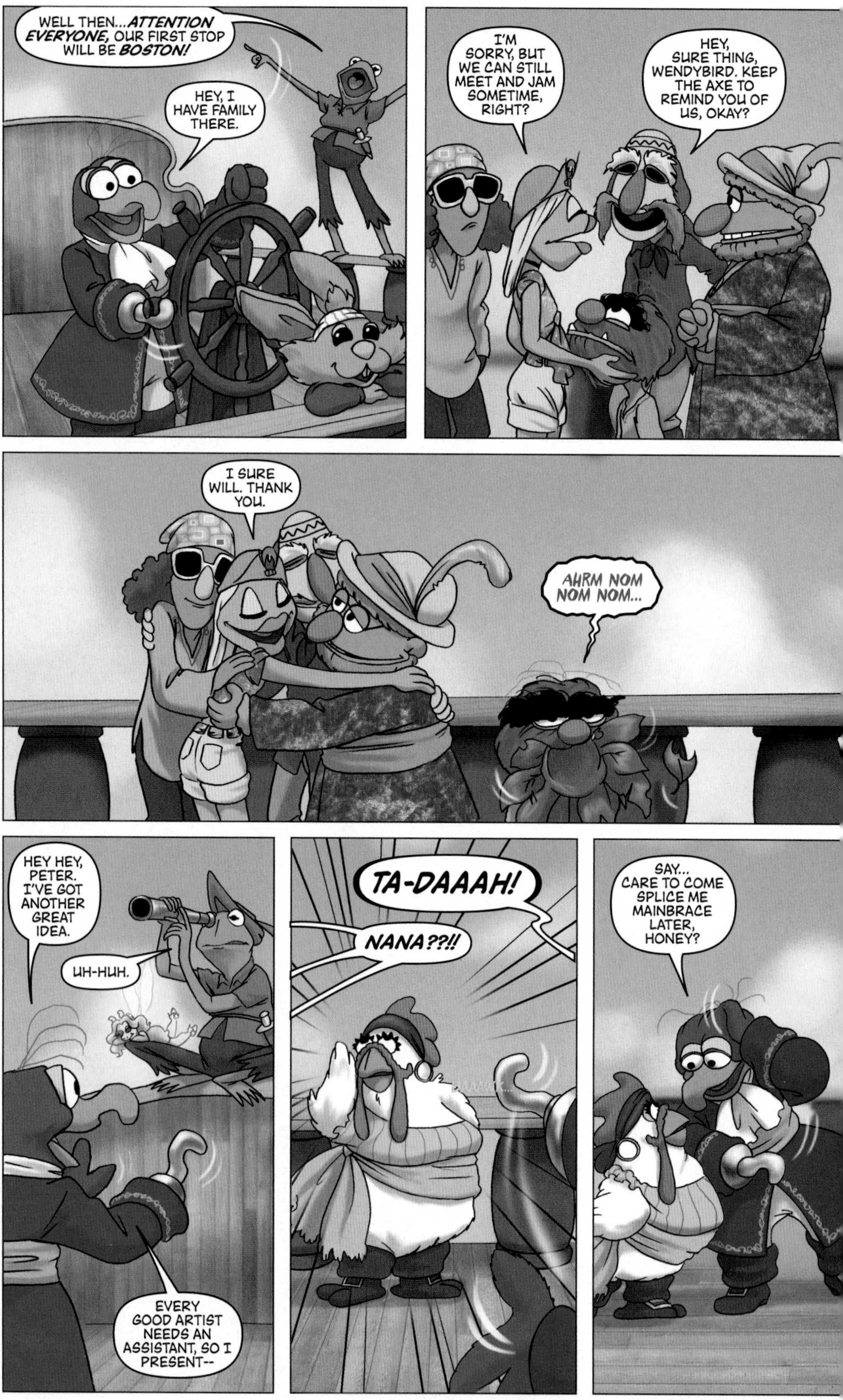
WELL THEN...**ATTENTION EVERYONE,** OUR FIRST STOP WILL BE **BOSTON!**
HEY, I HAVE FAMILY THERE.
I'M SORRY, BUT WE CAN STILL MEET AND JAM SOMETIME, RIGHT?
HEY, SURE THING, WENDYBIRD. KEEP THE AXE TO REMIND YOU OF US, OKAY?
I SURE WILL. THANK YOU.
AHRM NOM NOM NOM...
HEY HEY, PETER. I'VE GOT ANOTHER GREAT IDEA.
UH-HUH.
EVERY GOOD ARTIST NEEDS AN ASSISTANT, SO I PRESENT--
TA-DAAAH!
NANA??!!
SAY... CARE TO COME SPLICE ME MAINBRACE LATER, HONEY?

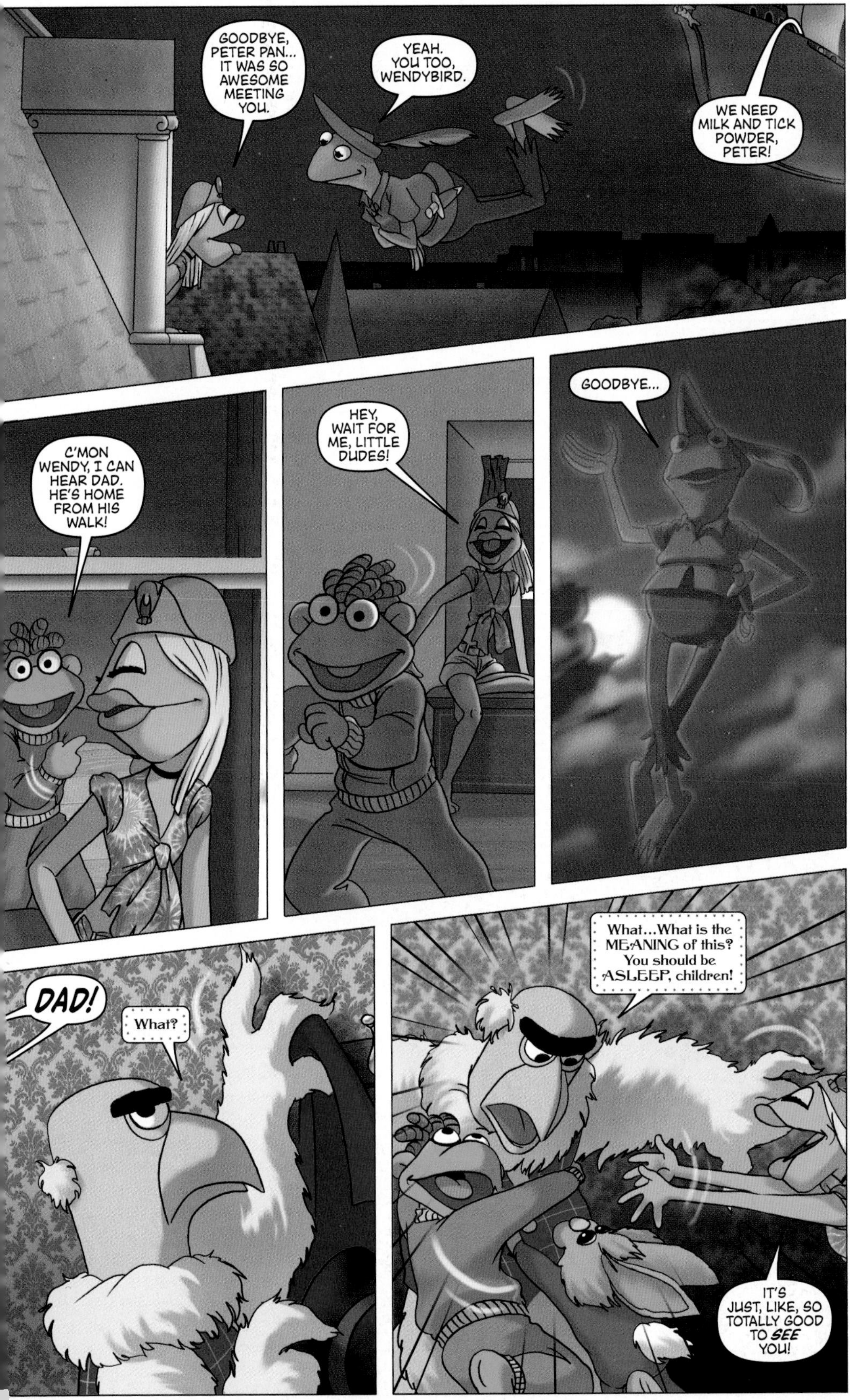
GOODBYE, PETER PAN... IT WAS SO AWESOME MEETING YOU.
YEAH. YOU TOO, WENDYBIRD.
WE NEED MILK AND TICK POWDER, PETER!
C'MON WENDY, I CAN HEAR DAD. HE'S HOME FROM HIS WALK!
HEY, WAIT FOR ME, LITTLE DUDES!
GOODBYE...
DAD!
What?
What...What is the MEANING of this? You should be ASLEEP, children!
IT'S JUST, LIKE, SO TOTALLY GOOD TO SEE YOU!

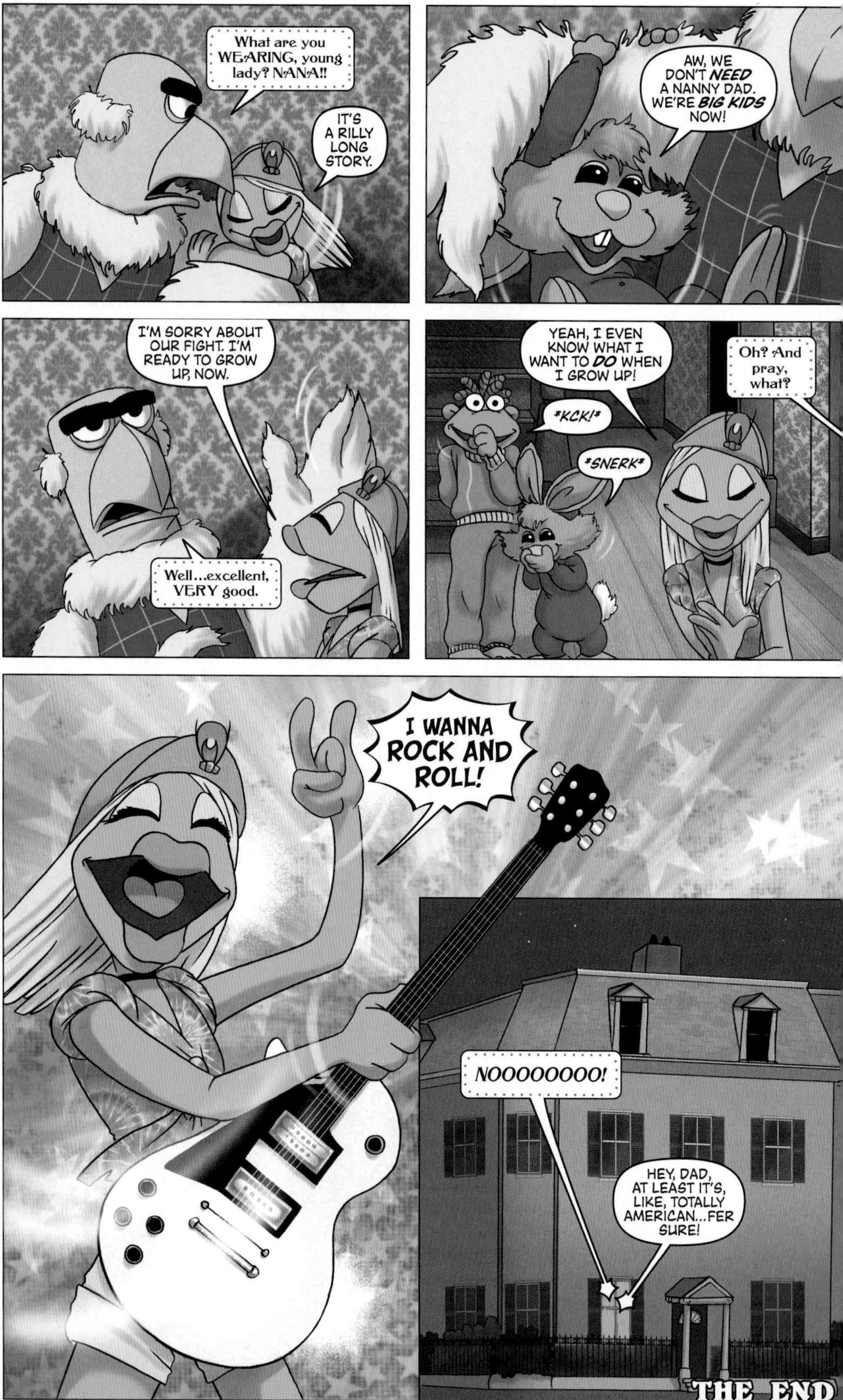
What are you WEARING, young lady? NANA!!
IT'S A RILLY LONG STORY.
AW, WE DON'T NEED A NANNY DAD. WE'RE BIG KIDS NOW!
I'M SORRY ABOUT OUR FIGHT. I'M READY TO GROW UP, NOW.
Well...excellent, VERY good.
YEAH, I EVEN KNOW WHAT I WANT TO DO WHEN I GROW UP!
KCK!
SNERK
Oh? And pray, what?
I WANNA ROCK AND ROLL!
NOOOOOOOO!
HEY, DAD, AT LEAST IT'S, LIKE, TOTALLY AMERICAN...FER SURE!
THE END

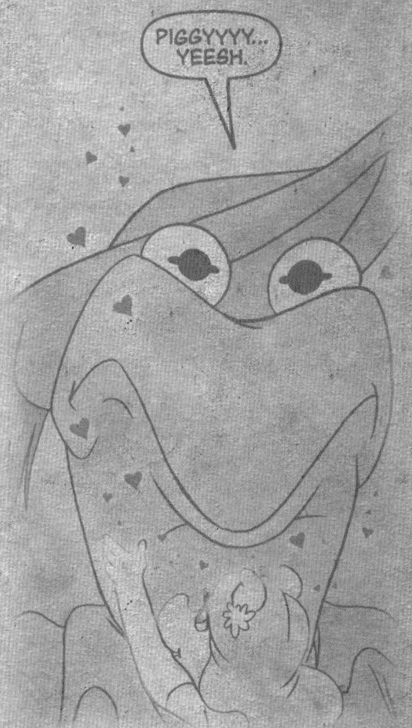
PIGGYYYY... YEESH.

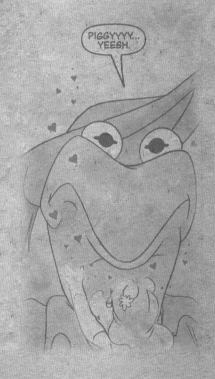

cover gallery

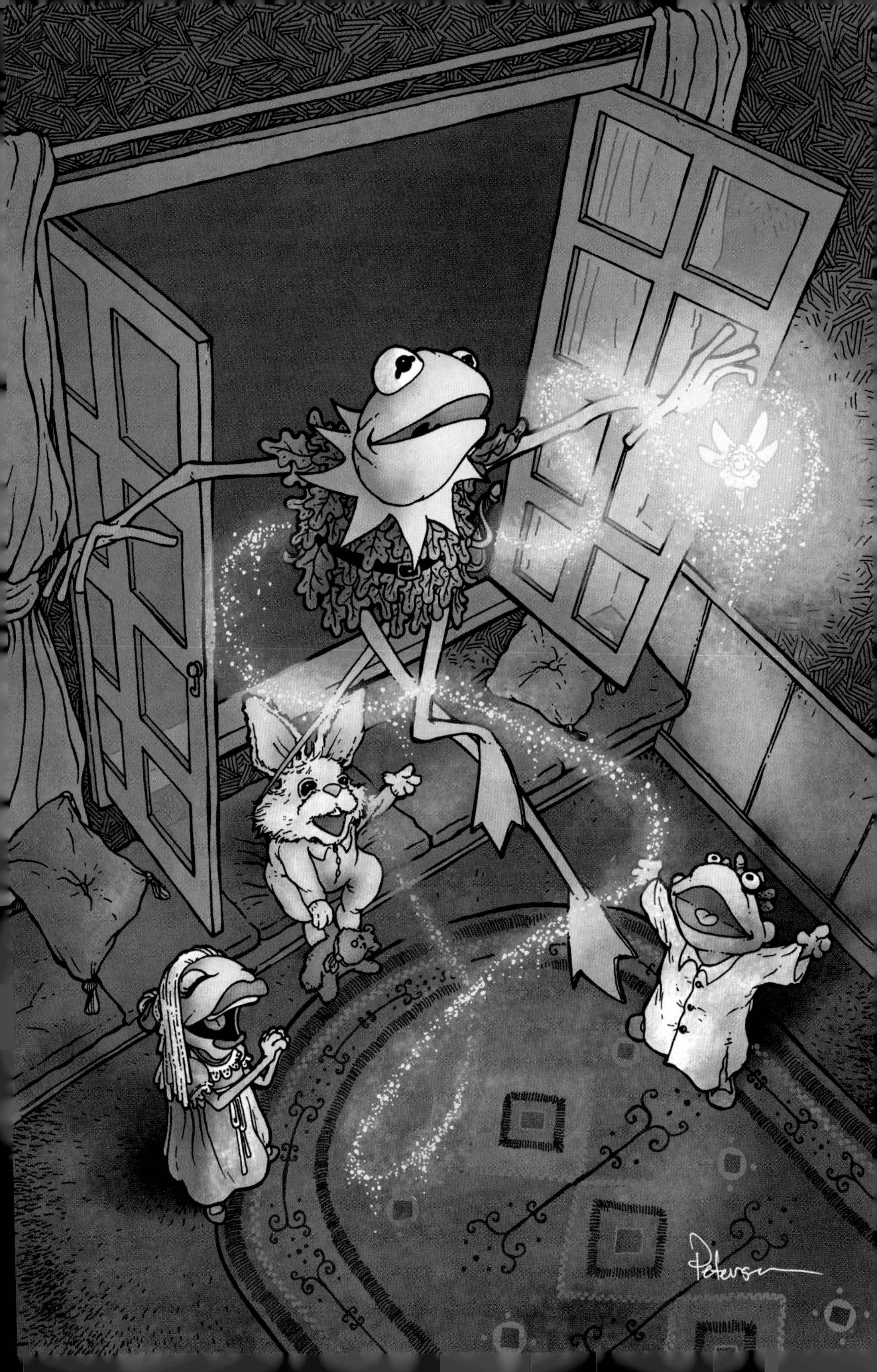
Peterson

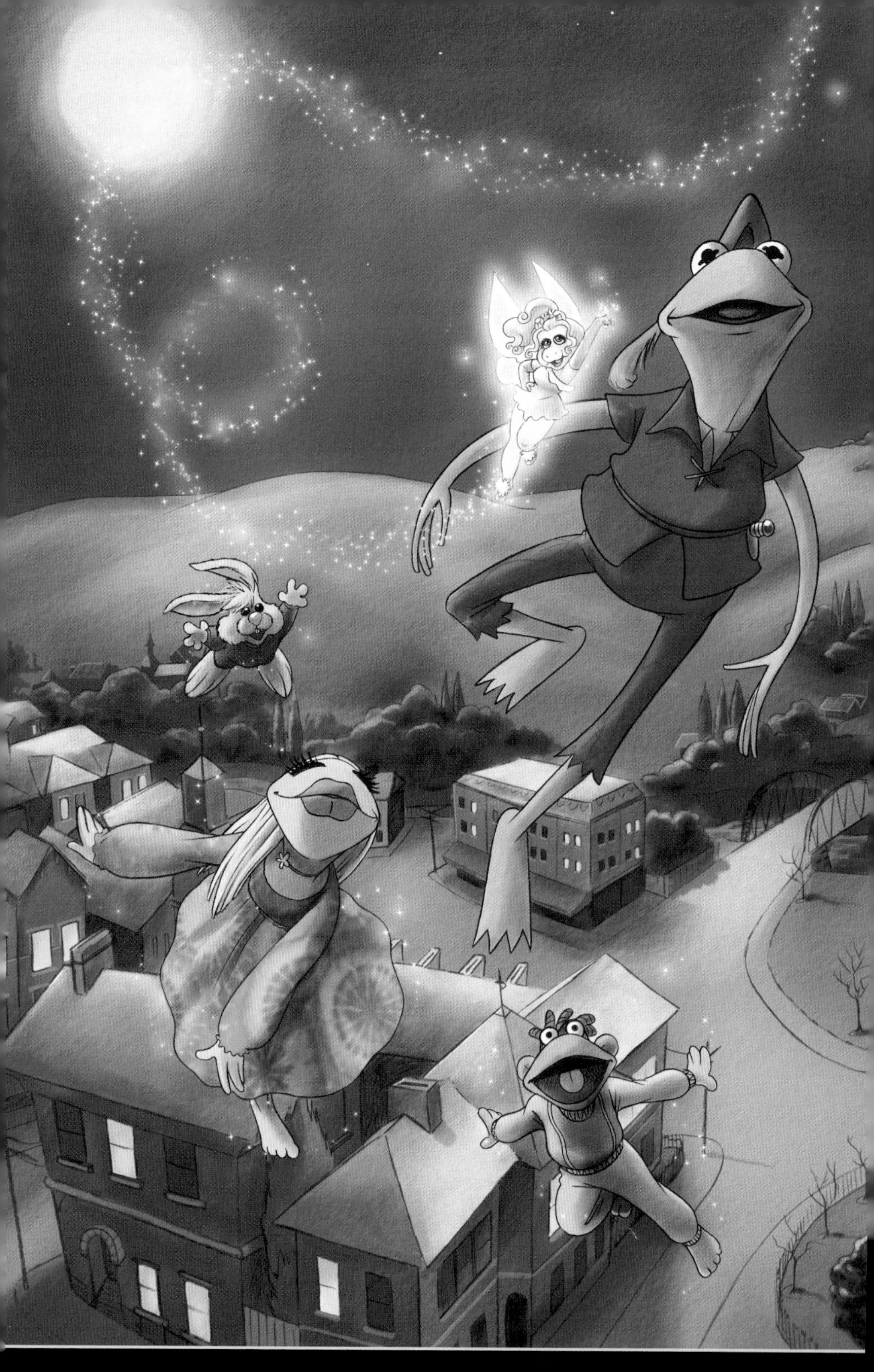

COVER 1B: AMY MEBBERSON

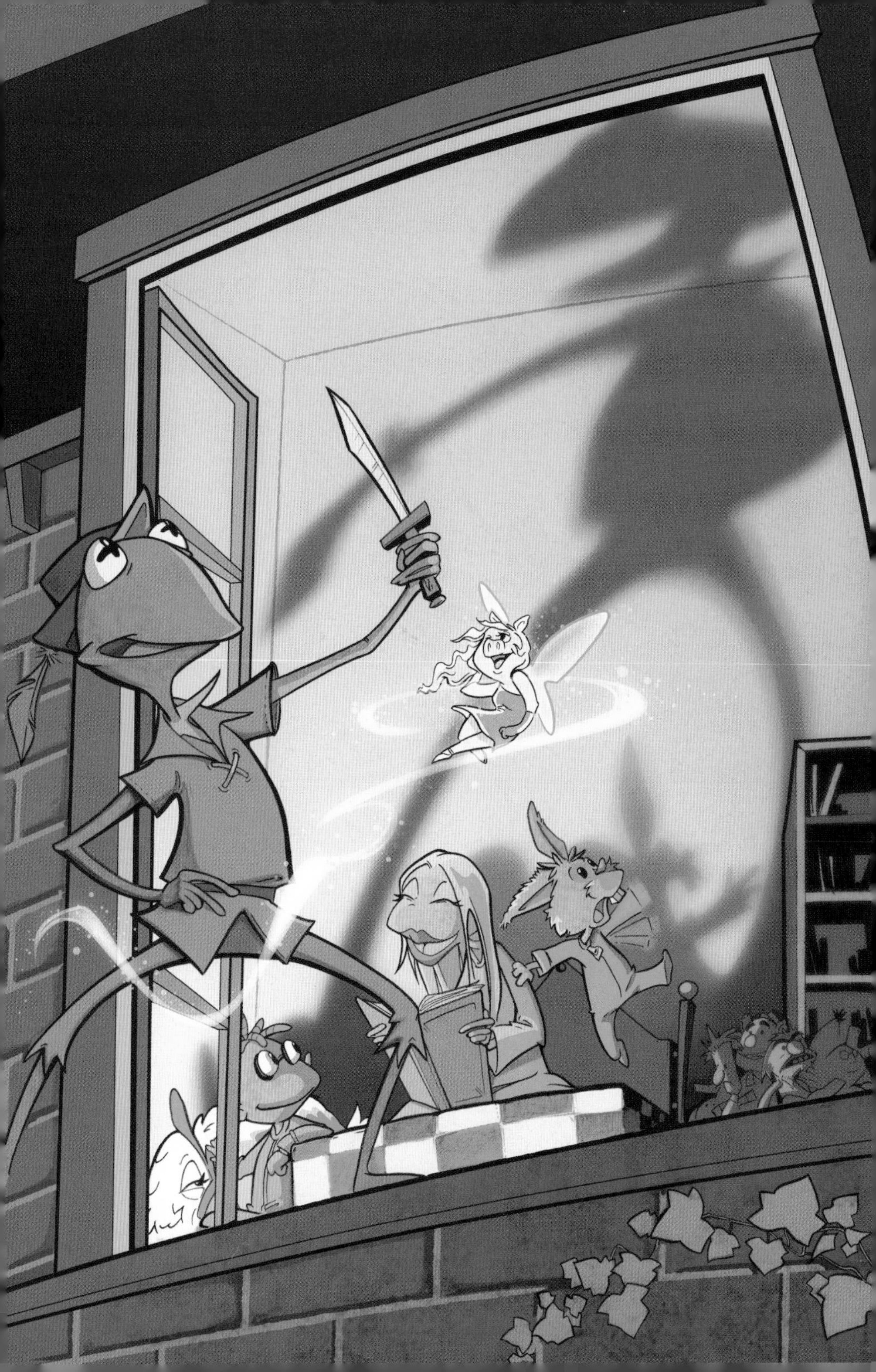

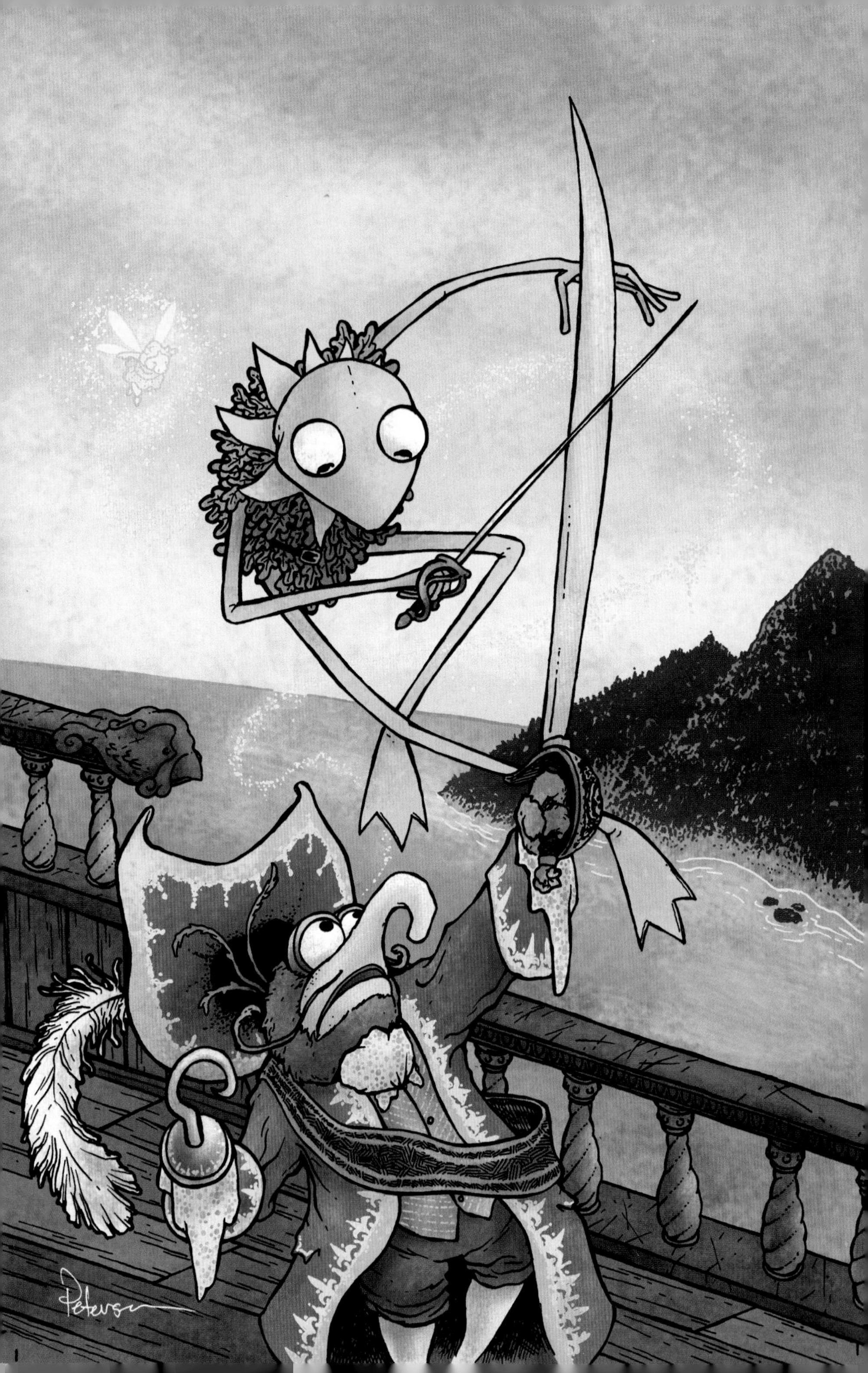
Peterson

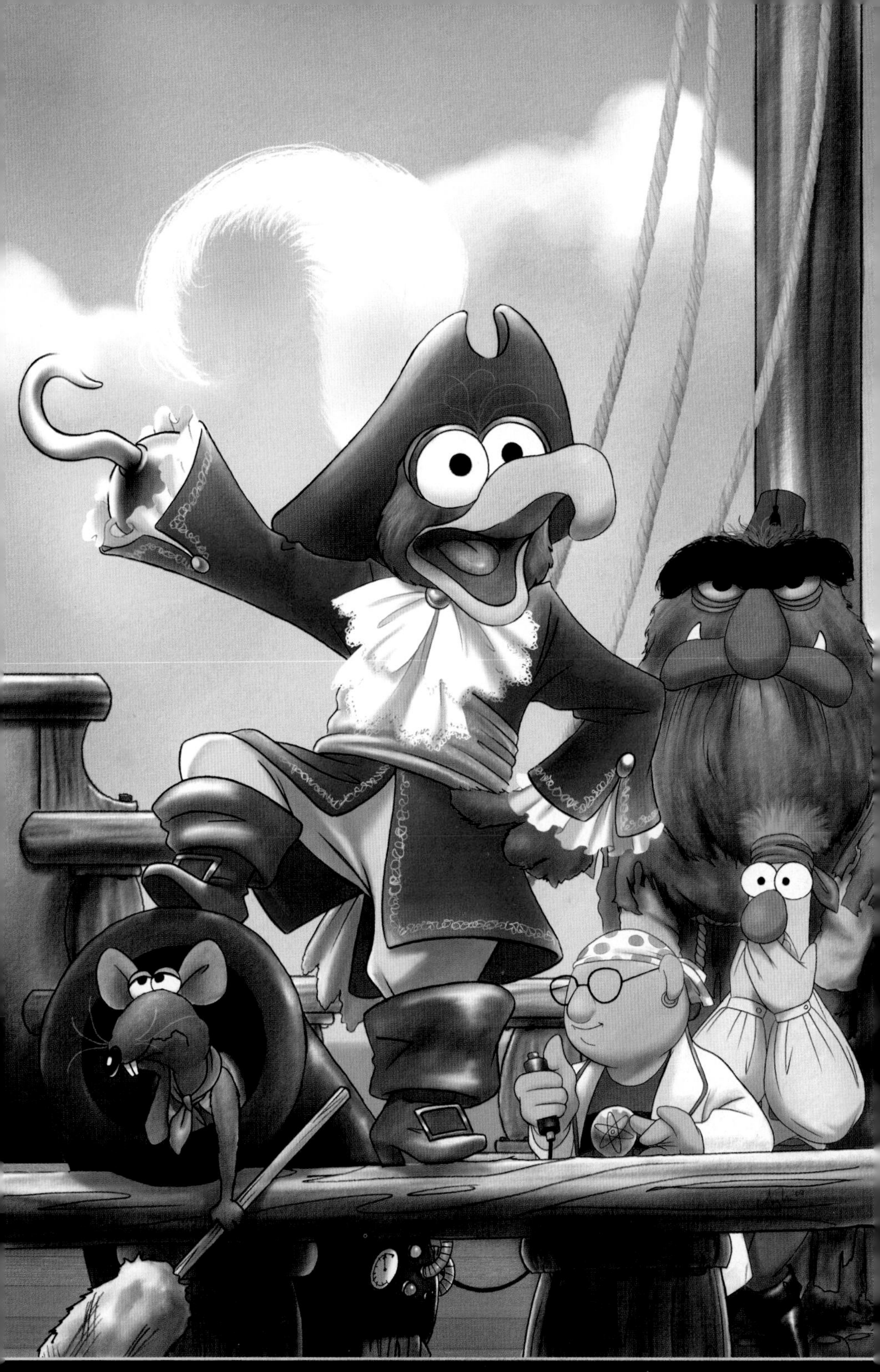

COVER 2B: AMY MEBBERSON

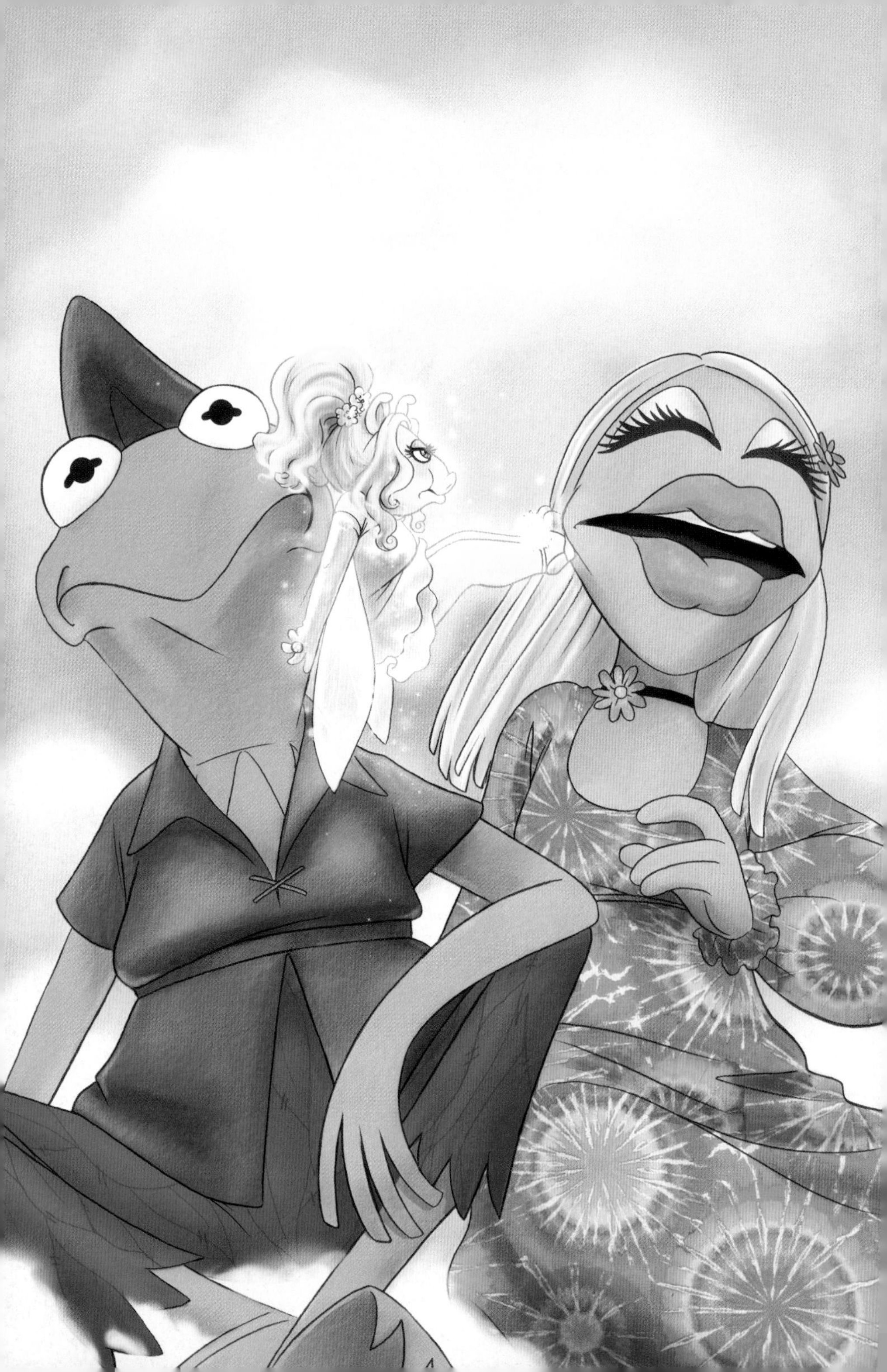

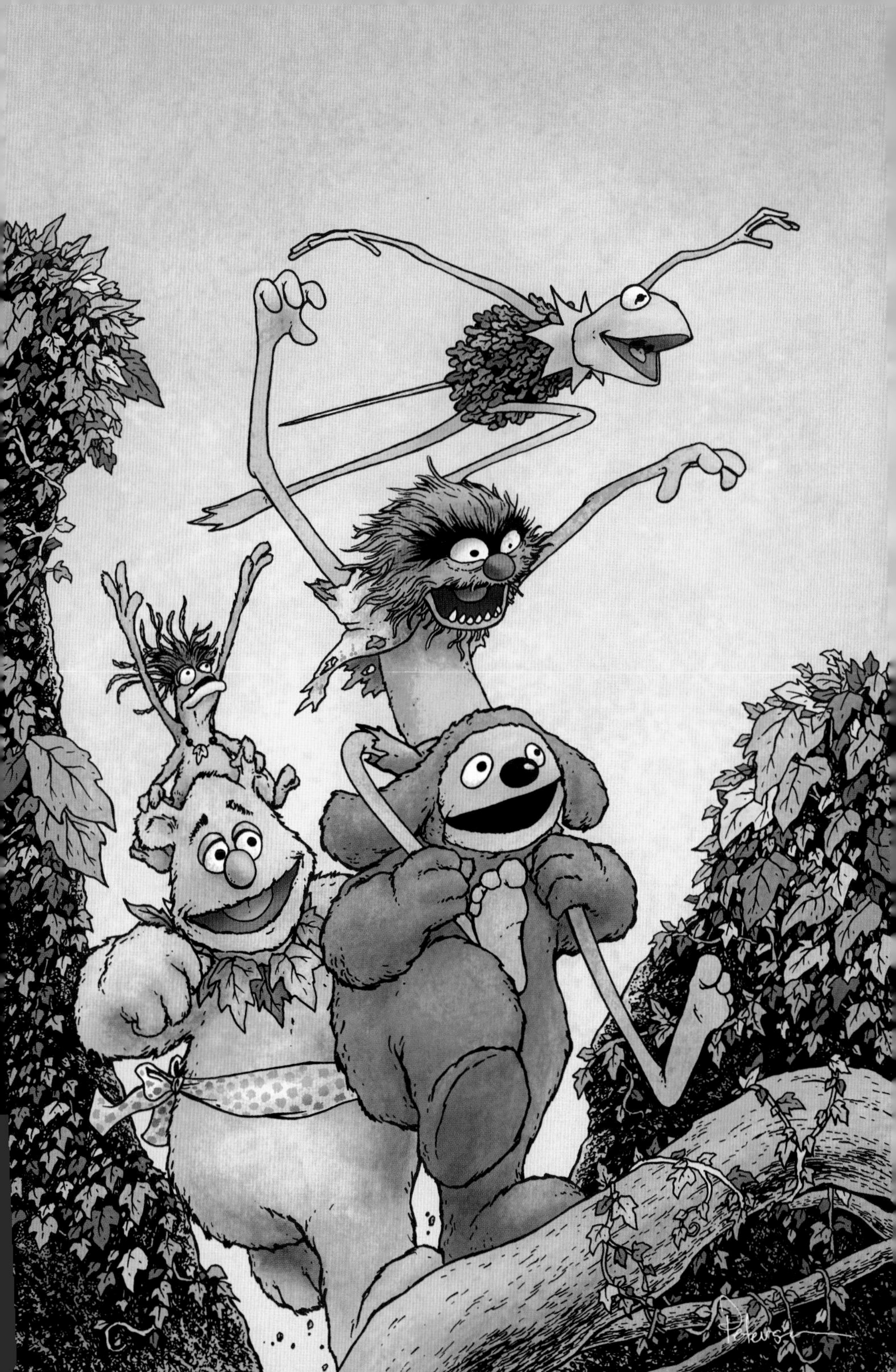

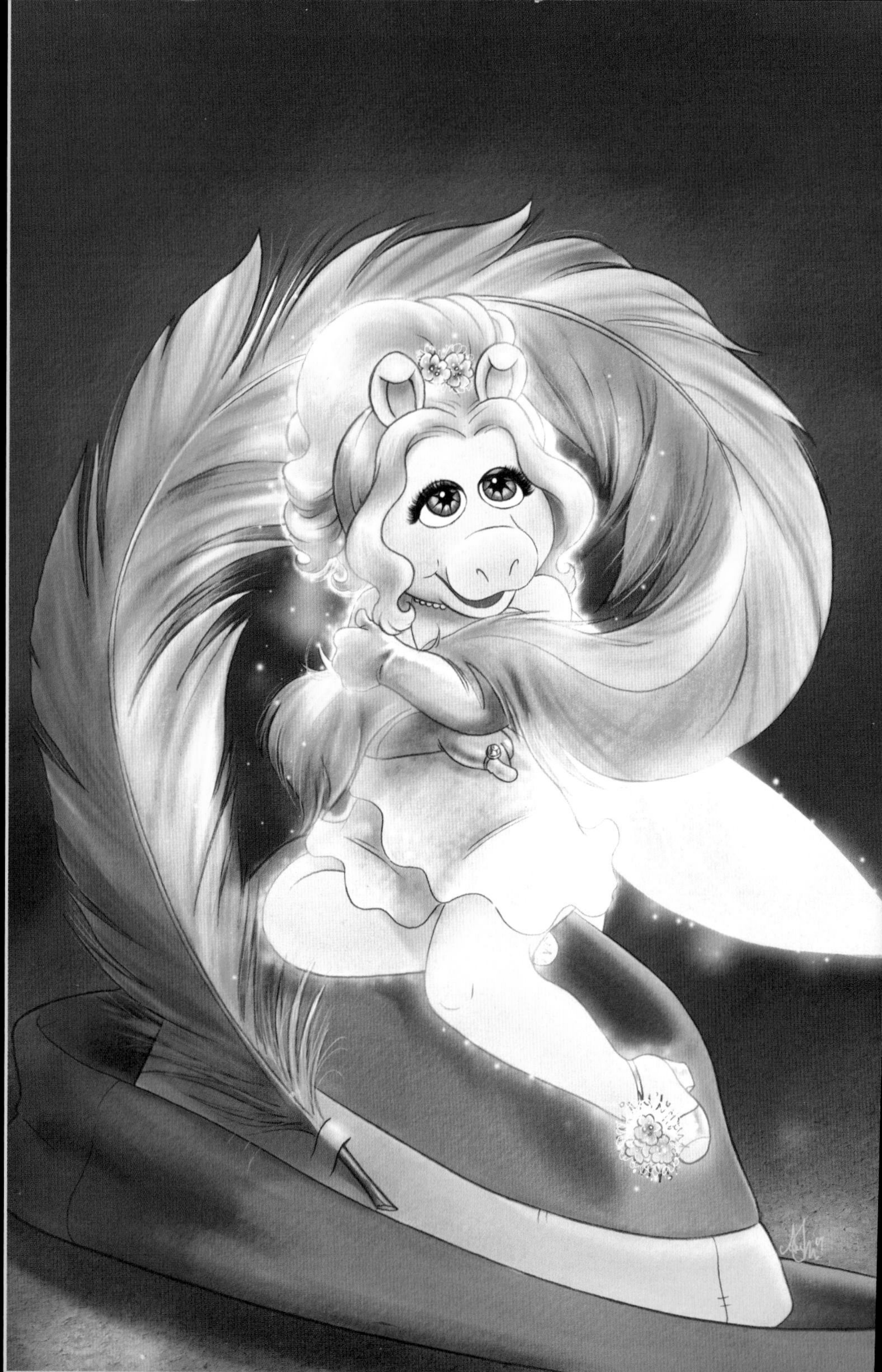

COVER 3B: AMY MEBBERSON

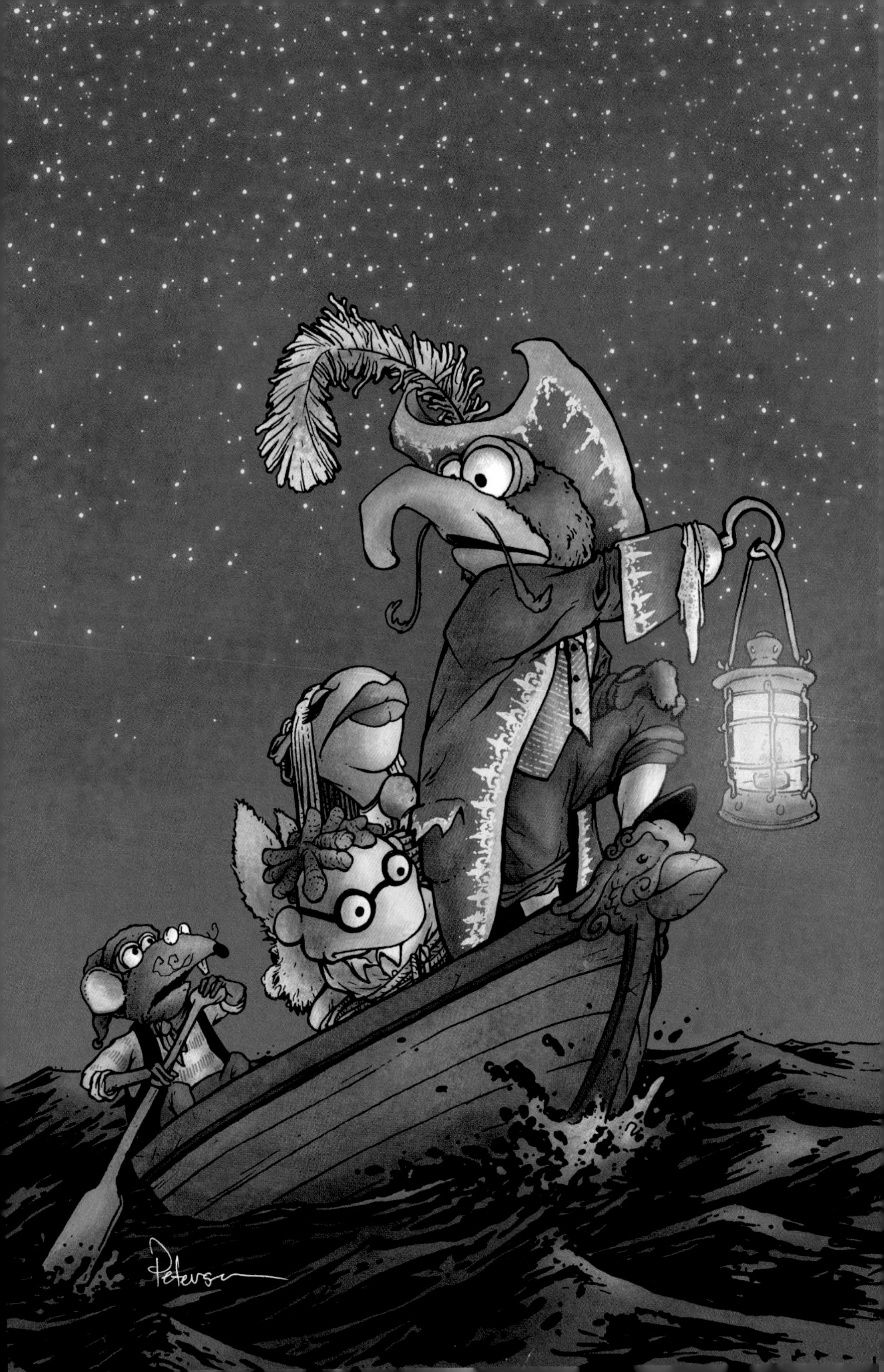

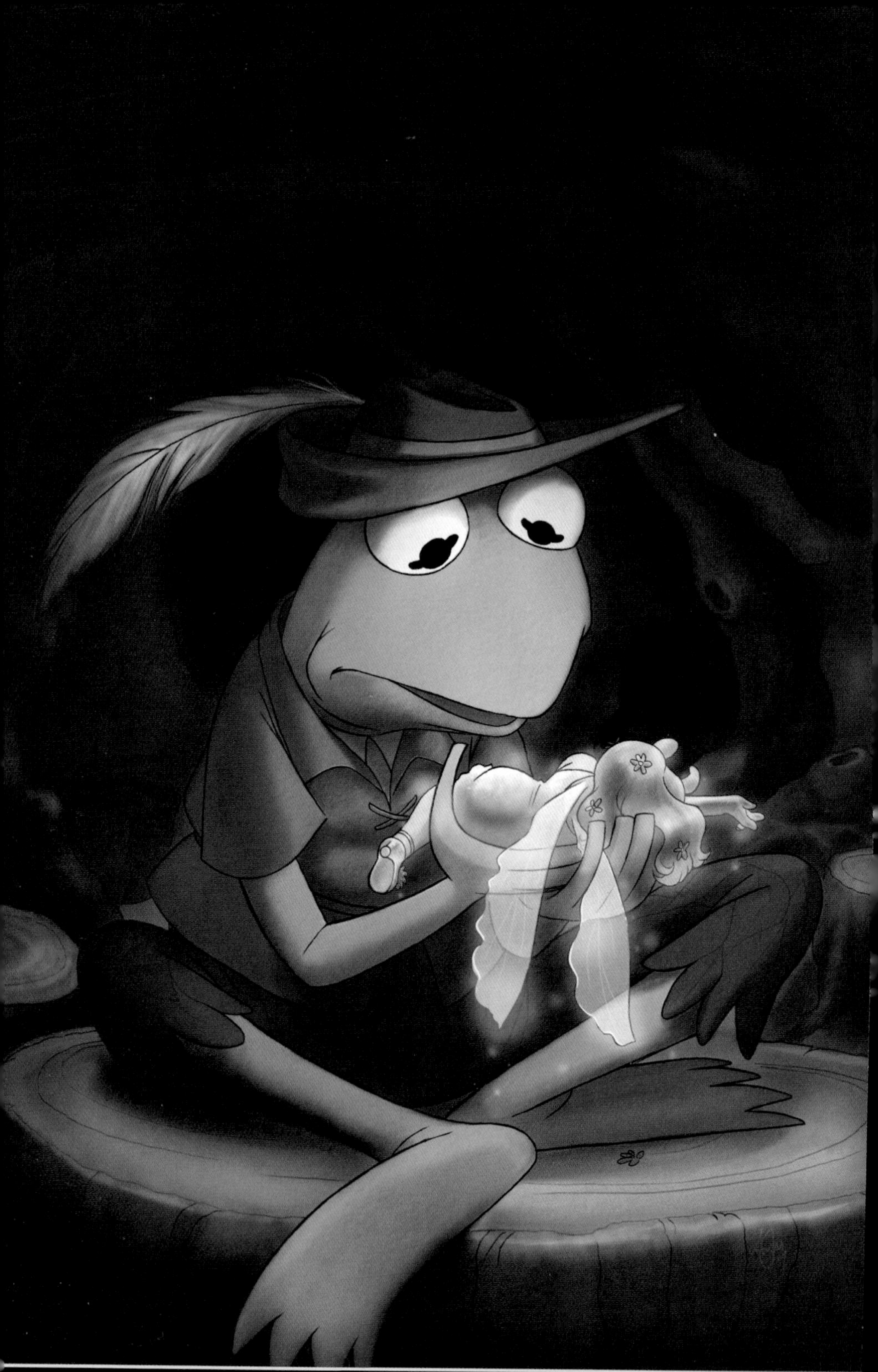

COVER 4B: AMY MEBBERSON

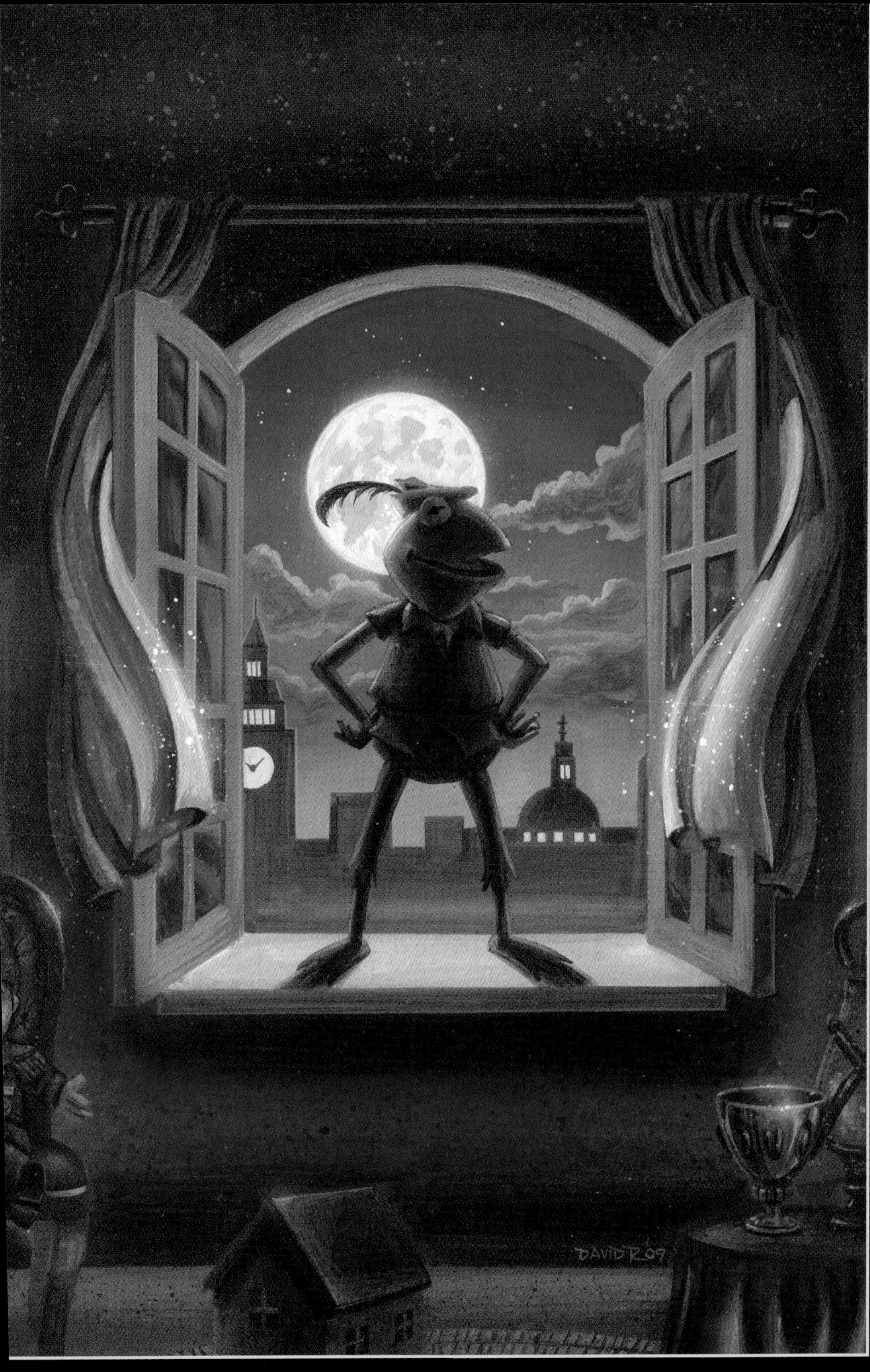
DAVID R '09

CASE WRAP BACK COVER: DAVID RABBITTE

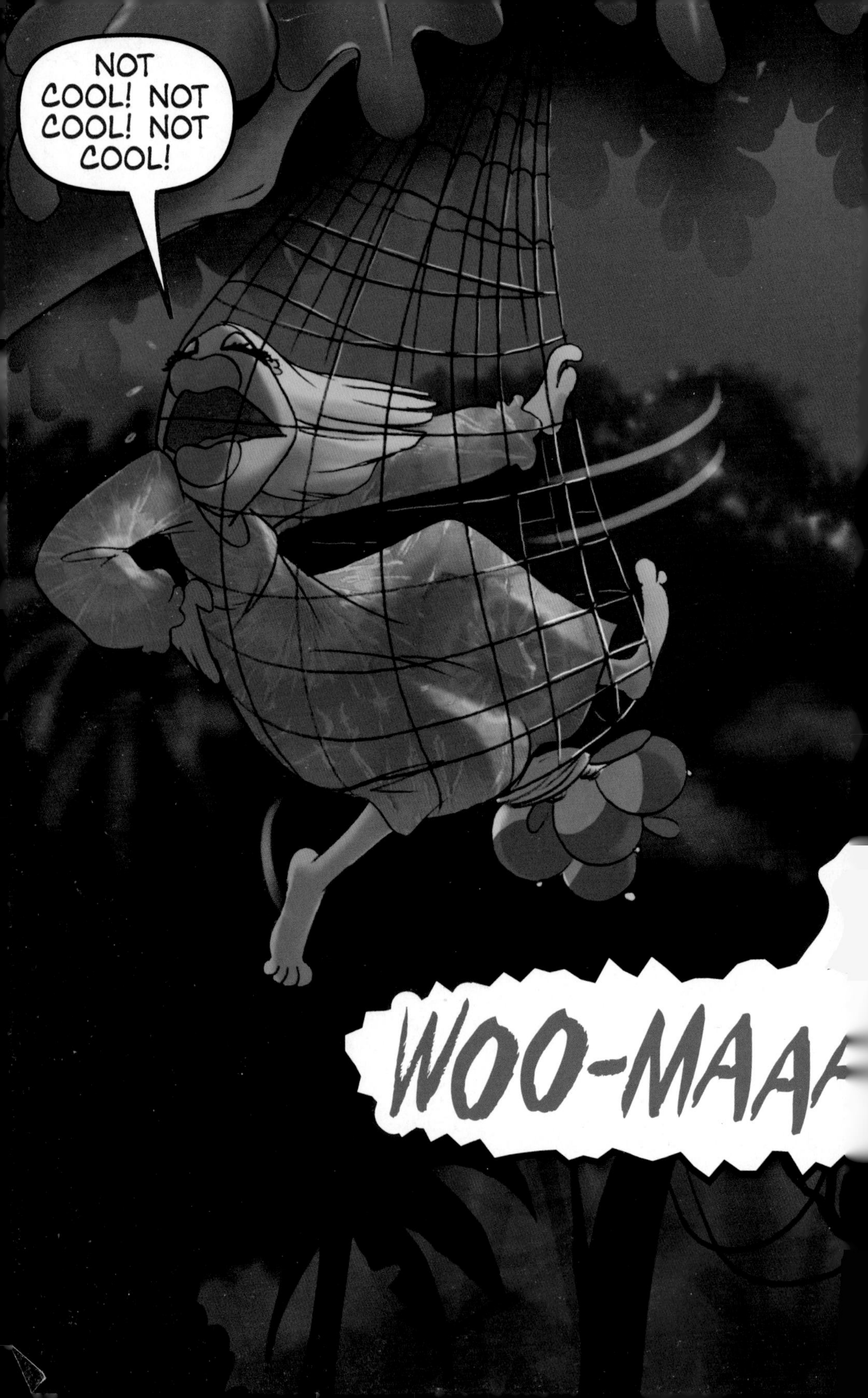
NOT COOL! NOT COOL! NOT COOL! NOT COOL!
WOO-MAA